In the Fullness of Time

Marcus Coles

ACKNOWLEDGMENTS

Fiona spends countless hours reading and editing these books when she has much better things to do. I am so grateful to her for all the help and support she has given me. This trilogy would never have been completed without her.

Also by Marcus Coles

Murder on the Titanic

The Breaking Dawn

Land of Promise

To Benjamin

Chapter I

Asher shivered in the corner of his small, dank cell. It had grown noticeably colder in this rotten hole, and it hadn't been very warm to begin with. The change in the weather was another depressing sign of how long he'd been there. He felt he'd been there for weeks but had no idea how long it had actually been. The soldiers who guarded him never spoke; they simply grunted something unintelligible when he tried to speak to them.

Tormented night and day by the memories of what happened, he had been a nervous wreck. How he rued the day he had ever set eyes on the beautiful Diana. His pursuit of her, the daughter of an old Roman General, had almost been the end of him. The man had a reputation for aggression and even violence, but to command Asher to be crucified was a level beyond! He still couldn't believe it. Sometimes he felt it had all been a dream, or a really vivid nightmare. But then he looked at the scar he'd been left with and he was reminded of the ordeal. He ran his fingers over his wrist, just like the soldier had before he'd driven the nail into him.

The pain of that moment was indescribable. It had returned to him a thousand times. The fear was worse. He couldn't help but recall the utter terror he had gone through when he realised what they were doing. That fear still kept him awake at night, despite the cold. And if not the fear, then the pain robbed him of any rest.

This had gone on for weeks - how many, he didn't know. The pain had mostly gone but he still ached all over. His wrist in particular felt weak and he lacked strength in his hand. Sleeping on the rough straw mattress they'd supplied was gradually getting easier. He no longer groaned in pain every time he had to move or turn over.

He hadn't talked to another living soul the whole time he'd been incarcerated. His last meaningful conversation was with Diana! How badly he had misjudged her and that whole sorry affair. He'd had to endure different types of pain: the scourging he'd received from the Romans and the painful memory of the fool he'd made of himself over Diana.

Perhaps he should have worked it out sooner. He had seen with his own eyes the vile way in which she had spoken to her slaves. There was something abhorrent about it even then. It had chilled him to the bone. Yet his desire to be with her had overridden any moral objection he might have had to their flirtation. Then there was their final moment together in the garden. He had tried to evince some sort of emotional response from her by sharing with her how he truly felt. It had become obvious quite quickly that she didn't care. Her final comment to her father was the final stab wound in his already bruised and battered heart.

He had had hoped that Varius would have come to his rescue before now. Surely his friend would come and find him and secure his release. He felt sure he would. Despite their differences, they had become good friends and Asher knew that Varius would do all he could to get him out. Something must have gone wrong, that was the only plausible explanation. He hadn't even come to see him.

Chapter II

Varius had been in the Galilee for several weeks now. The area was known to be very quiet and humdrum: a region which rarely saw any excitement. He still wasn't sure why he had been sent here but he knew it was intended as a punishment.

It had to have been his meeting with Pilate. The Roman Prefect hadn't seemed angry at the time, but Varius must have angered him when he petitioned for Asher's release. Pilate was known to be hot-tempered and unpredictable, but Varius couldn't let Asher rot in a cell because of that idiot Flaccus without trying something.

Now he found himself here, in the Galilee, with no idea what had become of Asher. Maybe their paths would cross again, if he ever made it out of that Roman prison.

He gazed out across the great lake and marvelled at where he now found himself. He had been thrust from the family home in his mid-twenties and sent to Egypt. He had marvelled at the Great Library and Pharos, the lighthouse of Alexandria. His memory of the pyramids was scarred by the death of his friend Gaius. But it was Safiya, the woman who had broken his heart, that had soured the whole Egyptian adventure.

From there he had ended up in Joppa and the land of the Jews. He had fought for his life in the desert of the Negev and encountered hostile mobs in Jerusalem. Then he had been posted to Caesarea, which he had loved. Now here he was in the Galilee and he was yet to reach his thirtieth year.

Varius was based in Tiberius in the small barracks near Antipas' palace. The weather was cool and dry, most of the locals seemed to be fishermen and the small towns that sat around the circumference of the lake were small and nondescript. He had often ridden as far as Chorazin on the northern shore, travelling through Magdala and Capernaum. It seemed to him to be a sleepy, laid-back area. There would be no trouble here. He'd heard a few whispers from the locals about a preacher who appeared to be growing in popularity but that was of no concern to him.

He had attended, in official capacity, some of the parties thrown by Antipas. They were wild affairs that would have shocked the faint-hearted. Not Varius. He was used to the decadent orgies that were a daily occurrence among Rome's upper crust. Had Antipas learned it from them or had he always had a penchant for depravity?

His wife, Herodias, seemed to be the orchestrator in chief. The wine flowed freely, the guests ate to excess and as the evenings wore on they seemed to become more and more inhibited by their clothes. These they discarded with enthusiastic abandon as the revelry increased. Salome, the fourteen-year-old daughter of Herodias could dance as provocatively as anyone there. Despite the fact she was of marriageable age, the deliberately seductive moves of the young girl made Varius deeply uncomfortable. Herodias seemed to have no such qualms; she watched on with pride.

If Pilate had known that one of Varius' duties would be to attend such soirees, he never would have exiled him here. Despite the cavorting Salome, he would have been quite happy to join in with the merriment.

He did regret what had happened to Asher. He knew that Diana was up to no good and that his friend had been sucked into something he couldn't handle. Perhaps he had waited too long to warn him. He had only found out about Flaccus' overreaction days later when he had gone looking for Asher. He had hoped to get Pilate to secure his release and had left the palace hoping he had done so. It was only later he had discovered otherwise. His superior had told him he was being sent to the Galilee and therefore that he almost certainly had not managed to get Asher released. He hoped he would be alright and that the moron Flaccus hadn't done something stupid.

Chapter III

Asher continued to fester in his melancholic state when the door of his cell burst open. An old man dressed in rags was shoved in roughly by one of the soldiers. He barked something barbaric and indecipherable and then slammed the door closed.

The old man had stumbled over. Asher had leaped to his feet as soon as he saw the man enter but was too late to stop him crashing to the hard stone floor. He rushed to his side and helped him sit up against the wall. The man groaned in pain. He was of average height but very old and very frail. His frame was skeletal, his skin stretched tightly over his aged bones. He had a long grey beard, and huge black bags underlined his dark blue eyes. His clothes were simple, dirty and worn.

'I'm sorry - if I'd known you were coming I would have tidied up a bit.'

The old man peeked out from underneath one of his drooping eyelids and mustered a smile. 'Hospitality is not what it was in my day.'

Asher admired that the old man, weak as he was, could still crack a joke and smile.

'I'm afraid I haven't got much here to make you more comfortable. You can have this old straw mattress. It's all that I have.'

'If it's all that you have then you have given me more than enough. Thank you, young man.' He slid down the wall slowly and painfully so that he was lying down. His eyes remained closed and in a few more minutes he was asleep.

Asher stared at the sleeping patriarch in wonder at what he had could have done to earn such treatment. An anger swelled within him as he thought of the heartless Roman soldiers and their treatment of others.

It was more than an hour before the old man awoke. He moved slowly and stiffly as if his joints had seized. Asher helped him sit up once more. He was much more alert now; his eyes were open and he was surveying the scene with interest.

He looked at Asher intently. 'So you're my new cell mate, eh?'

'Asher,' he said and thrust out a hand in the direction of the old man.

'Hello Asher. My name is Elkanah.'

Asher could barely contain himself. He had been starved of company for weeks and now he had someone with whom he could talk.

'I have to admit, sir, I am curious why someone like you has been thrown in a cell like this with me.'

'Why curious?' the old man immediately asked. There was a sharpness in his voice and a cheeky twinkle in his eye. 'How do you know I am not an infamous rabble-rouser or the fearless leader of a band of desperate rebels?'

Asher smiled. 'Because you look too old, kind and wise to be anything of the kind.'

'Perhaps I am a master of disguise. I have become adept over my many years at tricking people and deceiving them into thinking I am a frail old man. The reality is, I am a cunning con-man, like Jacob of old. I know how to mislead and manipulate people until I get what I want.'

There was a brief moment's silence when both men stared at one another earnestly. Then suddenly, in complete unison, they burst into fits of uncontrollable laughter.

Asher felt as if a well of joy had broken forth within him and the laughter was healing his wounds. Weeks of despondency and dismay were melting away in the company of this eccentric old man.

'I have sat alone in this cell for many weeks longing for a companion,' Asher smiled. 'You, sir, are an answer to my prayers.'

'I like you already, young Asher. You're very different from most of the thugs and roustabouts I usually meet in here.'

Asher was surprised. 'You stay here often then? I should have thought you would be able to find more respectable lodgings.'

'I am a most unwelcome guest in this town and I have slept many long nights in this very cell.'

The impact of the old man's words disturbed Asher and he suddenly became solemn. He stared at him, silently willing him to go on.

A few moments later, Elkanah got the hint. 'I have a very bad habit of telling people what I think,' he said finally. 'The problem is these Romans don't like hearing it, especially their illustrious leader, Pilate.' There was a long pause during which he looked more and more pensive, gazing into the distance as if he was looking straight into the past. 'I can remember a time before the Romans. Not many of us left now.'

'You're not their biggest fan, I gather?'

The old man allowed himself a mirthless smile. 'I can't help it. A man of my age should have more self-control. That's always been one of my biggest problems. I know that I should just shut up, but when the time comes I don't seem to be able to stop myself. If I see a Roman acting like a barbarian, I tell them. When Pilate marches past with his legions, all arrogant and domineering, I start bawling at them. It's like there's a hotbed of anger within me and when it explodes there's no stopping it.'

'I can admire that,' Asher smiled conspiratorially. 'Whom did you upset this time?'

'There was a young woman in the market square quietly trying to go about her business. Unfortunately for her, two of these brutes tried to take advantage of her. The whole thing unfolded right before my very eyes.'

'What did you do?'

'I started throwing things at them.'

Asher laughed. He was liking this old man more and more with each passing moment. 'What were you throwing?'

'I had just been to one of the market stalls and had a bag of fresh fruit with me. They weren't very happy when pomegranates started raining down upon them. They were even less happy when I discovered some rocks and stones lying conveniently at my feet.'

'You threw them too?'

'As many as I could,' the old man replied. It was evident in the tone of his voice that he was proud of himself. 'They didn't like it of course and marched straight over and grabbed a hold of me. A few minutes later I found myself here with you.'

'And the woman?'

'They had to let her go. She was lucky this time.'

'What do these women need to fear when you're around to defend their honour, eh?'

'I'm not long for this world, Asher. It's the young people like you and that young woman I fear for. A sick and perverted age, that's what it's become. Who knows what it will be like by the time you're my age - if you last that long.'

'I'm not planning on going anywhere just yet,' Asher looked around morosely. 'I wouldn't mind getting out of this cell though.'

'How did you end up in this cell in the first place?' Elkanah asked, ready to change the subject.

'Nothing so noble as why you're here, I can assure you.' Asher was reluctant to share his story. In comparison to the old man's tale, it made him look weak and pathetic.

'Well come on then,' Elkanah said impatiently after several moments of silence.

'There's really not much to tell,' Asher said sheepishly.

'You're embarrassed,' the old man wisely observed. 'That can mean one of two things: you've done something exceedingly stupid or there's a woman involved.'

'How about both of those things,' Asher said dryly.

Elkanah laughed heartily. 'I knew it. There's nothing new under the sun. That's what King Solomon said. Young men are the same the world over and throughout the ages. Always getting into trouble over some woman. So what happened?' he asked, after he'd finally stopped laughing.

'I fell for her. I was besotted with her.'

'A Roman?'

'Yes.'

'Rich?'

'Yes.'

'Beautiful?'

'Very.'

'You thought you had a chance?'

'I thought I had a chance.'

'Poor deluded young man,' Elkanah smiled shaking his head. 'What made you think a normal Jewish boy like you could ever succeed in the company of the Roman elite?'

'I don't know,' Asher sighed, reluctant to dredge up painful memories. 'She must have cast some sort of spell on me I suppose.'

'Rubbish! Don't go blaming her. It was you and your foolish notions that authored this calamity. So how did you end up in here?'

'Her father is a General.'

This new revelation was enough to set the old man off again. His head dropped to his chest as he tried to muffle his laughter in the thickness of his beard and the folds of his tattered old gown.

Asher couldn't help but be amused at the sight of the old man to whom he'd brought such pleasure. The weakness and frailty that seemed to ooze from every pore had been jostled away by the sniggers and guffaws that Asher's story had elicited.

'So, he found out and had you thrown in here?'

Without thinking, Asher massaged the scar on his wrist. Elkanah noticed.

'Roughed you up a bit, did they?' he asked.

'Just a little bit,' Asher said with a weak smile.

'And how long have you been here?'

'I'm not sure. Several weeks at least.'

'So was she worth it?'

Asher thought for a while. His delay in responding sent Elkanah into another fit of laughter from which it took him some time to recover.

Chapter IV

The palace of Herod Antipas was as grand as anyone might expect. The family had certainly had an enormous influence on this region and beyond. The legacy of Herod the Great was everywhere. Varius had learned that Herod Antipas had been Tetrarch of Judea and Peraea for some years. He had presided over an era of peace and prosperity. The Jewish revolts which had taken place elsewhere had not erupted in the Galilee. Antipas had inherited the land and title from his father, Herod the Great. He had bequeathed Judea and Peraea to his son on his death. This had been ratified by Emperor Augustus.

He had three main palaces from which he governed the area on behalf of Rome. For many years, his base in the Galilee had been the town of Sepphoris, a few hours walk from the nearby Nazareth and a few days journey from the Sea of Galilee. Sepphoris had been badly damaged in the Jewish revolt. Now it was an impressive town with much Greek and Roman influence. It was where the region came to do business and an important stop on the Via Maris. Varius had bivouacked there on his way through the Galilee. It was his sort of town: a large Roman presence and lots of pillared temples and wide colonnades that reminded him of home.

Antipas, however, had determined to move his regional capital to the shores of the Sea of Galilee. He had, for many years, been building a town on the western shore which he had named Tiberius. The lavish palace he had built for himself overlooked the great lake. He was encouraging all people to make their home there. It had been a great building project and had provided much work for the people of the area. The carpenters and stone masons loved Antipas.

He also had a palace in Jerusalem in the upper city near the Praetorium. He, like everyone else in this country it seemed, travelled to Jerusalem for the big religious festivals. Now that Pilate, as the reigning Roman Prefect, occupied the old palace of his father, Antipas had to be content with the palace of much lesser size and opulence.

As Tetrarch of Peraea also, Antipas spent some time in Machaerus. Varius hadn't been there but had heard it to be a formidable and impregnable fortress on the eastern shore of the great salt sea. Antipas was on constant guard against the Nabateans in the east.

Varius had done his research and discovered that on account of some dirty dealings, the old Jew was both unpopular with his own people and reviled by King Aretas IV, overlord of the Nabatean kingdom.

Varius found it hilarious that the rich and powerful the world over were just as dysfunctional as everyone else.

Antipas had married Phasaelis, the daughter of the Nabatean King. However, after many years of marriage he had taken a fancy to his brother's wife, Herodias, who was also his own niece. She had agreed to marry Antipas as long as he divorced his Nabatean bride.

How was it that women were able to tie even the most powerful men up in so many knots that they committed such reckless and stupid mistakes?

She got wind of what Antipas had in store and made her escape from the fortress at Machaerus. Although annoyed at his wife's escape, this liberated Antipas from his marriage and therefore he was free to marry Herodias.

The whole sorry tale was an example of complete family dysfunction which the Herodians were known for. Yet despite the brazen way he'd humiliated Phasaelis, Antipas was still securely embedded in his position as Tetrarch of Galilee and Peraea.

The affair had made him unpopular though and the Jewish people were unforgiving. The sins he'd committed against his wife and against his brother were unforgivable.

Varius wondered which concerned Herod more: how he was viewed by his own people or the possible vengeance of King Aretas. He was bound to be incensed by the treatment of his daughter. Would he pursue revenge? And if so would Varius have to get involved in defending him? That would be sickening. There were many reasons for going to war. Fighting to defend an aging idiot because he had an unhappy marriage was not one of them.

Chapter V

The following day Asher and Elkanah were sitting chatting in their cell. One of their captors arrived early, threw them two small rolls of stale bread and dropped a small jug of water on the floor. Half of it spilled out before Asher could scramble along and retrieve what was left. 'It warms your heart, doesn't it? The way they take care of us?' Elkanah said sarcastically.

'He's one of the nicer ones.'

Asher sighed. He'd enjoyed the time spent with Elkanah yesterday. He would have enjoyed a normal conversation with anyone having been isolated for so long. The old man was genuinely good company though and Asher was secretly very grateful that he'd been locked up with him. However, as the sun rose over the earth once more a new wave of melancholy washed over him.

'How long have they kept you here all those other times?' Asher asked, once he'd digested his sorry excuse for a breakfast.

Elkanah thought for a moment. 'Sometimes a few days, sometimes a week or more. There doesn't seem to be any rhyme or reason to it. I think they just let you go when they feel like it or when they need the cell for someone else.'

'Great! I've already been here for weeks! How much longer can it be?'

'I loathe to be the bearer of bad news, Asher, but you could be here for months or they could let you out tomorrow. What would be really bad news would be if the General who had you thrown in here forgot all about you. Then you could be here for years.'

Asher was horrified. 'Please don't say things like that. It's taken all the mental strength I have not to lose my mind in here already.'

'You mustn't lose hope. Any minute, any day now, someone could walk in here and set you free.'

'That's easier said than done. Hope can be agonising, painful if that's all you have. What was it King Solomon said? Hope deferred makes the heart sick?'

'You know the wisdom of Solomon? I'm impressed, young man. Of course, it depends on where, or in whom you place your hope.'

'What do you mean?'

'In my experience you should never hope in man. You are destined for disappointment if that's where you place your trust.'

Asher was confused. 'In what is your hope placed?'

'In whom.'

'In whom?'

'In whom have I placed my trust would be a more appropriate question.'

'Very well. In whom have you placed your trust?'

'The Almighty. El Shaddai.'

'Ah! I see where this is going. I should put my hope in God. He'll rescue me from this prison as he did for Daniel or Joseph.' Asher didn't mean to sound so dismissive and scornful but he realised as the words were leaving his lips that that was exactly how he sounded.

'I shan't imagine you will be taken from here and given one of the most powerful positions in the land as happened to them,' Elkanah said chuckling. 'But the one who rescued Daniel and Joseph is more than capable of rescuing you too.'

Asher sat quietly for several moments studying the old man. He didn't really know what to say in response to his words of wisdom. He had never been one to mock the faith of another and he had spent many long hours in the synagogue in Bethany. He probably knew the scriptures better than most. Yet when he pondered the old man's words it suddenly dawned on him that he hadn't visited any synagogue for some time. Not once in Caesarea and barely before that. He felt a pang of guilt course through him.

'Have you petitioned him for your release?'

'Who?'

'Yahweh. He is the sovereign I AM. You have had much time sitting in here on your own. You must have been crying out to him to set you free?'

Asher felt foolish. The thought had never occurred to him. Why had he not thought to cry out to the Lord to come and deliver him in his hour of need? He had forgotten. Had he really fallen so far?

'I confess I haven't,' he finally said. 'The notion never occurred to me.'

Elkanah looked at him pensively for some time. 'That is strange, don't you think?'

'Yes, I suppose. I think I've been waiting for them to just release me. I had hoped that my friend Varius would secure my release but that didn't happen.'

'Like I said,' Elkanah continued. 'Don't put your trust in man.'

Several minutes' silence followed, during which both men pondered their words. Asher felt a fool for having neglected what to most would have been the obvious strategy. But had he prayed and petitioned God for his release, would God have granted it? Asher had obviously been rather faithless of late.

'How did you come to be in Caesarea?' the old man finally asked, breaking the heavy silence in the cell which had threatened to crush them both.

Asher was now in no mood to tell his story but out of respect for the old man he half-heartedly launched into his epic tale. 'Well,' he sighed, 'I left my home town of Bethany about two years ago. Do you know it? It's just south of Jerusalem.'

'I've heard of it, but I confess I have never been.'

'You're haven't missed much. It's on the cusp of the desert, not far from the great salt sea and the river Jordan.'

'Why did you leave?'

'The short answer is I became disillusioned with my life there. Whenever I thought about the future all I could see was me walking my father's vineyards, marrying, bringing up children, looking after the family.'

'All noble pursuits in their own right,' Elkanah interjected.

'I know that and I have great respect for my father and the others in the family. Yet the more I thought about my future the more restless I became. People were always asking me when I was going to do this and when was I going to do that, when was I going to marry such-and-such and telling me it was high time I was the head of my own family. My brother's wedding exacerbated the whole problem.'

'He's younger than you?'

'Exactly! Anyway,' he sighed, 'I determined to leave. My parents were disappointed, of course, but gave me their blessing. I am sure they expected me home long before now. I just hope my mother hasn't worried herself into an early grave.'

'So you left and went where?'

'I spent some time in Jerusalem. I had always been fascinated by that city but the more time I spent there the more the novelty wore off. I did spend a lot of time in and around the temple though. You would have been proud of me.'

'It has been a long time since I have been to the temple in Jerusalem. Is it still crawling with the great and the good? The Pharisees and Sadducees, the priests, scribes, rabbis and teachers of the law?'

'Unfortunately, yes. They were part of the reason I decided to leave. There seemed to be something so phoney about them. They try so desperately to maintain a façade of piety.'

'We all do that.'

'Well I bet they're all masking a multitude of sins.'

'Aren't we all?'

Asher was somewhat irritated at his friend's attitude but soldiered on. 'Anyway, I left and went to work for a friend in the Galilee. I stayed there for a few months but soon got bored. I did run into a bear though!'

'A bear? You were up in the mountains?'

'Nowhere near. I hadn't even made it through Samaria when he accosted me. I lived to tell the tale though!'

Elkanah smiled briefly before asking. 'So you left the Galilee and came here?'

'Yes. I found work in a guest house catering mostly to the wealthy Roman set.'

'And it was there you first laid eyes on your beloved?'

Asher couldn't help but smile at the old man. 'Have you heard this story before?'

'More times than you know,' he answered cryptically. 'If I had a denarii for every time I'd witnessed a young man heading off on some foolish adventure, I would have accrued enough to buy Herod's Palace!'

Asher was hurt. 'I don't think I've been engaged in a foolish adventure.'

'Then what have you been doing?'

Asher thought for a moment and didn't know what to say.

'Why did you leave? To move from one mundane job to the next? To find and marry a wealthy Roman heiress? To live a carefree life in pursuit of pleasure and riches? To avoid going to work in your father's vineyards?'

'None of the above,' Asher snapped, growing more irritated at the old man's tone.

'Then what?'

'I don't know!' he said crossly. 'I can't remember. I just wanted to get out of there.'

Elkanah waited for several minutes, sensing that his young cellmate was getting exasperated and fed up.

'You've lost your way,' he said gently. 'You left home searching for something you couldn't define. You were looking for some meaning in life, a purpose to which you could be devoted.'

Asher felt as though someone had just slapped him across the face. He suddenly remembered his old friend Zeke and the words he'd spoken to him that day on the hillside overlooking Jerusalem. He had said the same thing then. Meaning and purpose.

'But you've lost your way,' he repeated. 'Somewhere along your journey you got distracted and you forgot what it was you were looking for.' He paused to let the words sink in. He could tell from Asher's demeanour that something was stirring within the young man.

'When you get out of here you need to get yourself back on track. You will find what you seek but not in the places you've been looking so far.'

Asher was amazed and couldn't hide his astonishment as he looked at the old man. How was it that he could be so perceptive? He felt as if his carefully chosen words had refreshed him somehow. A warm feeling kindled inside him. His words had caused new life to bud up from deep within. For the first time in who knows how long, he felt as though a burden had been lifted from his shoulders. He had toiled under a yoke he hadn't known was there. The wise, thoughtful words of an old man had released him from a wandering hopelessness. He felt as though he'd been liberated from a prison cell far more constrictive than the one in which he now sat.

'I'll leave,' he finally said, a new hope evident in his voice. 'I'll go to Rome, Athens and further still. I'll find whatever it is I'm looking for and I won't stop looking until I find it. Only this time I'll remain focused. I won't get distracted and I won't lose heart.'

He beamed as he turned to the wizened sage. What he saw saddened and confused him. The old man was shaking his head sadly or solemnly, Asher couldn't tell.

'You need to return to the Galilee,' he finally said.

'Galilee! Why would I want to do that? There's nothing for me there!'

'That's where you'll find what you're looking for.'

Having been amazed at the old man's sage brilliance, Asher was now doubting his sanity. 'But I spent months there. Nothing but fishing villages, shepherds and farmers. It was boring, mundane. I have no desire to return.'

'Trust me,' Elkanah said, and for the first time Asher could see in his eyes a firm resolve, a seriousness that hadn't been there before. Asher could tell that the old man wasn't just offering him some travel advice. He knew something and he was imparting it to Asher.

He felt it was no longer appropriate to protest but merely nodded and accepted the old man's advice.

The discussion seemed to tire Elkanah out for he soon slumped to his mattress and fell asleep. Asher was left to silently contemplate the old man's words. He was grateful to him. He felt he had put him back on the right path. He thanked him quietly. He thanked Yahweh too, for bringing him into his cell.

Chapter VI

Several hours passed in the cell but the old man slept soundly. Dim rays of light were eking their way through the narrow opening in the wall and there was commotion to be heard outside the cell. It sounded like lunchtime. Asher had been there long enough now to recognise the sounds. The soldiers would be making their way from cell to cell hurling broken pieces of stale bread at the prisoners.

His mind was still a whir of excitement following the conversation with Elkanah that morning. He was a lot wiser than he looked in those tattered old robes. His long grey beard might have made him look distinguished were it not so dirty and unkempt.

He looked at him again. He hadn't moved a muscle since he had fallen asleep after breakfast. In truth, Asher was pleased for it gave him time to ruminate on all the old man had said. He had reminded him of old Zeke and how he had encouraged him all that time ago when Asher was struggling over what to do with his life.

Asher heard the soldiers approaching their cell door. It was flung open with some aggression and one of them marched in. He was middle aged, surly and violent. Perhaps he felt he had served in the army long enough and deserved a better job than looking after scumbag prisoners in a Roman backwater.

'You! Old man!' he growled. 'You're leaving.'

Asher looked at his friend with a huge grin on his face. He was getting out. He was going home.

Elkanah didn't move.

'Did you hear me, old man?' he yelled and prodded the sleeping prisoner with his foot.

Still Elkanah didn't move.

A sudden wave of fear washed over Asher and he leaped to his feet. Rushing over to his friend, he shook him gently by the shoulder. His arm was rigid. It was though it was locked in place by powerful muscles. Asher shook him again.

'What's going on?' the soldier bellowed.

Asher lifted Elkanah's head gently with his hand and then let go. The old man's head dropped back. Asher's fears were confirmed. The old man was dead. He backed off, stunned.

'Well?' the man shouted again. 'What's wrong with him?'

'He's dead,' Asher said quietly. He had to fight to hold back the tears. He had only known this man for a matter of hours but he felt Elkanah had changed his life. How could he be dead – the man who was speaking with him and laughing only hours ago?

'He's dead?' the soldier repeated roughly. There were a few moments of silence.

'In that case you can go instead.'

Asher thought he'd misheard. He remained motionless, staring at the floor.

'Did you hear me?' he roared. 'Get out of here! I've got to release a prisoner today so it might as well be you!'

Asher got to his feet nervously. He couldn't take his eyes off his fallen friend but he could sense the soldier was growing more impatient.

'So, because this man has died, I can go free?'

'That's what I said, now get out of here before I change my mind!'

Asher walked toward the door, passed the soldiers who were both eyeing him aggressively. He turned to look once more at the lifeless body of the man whose death had brought him life. A whirlwind of emotion raged within him so before he lost control he turned quickly and walked out.

He hurried along the dark corridors, past the cells from which the pained cries of the prisoners rang out. It wasn't long before he spotted an enormous shaft of light at the end of the corridor. When he stepped outside a gust of cool, fresh air hit him in the face and he gasped. He may have only been there for a few weeks but it had felt like an eternity. The sun was hidden and a forceful breeze was blowing in off the sea. It may have been winter but it was both pleasant and refreshing.

He left the barracks quickly and walked out into the street. He was a free man again. He stopped and turned, once more looking at the barracks in which he'd been held for the last few weeks. Only now he was no longer feeling anger and the cruel sense of injustice. He was thinking of the short time he'd spent with Elkanah and how those few short hours had impacted him in an incalculable way. Not only had his words helped to wake Asher from a slumber and put his life back on track, but he had been instrumental in his release. The old man had saved him in more ways than one.

He stood still in the middle of the street pondering the old man's legacy for some minutes. Passers-by looked at him strangely, as if he was a man who'd lost his mind. Asher had never felt so alive.

After a few moments contemplation he decided to go straight to Ezra's guesthouse. He wouldn't be able to hire him again after what had happened but he was sure the old man would give him a bed for the night. Then he would have to decide what to do and where to go next. Should he look for Varius and find out what had happened? Maybe he should leave Caesarea immediately and close this chapter of his life for good. The old man had told him to go back to the Galilee. He said he would find what he was looking for if he returned.

That decision could wait. First, he had to find somewhere to sleep for the night, then he would decide where his future lay.

Chapter VII

The prison cell was cold and dark, just like her soul. Shifra never got to speak to anybody and was never paid any attention. A few days ago, one of the soldiers had thrown a blanket at her. He didn't want her to die. That was nice of him. It had almost certainly been winter for a few weeks already. She had been forced to curl up into a tight ball to keep out the cold. Sometimes she was tempted to embrace it. Maybe the cold temperatures would freeze her heart solid. Then she would be free. Free from the feeling, free from the pain. Free.

She had been in this prison cell for months - almost a year, in fact. There were times when she thought she would go crazy. There were moments when she thought if she shed any more tears, she would dehydrate. It had given her plenty of time to mull over the last two years. She felt as though she had lurched from one disaster to the next. Unrelenting pain and misery had been heaped on her over and over again.

It had started when her father died. He had been a kind and generous man, a loving father and devoted husband to her mother. They were a happy family. Elishama was popular in the community: successful and esteemed. When the wasting disease took his life, she had experienced a pain and sorrow she had never hitherto known.

They thought they would have to become the chattel of her father's brother, Eliashib. He was a distinguished scribe from the local synagogue, highly thought of in their home town of Joppa. He was a snake. He essentially paid them to go away. He made it sound like he was doing them a favour but something about that transaction had always bothered Shifra.

She and her mother ended up working in the fields but decided to move to Jerusalem to start a new life for themselves. It was on the way that they were attacked by desert bandits. She had been violated and sold into slavery by someone they had trusted. She had never seen her mother again.

Her life as a slave to a wealthy patron of Hebron was soul-destroying. She had escaped when on a visit to the Holy City and made a genuine friend in Keziah. They had gone on the run together and returned to Joppa. There, Shifra had rediscovered happiness, friendship and the love of people who genuinely cared about her, but it hadn't lasted long.

Eliashib turned up again. It had been her cursed bad luck to happen upon her wicked uncle when entangled in an illicit tryst with a local prostitute. She had tried to help him but had ended up a prisoner. He had left her to rot in this jail cell.

Night after night, as she sat alone, shivering in the dark, she couldn't help but feel that this was her destiny. This was the way it was meant to be. She was one of those people who seemed to be cursed. Perhaps she deserved it. Perhaps there was something deeply wrong and God was punishing her.

She had given up hope. The prostitute had been released an age ago. Yet she remained. Was Uncle Eliashib still vindictively ensuring she was kept there? After all this time? How cruel could the man be? Nobody had come to find her, not Tabitha, not Keziah - nobody. She spent the days and the weeks and the months staring at the stone walls. Perhaps she had lost her mind.

It was breakfast time. She could hear the soldiers moving from cell to cell hurling rank food and vile abuse at their captives.

Her door was flung open and the soldier whom she saw every day marched in. 'You!' he yelled. 'Out!'

Shifra didn't move, confused as she was at the alteration in the routine. Usually he threw a piece of bread at her and scowled. Sometimes he shouted something obscene or when he was hungover (which was often) he slurred something unintelligible and slouched off.

'I said move!'

'Why? Where are you taking me?' she managed to ask, though she was terrified of the man.

'I'm not taking you anywhere. You're leaving. Your time's up.'

'I'm getting out of here?'

He didn't like her tone. He marched into the room and grabbed her roughly by the hair. She screamed as he dragged her out of the cell and along the hallway. She stumbled and fell but his vice-like grip on her hair didn't weaken. Eventually they emerged into the open air. She recognised it as the courtyard in which she'd been beaten. She had to close her eyes, for the brightness of the sun blinded her.

Her ordeal ended when they reached the gates to the barracks. The soldiers who were on duty opened the gates and her captor marched through. With one final wrench of her hair, he hurled her to the ground.

'The old vulture who paid for your upkeep hasn't been seen or heard from in weeks!' he shouted at her angrily as she scratted about in the dust, tentatively touching her aching head. 'We're not keeping you here occupying a perfectly good cell, so you can be on your way!'

With that parting gesture he returned to the barracks. The sentries guarding the gate slammed them shut and she was left, crumpled in a heap crying and holding her aching head. She had blood on the ends of her fingers and clumps of hair in her hands. She sat sobbing for several minutes before she managed to look around.

Suddenly the delightful realisation dawned on her that she was free. The sun was shining in the vast blue sky and a cold wind was blowing in off the sea. There were a few people in the street, all of whom were giving her a wide berth. The soldiers in the barracks were still eyeing her suspiciously through the gates.

Suddenly the pain didn't seem so jarring. The relief she felt now was overwhelming. It was over! It was finally over. Yet there was no joy. Looking around her at the buildings and the people she suddenly felt alone. She had been released into the vast openness of the world but it was just her. Now where would she go and what would she do? She got to her feet, pulled the hair back from her face and the scarf over her head.

Her thoughts turned immediately to Tabitha. She had to go there and tell her what had happened. Keziah too would want to know where she'd been. They would welcome her back. They would be overjoyed to see her. Or would they?

She had been gone for what felt like the best part of a year. She had no hint that Tabitha or Keziah had even come looking for her. They would have moved on with their lives by now. They may have even forgotten all about her.

Or worse: what if they had found her and knew exactly what had happened. What if they knew she was in there but had left her there on purpose and not tried to get her out. They probably thought that she deserved it. If she was involved in a heinous attempt to trick and seduce a respected Scribe then they probably wanted nothing more to do with her.

If she turned up there now it would be humiliating. They would turn her away and shout at her. They would say they wanted nothing more to do with her and never want to see her again.

But Tabitha wasn't like that, was she? She had been so kind and welcoming the first time. She had gone out of her way to help her, providing her with a home and a job. More importantly, she had been a good friend or even a mother to her. She was always helping the poor and destitute. Why would she not want to help her now?

She didn't deserve her kindness. Look what had happened. Despite the help and favour she'd been given, she'd still ended up in a prison cell. There was something deeply wrong with her; she was cursed, bedevilled, damaged goods. It would be better for Tabitha and Keziah if they never set eyes on her again. She would only cause them more pain and embarrassment. They would be better off spending their time and effort helping others who were actually worthy of their kindness.

The desperate thoughts tormented her as she tried to figure out what to do. In the end she couldn't bear the thought of what might happen if she turned up at Tabitha's house and she was unwelcome. She had been abused and rejected by so many, so often. To be sent away by the one person who she thought might have once really cared about her was too heartbreaking to contemplate.

She would leave. Go somewhere else. Turn her back on Joppa once and for all. She had no money, no family and no prospects. At least she had been here before. This time it was less terrifying. She knew what to do to survive.

She thought some more until she remembered the way to one of the local markets. Once there she enquired if any of the merchants were on their way to another town and, if possible, could she accompany them.

Most of them wanted nothing to do with her. Highly suspicious of a young woman her age, alone and without a husband or family, they gave her short shrift. At last a family took pity on her. They were going to Jerusalem to visit family and she was welcome to join them.

Shifra was relieved. She had been prepared to go with anyone and accept the risks she knew only too well. However, travelling with a family seemed to be one of the safer options.

There were dangers in Jerusalem for her too, of course, such as bumping into anyone from the household of Ahlai, or anyone associated with Hodesh and Kenan, her old master. Yet getting out of Joppa was her priority and so she accepted with alacrity the family's offer.

They left almost straight away, having picked up some fruit from the market. They had a donkey, a small cart and three small children. Soon they were on the road Shifra had travelled many times before. Here we go again! She thought, with resignation.

Chapter VIII

Sarah was back in Jerusalem. It was the time of Pesach and so Pilate was expected to be there to ensure the heaving crowds of Jewish pilgrims behaved themselves. He wasn't always successful, of course; in fact he often made matters worse. In the past it was his stupid actions which had inflamed the people and led to scores of unfortunate deaths.

She liked returning to Jerusalem. Caesarea had grown on her but she had many fond memories of coming here with Elishama and Shifra. Despite the pain of recent years those memories had remained intact and unsullied.

Claudia wanted some time alone so Sarah had been told the time was her own. As Eve didn't need any help, Sarah decided to walk into the city. The streets were crowded with people. The merchants in the marketplace were shouting excitedly, drawing customers to their stalls. There were animals everywhere. Offering a sacrifice for Pesach was mandatory and so, no matter how wealthy you were, you had to offer an appropriate sacrifice lest Yahweh be displeased.

Sarah was conflicted when she looked upon the crowd. On the one hand she enjoyed the buzz and infinite energy that crowds of this size created yet she couldn't help but feel for them. Most of them were very poor yet they were desperate to do what was right. They must offer the sacrifice. It must be perfect, without spot or blemish. They must abide by the traditions and customs of their forbears. Their devotion to Yahweh must be tangible and heartfelt.

Sarah was more sceptical than she had ever been. There was something about this behaviour that she abhorred, though she could never quite put her finger on why.

As she surveyed the scene, a retinue of religious leaders walked by. They were probably making their way toward the temple. No doubt they felt they had something of earth-shattering importance to do there. They weren't blind to the needs of the crowd. They saw it and they were indifferent. It was awful, the way the so-called leaders showed such apathy toward the people, the flock for whom they were supposed to show compassion and give guidance to.

She watched as they swatted away those who had the audacity to approach them. She shook her heard silently as they berated those who got too close or who unwittingly slowed them down. Suddenly one of them caught her eye. She felt as though she recognised him.

She edged closer through the crowd. She quickened her pace so that she could get a better look at these men, especially one of them in particular.

The crowd was about ten people thick. Then she spotted him. Her blood ran cold and a horrible feeling rose up in her stomach. It was Eliashib, her old brother in law. He was here in Jerusalem. And, to her horror, it looked as though he was someone of influence. He was dressed in the ornate garb of the Sanhedrin. They were the much-revered teachers of the law, the scribes and lawyers whose job it was to explain scriptures and interpret God's word. They wielded an enormous amount of power and she was horrified to see that Eliashib looked to be one of their ranks.

Rooted to the spot, she watched as he and the others pushed and barged their way through the crowd. Dumbfounded, she recalled all the horrible altercations she'd had with him in the past. What was he doing here? If he was a member of the Sanhedrin, he had the opportunity to cause an unapparelled amount of distress to many people.

Deciding she had to know more, she shook herself from the dazed stupor she was in and made her way in his direction. Having rounded a few corners, she spotted him and his cronies obviously heading toward the temple. She followed him, not knowing what she was going to do. She was seized by a desperate desire to find out exactly what he was doing in Jerusalem. Maybe then she could figure out what to do. At the very least she could warn somebody about what he was like and what he was capable of.

She passed into the temple area which was thronged with people. Most people who didn't live in Jerusalem visited at least three times a year for the major festivals. Pesach was one of them and so there were crowds everywhere.

She kept her eye on the man who had caused her so much angst over the years. He disappeared with his fellow Scribes into an area in which she was forbidden to enter. Women didn't have the same rights of access as men. They were deemed less worthy and therefore had to remain in the courts of the women, while the men were granted the privilege of edging closer to the Holy of Holies.

Standing disconsolately in the outer courts she wondered what to do next. The more she thought of Eliashib as a member of the Sanhedrin, the more her blood ran cold.

However, she was also reminded of an old family friend. He was a member of the Sanhedrin and, if still alive, he may remember her.

As if by the blessed hand of providence, as she cast her eye around the outer court her eyes alighted upon the very man.

'Nicodemus!' she said out loud and, in an instant, rushed toward him. He, unlike the others, was alone but he too was busily trying to make his way through the crowd.

She managed to draw alongside him quickly. 'Rabbi, do you remember me? It's Sarah!'

He stopped and looked at her carefully.

'We are old family friends, you and I. Though I confess you knew my husband, Elishama, better than you knew me.'

'Elishama,' he said out loud as if it would help him remember. He looked closely at Sarah once more and a broad smile stretched across his face. 'Sarah!' he said confidently.

'Yes, Rabbi, you remember me?'

'Of course I do, Sarah. How are you and how is your husband?'

'I'm afraid he died almost three years ago.'

Nicodemus sympathised. 'Oh, I am sorry to hear that, Sarah. He was a good man.'

'He was a good man and I am thankful for the years we had together.'

'How are you then?'

'I am well thank you, Rabbi, I am well.'

'And you had a daughter, didn't you? It was a daughter wasn't it?'

Sarah paused. She thought about Shifra every day but she hadn't spoken about her for a long time. 'Alas that is a long story Rabbi and you are a busy man.'

'I'm sorry Sarah. Not a painful story, I hope?'

Sarah decided to sweep past that comment and move the conversation on. 'When I saw you, I rushed over for there is something I must discuss with you urgently.'

His face lit up. 'Is it about Jesus?'

His face was animated with expectation. Without saying a word, he was imploring her to confirm his hopes.

'Who?'

'Jesus the Nazarene?'

Sarah was bewildered. 'I have no idea who that is.'

Nicodemus overcame his disappointment and began to smile. 'Apparently he's causing quite a stir in the Galilee. I met him, you know?'

The thought briefly passed through Sarah's mind that her old friend had taken leave of his senses.

'I need to talk to you about Eliashib!' she said firmly.

'Who?' he replied.

'A few moments ago I saw Elishama's brother, Eliashib here in Jerusalem. He was with some members of the Sanhedrin.'

'Eliashib,' he repeated. 'Yes, I know him. He was inducted into our fellowship a few weeks ago. From Joppa I believe.'

Sarah had heard enough to make her heart sink. 'So it's true?'

'What's true?'

'Eliashib is a member of the Sanhedrin?'

'Yes. He has been for a number of weeks. Why?'

'How could this have happened? I thought you and your esteemed brothers were wise. Not just anyone can be on the Sanhedrin, can they? It's a position of great power and privilege. I don't understand why you would admit him to your number.'

Nicodemus was puzzled by her attitude but he tried to appease her. 'As I recall, he was nominated by Rabbi Tobiah in Joppa. He's highly thought of, you know. A seat opened up on the council and there weren't many names forthcoming - no suitable ones anyway. I believe that was when someone mentioned Tobiah and that he might be able to nominate someone appropriate.'

Sarah listened intently without saying anything. She was resigned to the depressing reality.

'He nominated brother Eliashib and when the delegation returned from Joppa his appointment was ratified by a majority of the brothers. Myself included, I should add.'

He paused and stared at Sarah, trying to ascertain what the problem was. 'Why Sarah? What is your interest in this?'

'He's no good Rabbi. I shan't bore you with the details, especially when the deed's been done, but he is not fit to hold such a position.'

Nicodemus was shocked. 'But why ever not, Sarah?'

'He's sly and conniving, greedy, unscrupulous, uncaring, arrogant and selfish,' she chose her words carefully, delivering her condemnation slowly and enunciating each word with venom.

He was appalled. 'Sarah!' he protested. 'You shouldn't say such things, especially about someone who now holds a position of great honour.'

'There is nothing honourable about that man, Rabbi. Heed my words and stay away from him.'

She had no desire to pursue the conversation any further. She started to back away, keeping Nicodemus fixed in her solemn, melancholic gaze. Eventually she turned and walked off.

Why was it that this world seemed to reward people like Eliashib? They were rotten to the core but still managed to benefit from all the wealth and privilege this world had to offer. It wasn't right and it made her feel sick to her stomach. Was there any justice in the world? If there was, men like him and Pilate and the men who took Shifra would get what they deserved. Retribution and revenge, that's what she wished for them.

Thoroughly depressed and worn out, she cut a forlorn figure as she made her way back to the Praetorium.

Chapter IX

Varius relaxed in the sun, looking out over the Sea of Galilee. The sight had grown on him and now that summer was coming he liked nothing better than to sit in the morning sun looking out over the magnificent vista. He sat in the shade of a gnarled old sycamore tree and watched as fishermen toiled in the morning sun, bringing home their catch.

He had come here often when off duty and had become known to some of the local fishermen. They often mended their nets near where he liked to sit. They were understandably wary of him at first, which Varius liked. They were always on their best behaviour when he showed up and were at pains to offer him a portion of their catch and wine too. He concealed the fact that he spoke their language for some time, hoping that he would catch them saying something untoward. He thought he might overhear them criticising the Emperor or the Roman presence in the region. Perhaps he would overhear them deriding him.

He never did though, which caused him to conclude they were genuinely nice people who just wanted to be left alone to get on with their lives. The day he spoke to them in Aramaic was a fine memory of his he would cherish forever. A number of them were dragging their small boat ashore, one of them perched precariously on the end. Varius had walked over casually and in his best Aramaic had offered to help. The men were so shocked they let go of the boat and their friend fell off the back and into the water. It was a scene of great hilarity and Varius was grateful for the chance to share in the good-natured banter with the fishermen.

Once he had explained to them that he had learned Aramaic in Joppa and enjoyed conversing with them in their own tongue, their affection for him seemed to grow. They were still overly respectful, of course, and always a little on their guard. No matter how affable they became, the truth was that he still represented the Roman oppressors.

The man with whom he spoke the most was an older fisherman by the name of Banaah. He was in his sixties but strong as an ox. He had worked as a fisherman by the Sea of Galilee his whole life and so had generations of his family before him. His face and hands were worn and weather beaten, proof of a life spent outside, battling the elements. The other men willingly submitted to his authority which seemed to imbue him naturally. There was nothing harsh in his manner but he seemed to exude a gentle kindness which Varius had never seen in a leader before. And that is certainly what he was, for the other men had the utmost respect for him.

Varius had spent many lazy mornings talking with him, while the others were out fishing. Now that he was advancing in years, he was the one who volunteered to mend the nets while the others brought in the catch. He always had his grandson with him, a boy named Heled. He would sit by himself most days, small knife in hand, carving a piece of wood his grandfather had procured for him.

Banaah had explained that he carved small toys for his siblings and cousins. It was all he was good for. He was lame in one leg and had only half a brain. It had always been so with him and had brought much shame on the family. His father, Banaah's son in law, had no time for the boy. That was why he hung around his grandfather like a little lost puppy. He was the only one who showed the poor wretch any kindness.

This particular morning was similar to many others. Varius, sitting in the shade of the sycamore tree, watched as Banaah approached. He had a bundled fishing net in his hands and an old leather pouch hung loosely from his neck. His powerful arms and shoulders were dark brown, his hair and beard, dark grey. Heled hobbled behind him, using a crutch for support.

'Good morning, Varius my friend,' he called out jovially, before plonking himself down nearby to begin his work.

'How are you, Banaah?' Varius replied in flawless Aramaic.

'Glorious, my friend, glorious. There's air in my lungs and strength in my bones.'

It was a typically enthusiastic response from the old timer.

'Where are the men? They haven't returned yet?'

'They weren't having much luck out there last night so they returned just after midnight. They went out again just before dawn, hoping for better luck.'

'It's a tough life, eh Banaah?'

'I wouldn't change it for the world,' he sighed contentedly. 'I don't get out there much anymore but this great lake has provided for me and my family for generations. As a young man there was nothing I liked better than sailing out there just as dawn was breaking, the wind rushing through my hair and the spray soaking me to the bone.'

'It's not for me,' Varius winced at the thought of being a fisherman. All that hard work, toiling day and night, stinking of fish and covered in slime. It wasn't that long ago he and Asher had nearly been killed by the ferocity of the ocean.

'You and I are from different worlds. I dare say I would not like Rome or the other big cities you have ventured through on your travels. I like the quiet life. You can keep the eternal city.'

Varius laughed. 'You country folk up here are all the same. You prize your seclusion. The rest of the world can go hang.'

Banaah grimaced. 'Not the expression I would have used, but you're right. We've no desire to get embroiled in the troubles of the outside world.'

'Though there has been rumours of unrest recently, has there not?'

'Unrest?'

'I don't mean violent unrest,' Varius clarified. 'I mean this preacher that I keep hearing whispers about. What's his name?'

'Ah! You mean this fellow Jesus?'

'So you've heard of him too then?'

'My daughter keeps talking about him. She often wanders up to the northern shore and returns with fancy tales from Capernaum.'

'What do you mean by fancy tales?'

'Well this man they call Jesus goes about preaching, not just in the synagogue but out in the countryside too.'

'Is there anything special about him? There is no shortage of wandering preachers, is there?'

'This one's different, if you believe what people say.'

'What do they say?'

'My daughter says he's not like the others. He's different.'

Varius was intrigued. 'How so?'

'From what I can gather, he's not a trained Rabbi. He's not a scribe or teacher or someone who's studied the scriptures.'

'Well what is he then?'

'A tradesman I think, some sort of carpenter or potter. Something like that.'

Varius was incredulous. 'You're suggesting that people are becoming besotted by a wandering craftsman?'

Banaah shrugged his shoulders. 'All of my information comes from my daughter. She seems to think he's something special. He performs miracles according to her.'

'Miracles!'

'That's what she says.'

'What kind of miracles?'

'Healing people,' Banaah shrugged with affected nonchalance.

Varius couldn't help but laugh. 'Don't tell me you believe all this Banaah!'

'I don't know what to believe,' he answered sheepishly. 'I have always said my daughter was level-headed and not given to puerile flights of fancy, but she seems smitten with this one.'

Varius shook his head in dismay. 'A miracle-working handyman who can heal the sick! The gullibility of my fellow man shall never cease to amaze.'

'No doubt you'll see him soon. If his reputation continues to rise he might be a threat to you and your kind.'

'Come on, Banaah! What could the might of Rome possibly have to fear from some half-baked fruitcake and his mindless devotees?'

'There have been rebellions before and they all start with a charismatic leader who can command a following.'

Varius dismissed the notion out of hand. 'I shan't lose any sleep over this man, Banaah. Before too long he will have vanished back into obscurity like all the others.'

Chapter X

The last few months had been exhilarating for Eliashib. Moving to Jerusalem had been nerve-racking at first, but he had quickly found his feet. His position on the Sanhedrin had been ratified quickly, despite some members of the brotherhood publicly questioning his suitability. He sensed they had their own preferred candidate and would have opposed anyone regardless of who they might have been. Eliashib knew he was clearly and impeccably qualified for the role.

The initial nerves soon passed and he began to feel at home among these men who wielded such power and commanded so much respect. This was where he belonged after all. These wise and learned men were the ones with whom he felt a kinship. In the first few debates and discussions they'd had, he had watched and listened closely. It hadn't taken him long to realise that they were no wiser nor more intellectual than he. Their deliberations often centred upon the meaning of scriptures and the relevant interpretation of them. These were areas in which he excelled, and he soon found he was quite comfortable discussing all manner of subjects in public.

Many of the brothers had spoken to him after these discussions. They had said that his thoughts and comments had been most insightful. He was truly in the right place.

He thought back to his last few weeks in Joppa. It still thrilled him no end to think of how he had outmanoeuvred

Joktan and Tobiah. He would have been content with the leadership of the synagogue but the more he had mulled it over and the more he thought of that arrogant Joktan, his plan changed. It wasn't until he had been called into Tobiah's office that he had been inspired to alter the course of his mission.

It was the insipid and weak character of the delegates from the Sanhedrin that had changed his mind. He worked out within a few minutes of entering the room that these men could be easily manipulated. They did not have the astuteness or political nous that he possessed. He remembered fondly those minutes when he schemed silently, considering his options over and over in his mind. They hadn't the least idea what he was thinking and planning. Even if they had, they would not have been able to stop him. It was then that he realised that he could secure the position on the Sanhedrin. Why should he accept the lowly position of synagogue leader in comparison to such a prestigious post? It came to him suddenly as if it had been deposited from above: Jehu could lead the synagogue and he should go to the Sanhedrin. It was brilliant. In one master stroke, he could sweep aside the senile old fool and his arrogant acolyte.

He smiled fondly, remembering the thrill of those hours. He could still see vividly in his mind's eye, the look on Joktan's face when he realised he would be getting no promotion. Eliashib had taken the spot that Joktan most coveted and he would probably never get another opportunity. It was so delicious it made his heart sing.

He was overjoyed to be in Jerusalem. This was where the power lay. This was where decisions were made that affected the course of countless lives. He was thrilled to the bone that he would get to play such a pivotal role in shaping and protecting the future of his people.

He was on his way to the temple now, to the Hall of Hewn Stones, where the Sanhedrin met. They sat there every day, hearing cases that had passed through from the minor courts.

He was always relieved to make it into the inner sanctum of the temple. He could escape the clutching, fawning rabble that filled Jerusalem's streets. Often, when they saw him coming, the crowds parted like the Red Sea parting around Moses. They were in awe of him. He cut a fine figure in his expensive garments and bejewelled fingers and he was pleased to see them scurry out of the way when he approached.

Occasionally, however, someone would have the temerity to approach him. It was usually the poor or the sick. The idle scroungers never got any satisfaction from him. Had they known their scriptures they would have heeded the advice of King Solomon. 'Go to the ant, you sluggard. Consider its ways and be wise!'

They were only marginally better than the cripples and half-wits. Their weaknesses and deformities had been decreed by God. If he had seen fit to curse them with such afflictions then they must have deserved it.

Sadly, Jerusalem was full of them and their numbers seemed to increase by the day. That was one of the reasons he dearly loved the sanctuary of the temple. Once you crossed the threshold of the inner courts, you were safe from the rabble.

He took the seat he had grown accustomed to, next to brothers who had sat on the Sanhedrin for many years. Caiaphas the High Priest was in attendance, as was his father in law, Annas. He had four other sons, all of whom were there, thick as thieves. Gamaliel was an imperious figure, tall and indomitable. There was something about him Eliashib didn't like.

Eliashib relaxed in his chair and prepared to concentrate on the disputations at hand. There was invariably some matter regarding Shabbat. How was it to be best observed and under what conditions could the rules be relaxed?

He looked around the court once more and an excitement built within him. This was his world and he loved it.

After a long morning of listening to prolonged discussion and debate, he relaxed in a meeting room in the temple. Surrounded by the brothers of the Sanhedrin, he talked with his new friends about all manner of topics. He didn't know all of their names yet and sometimes felt as though he was stuck on the periphery of their conversations.

He sidled up to a group of men who seemed to be listening intently to the one who was addressing them. 'Gather in brothers,' he said conspiratorially. 'Gather in.'

Eliashib huddled in with the half dozen other brothers, eager to hear what the man had to say. He was advancing in years, with a hunched stature and face like a wrinkled prune. His eyes were shifty and alert.

'There is something brewing in the Galilee,' he whispered. He paused, waiting for someone to ask him what it was. None did.

Frustrated, he continued. 'There is a man by the name of Jesus, travelling all over the region, preaching and teaching the people.'

'Preaching and teaching what?' one of them asked.

'Teaching from the scriptures of course. He has done so from the synagogue in Capernaum.'

'Well is he trained? Is he educated?'

The old raconteur laughed. 'Educated?' he mocked. 'You must be joking, brother. They say he's a carpenter from Nazareth.'

'A carpenter!'

Some of them were shocked and some indifferent.

'So what?' one of the men scoffed. 'Let him talk to the ignorant farmers and fishermen up there. What do we care?'

Another of the men was clearly annoyed at his apathy. 'We care because of our commitment to protecting and preserving God's word!' he said. 'Are we to allow this uneducated fellow to travel about the place preaching and teaching? And in the synagogue too! It's repugnant!'

Eliashib thought the man was going a bit too far. A wandering peasant in the Galilee was hardly any of their concern. However, he did think it important to defend the integrity of the scriptures.

'What is the essence of his sermons?' someone asked.

The old man smiled. 'Now that is an interesting question, brother. Apparently only a matter of weeks ago, he delivered a large, open-air sermon on the banks of the great lake. My sources tell me that he was announcing a blessing on all sorts of different people.'

'Announcing a blessing!' one of the younger men was horrified. 'Who does this man think he is? What kind of blessing?'

'All the man could remember was that he said, 'blessed are the poor''

'Blessed are the poor!' there was a round of laughter.

Eliashib thought it the most absurd statement he had ever heard and said so. 'Now we know the man is insane. Blessed are the poor!'

'The people up there don't think it's insane,' the old man replied solemnly. 'He gathers quite a crowd.'

'So does the lunatic in the marketplace, dancing and juggling with fruit.'

'He inspires devotion.'

'That's because they lack direction,' Eliashib replied. 'Perhaps we need to send someone up there who can open their eyes to the true meaning of scripture? Blessed are the poor indeed!'

There was a few moment's silence while the few men contemplated Eliashib's suggestion.

'Wait a minute!' one of them suddenly blurted out angrily. 'This isn't the same fellow who has been causing trouble here in Jerusalem lately, is it?'

A few of them nodded assent and another chimed in. 'A while ago I heard an account of a man who had seemingly gone quite mad in the temple. He attacked the merchants, flipped over the tables and made quite a scene.'

'That was over a year ago, it can't be the same man.'

'I have heard more disturbing accounts that happened not long ago.'

'Well go on then,' their impatience was wearing thin. 'What have you heard? I can't say I've heard anything.'

'That's because you spend your whole time cooped up in here. You ought to get out of here once in a while and see what happens in the real world.'

'Will you two stop bickering and get on with it?'

'Well there was an account of a most grotesque violation of Shabbat.'

The men, as one, recoiled in horror as if they had all been stabbed. A desecration of Shabbat was as heinous a crime as one could commit. Eliashib was disgusted.

'So, what happened?' one of them managed once they had regained their faculties.

'This man, if it is the same man, apparently prayed for someone's healing at the Pool of Bethesda and then did the same thing in the synagogue.'

'On Shabbat?'

'On Shabbat!'

'Terrible!'

'Disgusting!'

'Shameful!'

'An abomination!'

'Did they get healed?' a dissenting voice dared to ask.

The other vultures turned on their errant friend. 'Well of course they weren't healed!' one of them droned.

'That's not what I heard!' another goaded.

'Well it can't be true. It just can't be!'

'Why not?'

'Because Yahweh wouldn't sanction the violation of Shabbat. It is holy. Precious. It is sacred, brother. You know that.'

There was several moment's silence while the men comprehended the distressing news, each trying to figure out what they had heard and why it couldn't possibly be true.

Finally, the original instigator of the discussion piped up. 'I haven't told you the full story yet,' the old man continued. 'about the man in the Galilee.

'Well go on then,' one of them sighed.

'He's not just preaching and teaching.'

He paused for dramatic effect.

'Well what else is he doing?' someone snapped.

The old man delivered his next lines slowly, methodically and with great relish. 'He's healing people.'

The men, of one accord, looked at the old man with a look of disgust and incredulity.

'Not you as well! Not more of this healing nonsense!'

Eliashib questioned whether he himself had taken leave of his senses. Why was he listening to this doddery old fool?

With flamboyant gesticulations and animated cries of offence, the men rounded on the old man.

'What are you talking about?'

'Don't be so ridiculous!'

'You should be ashamed of yourself.'

'Healing people!'

The old man struggled for several moments to retain the command of the group. Some of them sought to leave but he pulled them back.

'I am telling you just what I heard from those who were there,' he pleaded. 'The man who told me all this is a sensible, God-fearing, down-to-earth businessman, now living in Tiberius. He is not the type to cook up some fanciful story and he wouldn't be willing to talk about it if he hadn't seen it with his own eyes.'

The men fell silent, realising for the first time that the old man was in earnest.

'Are you telling us you actually believe all this?'

'I don't know what to believe,' the old man answered. 'But what I can say is this: I have never had any reason to mistrust this man in the past.'

The seriousness of their friend's words and the respect they had for him caused the men to pause and think.

Eliashib felt the need to say something quick, lest the men actually start to believe this nonsense. 'What kind of healings?

'The sermon I was telling you about? Where he spoke about the poor being blessed?'

'Yes, go on.'

'Immediately afterward, he healed a man with leprosy,' the old man said it matter-of-fact.

'Leprosy!' the chorus of disagreement erupted again.

'The man can't be consorting with lepers,' one voice rose above the din. 'That's sinful!'

'He also healed a centurion's servant!' the old man continued, ignoring their protestations.

'A Roman!'

'This story is confounded nonsense and you ought to be ashamed of yourself for regurgitating it!'

'First a leper then a Roman! Of all the wicked absurdities you could conjure up! You've outdone yourself this time!'

A few of them men started to laugh, though none of them drifted away.

Eliashib was pensive. When the derision died down, he asked, 'Does this man believe himself to be the Messiah?'

The men stopped laughing and turned to look at Eliashib who was searching the face of the old man for an answer. Before long everyone's gaze was fixed on their old friend.

'There are some who believe he is a prophet. I am not sure any are attributing to him Messianic qualities.'

'Give them time,' one sneered.

'They love a false Messiah up there. They've embraced enough of them.

'He's obviously just another fruit cake. He'll be gone in another few weeks and his crazed followers will crawl back to the huts and hovels from whence they came.'

'I'm not so sure,' the old man said thoughtfully.

Eliashib was perturbed by the old man's demeanour. 'Do you think he's dangerous?'

He thought for a while before answering. 'I don't know, but I am certain this is a situation that needs our attention. If someone up there is causing trouble and whipping the people up into a frenzy then we need to know about it. Imagine if he came down here and did the same.'

Most of them looked at the old man with thinly disguised disdain.

He ignored them. 'If he is dangerous, he'll need to be stopped. And the sooner the better.'

No sooner had the words drifted theatrically off the old man's tongue than the men were once more called into the hall. They had more cases to hear in the afternoon and their presence was required.

Eliashib was unable to concentrate on proceedings and heard little of what was discussed for the rest of the day. He couldn't deny he was interested in what the old man had said. He'd heard of deranged preachers claiming to be the Messiah but he'd never seen one. He was intrigued by the idea of travelling to the Galilee and seeing this all for himself.

There was another idea percolating in his conscience though. This could prove an exciting opportunity. If he orchestrated this properly, he could ingratiate himself with the most influential members of the Sanhedrin. Caiaphas, the High Priest, might want a first-hand report of all that was going on in the Galilee. If he could inveigle his way into his confidence, it might pay off handsomely in the future.

The more he thought about it the more he was convinced it was a workable plan. He would impress upon his elders the need to investigate this Nazarene and by so doing, he would elevate himself among the brethren.

Chapter XI

Night gave way to a grey dawn. Varius had been on duty all night, guarding the residence of Herod Antipas. The gathering had been quiet by his standards: he was a notorious hedonist. Nothing stirred in the palace now. It would be hours before the family awoke. Often, they didn't appear until noon. Fortunately, his shift was almost over and someone should be coming to relieve him any minute.

He hated the night shift and cursed it every time it was his turn. He found the long night hours interminably dull and the darkness seemed to never end. He longed for the approaching dawn but it never arrived as quickly as he hoped. The worst of it was, he was captive to his thoughts. Standing or walking alone for the whole night invariably led him to think. It was frustrating and inescapable. He didn't want to think. He just wanted his shift to be over.

His thoughts usually turned to the dramatic events of the last few years. His father had forced him out of the house and his mother had done little to stop him. He had been exiled in Alexandria where he had been teased and seduced by a local. The savages of that land had killed one of his best friends and then he had been banished to the land of the Jews. He thought of his time in Joppa. Surprisingly, learning Aramaic had redeemed that period in his life. He had prevailed in the Negev against a savage desert horde. His father would have appreciated that. There had been more action in Jerusalem, which would have pleased him. In

Caesarea and now in Tiberius, he had it easy. It had been quite the adventure. He was sure he had finally made his father proud. Almost sure.

His replacement arrived and finally Varius was able to leave the den of iniquity, return to the barracks and get some rest.

The morning air was invigorating yet dense, laden with the promise of a violent downpour. As he glanced toward the Sea of Galilee he saw thick, heavy grey clouds forming in the distance. A storm was coming. He shuddered as he remembered the monstrous storm that had sought to envelop him and Asher. That was possibly as close to death as he had ever come and it had been terrifying. He was still able to make out some boats on the lake. Their owners had obviously been too drunk or too stupid to realise that a storm was coming. Some of them might never return to shore. He had seen numerous shards of boat and smashed vessels littered around the shoreline on his many walks. Those familiar with the area knew these storms could be vicious.

He quickened his pace and returned to the barracks as drops of rain were growing in intensity. Many of his colleagues who were about to start duty were having their breakfast. He had no appetite and so headed straight for his bed. By the time he did, the rain was lashing down outside. He could hear it pounding on the roof and walls. It must be an almighty squall, he thought to himself as his head hit the pillow. It wouldn't stop him from sleeping though. The foundations of the building could be torn asunder and he wouldn't wake.

When he finally did, several hours had passed. It was almost noon and he was hungry. His stomach growled in annoyance at having been denied sustenance for so long. He dressed quickly and went straight to the canteen to pacify it. There were few people there. Most of his colleagues on night shift were probably still in bed and most others were either out on patrol or involved in some training exercise.

He ate alone and then decided to go for a walk by the lake. He was pleased to find the sun was shining and all traces of the violent storm had passed. The ground was bone dry, the yellow grass withered in the heat and small lizards scurried along in search of shade. The storm must have passed quickly for there was no sign it had ever happened.

As he approached the water's edge he could smell the fishing vessels nearby and see some of the men still unloading their catch. He hadn't been down here for some time. The last time he'd come he'd been annoyed by Banaah's story.

The fact such a well-respected man was giving credence to all this Jesus nonsense was infuriating. To make matters worse, he had heard more people whispering about him. He had heard soldiers he didn't know talking about him in the canteen and overheard the muted conversations of people in the street discussing the man too. Whatever he was, he certainly had people talking.

Varius had toyed with the idea of finding the charlatan and arresting him. That would give the people around here something to talk about. His superiors wouldn't go for it though. They were here to preserve the peace, not instigate a ruckus.

Religion angered him now like it never used to. He had always dismissed it as an irrelevance. When people at home had fawned over their favourite deity it hadn't bothered him. He didn't care what gods people prayed to or how many shrines they had in their homes. It was different now. He had seen too many examples of the absurdity of it all. He had observed the strong using religion to abuse the weak and the hypocrisy of it galled him. And through it all he couldn't escape from the memory of Safiya. She had chosen her religion over him.

Banaah was sitting by the shore. He was alone, doing nothing.

'How are you, old man?' Varius asked as he approached.

Banaah turned and smiled at his approach and thrust out a hand in greeting. 'I am well, Varius, very well. How are you?'

'I have been on duty in the house of Antipas throughout the night. I loathe the night shift, though at least when I do it there are some distractions.'

Banaah nodded in acknowledgment. 'Another wild party?'

'Not last night, which is why the night seemed longer than most. You have no nets to mend?'

'Not today. The men had a rough night. They caught little and wanted to stay out longer but a storm rose up. They had to race back to shore before it enveloped them.'

'I saw the storm clouds gathering as I made my way home. It looked like it was going to be a big one.'

'That's the surprising thing,' Banaah answered. 'The men said it looked terrifying and at one point they actually feared for their lives. It was a monster. The sky turned black and the waves were crashing in all around them. Thankfully they made it back and reached shore safely. Yet once they had done so and fastened the boats, the storm had died down almost completely. They said they had never seen such an angry and dangerous storm diffuse so quickly.'

Varius shrugged. 'I'm glad to hear it. I was out at sea in a storm once and it is not something I should like to repeat. Are you going out with them later?'

'No, not today. I rarely go out anymore. I'm getting too old.'

'Well in that case, old man, you should get yourself indoors out of this heat. Only lunatics and scoundrels are outdoors at this hour of the day.'

Banaah smiled. 'Which one are you?'

'Both! That's why I've been exiled up here in this godforsaken land!'

'This godforsaken land is my home don't forget and has been all my life.'

Varius was about to further his remarks when he noticed a number of people walking along the road nearby. They were all headed south and though there wasn't a multitude, there was enough to look unusual.

'Speaking of lunatics,' he said. 'What are all these people doing out here at the hottest hour of the day?'

Banaah looked and shrugged his shoulders. 'I could guess.'

Varius didn't hear him. There was a group of three men and two women passing nearby. 'Hey!' he shouted. 'What's going on? Where are you all going at this hour?'

'It's the Nazarene!' one of the women shouted back, enthusiasm evident in her voice.

Varius' heart sank, he curled his lip and growled. 'What about him?'

'Someone said he's in the region of the Gadarenes. We're going to see if we can find him.'

Varius could feel the anger rising within him. 'Why?'

The woman just shrugged her shoulders and they all laughed.

He turned from them and looked to Banaah for an explanation. 'By the gods, Banaah, what is going on?'

'Like I told you last time, he's creating quite a stir around here.'

He glanced at the crowd. There was a steady stream of people all moving in the same direction. He was suddenly caught in a quandary and didn't know what to do. He felt like chasing after them and remonstrating with them wildly. Even though there was only one of him and many of them, the fact that he was a Roman might be enough to guarantee their obedience.

Yet what he mostly felt was utter frustration. Why are these people all running after this mindless fool? How desperate and stupid must they be to wander all over the countryside looking for him? Don't they realise he's just another would-be Messiah? Don't they realise they're all being conned? Duped?

'Why don't you go with them?'

The voice was Banaah's. Varius spun around, a look of disgust on his face. 'Excuse me!'

'I said why don't you go with them.'

'Why would I want to do that?' he snapped.

'See for yourself,' Banaah shrugged. 'See what all the fuss is about.'

Varius looked confused and agitated. 'I don't care what all the fuss is about! I'm not traipsing along like the rest of these demented sheep after some deluded nobody!'

Banaah's voice remained calm and composed despite the rising tension of his Roman friend. 'You seem to be getting quite agitated for someone who doesn't care.'

For a moment Varius was taken aback by the man's insolence. He was about unleash a tirade of abuse when he stopped, remembering that this man was practically a friend. Instead he slowly pointed a finger at the old man, trying hard to control the shaking. He was full of rage. 'Mind your tone when you talk to me Banaah, mind your tone and mind it well.'

Banaah half raised his arms in surrender and said no more.

Varius sat down once more, making a concerted effort to control his temper. There was a few moment's silence while he composed his thoughts and stilled his nerve.

'Have you seen him?' he finally asked.

Banaah was quiet for several moments as if wrestling with his own thoughts. 'I haven't.'

Varius was surprised. 'Why not?'

Again, a long thoughtful pause. 'I'm not sure. There's something about this whole business that makes me uncomfortable. Like you say, there have been many come and gone claiming to be this and that. They have all disappeared as quickly as they arrived. Yet I can't help but feel there's something different about this one.'

'How different?'

'I don't know. There's just something I don't like about the whole thing.'

Varius looked at the old fisherman, trying to discern the meaning of his words.

'You're scared,' he finally said.

Banaah continued to stare out across the Sea of Galilee and then finally turned to Varius nodding and said. 'I think you're right. I am scared.'

Varius' anger and frustration had dissipated. He was now genuinely trying to figure out the motive of the old man.

'But why?' he asked, his voice laced with confusion, 'What's there to be scared of?'

Banaah shrugged his shoulders sheepishly. He was uncomfortable talking about his emotions in this way. 'I don't know. Maybe I think that if there is any truth in what people are saying about this man, then it is very serious. Very serious indeed.'

'But you don't believe there is any truth in it all, do you?'

'Have you noticed anything different about me today?' Banaah asked in response.

Varius looked puzzled. 'No, what?'

Banaah looked at him and smiled. 'I'm alone.'

It took Varius a few moments to realise what the old man was saying. For the first time he noticed the man's grandson wasn't with him.

'Heled!'

Banaah nodded solemnly. 'He's not here.'

'But I don't think I've ever seen you without him. Wherever you go, he goes. He hobbles around after you like he can't bear to be separated from you.'

Banaah smiled. 'Well all that's changed.'

Varius was suddenly concerned for the old man. 'What's happened? Has his condition worsened?'

The fisherman laughed, a loud explosive, uncontrollable laugh. 'Worsened! My friend, his condition hasn't worsened, the complete opposite in fact.'

'What do you mean?' Varius asked tentatively.

Banaah fixed him with an intense stare that made him feel uncomfortable. 'He has been healed Varius.'

He remained silent for several moments, struggling to grasp what the old man was saying. 'What do you mean healed? His leg has got better?'

'Not just his leg, his mind too. He is not the crippled half-wit you know.'

Varius laughed mirthlessly. 'That's impossible.'

Banaah nodded. 'Yes, impossible.'

'Where is he now?' Varius asked after several moments.

'He's out there fishing with the others. He can't get enough of it. He wants to stay out there all the time.'

'I don't believe it.'

Banaah didn't try to convince his young friend. 'Now do you see why I am afraid?'

Varius was repulsed. 'No! I don't see why at all. You have been taken in by this foolishness, Banaah. I am surprised at you. So something unusual has happened to your nephew. It is no reason to take leave of your senses.'

'It is more than unusual, Varius. Some of our ailments get better in time. I have seen that on many occasions over the years. I have seen friends who appeared to be on death's door make a complete recovery. I have even seen mothers survive the most traumatic of births. But I have never seen, Varius, never seen, the complete restoration of a man's mind. The boy is like a different person. I don't know him anymore. I have no idea who he is!'

'Then that is what you are afraid of. Something has happened which you cannot explain. It is understandable that you would fear it.'

Banaah shook his head. 'That is not what I am afraid of Varius. I am scared that this man is who people claim him to be. If what they are saying about him is true then I have every reason to be afraid. And so have you.'

Chapter XII

Shifra watched the crowds as she always did. She had been back in Jerusalem for almost a year and was now well accustomed to the city. She had many favoured spots throughout the city where she would just sit and watch the people. Thousands hurried back and forth, some of them working hard, some of them trying to maintain a pretence of industry.

She often fixed her gaze on one person for as long as she was able, imagining what kind of person they were, what their lives were like and what kinds of troubles they were forced to endure. She watched the people crowd into the temple to offer their sacrifices. She didn't sneer but she did feel a sense of pity for them, wasting their time in such an expensive manner.

She watched the slave girls and the servants hurtling up and down the streets in a desperate bid to please somebody - a demanding master or a surly mistress. She watched with apathy the beggars and cripples hoping that someone would show them some compassion. The only residents lower than them were the old donkeys and stray dogs. She looked down upon the religious leaders, these hypocrites who cared only for themselves but nothing for the suffering people they were surrounded by. There was a never-ending procession of them through the streets of Jerusalem.

She had spent many hours gazing upon and walking among the crowds. Yet despite taking up residence in a city of a few hundred thousand she had never felt so alone.

She often thought back to her time in Joppa and for a time had wondered whether she had been right to leave. Tabitha and Keziah would have forgotten all about her by now, but perhaps she should have gone to see them one last time. In the years of torment she had been through of late, her time in Joppa had been an oasis of peace. She had made friends and lived happily and safely. Everything seemed to be going so well until that fateful night when she had unwittingly stumbled across her wicked uncle.

Now she had been in Jerusalem since last winter and, thanks to Tabitha, she had been able to find employment. The skills she had learned from her had enabled her to find work with a weaver working in the southern part of Jerusalem. He had a shop on a busy street full of market stalls and did good business. She wasn't allowed to use his loom but she did do some sewing for him. She ran errands for him too all over the city and the poor wage he paid her was enough to rent a small room in the east of the city, near the Kidron Valley.

He approached now. She sat in the shop looking out at the people passing by. Her employer was a small man, fat and grotesque. The offensive arrangement of his features was matched only by the repugnant odour of his character. He was surly and mean, growling and barking orders like a rabid dog. She had never had a civil conversation with him and he was almost as rude to his customers as he was to her. He had a good reputation it seemed, so he was free to talk to them in any way he pleased.

She observed him as he fought his way through the unyielding crowd, dragging his corpulent, sweaty carcass along, though it rebelled. Sweat was dripping from his drooping jowls and his face was tinged with red, like the circumference of an angry boil.

He pushed through a group of women, looking admiringly at some pottery in the adjacent stall. Shifra would have smiled at the sight of the fat oaf had she not been completely indifferent to the man. His aggressive nature and surly attitude made no difference to her. Perhaps that was why she had lasted in his employ so long. Not many would put up with his petulant nonsense. Life was too short and he was too obnoxious. She did put up with it though. He paid her and that was all that mattered. The hassle of trying to find another job was more than she could bear.

'The cockroaches in this city,' he snapped as he finally reached the haven of his shop. 'Full of miscreants, roustabouts and low-life scum.'

Shifra ignored him as she usually did.

'Well?' he yelled. 'What about it girl! Have you sold anything?'

'No.'

He sighed and shook his head in disgust. 'Just as I thought. Useless! That's what you are, my girl! Absolutely useless. I don't know why I bother keeping you on. I might as well have employed one of the lepers from that colony nearby. They probably wouldn't scare off the customers as fast as you do. Most people would probably rather be served by a highly infectious, disease-ridden social outcast than by you. And I'm not surprised either! You've got that permanent sour expression on your face. It's no wonder there's no men hanging around here wanting to talk to you. The only thing you attract are the flies. Just like a great big pile of camel dung, that's what you are!'

And so it went on. She was used to this kind of tirade. It was commonplace. He'd obviously failed to make a deal or had lost a client so he came back to the shop and took it out on her. It had never bothered her. She was past caring what people like him thought. As long as he paid her, that was all that mattered.

She remained at the shop with him for several more hours, fixing some old garments someone had entrusted him with. On her way home the sun was still lingering over the western sky. She paid for some salt fish from the Galilee and ate it as she walked back toward her little room. It was a pleasant evening and so instead of going straight home she decided to cross the Kidron Valley. She would sit alone at home anyway, so she might as well sit alone somewhere beautiful.

She descended into the valley, following a small dirt track that many others would have trodden that day heading to and from the city. There were few people about now. Most people would be at home with their families. They would be sharing a meal together or lounging on the rooves of their homes, in the warm evening air.

She had no friends and knew no one. Once she'd hoped that she might strike up a friendship with someone in one of the nearby shops or maybe a servant of one of her employer's clients. No such opportunity had arisen and eventually she had given up all hope.

On the other side of the Kidron Valley was the Mount of Olives. This was one of her most favourite places to go. As the name suggested, the place was covered in olive groves. The gnarled complexion of the old trees, some of them thousands of years old, gave her comfort. In a simple, indefinable sense, she felt safe and secure when she wandered through these peaceful gardens. It didn't seem to matter that she was alone when she came here. There was a comfort and tranquillity in the place.

She wandered and sat and slept and dreamed. She blocked out the world and forgot about her life. Just listening to the calming and cathartic sound of the gentle breeze drifting through the trees.

She stayed for an hour or more until the sun had made its retreat and darkness had fallen. Small fires could be seen in the distance, flickering radiantly through the trees. As she gazed at Jerusalem she saw it had come alive with the light of a thousand torches and candles. She had always found that a spectacular sight despite her indifference to the city itself.

She began to walk back to her room. There were few people out now, though she did see groups huddled around fires, talking and laughing. Some of them were singing while their children scurried about in the darkness, shrieking with delight.

She overheard more than one conversation about a strange preacher who was causing quite a stir in the Galilee. Some said he had been to Jerusalem more than once and caused a disturbance in the temple. She dismissed these notions as the fanciful tales of the desperate. People were so eager for excitement. They would latch on to anything that would lift them from the dreary tedium that was everyday life.

They should get used to it, she thought. Don't pin your hopes on anything exciting or adventurous. You'll only be disappointed. Get your head down and get to the end of each day. If you can do that you've won one small victory.

It wasn't long before she reached her room. Not bothering to light a candle or change her clothes for the night, she collapsed on the bed and lay there in the dark. Eventually, she slept.

Chapter XIII

Although technically Winter now, the heat was intolerable. The dry desert wind seemed to encircle Varius, antagonising and goading him into surrender. Endless coarse grains of sand attacked him incessantly, forcing him to cower and shield himself from the vicious onslaught. When he did manage to lift his gaze, all he could see was an endless barren desert, a lifeless wilderness of nothing.

He had gone on many long hikes as a soldier, carrying his weapons, his tools and all his equipment. He had learned to grin and bear it, push through the pain and discomfort, conquer the mental fatigue. Yet this journey seemed to have been longer and more arduous than most. The trek south from the Galilee had been simple enough but then they had crossed the Jordan. The endless barren desert had stretched out before them like an eternal wasteland. The Great Salt Sea vanished into the west. When he had allowed his imagination to run wild, he had almost expected to see the skeletal remains of ancient monsters, long-forgotten victims of this lifeless domain.

The journey south had been made all the more abhorrent by the luxury afforded Antipas and his family. The retinue forced to accompany the preening wretch was absurd and infuriating. Varius boiled with rage that he had to accompany the braggart, and potentially risk his life in the man's defence. They had stopped many times, which had slowed their progress significantly. Probably not often enough though for the poor wretches that had to carry Antipas' litter. He would be a few slaves short by the end of this journey if he didn't show them more compassion.

The sand storm eased off for a few moments, which gave him the chance to look ahead. A small mountain was rising out of the desert. His destination lay before him, towering over the landscape like an angry leviathan, guarding its forbidden fortress.

Varius could make out the palace at the summit and a new hope kindled within him. In a few more hours they would have reached their destination at last: Machaerus, the mountain palace of Herod Antipas.

It was several more hours until they arrived. When they did so the distinguished family disappeared inside, fussed over by the staff who were eagerly awaiting their arrival. Varius was keen to get inside and have a cold bath. Having handed his horse over to the resident slaves, he retreated to his quarters without giving his surroundings a second glance. He was appalled to find that he was sharing a dormitory with his colleagues, some of whom had already nabbed the most private beds and were already removing their armour and discarding their weapons.

He hadn't been told the schedule and didn't know when he was next on duty. He breathed a sigh of relief as he heaved the breastplate from his body, the fellow in the next bunk, helping him do so. The thing weighed the earth and despite the fact he'd been a soldier for years, it never got any easier. He headed for the bathing area, spending more than an hour on the cleansing rituals that would make him feel human again.

He returned from the canteen as the sun was setting and was relieved to hear that he would not be needed that night. Some of his colleagues invited him to join them at dice and others for a saunter around the palace. He chose neither, preferring to rest and sleep.

After a hearty breakfast he was told by his superior that he would be on sentry duty in the afternoon, probably in one of the indoor reception areas.

In the meantime, Varius was encouraged to look around the palace and familiarise himself with the layout of the place. This he did eagerly, relieved that he didn't have to immediately present for duty.

As was to be expected with another of Herod the Great's building projects, this too was very impressive. He would probably never see them, but he imagined the bedrooms of the family would be large and ostentatious. The reception rooms were large, fit for holding big parties and entertaining many guests. Herod had made additions which ensured that whoever his guests were, however illustrious they may be, they would be suitably impressed and catered for. One of the outdoor courtyards was lined with Roman pillars and all manner of palm trees and exotic flora created a relaxed and luxurious ambiance. Elaborate mosaics adorned the walls and the furniture was made of the most expensive cedar wood that could be imported from the Lebanon. There was a Roman bath too, a sight which thrilled and irritated Varius in equal measure. At home he could enjoy such privileges as was his wont but here it was only for the delights of the pampered and privileged elite.

Salome was lounging in the courtyard as he passed. Surrounded by servants and slaves, she was pampered and doted on as though she were a princess. He had seen enough of her to know she was a precocious and seductive little minx. Even at the tender age of fourteen, she had already worked out how to manipulate people. She knew exactly how to get what she wanted, especially from men. He skirted the circumference of the courtyard, ensuring he stayed out of sight. One had to be careful traversing the palace for fear of disturbing the family.

He exited the lavish outer courtyard and walked to the top of the western wall. A spectacular vista opened up before him as he looked westward across the Great Salt Sea.

To the south he could just make out the fortress of Masada and,
 to the north, the River Jordan winding its way through the desert. He couldn't quite make it out, but on a clear day he wondered if Jerusalem would be visible from this vantage point. It was certainly an impressive sight and it was clear to Varius why Herod had chosen to renovate it and keep it in the family.

It wasn't just a palace though, it was a military fortress too - a formidable one. It had to be impregnable for Antipas had made a staunch enemy in the shape of King Aretas IV of the Nabataeans. Should he ever wish to avenge the outrage against his daughter, this would be his first port of call. Indeed, Machaerus was the place from which she fled, back to her father's house.

When he reported for duty after lunch he was told to take his position in the dining area. When he arrived to relieve his colleague, Antipas and Herodias were eating breakfast. From the corner of his eye he appraised the fat oaf. He wore a fancy robe that would be beyond expensive for most of the planet but which he had just thrown on for breakfast. His fingers were covered in flashy rings and he had a number of chains and necklaces hanging around his neck. His grey beard was trimmed and his thin lips made disgusting slapping noises as the honey he was gorging on dribbled from the corners of his mouth. He was an absurd creature, human refuse of the most revolting kind.

His wife was no better. She had probably been attractive once but her desperation to recapture the allure of her youth had failed. She usually looked like a wizened old hag, painted in such a way as to stave off the inevitable descent into irrelevance. She had failed spectacularly, succeeding only in making herself look like a hideous cadaver, recently escaped from the grave. Today she looked even worse. She had obviously only just awoken and hadn't had time to adorn herself with the paint and accoutrements in which she placed her faith.

Varius watched them silently from the corner of the room. They were oblivious to his presence, as they should be. He was pleased they wouldn't notice the obvious revulsion he felt when he had to look at them, nor know the contempt in which he held them.

He watched them closely for the next few days, his disdain slowly turning to indifference. The arrogant Antipas, obnoxious Herodias and licentious Salome were enough to make any sane person despise humanity. His growing apathy toward them helped him endure the next few weeks.

The endless parade of vacuous guests, all as shallow as their hosts, had increased markedly over the last few days. Antipas was having a birthday party and all the dregs of society were invited. The place was soon teeming with the rich and influential, Roman and Jewish alike, as well as some guests from the eastern reaches of the Empire. The preparations had been made, the wine stockpiled and enough food to feed a legion.

Varius had grown weary of their discussions. It was all Antipas could talk about and from his sentry position he had been privy to most of it. It was to be the party to end all parties, though he struggled to think how it could possibly be any more wild or licentious than any of the others. Where there's a will there's a way and Antipas was certain to be able to think of some way to make his party the most talked-about event of the year.

On the day itself, Varius was informed early that every soldier would be on duty from lunchtime until whenever all the guests had either fallen asleep or drunk themselves to death. As usual, Varius would be posted in the main reception room where the majority of the frivolity would take place. He used to like these assignments but familiarity had bred contempt and now he couldn't think of anywhere he would less rather be. Alas, he would have to endure yet another of Antipas' lessons in debauchery.

The soiree proceeded as every other. The endless flow of food and wine providing a suitable foundation for the wanton excess that followed, the dim torchlight creating an ambiance more than conducive to deeds that would normally be carried out away from prying eyes. The guests forgot what little reserve they already had as the night wore on. The men groped and squeezed to their hearts' content, salivating over the young women who appeared to adore their attention. The older women looked on with envy as their younger selves danced and cavorted at leisure with any who caught their eye. They too weren't beyond the grasp of lust's evil eye, as the younger men soon found out. Those who got trapped in a gaggle of painted ladies barely emerged with their clothing still intact.

As usual, Antipas was at the centre of the action. This time he had an extra special reason to be and he milked it for all it was worth. He guffawed and growled his way through the night, dominating one and all with his gregarious personality.

The party had been in full swing for several hours when Antipas raised his voice above the din. 'Entertainment, I say!' he slurred loudly. 'Entertain me!'

The noise died down as the founder of the feast spoke. Everyone looked at one another, wondering what it was he actually wanted.

'Who will dance for us?' he bellowed enthusiastically.

The crowd roared their approval and three young women were pushed into the centre of the room. Shedding their outer garments and displaying more flesh than would usually have been countenanced, they prepared to entertain their host. The rest of the guests moved back, falling over each other, spilling their drinks and crashing through furniture in order to give the girls room.

They danced with energy and skill, responding to the music, keeping their eyes locked on Antipas the whole time. The music became fever pitched, their actions and movements matching the exhilaration of the flute and lyre; their slender, perfect bodies commanded by the drums. Antipas whooped and hollered in delight as the girls gyrated before him, the crowd clapped in time with the music, the pace quickening all the time. They shouted their encouragement, willing them on, moaning and groaning with delight as the girls moved for their pleasure. Finally, they couldn't move as fast as the drums directed them. They threw themselves on the floor in exhausted exhilaration, ending the dance. Antipas applauded and the crowd cheered. The smiling girls, panting from the exertion, pushed through the crowd, yearning for their next skin full.

No sooner had they exited the arena than Antipas was eager to know what was coming next. He was just about to command for someone else to come and perform for the crowd when a hush fell over the room. It was Salome, daughter of Herodias who was walking slowly toward the centre. The crowd fell away before her until she stood alone in the centre of the room, all eyes fixed upon her. A calm had descended that Varius had never seen before at one of these parties. The air was thick with the anticipation of what she was going to do next. The look on the face of Antipas was a mixture of delight and desire. If he'd been a dog, he would have been saturated in his own saliva.

The musicians began to play a slow, mellow tune. Salome responded with the subtlest of movements, her bare arms curving and bending through the air with exaggerated slowness. She arched her back and pushed her chest forward in controlled, rhythmic movements, her hair draped over her face and shoulders. The crowd were spellbound. In contrast to the previous dance, this was slow and sensual, the movement of her young body hypnotising her admirers into a stupor of drunken desire.

She continued to move slowly around the floor, each movement carefully judged to obey the authority of the music and cause an unstoppable undercurrent: a sexual force. She now lay on the floor, sliding and turning, seducing her audience into a state of lustful adulation.

Varius was intoxicated, bewitched by the girl whom he had grown to despise. The silence in the room betrayed the fact that everyone else was likewise enamoured - all but Herodias, who had a look of malevolent pride etched into her gruesome features. The master puppeteer, gazing with satisfaction on her creation.

From the back of the large room Varius could hear the gentle thuds of the girl's body as it glided across the floor. Such was the enraptured silence in the room that all eyes remained fixed on the girl who had entranced them.

The music came to an end, she stopped, head down, face veiled by her long dark hair. Suddenly an explosion of cheering and applause broke forth. The spell was broken and all joined in the adulation for this young girl who had impressed them so.

She didn't smile. She took the adulation knowing she deserved it. It was hers. Salome understood that for a few brief moments she had captured the heart of every person in that room. Male and female, young and old, she had controlled them all; she owned them.

When the applause erupted, the spell was broken over Varius too. He shook his head as if to shake free from the effects of an intoxicating liquor.

Antipas was quietening the crowd. Salome stood there still, in the centre of the room, commanding the attention of all those present. He was thrilled, almost overcome with emotion. Varius couldn't work out whether it was admiration or pure lust.

'Ask me for whatever you want, daughter!' he yelled, his arms outstretched in extravagant posture. The crowd roared their approval. 'Whatever you ask of me is yours, even up to half my kingdom!'

The crowd resounded again with the noise of encouragement, all keen to see Antipas generously award the girl for what they'd just experienced.

Salome wasted no time but rushed to her mother's side. She clambered up to where her mother was sitting. She suddenly seemed like the young girl she was and not the embodiment of sexual desire she had just portrayed. She spoke to Herodias in hushed tones so that even those around couldn't hear what was said. The mother responded with alacrity and whispered into her daughter's ear. There was a knowing glance between them before Salome raced back to the centre of the room.

She visibly composed herself and prepared to speak. Dancing seductively in front of a huge crowd was no mean feat, but speaking in front of them was something altogether more terrifying.

'I want you to give me at once, the head of John the Baptist on a platter,' she announced.

The name meant nothing to Varius but it garnered an interesting and varied reaction from the crowd. Some gasped in shock, some covered their mouths with their hands while others merely smiled and nodded. It was obvious they all knew who he was and that this was going to cause quite a stir.

The most interesting reaction was from Antipas himself and Varius could tell immediately that he was conflicted. The smile which had been broader than the River Jordan, vanished. He glanced from side to side and around the room with his swift, devious little eyes. There was something about this request he did not like but he was loath to show it. Suddenly, as if to banish the doubt from his mind and conceal from his guests that he was perturbed, he began smiling again and nodding giddily.

'It shall be done!' he shouted, and the crowd cheered. Mother and daughter looked at one another, the look of the victor blazoned across their faces.

Varius looked on from the back of the room. His disgust for Antipas, rekindled once more. The man could announce someone's death so casually and calmly at a party to please a fourteen-year-old girl.

'You there!' he suddenly heard Antipas yell.

Varius looked around the room to see who was being addressed. It took only a few seconds for him to experience the horrifying realisation that it was he to whom Antipas was speaking.

'You!' he shouted again. 'Soldier in the back corner.'

Varius stepped forward.

'I want you to accomplish this task for my daughter,' he paused again for effect, ensuring he had the complete attention of everyone in the room. 'Bring me the head of John the Baptist!'

Varius was stunned. Despite the overwhelming noise in the room which had risen to deafening levels, he was rooted to the spot. The crowd were baying for blood, shouting and cheering as if in the arena.

Someone nearby prodded him sharply in the arm. He came to his senses, nodded in the direction of Antipas and walked out.

When he exited into the hallway he paused for a moment and basked in the cool night air. The contrast between it and the stifling heat of the party was wonderfully refreshing. He had little time to enjoy the moment before several servants came rushing up to him and also Polybius, one of his colleagues.

'Sir,' one of the servants addressed him. 'Would you like me to accompany you to the cells?'

Varius looked at him curiously. The blast of fresh air had momentarily robbed him of his memory. He suddenly remembered that he had been instructed to fetch the head of a prisoner.

'Yes,' he answered cautiously. 'Show me to the man's cell.'

Polybius was smiling. 'Are you ready for this, Varius?'

The questions startled him. 'Ready for what?'

'Ready for what? Ready to behead this Baptist fellow!'

Once more Varius was puzzled. 'You don't expect me to do it?' he said.

Polybius laughed hysterically. 'Varius, my naïve young friend. When Antipas said he wanted you to accomplish the task that is exactly what he meant.'

'But I'm not an executioner!'

'Nevertheless, this task is yours.'

'Nonsense! There must be an executiner in the cells or else someone else suitably trained.'

At this point the servant who had been leading them through the palace toward the cells stopped and turned to Varius. 'Excuse me, sir, but your friend is quite right.'

'What?'

'The master spoke with me as I left the room and said specifically that he wanted you to carry out his orders. He believes a well-trained Roman soldier will accomplish the task better than any other.'

Varius said nothing so the man continued, 'He is accustomed to getting his own way.'

'I am a soldier, not an executioner!' Varius protested.

'Be that as it may,' the servant replied haughtily, 'It is you who must behead the prisoner.'

Polybius was still chuckling. 'Come now, Varius, this will be a piece of cake for you. No problem.'

Varius was repulsed by this turn of events and now even more outraged that the fool Antipas could command him to commit such a deed. Fighting enemies in battle was one thing, even confronting rioting crowds, but this was totally different. This felt wrong, uncomfortable, and he was unsure how to proceed.

He said nothing for several moments as they continued to wind their way through the palace. 'Who is he anyway?' he asked finally.

'John the Baptist,' Polybius responded matter of fact.

'That name means nothing to me,' Varius snapped.

The servant spoke over his shoulder without stopping, 'He is a preacher, some say a prophet.'

Varius was halted in his tracks as if he had just been hit by a thunderbolt. 'A preacher!' He spat. 'A prophet?'

'So they say,' the servant replied apathetically.

'Not another one!' Varius growled, his voice rising. 'What is it with this place? Everywhere I turn there's another prophet causing trouble.' The anger was swelling within him.'

'What's this one's story?'

'I have no idea,' Polybius confessed.

'Who does he say he is?' Varius asked again.

This time the servant, sensing it was he whom Varius was addressing spoke again. 'He says he's just the voice of one crying in the wilderness!'

'Crying what in the wilderness?'

'Prepare the way of the Lord!'

'What's that supposed to mean? Does he claim to be this Messiah you lot are all waiting for?'

'Absolutely not,' the servant was emphatic. 'On the contrary, he has insisted that he is not the longed-for Messiah. He has merely been sent to prepare the way for the anointed one.'

Varius rolled his eyes. 'Not another one of these idiots! First the Galilee, now here. It seems one is never far from one of these crazed fantasists.'

'He is quite a celebrity in this part of the world. I hope the master knows what he's doing.'

'What does that mean,' Varius couldn't keep the irritation out of his voice. 'How did he come to be imprisoned here anyway?'

'The master had him arrested almost two years ago although it was Lady Herodias who was behind it.'

'Arrested for what?'

'There were numerous occasions when the man John, accosted them in public, haranguing them for their illegal marriage. He says it's illegal anyway. I think she finally got tired of it and impressed upon the master to have him thrown in jail. Do you know their family history?'

'I think I know most of the sordid details,' Varius answered, his voice thick with disdain.

'Well anyway,' the servant continued casually, 'I don't think the master likes it at all. I think he's quite fond of John and not because he has many followers either. I think he genuinely enjoys listening to the man. He's a passionate speaker, no doubt about that.'

'So he's kept him languishing in prison for the last two years to please Herodias?'

'I think so. She's probably wanted to get rid of John long before now. This time she's seen an opportunity and leapt upon it, the girl Salome proving the perfect accomplice.'

Varius sighed. 'Well she's going to finally get her way.'

They arrived in the dungeon of Machaerus. It was as to be expected: dark and forbidding. The air was rank with the smell of blood and faeces. No sound came from any of the cells. The men therein were either dead or insufferably weak.

Varius spotted what looked like a small office and headed straight for it. He was relieved to see a flagon of wine there. He snatched it greedily and began to drink. Wiping the excess from his face he addressed the servant. 'Drag the prisoner out into the courtyard and find the executioner.'

The servant paused, awkward and embarrassed. 'The executioner sir?'

'Fetch the executioner man!' Varius bellowed. 'I don't give a damn what Antipas wants. I'm not doing it!'

He took another drink of wine. Polybius stared at his friend, so too did the servant. There was an awkward silence. None of them spoke.

Irritated that the man hadn't moved, Varius yelled at him again. He could feel the tension rising and against his better judgment he knew he was nervous.

'With respect sir,' the servant stuttered sheepishly, 'there is no executioner.'

'What?'

'He's not here. I think that is perhaps why the master has instructed you to do it.'

Varius looked at Polybius, hoping for some support. He found none. Glancing past the servant at the door to the tiny office he noticed for the first time another servant standing there holding a large silver platter. Varius' blood ran cold.

'Get out of here!' he shouted.

Polybius sat down next to him on a rickety old chair. The walls were stained with blood and there was the hideous smell of body odour in the air. Who knew when the last time the men in this place had ever been properly treated. After a short while, Polybius broke the silence. 'You're troubled Varius, I can see that, but you have to look at it as another part of the job. We follow orders; we do as we're told.'

'We follow orders from that fat oaf?' Varius snapped.

'An order's an order. Just get on with it and then afterward forget all about it.'

He had not the energy to reply so he just sighed and drank more wine.

Several minutes later the servant appeared at the door. 'The prisoner is in the courtyard and bound to the block,' he said.

Varius looked up at the man with a mixture of resentment and defeat. 'Let's get this over with,' he said and marched out toward the courtyard.

When he got there, the man John the Baptist was hunched over the block. His face was hidden behind a tangled mass of dark hair, blood and dirt congealed in the mess. He was skeletal in appearance, his long arms and legs nothing but skin and bone. Evidence of the beatings and scourgings he'd received were all over his emaciated body. Yet for all that, Varius thought he might have looked worse given he'd been here for two years. Perhaps Antipas had favoured him. He may not have lasted this long otherwise.

Varius stepped forward so that he was an arm's length away from the prisoner. 'Lift his head,' he ordered to nobody in particular.

Someone scurried over, probably one of the workers from the prison. He yanked the head of the prisoner up and roughly wiped the hair from his eyes.

The man's cheeks were sunken and his face tired. Yet when Varius looked into his eyes he saw something there he had not seen before. There was strength - and peace. He had expected to see fear but there was none. The man was on the point of death yet he seemed not to care. Had the years in this prison broken the man completely? Did he long for death to end the pain? End the torment he'd suffered for so long?

No. It wasn't that. There was something indefinable in the man's eyes. Varius stared at him confidently but the more he gazed into the man's stare the more uncomfortable he began to feel. Then suddenly he realised what it was he saw. It was triumph. It was cool and understated, not arrogant or haughty. But confident. He could detect a sense of victory in the man. This prisoner, about to die a violent death, broken, in chains, and in a rich man's prison, believed he had won.

How do these people get enslaved by their own delusions? Varius thought. He opened his mouth to address the prisoner, yet as he did so he hesitated. A shiver of fear ran through his body. He didn't want to hear from the man, afraid of what he might say.

The sensation repulsed him so Varius, in a sudden fit of anger, turned, saw the attendant standing by holding a sword and swept toward it. He snatched it with such force the attendant stumbled back and to the floor. Varius recoiled and marched toward the prisoner whose head was now bowed. He stood in position over his helpless foe, gripping the sword tightly in both hands. He paused for a fraction of a second. The man was mumbling something. Then, with a mighty downward thrust of the sword he cut clean through the prisoner's neck, crying out angrily as he did so.

The head dropped to the floor with a sickening thud and rolled through the dirt. Bloody fluid spouted from the neck in an arching fountain.

In the Fullness of Time

And the sand was stained with the blood of John the Baptist.

Chapter XIV

Asher stood on the crest of a hill looking down upon the Galilee. The town of Tiberius lay before him. There was still a myriad of workers beavering away on the projects Antipas had dreamed up. Fishing vessels of all sizes were spread out across the lake, hoping that the day's catch would provide for their owners a handsome profit.

The air was cool and crisp, the deep blue sky sometimes visible through the layer of white cloud that covered the area. Asher threw a scarf around his head, shouldered his belongings and continued walking toward the great lake.

It had been almost two years since he'd left The Galilee, though it felt like he had never left. He recognised some of the towns dotted around the shoreline: Capernaum to the north, Magdala, north of Tiberius, and he could just make out Chorazin too in the distance. Gareb had been good to him there and he had spent many happy months in the employ of such a gregarious man. It hadn't lasted long though and he soon got tired of it. The easiest thing for him to do now would be to head back to his house and seek further employment. This he was loath to do, for he didn't want to feel like he was going backward. He wanted to do something new and, if possible, find this elusive something he was still searching for.

He had left Caesarea almost a year ago and thought for a time that he really had discovered what first old Zeke and then Elkanah, his cellmate, had discerned he was searching for.

On the first day of his departure from Caesarea he had walked for several hours through Samaria in the direction of The Galilee. It had been late in the afternoon when he had spotted the man sitting alone under an olive tree. His eyes were closed, the picture of serenity.

He seemed to sense Asher approach and rose to greet him. He had deep brown eyes, long dark hair and a full beard. He was dressed in simple robes and appeared to have no possessions. When he shook Asher by the hand and welcomed him, Asher thought for a moment that he would break his fingers, such was the strength of the man.

He invited Asher to join him around the fire he was about to prepare and eat with him. Eager to stop walking and rest awhile, Asher had agreed enthusiastically. Men who wandered in the wilderness on their own were usually lunatics or cutthroats. This man appeared to be neither and so Asher felt there was no danger from stopping with him for a while.

They ate bread and olives which the man produced from a satchel he had. The two spoke for hours until the sun had long since made its retreat over the horizon. Knowing it was too dark now to continue, Asher accepted the man's invitation to stay the night with him. He said he had been sleeping in a cave nearby which provided sufficient shelter from the cold winter air.

Asher marvelled at how he always seemed to end up in these situations. If he wasn't being investigated by hungry bears, fleeing naked from angry fishermen or surviving perilous storms, he was sleeping in caves with total strangers!

He slept poorly that night, the cave not really providing the adequate shelter that had been promised. His new friend seemed to have no such difficulty. When he awoke, he did so to the sound of several men who could be heard outside the small cave. He panicked momentarily, wondering whether this man was a criminal after all and he had lured him to this place where he would now rob and kill him.

His fears were swiftly assuaged as a few moments later, one of the men entered the cave holding a plate of fish and loaves of bread. Noticing Asher was awake, he promptly came over and offered him some breakfast. Eager to leave the cave and put the loathsome night's sleep behind him, he responded gratefully and joined the other men around the fire as they too tucked into their breakfast. They had baskets of bread and fish and so clearly had just returned from the market.

On enquiring who they all were and what they were doing out here, Asher was surprised to hear them describe themselves as disciples. They weren't merely friends of the man in the cave but they were his followers. They were a variety of ages but many of them were young, little more than twenty years of age. It became very clear, very quickly that they revered this man and believed him to be some sort of messenger or prophet. They spoke with a dreamy adulation as if he really were divine.

Asher had found him to be extremely friendly, though somewhat mysterious. Divine? That was blasphemous where he came from. The Romans were known to have no such qualms about ascribing god-like attributes to human beings but it was taboo for the Jews.

Eventually the man in the cave emerged and it was clear when he did so that he was very fond of these men who called themselves his followers. They adored him, hung on his every word and couldn't do enough to serve him in all manner of ways. In reply, he treated them with the greatest of respect, speaking to them kindly, encouraging them and laughing with them.

As the day wore on Asher felt like this was a company of men unlike any other. It had been suggested to him many times over the course of the day that he should stay with them a while. He had confessed that he was heading for The Galilee but had no idea what there was for him there. It hadn't taken long to persuade him to stay and so the days turned to weeks and the weeks to months.

It was a strongly held religious belief that held these men together. Some of them were fishermen, some were skilled labourers others had been farmers and one had owned an orchard. What bound them together now though was their belief in a coming kingdom. The one whom they all revered had an incredible knowledge of the scriptures. It didn't take Asher long to learn that he was expecting a great earth-shaking event to take place imminently. When it happened, it would shake the Roman world to its core and usher in another kingdom, a divine kingdom. There was a febrile excitement among his followers that Asher found contagious. Soon, he too was eager to hear of the coming kingdom and learn of how the Romans would be vanquished and the Jewish people set free.

After a few days in this atmosphere of excitement, love and expectation, Asher was convinced that this man and his followers were the answer to all his prayers. This is what he had been looking for. This man would give him the purpose for which he had been searching these past few years. Zeke and Elkanah had both said that he was searching for something. He'd found it.

It didn't last long. Doubts started to surface after about six months. He had always listened intently to what the men said, their leader in particular seemed to be the font of all knowledge. Gradually though, Asher began to spot contradictions in what he said. They were subtle of course and cleverly worded, but they were there and the more he noticed them, the more of them seemed to appear. He never said anything, of course, keeping his questions and concerns to himself, wondering and hoping that clarification would come. But it never did.

Gradually he began to study more and more carefully, not just what the men were saying but the men themselves. Whereas once he had just seen friendship and respect, he now began to discern underlying hostility and competition between them. The leader too, would sometimes be given to brief flashes of anger and frustration. It was never flamboyant or explosive but rather understated and hidden. To Asher this seemed all the more sinister.

About a month before he finally left, more and more stories were filtering into the group of a wandering preacher who was attracting large crowds wherever he went. The news of this man who was also said to be preaching about the Kingdom of God caused quite a stir among the group. Some of them said he was the genuine article, speaking with authority and healing the sick. Others said that he was an imposter and demon-possessed.

The effect on the group of these constant stories and rumours was fascinating to Asher. Although he had been with them for more than half a year he had not fully succumbed to their way of thinking. This allowed him to observe them as an outsider despite living among them. The effect these stories had on the leader was the most alarming. He seemed to feel threatened and every now and then he would say or do something to suggest that there was really a deep jealousy, a grotesque envy, bubbling away within him.

It was only a few days ago that events had taken a dramatic turn. One of the group, a younger man barely out of his teenage years had not been seen for more than a day. He was known among the group as the one who had spent the most time among the crowds of the wandering preacher. Now that he had failed to return, it was assumed among the others that he had abandoned them and joined the ranks of those who were touting this Jesus as a prophet.

The leader, who hitherto had managed to suppress the darker side of his nature was apoplectic with rage. Asher had never seen anyone explode in such anger and fury. That which he had kept bottled up for so long, maybe years, had finally erupted in a tirade of frenzied vitriol. The other men were shocked too and cowered before their volatile master.

Asher watched on with nervous fascination. Was he in danger? What was this man capable of? The gentle façade was gone. The wise and kind persona had been obliterated by this hideous monster, stung by betrayal and bent on revenge.

It was some time before his ire abated. When it did so he seemed intent on righting the wrong. Much to Asher's and everyone else's amazement he proposed a rebellion. It was at this point that Asher thought he saw the man for what he really was. A dangerous and unstable fantasist who, due to his natural charisma and intelligence, had been able to seduce men into following him.

Asher felt a sting of shame; a gnawing feeling of embarrassment that he too had been taken in by this charlatan. Fortunately, on the inside at least, he had been able to distance himself somewhat from the fanaticism of the others.

The plan was simple: launch a clandestine assault on the Roman barracks at Tiberius. They would have to overpower the sentries, access the weapons store and then create mayhem right in the heart of the seat of Roman power in The Galilee. Their escape would have to be swift for the retribution of their enemy would be terrible. Once news of the assault got out, people from all over the region would rally to their side. The followers of Jesus would abandon him and join them in their quest to rid the area of the Roman menace.

He had been called by God to lead them to victory against the Roman oppressors.

It was so ludicrous it was laughable. The leader shared his plan with them in all seriousness. Asher was forced to stifle laughter despite the seriousness of the situation. The man had clearly taken leave of his senses and was willing to go to his death and take others with him in order to heal his wounded pride.

Asher looked at the other men. Some of them were nodding in agreement, a docile look of excited anticipation written on their faces. Others had fear in their eyes.

The instruction was given that they were to pack up all their belongings straight after breakfast. They would all head into Tiberius where they would prepare to enact their plan at nightfall.

Asher went to bed that night knowing he had to leave before the sun rose. He couldn't sleep. Waiting until the darkest reaches of the night he lay still, listening to the muffled snores of the other men.

Suddenly a faint sound from across the glowing embers of the campfire kindled his interest. He stared through the darkness and made out the shape of one of the other men slowly rising from his bed. He was gathering his belongings as quietly as he could, obviously intent on escaping too.

Asher decided he had to move. If this man woke the others there would be no chance for him to escape too. Hastily he bundled his belongings into a bag and prepared to creep away. He glanced around him and was able to just make out the faint outline of the man disappear into the darkness.

Their leader would be incandescent with rage once he realised another two had deserted him. Asher had to move and he had to move now. How did he always end up in these insane situations?

He crept away from his sleeping comrades as quietly as he could. The darkness was penetrating and it was some time before he got his bearings. Once he'd done so, he moved off into the night in the direction of The Galilee.

He'd been walking for most of the day but now he could see the great Galilean lake stretched out before him. The welcoming vista of his former home brought a warmth to his heart.

He thought he'd found purpose in the wilds of Samaria. In reality, all he'd found was others who were in exactly the same boat as he: young men searching for meaning. In their quest for relevance they'd aligned themselves with a man who was eloquent and charismatic, inspirational even. Yet once one began to scratch beneath the surface, there was nothing there. Nothing attractive anyway, no character, no integrity, no substance. He was an empty vase.

Asher knew he'd had a lucky escape, but what now?

Chapter XV

Jerusalem was quiet. The stillness before dawn creating an eerie silence. A shroud of darkness covered the city. The people were still asleep, not yet willing to rouse from their beds and begin to prepare for another day's hard work. The only light came from the waning moon, intermittingly hidden behind dense rolling clouds. Rats and other small animals could be heard scurrying about in the shadows - the low growl of a dog or the faint whinny of an old horse the only signs of life in the slumbering city.

Eliashib walked quickly, eager to get home for some proper rest before spending another day in the temple courts. It always unnerved him, for the memories of that night in Joppa still tormented him.

In Jerusalem, as in Joppa, there were fallen women who sought only to seduce and defile the men. Important public figures like him were targeted more than any other. The wench he'd just been with was no different. The embodiment of everything in the world that was sinful and disgusting, she was just like the one who'd seduced him in Joppa. These harlots were the agents of the Devil; a lesser man would not have seen through their iniquitous ways. He, on the other hand, knew exactly what they were.

He arrived home quickly. If only the streets were this deserted during the day, he might be able to get to more places unmolested. He hated the feeling of the needy crowds pressing in on him, asking for prayer and begging for alms. They were a constant irritation.

He managed to get a few hours' sleep in his own bed before duty called. After a wholesome breakfast of fresh fruit, he made his way through the rabble to the Hall of Hewn Stones. There, for the remainder of the day, he sat with the other brothers of the Sanhedrin, hearing the cases brought before them. Most of them were mundane but some actually challenged his intellect and knowledge of the scriptures.

At the end of the day, before everyone separated to go their own way, another conversation struck up about recent events in the Galilee. The memory of the last such conversation was still fresh in his mind as it had vexed him exceedingly. The news out of the north was that this preacher, this Jesus, wasn't going away. If anything, he was gaining popularity.

This new information, supplied by those from the synagogue in Capernaum, was that he had healed the daughter of one of their officials. Indeed, it was even worse than that, for some were reporting that he hadn't just healed her, he had brought her back from the dead! What was truly terrifying was that some actually believed all this rubbish.

These wandering fanatics were usually harmless but every now and then one would emerge who was dangerous. Regardless of the threat, Eliashib boiled with rage at the stories being told about this man. It was an affront to the scriptures and an insult to Yahweh. He was clearly a wicked, blasphemous man, and by all accounts he was demon-possessed. Famous or not, popular or not, men like this man needed to be dealt with swiftly and punished harshly.

He swept through the outer courts of the temple. For once the rabble got out of his way, his sour mood and foul temperament clearing a path before him like a pig-farmer would through a synagogue.

He left the temple area and began descending the steps that overlooked the Kidron Valley. A familiar face caught his eye and he stopped suddenly. It was Varius, the Roman soldier whom he'd first met in Alexandria and latterly in Joppa. He was in civilian clothing, a clean white robe, expensive and pristine. Even out of uniform it was unmistakably him.

Eliashib watched him for a moment and then an idea began to percolate. He hesitated in going to speak to the man. His previous interactions with him hadn't been particularly enjoyable and he was a Roman after all. He may be an arrogant, pagan Neanderthal, but maybe he could be of some use. He dithered for a few moments more before plucking up the courage to talk to the man.

He walked over, feigning confidence. Varius was standing in the middle of the grand staircase looking out over the impressive vista that was the Kidron Valley and southern Judea.

'My friend,' Eliashib said tentatively, although he had meant to sound confident.

Varius turned toward him and recognised him in an instant. 'Rabbi!'' he announced, and then looking him up and down added. 'You do seem to have gone up in the world.'

Acknowledging his own ornate garb, Eliashib smiled. 'I am a member of the Sanhedrin now. An honour and privilege indeed.'

'Quite,' Varius replied, eyeing him keenly.

There were a few moments of silence during which Eliashib appraised his adversary. Something had changed. He didn't know what it was but it was subtle and undefinable. Something had changed in this young man. Perhaps there was a weariness in his eyes, an apathy that had not been there before. He looked tired, maybe not physically, but there was something about him that looked burdensome. 'Are you stationed in Jerusalem now?' he asked.

Varius shook his head with indifference. 'No. I am here with a retinue of soldiers guarding Herod Antipas.'

'Ah Yes, I heard he was back,' he paused. 'Is that a fulfilling enterprise?'

Varius laughed mirthlessly. 'Oh yes! It provides me with great fulfilment, standing guard over that fat, lecherous old tyrant.'

Eliashib could not help but smile. His time as Tetrarch had been peaceful but there were many who spoke of Antipas with disdain. He didn't command the respect that his father had.

Varius continued. 'I have just returned from Machaerus. He has a palace there.'

'Yes, yes and it was his birthday, was it not? I had heard there were many notables from Jerusalem heading over there to celebrate with him.'

'And oh did they celebrate!' Varius added.

'I have heard much of the parties thrown by Antipas. Debauched affairs, I hear. He is master in his own den of iniquity, is he not?'

'Rabbi, if I told you what went on at some of those parties, you would probably fall over!"

Eliashib nodded knowingly.

'But then again, maybe not,' Varius teased. 'Maybe you know all about the sorts of things they get up to there?'

He could not help but blush. The Roman was mocking him in a way no one else would dare. Varius continued before Eliashib had a chance to object. 'Would you believe me if I told you that he had a prisoner beheaded to satisfy the bloodlust of his wife and daughter?'

'At the party?'

'At the party. The man's head was served to him on a silver platter, to the delight and applause of all in attendance.'

Eliashib shook his head.

'He was hardly a dangerous criminal either. A preacher from around the area of the Jordan.'

'A preacher?' Eliashib was alerted at these words. Could it be the same man who he kept hearing about in the Galilee?

'Some claim him to be a prophet, I'm told. John the Baptist his name was. Have you heard of him?'

He was disappointed. Although highly unlikely, he was hoping that the dead man might be the same one stirring up trouble in the north. If he had been executed by Antipas, that would solve a lot of problems.

'Yes, I've heard of him. He was baptising people in the Jordan, gathering large crowds I believe. Some sort of wild lunatic, a crazed fanatic. There are a few of them about these days it seems.'

'How do you know they're not the real thing?'

The question surprised Eliashib. 'I'm sorry?'

'How do you know one of these prophets or preachers isn't the real thing? You're waiting for the coming of the Messiah aren't you? The anointed one? The Christ? This man might have been the one and Antipas has had him beheaded!' Varius jibed.

Eliashib shook his head arrogantly. 'You are correct when you say we are waiting for the coming of the anointed one. When he comes we shall know him. There shall be no doubt as to who he is, of that I can promise you. The whole world shall know it, including the Emperor of Rome!'

He winced inside, worried that he'd overstepped the mark and the Roman wouldn't take kindly to it.

Varius laughed but it was a derisory, piteous laugh. 'You're a fool, Rabbi, and so is everyone else who's hoping for some miracle-man to come and save you,' he paused. 'I'm sick and tired of hearing about these idiots and their mindless followers,' he spat. 'This country's diseased, and diseases need to be eradicated quickly, lest they spread.'

Eliashib remained quiet. The Roman's tone had changed. The light-hearted ribbing had been usurped by a subtle aggression: an undertone of anger. This was Eliashib's chance.

'I keep hearing of another,' he began tentatively. 'One far more dangerous than John the Baptist.'

Varius turned to look at him. He was stern and serious.

'He operates in the Galilee,' Eliashib continued, but was interrupted before he could say any more.

'So you've heard of this Jesus too, have you?' Varius snarled.

'Have you?' Eliashib was surprised.

'I'm stationed in the Galilee, I've heard all about him. The people up there are obsessed.'

'Is he dangerous?'

'Dangerous to whom?' Varius sneered. 'He's no danger to us.'

Eliashib was overjoyed at the direction of the conversation. Thank goodness he'd had the wisdom to approach the young man.

'I wonder if you might be able to help me in an endeavour I've been considering with regard to this charlatan,' he ventured.

'What kind of endeavour?'

'I want him arrested.'

Eliashib wondered whether he would be willing to help, for as the Roman had already said, Jesus was of no concern to them. There was something else though. Something discernibly antagonistic in Varius' attitude toward these men.

'Do you?' there was a flicker of enthusiasm in the otherwise hard face of the Roman soldier. 'Do you now?'

'Yes. I and several of the brothers believe he needs to be confronted; he needs to be arrested.'

'Why?'

'These men are dangerous. They lead the people astray and fill their heads with lies. They're not learned in the scriptures.'

'Like you are,' Varius interrupted.

Eliashib was irritated by the Roman's tone. 'Yes. like we are,' he repeated defiantly. 'I have devoted my life to the study of the scriptures. This man, whoever he is, is uneducated, and has no right to purport to know how to interpret God's word.'

Varius nodded apathetically. 'And Caiaphas? What does he think?'

'He will agree with everything I've said. We speak as one in the Sanhedrin.'

'But you've never actually spoken to him about it?'

'No, not yet.'

Varius smiled. It was a large, irritating grin. 'You're seeking to impress your superiors, aren't you? Arrest this Jesus, show yourself to be the defender of your precious scriptures and the top men will look favourably upon you.'

'That is not my motivation,' he said defensively. 'I merely seek to defend the veracity of the scriptures from those who would seek to pervert them for their own sakes.'

Eliashib was worried the conversation was getting away from him and that the Roman would decline to help. 'Surely your superiors would agree that this man is a menace and should be shut up?'

'I don't think my superiors care either way. It's not like he's leading an armed rebellion. He's no danger to Rome. His followers are farmers and fishermen. What are they going to do, throw fish at us?'

Eliashib was not amused. With this man's help he could track down this Jesus and have him thrown in a cell somewhere. And although it wasn't his primary motivation, it might look good for him among the brothers if he accomplished his task successfully.

There was a few moments' silence between them.

'I shall help you, Rabbi,' Varius finally said. 'I agree that these men are troublesome and perhaps dangerous. So what's your plan?'

'I shall have to discuss the relevant details with my brothers on the Sanhedrin. If all goes to plan I shall come north to the Galilee in the next few days.'

'I am returning there with my company tomorrow morning,' Varius said. 'Once you arrive and you have formulated a plan as to where and how you want me to arrest him, send word. You'll find me in the barracks at Tiberius.'

'Excellent!" Eliashib was thrilled. 'Then the next time we meet shall be upon the Galilee!'

Chapter XVI

Asher's surroundings were familiar, though not as comfortable as he had grown accustomed to in Caesarea. Carousing with the upper crust had been fun while it lasted but he had no desire for more of the same. He had never been materially minded and was just as happy roughing it with the lower classes as he was hobnobbing with the Roman elite. That was probably a consequence of his upbringing. His father's vineyards provided a handsome income but nothing lavish. He'd never known hardship but nor had he longed for the excesses of the rich.

Fortunately, he had always been able to find work quickly. This was partly due to the fact that he was southern. The people of Jerusalem and its environs looked down upon their northern neighbours. They were simple country folk: backward and uncivilised. They were easily spotted, shuffling awkwardly through the crowded streets of the great city. If there was any doubt based on their appearance, it quickly disappeared when they opened their mouths. The sound of their northern accent elicited scorn from the nastier elements of Jerusalem's populace.

Asher had detected a resentment towards himself when he had first arrived in the area and worked for Gareb. It had taken time to work out that people were suspicious of him simply because he was from the south.

Others were more courteous and he found that for some, the fact that he was a southerner was good for business. Gareb had liked introducing him to his well-heeled friends. He knew they would be impressed that he had a well-spoken, impressive young man from Judea in his employ.

He always carried himself with confidence, knowing that a pretence of it was just as effective as the real thing. He was prepared to do the hard work if he had to and imagined what it would be like toiling on one of the many fishing vessels that could be found on the Sea of Galilee. He had even been willing to offer his labour on one of the farms if needs be. That was certainly work he didn't relish, but he had to work somewhere and he didn't want to return to Gareb. That chapter of his life was closed and he had no desire to return to Chorazin.

He had approached the inns in Tiberius, looking specifically for the ones that catered to a more sophisticated clientele. If his time in Caesarea had taught him anything, it was that he had what it took to make it among the rich and powerful. The Via Maris was an important trade route from east to west and many merchants and businessmen stopped at Tiberius on their way through. He spent several days visiting the inns and restaurants of the new town, renting a cheap room to act as a base.

Many wouldn't give him the time of day despite his varied experiences, his confident demeanour and winning smile. Fortunately, after a couple of days, he had been introduced to Hiram, the cantankerous owner of a local olive yard. Asher was repulsed by the man's aggressive nature and sought to extricate himself from the conversation immediately. However, it quickly became apparent that the man needed an overseer and the job seemed like something Asher could do with his eyes closed. Once he'd informed Hiram of his time working in his father's vineyards, that he was fluent in Greek and had Roman connections in Caesarea, he was almost begging Asher to accept the job. His desperation was both pathetic and obvious. Using it to his advantage, he was able to negotiate favourable terms of service and so before long he found himself walking with Hiram to his olive yard.

It was situated an hour's walk from Sepphoris, the old capital of the region and a key trading post for locals and merchants travelling the Via Maris. A key part of Asher's job description would be to meet with merchants there and establish trade links and new customers. Hiram was always on the lookout for new opportunities and so every few days Asher was dispatched to the city to see what he could drum up. The rest of the time he was to supervise the activities on the farm. It was the end of the season and the olive harvest was beginning. Asher would be responsible for making sure everything ran smoothly. Labourers would be brought in from all over the countryside to pick the olives and drive the presses. It would be up to Asher to ensure they were suitable and hard-working.

Hiram was an ogre. He was similar in stature to Gareb, but that was where the comparison ended. In every other way they were completely different. Where Gareb was garrulous and warm hearted, Hiram was surly and obnoxious. He spoke to his workers with undisguised disdain, venom dripping from every word. He might have been handsome once but his features had been disfigured by a blackened soul.

Asher was curious as to what had made the man so bitter and cynical. He was rarely tempted to ask, preferring instead to spend as little time in the man's company as possible. Engaging him in conversation was foolhardy and only led to painful diatribes and acerbic monologues.

Until now Asher had been fortunate to work for kind and generous employers. Now it was his turn to work for an odious tyrant.

'You're sure these workers can cut it?' Hiram growled as he walked with Asher toward the olive yard. The harvest had begun and so it was understandable he was anxious and on-edge.

'I can't see there being any problems,' Asher replied.

'You can't trust the people around here, Asher, you must watch them closely.'

'Don't worry, Hiram. This is no different to the work I did for my father back home in Bethany. I know how to spot the indolent. The work shall get done.'

'Well see that it does!' Hiram barked. 'I'm paying you a lot of money to make sure this harvest goes smoothly.'

He marched off toward the house and left Asher to walk on alone. Patrolling the olive yard, watching the labourers picking the olives from the trees and carting them to the press, reminded him of home. He wondered what his family were doing now. He had left three years ago and never returned, not even for a visit. He wrote to his parents every once in a while, but he knew they would be disappointed that he had never come home. He wanted to and thought many times of returning but he didn't want to feel like a failure when he did so. How much had really changed since he'd left? He didn't feel like he'd accomplished anything, though he had definitely had some adventures. He still hadn't found what he was looking for and that pained him. If he went home now, with nothing to say or offer his parents, they would lambast him for having wasted years of his life. He had to accomplish something or he would bring shame on the family.

He approached the olive press where several men and women were busy crushing the olives that had already been harvested that day. It was different from what Asher was used to when treading grapes in the wine press. A large lever, weighed down by a heavy stone weight pressed down on a large, flat stone. This sat above a basket of olives, which, when crushed, squeezed out the olive oil. This was the precious commodity that provided an income for so many at this time of year. The oil would gather into a vat beneath the press. After a few days, the oil and water gathered there would be separated and the oil sold.

Asher watched from a distance, intrigued at how the process worked. He knew he had to remain aloof from the workers lest they question him and identify his ignorance.

At the end of the day he trudged back to the house with the others. They had been working harder than he but he still a felt a fatigue at having been out in the fields all day. The sun was beginning to disappear over the horizon, stunning stretches of pink and red blazing a trail in its wake.

A cluster of women were returning from the house. They must have been exhausted after a hard day's work but they showed no sign of weariness. On the contrary they were animated, their faces glowing with enthusiasm. It looked as though one of them was regaling the others with a story. Asher listened in as they walked past:

'I'm telling you there were twenty thousand of us there.'

'Twenty thousand?'

'Maybe more! The whole hillside was covered in people who'd been following him for days.'

'So where had they all come from?'

'I don't know. But believe me when I tell you, sisters, there was more than enough for everyone.'

He heard no more as the women continued their excited babbling all the way down the hill and away into the gathering darkness.

Hiram provided a meagre meal, which Asher ate out of necessity only. Upon returning to his room he collapsed upon the bed and went straight to sleep. Another time and in another place, he would have stayed up for many hours, drinking and conversing with his colleagues. Not here though. His own company was infinitely preferable to that of Hiram. He was looking forward to going to Sepphoris tomorrow. It should prove a refreshing change from the olive yard and Asher had always liked the big cities.

He rose early and made the most of the hour-long walk soon after the sun had risen. It ambled lazily through the eastern sky, reluctant to make its daily pilgrimage. The dullness in Asher's heart mirrored the apathy of the sun. He trudged along the dusty trail, a small bag slung over his shoulder containing a few pieces of bread and a skin of wine.

An uncharacteristic melancholy had settled upon him in the last few days and he could feel it. His senses were dulled, his energy sapped and he had not the patience for others he would normally have. Here he was back in the Galilee, doing a job that wasn't much different than the one he'd done back home in Bethany. The last year had been a depressing waste of time and he felt no further forward than when he'd left home all those years ago.

Had he been deceiving himself all this time? Was there really nothing more out there for him than to work in his father's vineyards? Should he end this fool's errand he'd pursued and return home? Perhaps his parents would be so pleased to see him return that they would overlook his stupidity. He felt sure his friends and siblings would not be so merciful.

Suddenly in the distance, the outline of Sepphoris rose before him like a gigantic sea monster rising from the ocean. No wonder it had been chosen from old as the capital of the region. It towered over the landscape, providing a focal point for all other little villages and hamlets in the area. Aided by the sun, a warmth rose in Asher's heart which fought to dispel the gloom which had descended upon him.

As he approached the city and the night drifted away, he was more conscious of others travelling along the road with him. Merchants from nearby towns and villages were lugging their wares with them, hoping to sell them in the Sepphoris markets. The more fortunate among them had donkeys to bear the load. Most, however, struggled with great sacks slung over their shoulders. Women carefully balanced upon their heads heavy containers of produce. They probably made this journey every day, knowing that the travellers along the Via Maris would stop and provide good custom.

When he entered the city, he could have leapt with delight. Antipas, and those before him who had designed the spectacle, had done a fantastic job. The influence of Greek and Roman culture was everywhere. There were long, paved colonnades. The exotic vines that draped themselves around the pillars and nearby walls looked divine. Grand buildings and temples reeked of affluence and prestige and there were marble statues everywhere. Fancy gardens could be glimpsed behind low-slung walls in which a plethora of birds flitted about among the flowers. Asher was reminded of the garden in which he walked with Diana all those months ago. Indeed, the whole place had his mind racing back to the times he'd spent in Caesarea with Varius. Sepphoris was not as modern and opulent as the coastal fort, but it was spectacular nonetheless.

There were some, like he, who were walking around open mouthed at the grandeur of the place. Most, however, had seen it all before. The great and the good were strutting along, eager to get to an important meeting or greet a favoured client. The most affluent were carried along in their litters, too important to share pavements with the commoners.

Most of the people, however, were ordinary folk, keen to do a day's business and then return triumphantly to their families. All kinds of goods could be purchased from the market stalls: from fruit and vegetables, to pottery and fabrics. There were even spices from the east which were getting much patronage from the well-heeled denizens of the city.

He walked and walked, taking in the sights and smells of the whole city. It was some time before he remembered he had a job to do. Hiram had sent him there to drum up business and as yet he hadn't spoken to anyone. He had no desire to either. Instead, he sat in a large open forum, watching the people of the city walk by. Munching on his bread and gulping down his wine, he suddenly felt happy again. Business could wait. For now, he was content to enjoy the moment. He'd had precious little to smile about recently so he was determined to take advantage of this, a most welcome diversion.

'Content to watch the world go by?'

Asher turned to see a little old lady sitting beside him. She was less than half his height and looked barely human. She stared at him through two beady little eyes and her toothless grin was surrounded by a number of rogue whiskers. She'd wrapped herself in old rags and round her head was wound a rough old garment that looked as though it had survived the exodus. She perched on the bench beside him like a mischievous child waiting for an opportunity to cause havoc.

He smiled at the old hag. 'I am for the moment, mother, but don't tell the master.'

She cackled with glee. 'You're new to Sepphoris then?' she asked.

'You can tell?'

'You can tell the people who just go about their business and never look up. You're not. You've spent the whole time gazing about you like a bird of prey.'

'I see I'm not the only one,' he smiled. 'How long have you been watching me?'

'Long enough to know you're a good man.'

Asher smiled. The old woman was probably mad as a bag of locusts. No doubt the customary request for coins was approaching the conversation with inevitable haste.

'I've lived here all my life, you know? Not far from here anyway. I could tell you some stories.' She became pensive and a wistful look appeared on her face as if some sudden fond memory had emerged from the dark recesses of her mind.

'I imagine you've seen a lot over the years.'

'I've seen this city rise and fall and the leaders come and go. The people are the constant, and the weather. The sun continues to beat down and ordinary folk like you and me go about our business no matter what. And for all that, I

110

have to agree with old King Solomon. There's nothing new under the sun.'

'Go on then,' Asher encouraged. 'What have you seen?'

She smiled again, her toothless mouth a dark chasm of horrors. 'How long have you got?'

'My boss isn't here to keep an eye on me, so I've got as long as I want.'

She stared straight at him, a cheeky, mischievous grin etched across her face. 'You young ones have got no respect for your elders,' she teased. 'I would never have said such a thing when I was your age.'

'You'd have said that and far worse, I'd wager,' Asher responded.

She nodded playfully, her naughty little eyes flickering with delight.

Eventually she said, 'You've heard of Judas, I suppose?'

'No. Who?'

'Judas the Galilean. He was a troublemaker some years back. He was one of these zealots you know, the ones who takes their religion more seriously than the rest of us.'

'I've seen plenty like that,' Asher said.

'Well he took umbrage at the Romans and their census, didn't he? Told his followers to refuse to pay their taxes. Led a raid on the city.'

'Here in Sepphoris?'

'Yes, right here. He and his followers rampaged through this very forum.'

Asher looked around, people were mingling freely, weaving their way in and out of the pillared colonnades. He imagined a time when the place was overrun by violent extremists.

'So what happened?' he asked.

'The Romans won't stand for that nonsense, will they?'

'They fought back, slaughtered his followers, burned down their homes and drove them into the wilderness. Judas was crucified in Jerusalem, I believe.'

'They're ruthless,' Asher replied, shaking his head. 'How long ago?'

She thought for a moment. 'Before you were born, though it doesn't seem that long ago to me.'

'You can't defeat the Romans. Not like that anyway,' Asher mused.

'Well how can they be defeated then, if not like that?'

Asher was surprised at the sudden combativeness of the old maid.

'I don't know. Maybe they can't be defeated. Maybe we just have to accept them.'

She shot him a look of undisguised contempt. 'You should be ashamed of yourself,' she snapped, prodding him in the arm with a minute, bony finger. 'A young Jewish man like you should be eager to take up arms against the Roman scourge.'

Asher couldn't help but smile at the latent ire of the old woman. 'It would have to be some leader who could raise an army of farmers and fishermen to take on the might of Rome.'

She shook her head sadly. 'These young men, their heads full of delusions, think they're the ones to break the Roman yoke. They convince themselves they're anointed, and persuade others to follow blindly after them. They have their grand dreams and visions, they speak with eloquence and charm. Yet in the end they get swept away like all the others.'

'He had messianic aspirations then?'

'Don't they all?'

'This area does seem to have its fair share of anointed ones,' he said dryly.

'Idiots. That's what they are, most of them anyway. As one dies or is executed, it doesn't take long for another to take his place.'

Asher sat silently, contemplating the sadness and failure of the human condition.

'There's another one wandering about at the moment, I hear,' said the old woman.

'Another what?'

'Another would-be Messiah of course!'

'Is there? I hadn't heard.'

'Some say he's from these parts. Nazareth, I believe.'

'Well maybe he'll have more luck against the Romans than this Judas the Galilean.'

'Maybe, young man, maybe.'

There was a pause in the conversation before eventually the old woman said, 'Aren't you interested? Maybe he's the real thing.'

'Who?'

'The Nazarene!' she said, an exasperated tone evident in her voice.

'Oh, I'm not interested in any of that,' he rebuffed her. 'I've had my fair share of holy men recently so I'm not about to go wandering around after another one.'

'Now that does sound interesting! Tell me about this holy man of yours!'

Asher rolled his eyes, wishing he'd never mentioned it. The last thing he wanted to talk about with this old crow was his wasted year in the wilderness with a secluded cult. It was an embarrassment he was never going to talk about, ever.

'Would you like some bread, mother? And I have some wine here too, if you would like?' he said smiling.

Despite her age, she wasn't completely tactless and accepted his obfuscation. 'As you wish. I knew you were a good boy,' she grinned, snatching the bread from him. 'The moment I set eyes on you, I knew you were a good boy!'

She accepted his offer gratefully. Asher watched on fondly as she wrapped her shrivelled little fingers around his rolls of bread and drank his wine as if it were the best she'd ever tasted.

Chapter XVII

The Festival of Lights was coming to an end and soon Jerusalem would return to some semblance of normality. It wasn't as bad as Sukkoth, which had taken place a few months ago, but it was bad enough. Now, as then, Jerusalem swarmed with visitors. Chanukkah wasn't one of the major festivals that people were commanded to attend, but it still caused Jerusalem to swell like a bloated sow about to give birth.

Her boss loved it, though you'd never know it given that his mood never changed. He was as surly and aggressive as ever. Yet the more people that arrived in the city, the more money there was to be made.

Shifra was pleased the whole thing was coming to an end. The city had been lit up for the last eight days, parties had been commonplace in the evenings leading to deserted streets in the morning. That was her favourite time of day, when the streets were abandoned by those who had drunk too much the night before. While they nursed their aching heads and vomited into their bowls, she could get some peace and quiet. She had no sympathy for them. These wretched people deserved all they got.

This evening she sat, as she often did, in an olive grove across the Kidron Valley. A thread of light wound its way through the valley as people celebrated the last night of the festival. It reached its zenith in the city, which was now aglow with a thousand torches. She had come out here every

114

night of the festival to escape the noise, the music but most of all the joy. She loathed the sound of people laughing and having fun and the greater the raucous shouts of jubilation became, the angrier it made her. At least out here in the darkness of the valley she could keep the revellers at arm's length. Tomorrow they would all start to drift back home and Jerusalem would once more get back to some semblance of normality.

One of her few small comforts was being able to gaze into the endless sky at night and stare at the starry host. On this occasion there was too much light radiating from the city and she could see little of what she usually loved to gaze upon.

From somewhere in the darkness came the sounds of people moving in her direction. It wasn't the sound of people up to no good, creeping silently through the recesses of the night. It was far worse than that, it was people laughing and singing. Shifra winced as the crowd drew near. She tried to shrink into the tree she was sitting beneath, hoping that they passed her by.

To her horror they stopped close by. There was about ten of them. They looked as though they had all had too much to drink for they were staggering and stumbling, through the undergrowth and under the trees. There was as many men as women and they all carried at least one wineskin. There was a clearing between the trees which the crowd had decided was their resting place. Shifra watched them from the shadows.

They passed their wineskins freely between each other and delighted themselves in swigging and guzzling huge quantities of wine as it was offered. They didn't seem to have any food with them. This was a liquid feast.

It soon became apparent that one couple in particular was at the centre of the group. They seemed to be the focal point, the others deferring to the man as he held court. He seemed to be telling some kind of story which had the others enraptured. When he reached the climax of his tale, a roar arose from the gathered party and the hilarity ensued once more.

Shifra watched, repulsed and intrigued in equal measure. Soon the leader of the group rose to his feet once more, only this time one of the females joined him. He seemed to be leading the band in a toast to the girl. It was then that Shifra realised they were newlyweds.

They were celebrating their new marriage and probably had been for days. They had snuck away from the rest of the family so they could be with their closest friends. Suddenly they didn't seem quite so annoying. It was difficult to see clearly in the darkness but there seemed to be genuine affection between the husband and wife. Their friends too seemed to display a genuine warmth toward them.

They clearly weren't reckless winebibbers at all but young people enjoying the company of their friends at a key turning point in their lives.

In the shadow of the great city, the light of a thousand torches illuminated the night sky. Shifra rebuked herself for the bitterness which had arisen stealthily in her soul. There was a darkness within her. She was enveloped by it. She looked at the happy couple and felt a weighty sadness, a heaviness in the pit of her stomach. A lone tear rolled down her cheek and she sighed wearily.

Chapter XVIII

The last two months had been ones of intolerable frustration. Eliashib had believed that others in the Sanhedrin would be as keen as he was to pursue this dangerous preacher in the Galilee. Instead, when he had approached some of the brothers with his plan to accost him in the north, he was met with cowardly hesitation. Even Caiaphas had been reluctant. There seemed to be a common feeling that the man was a minor irritant: a troublemaker, to be sure, but hardly a dangerous one. There were some who disagreed of course, who felt, as he did, that the man was a blasphemer and ought to be confronted and shown up for the charlatan he undoubtedly was. There was little agreement though, and as such he had not been given permission to pursue the man in the Galilee.

He had been forced to be patient. Fortunately, that was a characteristic he had in abundance. If the years of suffering for old Tobiah had taught him anything it was patience. He had worked for that old toad for years without any thanks or reward. Now that he was surrounded by others of a similar ilk and some that were even more inept, he was forced to be patient once more.

He had continued behind the scenes, coaxing and persuading others into his way of thinking. Fortuitously, he was a master negotiator and knew just how to speak to certain people in certain ways in order to reach a satisfactory outcome. His outcome. It had taken the best part of the last two months but he was sure he was gaining more support among the brothers for his plan. Once he'd assured them that he had the support of a high-ranking Roman soldier, they were more receptive to his calls for action.

There were some of course who he knew would never come around to his way of thinking. They were from the same school of thought as Tobiah: intransigent in their thinking and foolish in their outlook. Gamaliel was the worst of them and Nicodemus was another with whom he'd had no joy in convincing.

In the last week or so he'd felt a change. He'd continued to have his surreptitious conversations as usual, only he was beginning to feel more and more that the collective mood of the Sanhedrin was shifting.

Snippets of information kept reaching them from the Galilee of the tricks and deceptions the man was carrying out. The gullible and uneducated called them miracles, but he knew better. The latest was a report from the Decapolis that he had fed four thousand men with only a few pieces of fish and some rolls of bread. It was nonsense, of course, but not as preposterous as the other story he'd heard. A story was circulating among the ignorant that he had travelled across the Sea of Galilee with supernatural speed. His disciples had apparently entered into a boat – the only boat – and travelled to the other side without Jesus. When the crowd went looking for him on the other side of the lake, they found him in Capernaum with his disciples. Nonplussed as to how he had done it, rumours began to circulate that God had transported him in a blazing chariot like he had for Elijah. Others said that God had parted the sea so he could walk across on dry land, just as he had for Moses. Still others claimed that he had simply walked across the water as if it were solid ground. There really was no end to the stories these simpletons would invent.

Yet despite the ludicrous nature of the tales being told, they were having a profound effect. The Galilee was in uproar, apparently. Hundreds, if not thousands, of people followed him wherever he went. And he wasn't just confining himself to the Galilee either. They had heard of him throughout Samaria and Peraea as well as on the coast and across the Jordan. It seemed as though the man was having a far greater impact than any of the other false teachers who had gone before him. It was said he had even been as far north as Phoenicia and the cities of Tyre and Sidon.

When Eliashib spoke of him, people were finally starting to listen. The Sanhedrin was now abuzz with incredulity at the audacity of the man. And finally, yesterday morning, he had been given permission to track him down and question him. Of course, he was going to do far more than that. With the help of Varius, he was going to pursue the scoundrel through Samaria, Judea, the Galilee and the Decapolis or wherever he might be found. He would pursue him into Ituraea if he had to.

His attendants were seeing to his provisions at that very moment. Soon he would be off to the Galilee where he would confront the pernicious rogue and establish himself as a leading member of the Sanhedrin.

Caiaphas had granted him a small contingent of attendants to accompany him north. It was barely adequate, but it would have to do. He had been assured that the journey could be made in less than four days. It would be hard work for the slaves tasked with carrying him, but that was part of their role so they were used to it. One of the brothers had graciously procured a comfortable, Roman-style litter that he would ride in. He didn't ride horses and walking was out of the question. A more luxurious mode of travel was entirely suitable for someone of his stature anyway.

The plan was to stop the first night in Bethel and then make the long journey north through the countryside of Judea until they reached Shechem where they would spend the second night. His attendants had made arrangements to stay in Scythopolis on the third day. From there he would assess the situation further before ascending into the Galilee. He abhorred travel and as the weather was getting warmer he was sure to be bored and uncomfortable the whole way. Alas, sacrifices had to be made.

On the third day the weary company was struggling to keep pace and there was some concern they would not make Scythopolis by nightfall. His attendants had assured him the slaves were performing admirably given the arduous task required of them. He wasn't so sure. He knew most people were given to moaning and complaining at the first opportunity. Usually it was because they were indolent. He saw no reason why these slaves should be any different. There were murmurs that the two bodyguards were grumbling too. They'd been hired to accompany him wherever he went until his return to Jerusalem. They were big burly Thracians, ex-slaves who had earned their freedom. There had been nothing for them to do so far, so they should be thankful for that.

It was mid-afternoon and the sun was still raging. They were a long way from the summer months but that big blazing ball of fire could still make life most uncomfortable. Eliashib had never been this far north before and he was pleasantly surprised. It wasn't the barren wilderness he had imagined. They had travelled for miles through lush pastures and farmland, wooded areas where a myriad of trees crowded by gently flowing rivers. Once or twice he caught a glimpse of an ibex hurtling through the undergrowth and the sky was often filled with birds chasing each other without care. It was all part of Yahweh's grand design.

They had stopped for refreshment beneath a small cluster of trees, not far from the main trail. Unfortunately, it seemed as though they had left all the luscious scenery behind. He had been enjoying the green pastures of Judea as immortalised by the Psalmist. Now, however, his surroundings looked more like the Valley of the Shadow of Death. Perhaps it wasn't that bad but there were arid foothills everywhere, little vegetation and wisps of dust swirling erratically on the road.

Hur was his chief attendant. A capable, if slow, man who had proven not as incompetent as most. His family were keen that he get some experience working for members of the Sanhedrin. He was ambitious and hoped to one day elevate himself into just such a distinguished position. He had prepared for his master a seat in the shade. While Eliashib was keen to reach his destination, he was thankful to get out of the accursed litter for a few moments.

'Why Scythopolis?' Hur asked him while handing him a plate of olives.

'It's not far from the Galilee and has a good-sized synagogue that should be able to offer me suitable accommodation,' he replied.

'Has this Jesus been spotted there?'

'It's possible. I've had word that he operates all over the north, not just in the area around the Galilee.'

'I don't know anything about Scythopolis. I've never been.'

Eliashib detested idle talk but here saw an opportunity to educate his young aide. 'It wasn't always known by that name,' he began grandly. 'Scythopolis is the Greek name it was given to replace Beth Shan.'

'I recognise that name.'

'And so you should!' Eliashib scolded and clucked his tongue. 'Beth Shan was a very important city back when our people were first united under the leadership of King Saul.' He pointed into the distance. 'If we are where you have assured me we are, then very soon we should be able to see Mount Gilboa ahead of us. It was there that Saul and his son Jonathan were defeated in battle. The Philistines cut Saul's head from his body and pinned it to the wall of Beth Shan.'

'I thought Beth Shan meant, 'house of peace'?' Hur said with a chuckle.

Eliashib glared at him until Hur lowered his eyes in repentance.

'We revere our ancestors, Hur, we do not make light of their afflictions! Especially great men like King Saul.'

'I am sorry, sir. I shall be honoured to visit this auspicious place and, if you have time, I would like to learn more of the history of the area.'

He slunk away, leaving Eliashib to think of the matters they'd been discussing. It would be intriguing to visit the place even if it no longer bore the name of Beth Shan. Saul had failed to vanquish the Philistines on the slopes of Mount Gilboa but he would not fail. He was determined to track this Jesus down and hold him to account.

As expected, they only reached Scythopolis after nightfall. Eliashib sent the youngest and swiftest of his attendants on ahead to inform the synagogue leader of their arrival. They might have to forego the customary welcoming committee given the lateness of their arrival. Usually someone of his stature could expect a lavish welcome.

The synagogue leader looked flustered when they arrived. He was a small man, young and timid looking. He was probably terrified that a member of the Sanhedrin had shown up unannounced. Eliashib experienced a frisson of pleasure at how his mere presence could cause people to behave in such a manner.

'Welcome, your grace to Scythopolis,' he stammered. 'My name is Judah Bar Judah and everything here is at your disposal. Is there anything I can get you now? Some refreshment perhaps.'

'Not now. All I require is a bed and some comfort. For three days I have been on the road and I am tired and in need of a proper rest.'

'Of course, of course. My attendants have prepared my personal rooms for your comfort. I shall sleep elsewhere.'

Without further ado, Eliashib swept through the synagogue, guided by his new admirer. His attendants helped him disrobe and soon he was asleep, his dreams peppered with visions of ancient battles and fallen kings.

It was in the morning, over breakfast, that Judah Bar Judah finally plucked up the courage to ask what this retinue from Jerusalem was doing in his synagogue.

'I am on the trail of a charlatan, a con-man, a devilish cad, intent on deceiving the people and no-doubt making a great name for himself.'

'Ah! The Nazarene?'

'He is from Nazareth? This Jesus?'

'Yes, I am told he is originally from Nazareth but now has a base at Capernaum. It is from there that he carries out much of his ministry.'

'Ministry, is it?' Eliashib immediately shot back. 'I hardly think we should be calling this fellow's actions a ministry!' He looked upon his young host with scathing eyes.

The man was suitably chastised. 'Of course not, your grace, forgive me.'

Eliashib let his uncompromising stare rest upon the young man for a moment longer before asking, 'So it's Capernaum, then? That's where we should be headed?'

'Capernaum is a small fishing village, sir. There is a small synagogue there, I believe, but I doubt it would be suitable for you and your party. Although,' he paused, 'I have heard that the man Jesus preaches in that same synagogue quite frequently.'

'Does he indeed!' Eliashib was shocked but not surprised. The backward folk of the Galilee were probably far more susceptible to the man's trickery than their more educated southern neighbours.

'You might prefer to stay in Tiberius where Herod Antipas has his base. They would be far more accustomed to guests of your prominence than those in Capernaum. You could then make the short trip around the lake to speak to this Jesus in Capernaum or wherever else he may be.'

Eliashib nodded thoughtfully. 'Yes. I think that is probably the best thing for it. I shall stay here another night and then we shall head to Tiberius on the morrow.'

'You have travelled a long way to see him. Are you impressed or intrigued by what you've heard of the man?'

'Impressed!' Eliashib nearly choked on a fig, ending up spitting fragments of it all over his robes. 'Impressed!' he bellowed again so that the synagogue leader realised the foolishness of his words. 'Intrigued possibly, but certainly not impressed. Disgusted? Yes. Appalled? Yes. Indignant? Absolutely.'

Judah Bar Judah cowered in front of his older colleague, wishing he had used a different word.

'Is that what you have been?' he continued the tirade, 'Impressed?'

At that moment, one of the synagogue leader's attendants darted across the floor and whispered something in his master's ear. He seemingly felt the need to do something to help his master in the face of this unexpected eruption.

'It seems,' the young man began tentatively, 'that you may not have to go as far as Capernaum after all.'

Eliashib was breathing deeply, trying to calm down. 'And why is that?'

'The word around the synagogue in the last day or two is that he has been spotted in this area, not far from Mount Gilboa.'

The news settled on Eliashib like a warm blanket. This was a clear sign that his mission and purpose were blessed by divine providence. The great Yahweh had known the impostor would be in the vicinity and so had guided Eliashib his servant into the area in order to apprehend him. Just as the hand of God had guided Joshua into the Promised Land, so too had the Almighty guided him into Beth Shan in order to deal with this fraudster, this Jesus. He was on a mission from God.

'Hur!' he yelled.

'Yes sir?'

'Find a horse and ride as quickly as you can to Tiberius. Go to the Roman barracks and ask for a man by the name of Varius. Tell him that I am here in Scythopolis and that the man we're looking for is nearby. He is to meet me here at once with a company of soldiers.'

Chapter XIX

Varius had forgotten all about the Rabbi when he at last got the message that he had travelled north and was staying at a synagogue in Scythopolis. He was relieved, for the past few weeks had been mundane and he was itching to do something. The prospect of tracking down this wandering preacher was an intriguing one. The Rabbi was anxious to arrest the fiend and impress his superiors. The man's motives made no difference to him. He was surprised that an influential contingent of priests and rabbis hadn't come north sooner. The Galilee was obsessed with this preacher and he had travelled to Jerusalem before, so he'd heard. Yet it had taken the religious authorities a while to take the man seriously.

He had agreed to help the Rabbi not just because he longed for something to do but because he was irritated by the religious fervour of this people. He had become sickened by their preening priests and the obscene control they seemed to have over the people. The crowds followed them everywhere begging for prayers and alms, hoping that their ancient deity would grant them favour. This Jesus was no different from all the other religious leaders. He commanded a following as they did and would no doubt expect their unwavering devotion and loyalty. Meanwhile he would fleece their pockets and, in the end, convince them to do whatever he wanted.

It hadn't been difficult to secure the agreement of his superior. He was a cruel and uncompromising man and hated the Jews more than any other he knew. He resented being posted to Judea and would jump at the chance of lording it over the inhabitants of this despicable land. Varius had told him of his plan and had been given his blessing.

He was given a dozen soldiers and told to tell them they were going on a training exercise which Varius would lead. They were to bring belongings for an overnight camp, full armour and weaponry. They were used to going on long marches carrying all their gear and weapons. It was part and parcel of a Roman soldier's training and so they didn't question their orders for a second. Varius kept to himself what their real mission was and what they were going to do when they got there.

He received the message from Hur, the Rabbi's assistant just after lunch. Having obtained permission to proceed, he assembled the men and told them to be ready to depart at sunrise the next day.

Now they were approaching Scythopolis and Varius was eager to meet the Rabbi and find out where the preacher was lurking. He had noticed small groups of people in the distance as they had made their way past Nain and toward Jezreel. It was possible they were following or going to meet Jesus. He had briefly contemplated diverting their route and following the distant crowd. On reflection, however, he decided it was better to speak with the Rabbi first.

On entering Scythopolis he made a few enquiries as to the location of the synagogue. It didn't take long to find and so as soon as they arrived, he sent word for someone to fetch out the Rabbi. He only had to wait a minute or two before a commotion inside signalled the arrival of his Jewish accomplice. A broad, fake grin broke out across the Rabbi's face when he saw him.

'Varius, my friend,' he yelled, raising his arms in the pretence that he was genuinely fond of him.

'So you finally made it, Rabbi,' Varius said dryly. 'I was beginning to wonder if you'd changed your mind, or was it that you found it a challenge to get the agreement of your superiors?'

The Rabbi visibly bristled at his insolent tone. He did not like those around him to be reminded that he too was someone else's supplicant. Varius didn't care what the Rabbi thought. He didn't have to impress anyone, least of all a Jewish teacher.

'Some things are more complicated than they appear, my friend,' the Rabbi replied through gritted teeth, 'Especially when dealing with delicate matters of a sensitive nature.'

Varius rolled his eyes. 'Shall we get on with it?'

'Of course, step inside.'

Varius told his men to wait outside. They would be grateful for the rest having marched all day. Loath to remain in the synagogue, they sought shelter nearby while Varius followed the Rabbi down a dark corridor and to a small office. There were a few people hanging around, waiting to spring into action should the old man demand something. One of them looked of some importance but the Rabbi barely noticed him.

'I am Judah Bar Judah,' he said to Varius. 'Welcome to our synagogue.'

Varius nodded firmly but before he could utter a word, the Rabbi broke in. 'Leave us!' he barked. The man looked crestfallen. He left the room sheepishly, his eyes fixed on the floor.

'So, do you know where he is?' Varius asked as the old Rabbi eased himself into a chair.

'He's not far from here. I was told the news yesterday as soon as I arrived. He's apparently been preaching on the slopes of Mount Gilboa.'

'And he's still there? I've heard he likes to move around.'

'He's still there. I sent someone out there this morning and again this afternoon. He's still there and there are crowds of people flocking to him. Poor, ignorant fools.'

Varius smiled. 'He's really got under your skin, hasn't he?'

'He's a menace. With your help we shall deal with him swiftly and thoroughly.'

Varius was gratified. He was more than willing to do the Jew's dirty work. In fact, he would enjoy it. 'Tomorrow then?'

The Rabbi nodded. 'We shall dine early and leave straight away, as soon as the light allows. How many men do you have with you?'

'A dozen.'

'A dozen! Is that all?'

'That's enough. What do you think is going to happen?'

'He has many followers. What if they become nasty?'

'Nasty!' Varius couldn't help but laugh, a deep laugh that rumbled from within. 'They're farmers and fishermen, not soldiers.' He shook with laughter at the absurdity of the old man's suggestion. He obviously hadn't seen the Roman Army in action. They were formidable. Every army in the world had bowed before them eventually. The peasants of the Galilee would be crushed like insects if they dared to offer any resistance.

The Rabbi shifted uncomfortably in his chair as Varius struggled to suppress his amusement.

'Are they fully briefed on what to do?'

'No! they know nothing. I have them down here on a training exercise. They know nothing of this little plot of yours. Besides, it will be good practice for them when the times comes. I don't want them to know in advance what they might have to do.'

'You know best,' the Rabbi offered. 'So what are you going to do?'

Varius had always known he would be the one who would have to come up with the plan of attack. The Rabbi was all about talk, not action. He was quite happy for Varius to take over and then, once the deed had been done, he would return to Jerusalem and accept all the plaudits.

'All we have to do to find him is follow the crowd. When we do, we'll arrest him for disturbing the peace or inciting a riot or something and take him back to Tiberius and lock him up.'

'It'll be that easy?'

'Don't worry, old man,' Varius said confidently, rising to his feet. 'Tomorrow you'll finally get a good look at this man who's got you so terrified.'

'Terrified!' the Rabbi leapt to his feet to remonstrate but Varius, predicting and encouraging just such a reaction, was already closing the door and heading out into the dark corridor. Tomorrow was going to be fun.

Chapter XX

Asher had been given the day off and had decided to spend the time walking in the hills of southern Galilee. He could see Mount Tabor in the east, the site of Deborah and Barak's victory over the Canaanites many centuries ago. It towered over a lush green valley. Small houses were scattered across the landscape, evidence of a farming community that had been there for generations. He was approaching Nazareth, a large bustling town in the middle of the countryside. It was intimidated by its more sophisticated neighbours of Sepphoris and Tiberius but it had an allure of its own. It was full of hard-working folk and had the feel of a no-nonsense sort of town where people said what they meant and meant what they said.

He had never been one for walking, especially on his own. At home he was always with someone, whether he was working in the vineyards with his brother Daan or chatting on the rooftop with his sister Hannah. Other than that he would be in pursuit of some new adventure with Asa and Lahahana. He had thought about them often in the last few weeks, wondering if anything significant had happened in his absence. They might all have been married off by now for all he knew. He would be disappointed if Hannah had been. As her older brother, he felt he should have some say in who she married. Yet he couldn't blame them if they had all moved on with their lives while he had been away.

It was the odious presence of Hiram that had driven him away this day. The man was a people-repeller. If anyone could stand to be around him for more than a few minutes, it was evidence he was unhinged. The bitterness and aggression that exuded from his every pore was enough to offend and ward off even the most thick-skinned acquaintance.

He had left early and started walking. He planned to get to Nazareth for breakfast, which he had, and then decide what to do after that. He often walked by the great lake but there was so much commotion around there these days that he had been put off. Wherever he went someone was talking about Jesus. From the fishermen to the farmers, they all had one thing on their lips and that was this miracle-working preacher from Capernaum. Asher was amazed he hadn't yet seen him for to hear everyone speak you would think he was everywhere. He had witnessed many an impassioned argument about this Jesus. More than once he had seen fights break out, people passionately arguing that he was either a prophet, a harmless oddball or even the Messiah.

He had myriad stories of the good works he had done all over the region and beyond. He had been north into Phoenicia, south to Jerusalem, east to the Decapolis but more often than not, he could be found around the shores of the Sea of Galilee. At first, Asher had dismissed the stories and so-called miracles as the ignorant ramblings of poor people who didn't know any better. He assumed they and he would disappear sooner rather than later. Yet they persisted.

Now, as he walked through a Nazarene marketplace eating fruit and almonds, he could sense the place was buzzing. He couldn't hear what people were saying but there were many small groups dotted about, the people whispering to each other excitedly. Some were hopping from one group to the next like a bee in search of pollen. It's bound to be Jesus, he thought. What else could elicit such excitement in these people? Soon the marketplace began to empty and people started moving off in groups toward the south.

Two young men were about to break into a run when he nabbed one of them. 'What's going on?' he asked. 'What's all the excitement about?'

'It's Jesus,' one of the men replied excitedly. 'He's been spotted not far from here, we're going to see him.'

'Where?'

'Just south of Nain, near the slopes of Mount Gilboa'

'You're going there now?'

'We'll be there in a few hours if we walk fast.'

Asher nodded and said no more. The young men smiled pleasantly and then walked away. They had only gone a few steps when the one he'd spoken to stopped and turned around. 'Come with us?'

Asher shook his head. 'No thanks, it's not for me.'

'You haven't seen him before, have you?'

That was an unusual question, Asher thought. 'No I haven't. I have heard much about him though.'

'You should come,' the man smiled. 'You won't regret it.'

'No thanks.'

The man looked dejected but he was eager to get away so he nodded his acquiescence and fled.

Asher was intrigued, there was no point denying it. He had heard so much about this man both positive and negative. Yet he still felt wounded and embarrassed by his sojourn in the wilderness with someone who he thought had all the answers. That had been a colossal waste of time and he still cursed himself every time he thought about it. Could this Jesus be any different? He was certainly courting controversy. People all over the region were up in arms about him. It was only a matter of time before he would start to garner the attention of the Romans. Then he would regret causing such a fuss.

His friend and former mentor had never commanded such a following. They had always remained a small group of committed followers hidden in the Galilean wilderness. They had never made much of an impact on anyone. So maybe this Jesus was different. Maybe he should go and see for himself.

In a moment of spontaneity, which had once been his hallmark, he decided to follow the crowd. It was time he found out for himself what this was all about. What was so special about this Jesus of Nazareth?

Chapter XXI

They had been walking for about an hour. Varius had known crippled donkeys walk faster. The Rabbi was being carried in a litter by four muscular slaves, his attendants hovering nearby in case he needed something, which he frequently did. The men weren't complaining. He had worked them yesterday, walking them at speed through the Judean countryside to get to Scythopolis. Today would feel like a picnic in comparison.

There had been little traffic on the road as they went south west from their base. Mount Gilboa loomed large on the horizon. The countryside often resembled an old patchwork blanket, sewn together by one of the old Jewish widows. Lush green pastures, arid wasteland and wooded enclaves combined to make a unique environ. Small huts looked like they'd been dropped there randomly from the sky and all kinds of trees and bushes made lonely vigils, waiting for the next drop of rain.

The landscape undulated erratically so that it was often difficult to tell what was ahead. Varius had hoped he would have seen a large crowd by now, evidence that the preacher was nearby. There were people dotted about in the distance and all seemed to be heading in the same direction. Perhaps they were on the right track after all.

Varius walked at the head of the company, straining his eyes to see into the distance. The sun was behind him and was just beginning to provide a comforting warmth. He would be cursing it soon, wishing it would retreat behind a cloud so that he could get some respite.

He was walking up a small incline, the others following. When he reached the top he stopped suddenly, his heart skipped a beat and his stomach fell through his sandals.

Standing in front of him on the crest of the next hill was a gang of fifty men, angry, snarling and armed to the teeth. They looked dishevelled and hungry, itching for a fight. Were these the followers of Jesus? Was he amassing an army out here in the countryside? Had Varius stumbled across a threat to Rome after all?

'Positions!' he yelled.

The men around him dropped their gear, unsheathed their swords and readied their shields. Varius did the same. He heard a whimper from somewhere behind him. He assumed it was the Rabbi. He wouldn't have been expecting this. Farmers and fishermen? These were armed men and they looked dangerous.

Varius glanced to his side. His men had positioned themselves on either side of him. There were twelve of them and one of him. The militia on the opposing hill looked fifty strong. It was a fair fight.

'Advance!' he commanded and they all started walking slowly forward. They passed the crest of the hill and began walking down, ready to ascend the next incline and face the enemy.

He could hear the voices from the men on the hill. They sounded savage, animalistic, primitive. They mounted the crest and prepared for battle. There were no more peaks and troughs. This skirmish would take place on level ground.

Varius noticed the leader. He was taller than most, a thick bushy brown beard, torn rags for clothes wrapped around a muscular frame. His authority was all that was holding them back. They looked like a pack of animals, waiting for permission from their leader to charge. He hoisted his sword in the air and shouted something unintelligible. His men responded in an instant. As one, they hurled themselves forward.

'Go!'

Varius and his men surged forward too, into the fray.

Chapter XXII

Asher was now certain something had gone wrong. He thought he'd been following a group of people he was sure were going to meet Jesus but now when he looked about him, they were nowhere to be seen. He must have been daydreaming, for how else could he lose sight of people out here in the countryside, where it was mostly flat and dry?

Only now he realised it wasn't flat and dry. It had grown hillier and Mount Gilboa had grown bigger than ever. He passed through Nain, hoping that would be as far as he would have to go. He'd heard a story of Jesus stopping a funeral procession in the town and raising a young boy back from the dead. Nonsense of course, but maybe he had returned and Asher wouldn't have to wander all over the countryside looking for him.

He stopped and looked about him, hoping to garner some clue as to where he should go. Fortunately, on a nearby hill, he spotted a crowd of people. They looked quite animated but he couldn't work out what was going on. He decided to walk in their direction. If they weren't with Jesus, someone was bound to know something.

As he approached he got the distinctly uneasy feeling that all was not as it should be. There was something in the air, a tension, a foreboding, and the closer he got to the crowd the more nervous he felt. He could hear them now and the noise being emitted from the crowd was not a friendly one. He stopped in his tracks and looked closer. Romans! They were in amongst them, swallowed up by what was now undoubtedly an angry mob.

Asher froze. Some of the men were running from the soldiers, there were people running in every direction. He could hear the growls and the moans as they grew closer. Soon they were only a few metres away and he hadn't moved. He was close enough to see blood spurting and people falling. There was panic and fury; the crash of swords was horrifying and the screams of the fallen, horrific.

He was in danger but he couldn't move. He had to run but his legs no longer worked. His gaze was fixed on the battle which was about to envelope him.

Chapter XXIII

Eliashib couldn't speak, couldn't breathe. What was going on? What had just happened? One moment he was following the Roman soldiers, hoping that Jesus and the rabble would soon appear from somewhere. Then, before he knew what was going on, the Romans had surged forward. There was a crowd on the neighbouring hill and they looked angry. It was Jesus' followers. It must be. The man was more dangerous than anyone thought.

While struggling to understand this dramatic turn of events the Romans, led by Varius, had flown at the angry mob. He had realised belatedly, that he was too close to them. When the Romans clashed with the mob he was close enough to see the swords and shields clash. He heard the painful cries of the first victims and saw the ferocity in the savage faces of the mob. He panicked, realising suddenly that his life was in danger.

'Get me out of here!' he yelled at nobody in particular. Fortunately, Hur and some of the others were close by. They grabbed him, spun him around and began to march him away from the battle.

He winced in fear, tears welling in his eyes as he heard the sickening noise of the conflict behind him. Some men were screaming, others shouting and the constant sound of clashing swords and the thud of shields seemed deafening to him.

He couldn't die. Not here. Not now.

He was running now, yet he hardly knew how. There was someone on either side of him almost lifting him from the ground. They were hurrying him away and gradually the noise of the battle began to die down. He was exhausted and having trouble breathing. Commanding them to stop, he tried to compose himself. He turned around but couldn't see over the crest of the hill to where the fight had begun.

He would have to get back to Jerusalem and report what had happened. The Sanhedrin would need to know that this man Jesus was raising an army. He was far more dangerous than any of them had thought. This was sedition and would attract the vengeance of the Romans too. The Romans! What about Varius? If he didn't make it, he, Eliashib would be the only one who could inform the elders of what was going on in the Galilee. Perhaps then he would get the recognition he deserved.

Chapter XXIV

Varius hadn't expected to be fighting for his life in the Judean countryside. Yet when the mob had appeared, he experienced a sudden rush of blood, a heightened excitement that he rarely felt these days. The big man, the leader had led the charge. Varius had gone straight for him but in the chaos of the initial advance he couldn't tell whether he'd made contact with him or not.

He and his men were well trained. Their attackers may be greater in number but they had neither the skill nor the discipline of Roman troops.

They stuck together as the savages attacked. There were spears, swords and daggers all being thrust in their direction. They stood firm, shields held tight. The roar of the men as they attacked sent a momentary shiver down his spine. Memories of the bandits in the desert returned but even they didn't have this savage intensity.

There was a brief pause in the onslaught. As one, the Romans advanced. Varius thrust his sword forward. He connected with the unprotected bare chest of a man wielding a spear. He groaned in pain and fell to the floor. With some effort, Varius jerked the sword out of the man's chest. He was dead before his body hit the ground.

The scene soon descended into chaos and to Varius it was all a blur. He was cutting and thrusting with his sword as men approached. He was ducking and dodging as an array of weapons were either hurled or swung in his direction. He was conscious of his men being close by but his focused gaze darted from side to side as the battle quickly descended into mayhem.

He spotted the big man. He was an intimidating figure, fearless and imposing. He was locked in battle with one of Varius' men but he couldn't tell who. He wanted to get over there and help, cut the man down and help his colleague. Yet he was almost surrounded and there were too many of the barbarians in the way.

He continued to raise his sword, parrying the blows that sought to dislodge his head from his body. He sliced through a hamstring, brought his sword crashing down on a neck and slashed across a man's chest. One of the savages had fallen. Varius lurched forward, sword raised, ready to finish him off when he felt a sudden pain flash through his body. It was his arm. He spun to his right to see a short, muscular man with ragged clothes and a disfigured face. He was twisting and swirling a dagger in each hand. The pain was incredible. He could see the blood running down his arm. A violent surge of fury engulfed him and he stepped forward, using his shield to crash into the crazed lunatic. The man lost his balance and fell backward. Varius seized the advantage. He leapt forward, slashing the daggers out of the man's hands with a swift, sweeping motion. He was defenceless yet he looked up at Varius who was towering over him with not a hint of fear. Disgusted and disturbed, he took his sword and drove it through the man's chest. Blood spurted from the man's mouth, his eyes rolled back into his head and he fell back, motionless.

Varius had only time to savour the moment for a second. He looked up and saw the ground was littered with the dead. Among them were two of his men. Yet the battle continued to rage. He raced over to where another of his colleagues was fighting off three of the barbarians. He approached his foe from behind, swinging his sword at the man's neck. He felt a twinge of disappointment that the head didn't sever completely but was left dangling by a resolute strand of bloodied muscle. He yanked his sword free, sending fragments of his victim's spinal cord flying through the air.

His compatriot had bested the other two, galvanised by Varius' timely intervention.

He looked around for another assailant. Where was the leader? Where was the enormous savage warrior whose reckless arrogance had caused this carnage?

He searched the scarred battlefield for the rebel leader. Instead his eyes alighted upon a man, standing not far from where he stood. He wasn't dressed like the others and was stood as if frozen in fear. He clearly wasn't one of them. Someone caught in the wrong place at the wrong time. He turned to look for the leader once more but then a flash of recognition assailed him. Before he could turn to confirm this sudden notion, he spotted the pack General.

He was hurt but unbowed. The body of a Roman soldier lay at his feet. Varius scanned the battlefield. There were few left alive. Countless bodies strewn everywhere, the bloodstained ground a silent witness to the senseless slaughter.

He could see some had already fled, pursued by his comrades across the undulating hills. Varius ran forward, dodging the bodies of the slain in his attempt to reach the leader. He got there slower than he would have liked. When he did, he realised the man, big as he was, was in no state to continue the fight. He turned when he heard Varius approach, the fiery light of rebellion still in his eyes. Yet his strength was failing. He stumbled and fell to one knee. Varius approached, his sword drawn, ready to relieve the man of his head.

He paused before decapitating the wretch. The fool had a wicked grin hidden behind his disgusting, gnarled features. He was almost covered in blood, yet he was chuckling quietly. Maniacally.

Varius changed his mind. A swift death was too good for the likes of him. He would drag him back to the barracks if he had to, and if he survived he would suffer indefinitely for what he'd done.

Varius spun his sword around in his hand and brought its hilt crashing down on the man's face. He groaned sharply and collapsed to the dirt, the crazed grin wiped from his face.

Chapter XXV

Having finally come to his senses, Asher was running as fast as his legs could carry him away from the violence. Resisting the temptation to ditch his robes, which were only slowing him down, he ran north, away from Mount Gilboa and toward Nain.

After a few minutes he had to stop. He had drastically overestimated his ability to run for more than a few minutes. He found a cluster of small trees and collapsed in the shade beneath them. Out of breath, panting and clutching his chest, the thought crossed his mind that his heart was failing. He glanced to the hill on which the battle was taking place. He could still see the figures moving about on top of it. He hadn't run that far – they were only a few hundred metres away.

Several minutes passed and he managed to catch his breath. He was still alive. The sprint hadn't killed him and neither had the armed rebels or Roman soldiers battling for supremacy under the shadow of the mountain.

It was the sight of Varius that had broken him out of the ridiculous stupor he was stuck in. Until then he had just stood there like a small child, frozen with fear and vulnerable to any sort of attack.

It was definitely Varius though. What had he been doing there? He couldn't believe what he'd seen. His old friend, his Roman friend, was a soldier, a killer. He had never really thought about what that actually meant and what these soldiers often had to do. Varius was his friend with whom he had shared drunken evenings out. The man who had shown him all the illicit pleasures of Caesarea. Together they had survived a violent tempest.

Now he had seen Varius stabbing and killing people. He had watched as he had driven a sword into a man's chest and almost decapitate someone. His face was splattered with blood and there was a gaping wound on his arm. He was there in the midst of the battle - there, at the centre of a violent and terrifying episode, and he looked at home. He looked as though he belonged. Perhaps that was what had shocked him as he watched his friend brutally cut down all who stood before him.

He recalled the look in Varius' eyes as he stared at him. There had been no hint of recognition. They had looked at each other for several moments but there had not been a flicker of acknowledgment in his old friend's face. Had he really forgotten about him already? Or was he consumed with vengeance, his mind focused on meting out death upon his foes?

That was not all he had discerned in his friend's face. There was an excitement there, a relish for what he was doing. He looked like someone secure in his calling, established in the purpose for which he had been put on this earth. He was doing what he had been born to do: kill and wage war.

He couldn't help but become philosophical as he sat, ensconced in the safety of the small trees. He thought of the men against whom Varius was fighting. They looked dishevelled and unkempt. Many would dismiss them as wild savages, no better than animals who deserved the violent end they were destined for.

But what were they fighting for? What had led them to take on the might of the Roman Army? Were they angry? Disillusioned? Frustrated and fed up with a life that brought nothing but hardship and suffering?

Maybe there was something admirable in their barbaric ways. If they were dispirited and undone at least they hadn't given up. At least they weren't lying on their beds wallowing in the mire of apathy and self-pity. They had determined to fight. They had resolved to do something to change their circumstance and alter their future. But what would it bring them but more heartache? More frustration. More bitterness and resentment.

They were violent, disturbed, even degenerate individuals. But they were living. Well, not anymore obviously, but they had lived, they had acted. They'd had meaning and purpose. Something which he still hadn't found.

But who were they? The followers of Jesus? They couldn't be. He'd heard snippets of information about the wandering preacher but what he'd just seen was incongruous with what he'd heard. He was supposed to be a teacher not a warrior. He spoke of love not war. He healed people; he didn't kill them. Could these crazed men really be followers of this Jesus? It seemed impossible.

He sat for some time pondering what had happened and wondering as to who they were. Concluding that they couldn't be the preacher's devotees, he wondered if there were others like him. Were there more men hiding in the Judean countryside, commanders of large crowds, ready to wage war against the Romans?

Whoever they were, they had something he didn't: passion and purpose. Their methods might be suspect and their beliefs warped, but they were fused with energy and bold enough to act. How did he compare? Was there anything he was willing to die for?

Chapter XXVI

Varius lay on his back, shielding his eyes from the afternoon sun. The battle was over and four of his comrades lay dead. Another was sure to die before nightfall. He had done everything he could and they had fought bravely, but in the end the savages had managed to murder four of his friends. They were his responsibility, they had died on his watch. His thoughts returned to that day by the pyramids when his friend Gaius had been killed by a mob of bandits. That was bad enough and had caused him much pain, but this was worse. He hadn't been responsible for Gaius, but the young men he'd brought down here had thought they were coming on a training exercise. They had no idea they would encounter a militia of crazed reprobates. But neither did he! He cursed himself. Should he have known that the followers of Jesus were armed and dangerous? He was expecting to confront farmers and fishermen, not wild rebels armed to the teeth.

He had sent one of his men to Scythopolis to fetch men and servants. He had just returned with medical supplies, food, fresh water and a wagon on which to transport the dead. One of the servants had just finished sewing up the wound in his arm and bandaging it. It hurt like hell and would leave a nasty scar. Perhaps if his father had lived to see the scars, he would have admired the fact he had been wounded in battle.

Most of the enemy were either dead or had fled. The ones that remained were now shackled and sitting in a row not far from where he now lay. He was going to personally escort them back to the barracks in Tiberius where he would make sure they paid a heavy price for their little rebellion.

'We're ready to go now, sir, if you're ready.'

Varius eased himself up on his good arm and peered into the tired face of his compatriot. 'Have the bodies been loaded onto the wagon?'

'Yes sir.'

'And the others? Has someone seen to their injuries?'

'Yes sir. We've all been pieced back together. We'll be fine until we get back to barracks.'

'And the prisoners?'

'Seven of them, sir, including the leader.'

Varius growled under his breath, remembering the twisted, evil face of the main protagonist. 'Bring him to me!' he commanded before struggling to his feet.

He watched the man turn and walk to the row of prisoners. They were all shackled and caked in mud and dirt. Dried blood covered their limbs and flies swarmed around their still open wounds. Nobody had seen to their injuries and nobody would.

The leader was brought over, limping wearily but with a defiant gait. He was trying to hold his head high but was struggling. They stopped in front of Varius who could barely contain his disgust. It took all the self-control he could muster not to run the man through. The man was tall and even though he was shackled and defeated he was not broken. There was still something intimidating about the fiend which irritated Varius.

'Name?' Varius barked.

The man said nothing, staring at the floor and moving his head from side to side.

'Answer when you're spoken to you wretched piece of filth.'

Varius responded to the next bout of silence by whacking the man across the head as hard as he could. The force of the blow caused the wretch to lose balance and he tumbled to the floor, groaning as he did so.

'Stand him up!'' Varius yelled.

'What is your name, dog?'

This time the man summoned the strength to raise his head and look Varius directly in the eyes. There was an insolent arrogance about his stare. He had the temerity to look him in the face far longer than was respectful.

Varius raised his hand to strike him again, but before he got the chance, the cur murmured in his own tongue, 'I am the son of my father.'

His swollen lip curled into a snarl and he emitted a chuckle of defiance.

So he prefers to hide his identity, Varius thought.

'Barabbas then,' he announced boldly.

The man looked up sharply, shocked to hear a Roman soldier repeating his words in perfect Aramaic. Varius smiled, pleased he had been able to garner such a reaction from so despicable an animal.

'So Barabbas, your rebellious days are over,' Varius was feeling more confident, now he felt he had the upper hand. 'No more insurrections for you,' he said. 'You will now experience Roman hospitality the likes of which you have hitherto never known.'

Barabbas was struggling to control his ire, angry that his brazen act of defiance had achieved nothing.

'Take him away,' Varius said calmly to his colleague. 'Let's get moving. We have a long walk ahead of us.'

Chapter XXVII

On days like this, the heat in the city could be unbearable. It hit you like a solid mass when you stepped outside. It was well into autumn now, yet the summer warmth refused to yield. Shifra couldn't remember the intense heat lasting so long. She still had to battle through the busy streets though. There was a never-ending list of errands to run, messages to deliver and customers to appease. The incessant heat caused temperatures to fray. Even those who were normally placid and easy-going were irascible, liable to fly off the handle or launch into a tirade of abuse at the slightest provocation. Her boss, who was highly irritable at the best of times, was like a wounded animal. It was best to give him a wide berth, which she did as a matter of course anyway.

The Feast of Booths was over and people were beginning to return home. The temporary shelters had been taken down and the city was returning to normal. She loathed the big festivals when people from all over the country descended upon Jerusalem. This festival seemed to be particularly ludicrous. Erecting shelters made of leaves and branches and eating in, or even living in them for a week, was madness. Yet that is what they did, by their thousands.

Sometimes the city went crazy even when there wasn't a festival on. There was more and more talk of this preacher from the Galilee who was supposedly able to heal the sick.

It was obvious when he was in town because the whole place was in a tumult. The religious leaders hated it and despised him. That gave Shifra a morsel of comfort. Anything which agitated and infuriated them must have some merit.

It was early, just after dawn, and the streets were not as crowded as they would soon become. Shifra had to see one of her master's clients beyond the Antonia Fortress to the north. If she made this journey later in the day it would irritate her even more. Best to get it out of the way early.

The temple cast a gigantic shadow in front of her, dominating the city like an ancient behemoth. She couldn't help but look up in disgust as she approached. That place seemed to sum up much of what was wrong with the world.

As she drew nearer and readied to circumvent the great temple area, she noticed a strange absence of people in the surrounding streets. It should be quieter at this time of day but not this quiet. The few people that were about, were running. They were all headed in the direction of the temple. That wasn't all that unusual either but something about this seemed odd. Something unnerved her. There was something about the frantic way in which these people were running. It was out of the ordinary. It felt as though they were desperate not to miss something. What could it be? More people kept appearing, men and women, young and old, couples and cripples, women dragging children, men dragging their fathers, all hoping to get into the temple courts to see what was going on.

And then it hit her. There was only one thing that caused this sort of behaviour outside of a major festival. Jesus. It had to be him. What else could it be? Would he appear in the temple courts? Everyone knew that the religious authorities were getting more and more irate at what he was doing. What he was saying was even worse. It was said that his life was in danger, that if these people got their hands on him he would be killed. She wouldn't put it past Caiaphas and the rest of that mob. Murdering a preacher from the countryside was probably just the sort of thing they would revel in, no matter how deluded and irrelevant he was.

She paused for a moment, watching the people rush up the steps and disappearing into the outer courts of the temple. She thought about joining them. She had heard of this Jesus many times. It seemed these days that everyone had a story about him. She had never seen him though, had never really been that interested. She shook her head and began to walk on. What did she care what this man was saying and doing? She wasn't like the other mindless sheep that followed him around. And if he was stupid enough to show up at the temple in Jerusalem then he deserved all he got.

She took a few more steps but something was tugging at her soul. In spite of herself, she was curious. She wanted to see what was going on. If it was Jesus up there then maybe she should go and see what all the fuss was about. At least she could judge things for herself instead of having to rely on the infantile notions of others.

She turned around and began climbing the steps toward the Court of the Gentiles. There were people running past her on both sides as well as the old and infirm struggling just to make it up at all. When she reached the zenith, she was amazed at the size of the crowd. She had never been good at estimating how large a crowd was but there were definitely hundreds of people here. All she could see was the backs of everyone. The focus of their attention was unclear. For a moment her heart sank. She didn't like people and hated crowds. Momentarily she thought to turn back and continue on her errand but something made her stay. More than that, she decided to push through.

Being a small woman was finally beginning to pay off. She squeezed through the crowd, edging past men and women, easing them out of the way and shuffling through. Men were grumbling at her and old women hissing. At one point she contemplated crawling through their legs but hesitated. She was getting closer but was still unable to see above the heads and shoulders of those blocking her way. She kept going. She was forcing her way through now. People were shoving her back and pushing her away, deliberately trying to block her. She kept going. At last she felt herself edging closer to the front of the crowd. There were only a few people in front of her now.

And then she saw him. He was too far away to get a good look at his face but he looked very plain, almost nondescript. He had dark brown hair which reached to his shoulders and a beard. He looked very much like every other man in this country. In his clothing too, there was nothing to distinguish him from anyone else. Had he not been sitting in the midst of a large crowd, their focus trained on him, there would be nothing to distinguish him from anyone else.

She couldn't hear what he was saying. He was definitely saying something for she could see his lips moving and he was gesticulating with his hands. He was almost smiling, yet what he was saying seemed serious. There were murmurs in the crowd, some people nodding their heads, others looking bemused. There were still more, frowning, shaking their heads and clicking their tongues. They could obviously hear what he was saying, but she couldn't.

Suddenly, there was a commotion in the crowd. It was nowhere near her but off to the side somewhere. The crowd was reacting to it, she could hear people shouting, grumbling, complaining. She had been on her tiptoes trying to see Jesus and now her legs were aching. She tried to look over the heads of the crowd to see what was going on but she couldn't. She turned to look at Jesus. He was now standing and had moved forward. There was a curious expression on his face. The placid demeanour was gone, usurped by a look of anger.

Suddenly some men burst through the crowd and stopped in front of him. They were Pharisees. Some old, some young, about a dozen of them. Then she noticed one of them at the rear was dragging a woman by the hair. He was tugging at her roughly, she was stumbling along trying to keep up. No doubt she was crying and wincing in pain. Shifra shuddered to think of the times she'd been treated like that.

The man threw the woman to the floor with a callous indifference that made Shifra feel sick. This was how these men treated women, she had experienced it first-hand. But what were they doing here? Why had they brought her before Jesus? What did they want him to do?

She cursed that she couldn't get closer, she couldn't hear what they were saying. She had come a long way through the crowd but now it was like an impenetrable shield which she couldn't break through. Had she not been engrossed in what was going on before her, she might have panicked at the feeling of being hemmed in by so many people.

The woman remained in a crumpled heap on the floor. She was probably terrified. Her long dark hair was draped over her face, shielding her from the gaze of the expectant crowd.

The men were gesticulating angrily, many of them pointing at the woman and then at Jesus. One of the older Pharisees kept pointing at the temple.

A ripple of understanding began to filter through the crowd. Shifra kept overhearing the words harlot and whore, repeatedly whispered among those around her. They were shaking their heads, their anger evident in their scowls and furrowed brows.

For Shifra, the realisation suddenly dawned as to what was going on. The woman was being accused of some sexual sin. The men had dragged her before Jesus, before the crowd, in order to humiliate her. They wanted her to be punished. Shifra gasped in horror at what that could mean. The penalty for adultery was death. According to the law, the woman deserved to be stoned. Was that why they had brought her here? So she could be stoned by the crowd? By Jesus?

That didn't make sense. The Jews didn't have the right to administer the death penalty. They would know that. What then, was their plan?

They were still gesticulating wildly at Jesus. He looked surprisingly calm, though she could have sworn that the look of anger on his face had been replaced by sadness. The woman still lay at his feet.

Then Shifra thought she understood. This wasn't really about the woman. This was about Jesus. It was a test, a trap. They knew they couldn't lawfully execute her and they knew he wouldn't condone it. Everyone knew he was always talking about love and peace. So what would he do?

Shifra looked at the woman. A desperate figure, crumpled on the floor, cowering in guilt and shame. The voices of her accusers ringing in her ears and a crowd of onlookers baying for blood.

The Pharisees seemed to stop their tirade. Jesus was crouching down, writing something in the sand with his finger. Shifra stretched painfully on her toes, eager to see what he was writing. She had no idea.

The Pharisees had gone quiet. Their demeanour had changed. Their obstinance had dissolved, their aggression evaporated.

'What is he doing?' she whispered to the people around her? 'Can you see what he's writing?'

Some people shook their heads, others told her to shut up. She was growing frustrated. What was going on?

A few seconds later the first of the Pharisees began to move. It was the oldest among them, the one who had been constantly pointing at the temple. He started backing away from Jesus as one would from a wild animal. He was scared. He turned swiftly and marched away, shouting at people to get out of his way. Then another followed him and another. Some of them looked simultaneously awed and terrified. Some of them turned and fled, others backed slowly away as if any sudden movement would kill them.

All of a sudden, one of them said something. It was one of the younger ones. He pointed at Jesus and said it again. The preacher stopped what he was writing and stood up. He said something which caused a sensation in the crowd. There were audible gasps and a collective, violent intake of breath.

'What did he say? What did he say?'

She was ignored.

Jesus crouched down once more and continued writing in the sand. It wasn't long before the younger Pharisees were leaving too. Soon they had all gone. Jesus was left crouching, his finger in the sand.

He stood up and moved toward the woman. She hadn't moved the whole time. Now Shifra could see the sand around her was wet, soaked in tears.

He took her by the hand and helped her to her feet. It was the most caring and gentle of gestures. He wiped the hair from her face and the crowd gasped again. He touched her. He touched the sinful woman. For a few timeless seconds, he looked at her. She struggled to lift her head, standing helpless before him. She took his hand and raised her head slowly so that her eyes met his. He said something to her and her posture changed immediately. In an instant she looked as though she was standing taller, her head aloft. He swept her hair back and Shifra caught a glimpse of her face for the first time. She was radiant.

Whatever she must have been feeling before, there was no trace of it now. No guilt, no shame, no embarrassment.

Shifra felt as though her heart was about to burst through her chest. Her whole body was tingling and there was a sensation inside which she couldn't fathom. She realised she was crying. Sobbing. She was surrounded by strangers, and she didn't care.

Chapter XXVIII

A multitude was streaming down from the temple courts. It was obvious from the myriad of expressions and demeanours that something had just happened up there. Sarah rarely went up there anymore. She'd lost her faith or rather abandoned it. She knew what it was anyway. Any sort of commotion in Jerusalem these days was invariably down to this Jesus.

She stared at the people coming down from the Court of the Gentiles. There were hundreds of them and they all looked like they'd experienced something different. Some of them were smiling or laughing. Others had looks of disbelief written across their faces, their eyes wide with wonder. Some were angry, some confused and some in the middle of intense conversations. Whatever had happened up there had got them all talking.

Despite herself, she was curious as to what it was. She had never been interested in the past. In fact, she had actively avoided going anywhere near this Jesus and his followers. It was whispers here and there to begin with, 'Did you hear that he said this?' or, 'I heard he did that.' But as his reputation grew, so did the stories and so did the commotion that was caused in the city. She had heard Pilate and Claudia discuss him once or twice. He seemed to think there was nothing to get worked up about. He thought the whole thing highly amusing. He loved to see all the religious leaders, the Pharisees and Sadducees, the lawyers, the teachers and the scribes, all upset and agitated about it. He couldn't fathom how a nobody from a backwater town like Nazareth could have them all in such an uproar. Claudia was more pensive. She would usually let him rant on without offering her opinion. He never asked for it anyway.

But now that Sarah was here, at the temple and so close to the apparent epicentre of the morning's events, she was tempted to wander up and see what was going on. The old her would have. The old her would have been up in a flash. Eager and enthusiastic to see what all the fuss was about. That old Sarah was a distant memory now. She'd been buried in a haze of pain and disappointment.

Now she found herself on the bottom step of this grand staircase. Something inside her urging her to go on. She stopped, steeling herself against the feeling inside and paused. It only took a few moments of self-discipline and the moment would pass. It did. She turned her back on the temple and walked away.

Chapter XXIX

Gradually the crowds subsided and Shifra found she was able to move. She had spent the last few minutes, head in her hands, sobbing uncontrollably. She was glad that nobody cared, that nobody asked her what was wrong. If they had done, she wouldn't have known what to say.

The hideous crush of the crowd was weakening by the second. She looked up and had to pull her sodden hair away from her face. Wiping the tears from her eyes, she could tell that Jesus was gone and the people were all leaving. She had no idea where he had gone or what was going to happen next. She began moving through the crowd until she reached the perimeter where a pillared colonnade ran around the outside. She sat down on a small step and watched as the remainder of the crowd fell away.

She began thinking about what had just happened, trying to figure out what had gone on and why she had reacted like that. She pictured again Jesus talking to the shamed woman, showing her compassion when everyone else had sought her demise. Then the tears started flowing again. She tried to stop it but she couldn't. She tried to control and compose herself but it was impossible. Eventually she had to yield to the surging pressure of emotion welling within her. She buried her head in her hands, tucked it between her knees and let it flow.

She might have been there for hours, she didn't know. When she finally found the strength to raise her head and look up, everything looked different. Everything seemed brighter somehow, and it was nothing to do with the fact the sun was much higher in the sky than it should have been.

'Are you alright?'

The voice startled her. She spun around to see a young man sitting next to her, an arm's length away. She said nothing but stared at him.

'Are you alright,' he repeated, a slightly bemused expression on his face this time.

Still she seemed unable to reply.

'The reason I ask is because you seem to have been sitting there crying for some time,' he paused, hoping she would say something, but she didn't. 'I've been here for an hour and you've been crying the whole time. The old woman who was sitting here before me said you'd been like that for a while.'

Shifra continued to gaze at the young man. He looked a few years older than she, tall with thick black hair, almost clean shaven with a slender build and kind eyes. He had a gentle smile and a cheeky face.

She turned away quickly. She could feel the tears welling up again. Would this never end? Was he talking to her? She couldn't remember the last time anyone had spoken to her.

'Tell me you're fine and I'll walk away. I just stayed to make sure you were alright. I didn't mean to upset you.'

She looked at him again, uncomprehending as to how anyone could be speaking to her in such a way.

'I'm fine,' she croaked finally, desperate not to seem impolite.

'Good!' he said rising. 'That is a relief. Now I shan't bother you any more.' He nodded at her in respect and began to walk away.

'Did you see him?' she blurted out suddenly, unwilling to watch him walk away.

'See who?'

'The preacher. Jesus.'

'Was he here? Here in the temple?'

'He was just over there a few minutes ago, surrounded by a huge crowd. You must have been there.'

He smiled kindly, 'I think you might have lost track of time. There's been nothing like that since I've been here. But he was here, was he? Jesus, I mean?'

She nodded silently, unnerved by the suggestion that she'd been there a lot longer than it felt.

'I've heard all about him, of course. He is quite the celebrity in the Galilee. Crowds of hundreds follow him everywhere he goes. Here too, it seems.'

Shifra nodded and tried to smile affably. She had not quite recovered her powers of speech and cordial conversation had been rarer than hen's teeth for her lately.

'What was he like?'

'What was he like?' Shifra repeated.

'Jesus. What was he like?'

'I'm not sure,' she said vaguely. 'I couldn't really hear what he was saying.'

'Did he do anything?'

'Do?'

'Did he do anything? Most people who've seen him say that he doesn't just say things, he does some pretty crazy things too. Someone told me once that he heals the blind.'

'Does he? Does he really?' there was a sudden urgency in Shifra's voice that she hadn't expected.

'I don't know. I've never seen him.'

There was a moment's silence between them. 'Do you want to? she asked.

Now it was his turn to be coy. 'To be honest,' he said quietly, 'that's why I'm here. That's why I came to Jerusalem. I do want to find him. I want to discover what all the fuss is about.' He paused again. 'Is he just another crackpot like all the others or is he different?'

'He's different,' she announced immediately, a confidence evident in her voice that she thought had long since vanished.

'What's different about him?'

163

'I don't know but I feel like I need to find out.'

'Why?' His question was abrupt but she didn't feel like he was prying. She got the impression he genuinely wanted to know.

'Something happened this morning. I can't explain it and I don't know what it was, but something definitely happened to me.' She was surprised at her own candour.

'Because of him?'

'I don't know. I think so. I don't know what else it could have been.'

'Well if you need someone to help you look, I'm in.'

She smiled. It was a strange, foreign feeling. She remembered it, liked it.

'What's your story?' she asked.

'I've been working like a dog in the Galilee for the last few months. Harvesting olives and grapes and figs. I just needed to get away for a few days. My boss is... difficult, so that was reason enough to get away.'

'You're from the Galilee?'

'No but I've spent a lot of time working up there the last few years.'

'You must have come across him, then? That's where he conducts himself, isn't it?'

'It is, and I've heard plenty about him, but I've never come across him.'

'Why not?'

'I didn't want to, I suppose. I've had my fingers burned to be honest,' he sighed. 'I suppose I just took him to be another charlatan, followed by gullible, empty-headed dreamers.'

Shifra didn't say anything. He could have been describing her.

'I went looking for him, you know.'

'You did? But you didn't find him?'

'No. I nearly got killed instead!'

Shifra was wide-eyed. 'What happened?'

'I was wandering around like an idiot, hoping to stumble across a crowd that was sure to be his followers. I stumbled across a crowd alright, a crowd of crazy maniacs trying to kill Romans.'

She couldn't help but smile, though she was shocked too. She covered her mouth with her hand to conceal her smile. 'What happened?'

'I ran as far and as fast as I could! I never did see Jesus or any of his followers. That was a few months ago. I've been thinking about it ever since.'

'Shall we help each other?' she asked tentatively.

He nodded, smiling. 'Now?'

'I have work to do, errands to run. My boss is going to kill me when he learns how much time I've wasted here.'

'Then we'll meet at the end of the day. Here?'

Shifra nodded. 'You see what you can find out and I'll do the same.'

They smiled at one another. She could feel an excitement building within her. This was something she had not felt for a very long time and it felt amazing. 'What's your name?' she asked.

'Asher. You?'

'Shifra.'

'Well, Shifra, I am very pleased to have met you. I shall see you here, at the end of the day.'

She stood up quickly, a sudden surge of excitement coursing through her. She nearly fell over again. He reached out and steadied her. She felt light, uncluttered and unrestrained. Free. For the first time in a long time she felt as though a great burden had been lifted from her shoulders.

Chapter XXX

It didn't take long for news of the morning's events to reach the Sanhedrin. The brothers were in the midst of discussing a violation of the Levitical law by a synagogue leader in Jericho, when one of their acolytes burst in. By the time he had finished regaling the group about what had just taken place in the Temple's outer courts, the Sanhedrin was in uproar. Caiaphas demanded to know who had dragged the woman before Jesus and if they were present among them. It was quickly concluded they weren't and assumed that they had each returned to their own homes. Who was the woman then? And where was she now? No one knew that either, which only exacerbated the feelings of anger and frustration which were now dominating the proceedings.

The prevailing mood among the Sanhedrin was that this Jesus needed to be stopped and the sooner the better. There were some dissenting voices who tried to claim the man was harmless and would be better off ignored. They were drowned out and told to be quiet by the angrier and more vociferous among them. Many called for his immediate arrest and imprisonment, some advocating a more clandestine and morally dubious approach. There were others who pointed out that he was very popular and to consider how the people would respond if he was arrested and imprisoned. They didn't want a riot on their hands. The last time one had broken out in Jerusalem, many had been killed at the hands of the Romans. They must avoid a repeat of that.

After a prolonged episode of rancorous debate, the brothers retired, ready to reconvene later in the afternoon. There were other matters to discuss but this matter of the Galilean preacher was casting a shadow over all their proceedings. Rather than going away, the situation was becoming more serious. Something needed to be done.

Eliashib struggled to control his ire when told of what the man had done in the temple courts. There was now a plethora of examples of how he flouted the law with impunity and taught as if was learned in the knowledge of the scriptures. The man was dangerous. If only his colleagues had listened to him sooner, he might have been apprehended a long time ago.

He cursed when he thought back to the incident on the slopes of Mount Gilboa. They had been on the trail of him then and surely would have been able to arrest him with a retinue of Roman soldiers in tow. Then his followers had shown up and that battle that resulted was terrifying. He reported it all upon his return to Jerusalem but the reaction was mixed. Some of the brothers agreed with him that they should speak with Pilate and organise a century of soldiers to arrest the fiend and lock him up. The more cowardly among them were more cautious. They feared the man and the following he commanded. It was bad enough they were mostly farmers and fishermen, but now it appeared as though they were armed. That was altogether more problematic. He had argued that was all the more reason he had to be confronted sooner rather than later. The larger the following, the more dangerous the man would become. Unfortunately, the more short-sighted of the brethren won and they had decided to do nothing. Eliashib cursed their ill-judgment, but there was nothing more he could do.

For the last few months he had tried to convince others that the man was more dangerous than they acknowledged but he was given short shrift. Even Caiaphas wouldn't hear of it, surrounded as he was by minions of intellectual lightweights.

'So, what do you think, brother?'

It was Saul, one of Eliashib's colleagues on the Sanhedrin. The two of them often conversed, being of like mind on various matters.

'You know what I think, brother Saul. I have been saying for some time that the man is a dangerous lunatic. He should have been arrested a long time ago. Unfortunately, there are too many factions around here who don't have the strength of character to do what needs to be done.'

'You still propose the man should be arrested then?'

'Without delay!' Eliashib snapped. 'Anyone with half a brain can see what must be done.'

'You believe we're too cautious?'

'I believe there are too many of our number who lack a spine. Unfortunately, those of us who have the ability to get things done, don't have the support of enough of the brothers.'

'Then what is to be done, brother?' Saul hissed.

Eliashib was silent for a long while, thinking carefully about an idea which had only just begun to take form in his mind. Saul waited impatiently. At last he spoke, 'Maybe we should take matters into our own hands.'

'Meaning?'

'Meaning that for the good of the people, this man should be removed, by force if necessary.'

'What does that mean?' Saul asked tentatively, a worried expression distorting his features.

Eliashib fixed him with an icy stare. 'How familiar are you with the Levitical law?

Saul took offence and puffed his cheeks out in disdain. 'More familiar than anyone else here!'

Eliashib looked at him in disgust, mocking the man's ludicrous and deluded assertion. 'Then you are familiar with the appropriate punishment for one who blasphemes?'

Saul nodded. 'He shall be stoned.'

Eliashib couldn't resist the opportunity to go one better and quote the exact words of the scripture. 'Anyone who blasphemes the Lord must be put to death. The entire assembly must stone him.'

Saul shook his head. 'We don't have the authority to stone anyone. It is our Roman overlords who must enact that sanction.'

'But you agree he is deserving of it?'

'Yes, the blasphemer deserves death.'

'So you agree he is a blasphemer?'

'It would appear so, from what I have been told, though I must confess, I have never witnessed the man's behaviour with my own eyes.'

'Irrelevant. He deserves to die. Agreed?'

'It sounds like you are thinking of taking the matter into your own hands and arranging the man's death'

Eliashib nodded. 'Would that please or displease Yahweh?'

'To do so without the consent of the Sanhedrin? Without the knowledge of Caiaphas and the other most esteemed brothers?'

He said nothing but looked earnestly at his friend who was patently struggling to accept what Eliashib was suggesting.

'I don't know, brother,' Saul continued. 'I don't know.'

'My conscious is clear,' Eliashib went on. 'Such an act would be in service to Yahweh and would see the end of a wicked and dangerous blasphemer. My allegiance, first and foremost is to God.

Chapter XXXI

Shifra darted through the streets of Jerusalem, her heart bursting with a new sensation. Was it hope? The streets were crowded now but she didn't care. She felt faster and lighter than ever before. It was as though a heaviness had been lifted and she could now move, breathe, live. She wanted to stop and think about what had happened in the temple courts, talk to someone, explain that something had happened. She wasn't sure what it was but something had definitely happened to her. She felt different.

She was hours behind schedule now. Her boss would be livid when she finally returned. She had been supposed to collect the money and return before the frantic action of the day began. She was way past that now and would have to endure another abusive tirade when she returned.

Her thoughts wandered relentlessly as she pushed and barged her way through the cramped, narrow corridors of the upper city. She couldn't force from her mind the events in the temple courts or the conversation with Asher that followed. He was a strange young man: tall and strong, yet warm and gentle. He seemed to have an interest in Jesus too. She would find out more when they met again in the evening. Another incredible occurrence! She'd actually had a friendly conversation with somebody!

It was some time before she managed to return to the shop. Midday had passed and many had retired indoors to escape the unusually fierce autumn sun. The customer had been unwilling to pay but she was used to every different kind of stunt people pulled in order to avoid settling their debt. She'd grown accustomed to using a combination of cajoling and encouragement to get what she wanted. She rarely had to resort to threats but had on occasion. Her employer was known as a hard man who could act like a rabid sow when he didn't get what he wanted. Most people were eager to pay their dues so as not to have any more involvement with him than was strictly necessary.

He was gnawing on a piece of fruit when she entered, his face stained with the juices. He looked up and snarled at her approach as if she was a rival beast encroaching on his territory. Anger flashed in his eyes and he threw the juicy carcass to the floor.

'Where have you been?' he growled, fruit residue flying in every direction.'

Shifra had to steel herself inside. She knew what was coming, she'd witnessed it many times before. 'I'm sorry sir, I got waylaid.'

'Waylaid! I'll say you got waylaid, you lazy little bitch. You were supposed to be back hours ago.'

'Well I'm back now,' she said calmly.

'I've probably lost out on some business because of you. I had to stay here and look after the shop because you were out gallivanting when you should have been working! Did he pay?'

Shifra threw a small bag of silver coins onto the table which stood between them. 'He paid.'

He snatched the bag from the table and poured the coins into his hand, counting them carefully once he'd done so. He muttered something indefinable under his breath and grunted, obviously satisfied that the whole amount was present.

'Where were you anyway?' he snapped.

Shifra had been longing to talk about what had happened but the thought of confiding in this wretched oaf was deplorable.

'I got caught up in the crowds around the temple that's all,' she paused. 'I'm here now. I can watch the shop for you if you like.'

'There's always crowds around the temple, that's nothing new. And you've never shown any interest in what goes on there before.'

She shrugged her shoulders.

He was not to be put off. Like a rat, entrenched in the gutter, he could smell something was amiss. His shifty little eyes bored down upon her. 'So what was it?'

'There was a commotion in the temple courts. I went to see what was going on, that's all."

'For several hours?'

She said nothing.

'So what was going on?'

She maintained her silence but so did he. She could feel him staring at her and could sense his growing agitation.

'Well? Out with it girl!' he roared with a sudden outburst of monstrous rage.

'It was Jesus. He was there.'

The mention of that name caused an instant violent reaction in the man. He leaped from his stool, snarling like a wounded dog and rushed across to where she was standing. So shocked was she by the speed and ferocity of the brute that she didn't move. He swept the back of his hand across the side of her head and sent her reeling to the floor, crashing through a cluster of pots which smashed on impact.

'Him!" he snarled and he hit her again on the back of the head. 'You were late for my customers because you were following him about?'

He dragged her to her feet and continued to bring his open hand down upon her head, over and over again and with increased vitriol. Cowering in fear and bewildered by his overreaction, Shifra sought to protect herself from the attack. There was no let-up and seemed to be no end to the man's anger. Having exhausted himself and hurt his hand, he dragged her by the hair and across the shop and hurled her across the room. She stumbled and fell, crashing into a table as she tried to recover. Then everything went black.

When she awoke he was gone. The room was in disarray and she was lying on the floor. She blinked a few times, turning onto her back to remove her face from the dust and dirt. Her head was pounding and she could see a blood stain on the floor beside her. Tentatively she felt around her head and winced as she touched a big bump protruding from the back of her skull. Her hair was wet and sticky and on closer inspection she could see the blood on her hands. Struggling to her feet she staggered into the back of the shop, found a jar of water and began to administer some first aid to herself.

As she did so she was suddenly assailed by the prospect that he could return any minute and then who knows what would happen. She made to leave but the throbbing in her head intensified so she stumbled toward a pile of thick blankets to the rear of the shop and out of the prying eyes of any would-be customer. Slouching back with her head against the wall she closed her eyes and within a few moments, she was asleep.

When she awoke for the second time it was much darker. Her head was still aching but she could think more clearly. She had obviously been here for hours for there was no noise coming from the street outside and she could see only the faint outline of the room around her. There was still no sign of her employer.

This time she was more alert. She moved through the shop swiftly, eager to get away. There was no way she was returning to this place. He could go to Sheol for all she cared.

Stepping out onto the street she paused. If he wasn't here and she wasn't coming back, she might just take a few things with her. She went back inside and the first thing she saw was the bag of silver coins on the table. In his fury, he had left without his precious money. Sweeping up the little bag, she revelled in the delicious sense of revenge. It would serve the tyrant right for treating her like that. It was the least she deserved for putting up with him for so long.

Her one room lodgings wasn't far and fortunately she had never told him where she lived. She would have to be careful, of course, because he would almost certainly come after her once he'd realised his money was gone. She would worry about that later. For now, she just wanted to get away from him and the stinking shop she'd had to work in for the last year.

At home she managed to clean herself up quickly but painfully. Her head was aching and the slightest touch to the affected area made her groan in pain. There were traces of blood on her robes which she didn't have the energy to attend to.

What had happened? She suddenly remembered the ferocity of the attack. He had been his usual angry but sullen self until she had mentioned Jesus. Then it was as though he had been possessed by something. She had witnessed many of his aggressive tirades and been on the receiving end of many more. Yet this seemed to be something altogether more disturbing. What had made him so angry? Why had the name of Jesus caused such a violent reaction?

She suddenly gasped in horror. Asher! She was supposed to meet him in the temple courts. They were going to look for Jesus together. Now it was dark. Would he still be there?

She raced from her room, bolted the door behind her and began running up the street. She hadn't gone far when her aching head reminded her that she was being foolhardy and she slowed down rapidly. Shuffling through the streets as fast as she could, she finally made it to the steps of the temple.

There were few people around now, most having returned to their homes after a bruising day's work. The flames of Jerusalem's myriad torches danced in the night, helping weary merchants find their way home.

She staggered up the huge staircase, using her hands for support. Eventually she made it to the top, panting and gasping for breath as she did so. She had overdone it but she was desperate to see Asher again, the first person since forever with whom she'd had a normal conversation.

She returned to the spot where they'd met but he was nowhere to be seen. She cursed loudly and slumped to the floor on the spot where she'd sat that very morning. Rogue tears began running down her cheeks, her heart aching with frustration and disappointment. Was normal human interaction too much to ask? Was she destined to be treated like dirt by everyone she met? Instead of the gentle, caring warmth of the stranger, Asher, she had to endure the cruel anger of her employer. Why couldn't someone treat her the way Jesus had treated that woman this morning?

And then, as if someone had unplugged a deep well of emotion, she burst into tears once more. And for the second time that day, on the exact same spot as before, she sat and she wept.

Chapter XXXII

Asher had been in Jerusalem several weeks now and was experiencing an inner turmoil that was unfamiliar to him. He had always been happy and easy-going. He never felt stressed or anxious about anything. Things always seemed to turn out well for him no matter where he was or what he was doing. Even though he hadn't found what he was looking for, he hadn't felt a complete failure.

Now though, things were different. He wasn't far from home and there was really no excuse for not returning. Bethany was only a short distance from Jerusalem and the walk south would take no time at all. He wanted to see his parents and his sister again, tell them about the adventures he'd been on, the places he'd seen and the people he'd met. But he didn't want to acknowledge that he'd achieved very little, if anything. It had been four years since he'd left and what did he have to show for it? What would his parents say when they realised his situation was no different than when he left? He didn't want them to be disappointed and he didn't want to admit to himself that these last few years had been a complete waste of time.

Then there was Jesus. Many people could talk of little else but he still hadn't seen him. He regretted it now, that when he had lived in the Galilee, he hadn't shown more interest. Now that he did want to track him down he couldn't find him. The preacher came to Jerusalem often apparently, but he'd never managed to be in the right place at the right time. Many people spoke of secret plots and machinations cooked up by the religious leaders. They wanted to kill him and get him out of the way. They were furious with him, called him a blasphemer and demon-possessed. No wonder Jesus liked to keep a low-profile sometimes when powerful people were out to kill him.

Yet he hadn't been hiding that day at the temple courts. That was the day he'd met Shifra, the girl who couldn't stop crying. She'd seen Jesus. She'd witnessed an altercation between Jesus and the Pharisees that had had a profound effect on her. When she hadn't shown up for their agreed meeting he had been bitterly disappointed. They were going to look for Jesus together. Perhaps she had just been saying what he wanted to hear to get rid of him. She probably had no intention of returning to meet him.

He found himself looking for her everywhere. As he walked down the street he looked at every young woman passing by, hoping he'd see her. He tarried in the marketplace eager to catch a glimpse of her buying a loaf of bread or some fruit. He had returned to the temple courts on numerous occasions but had never seen her there either. Sometimes he sat on the staircase inspecting everyone as they passed by, sometimes he stayed in the spot where they'd talked. Yet despite his perseverance, she had never shown up.

His response to her had surprised him and he had to ask himself constantly why he thought about her so much. Their conversation had been fleeting and she had been a gibbering wreck for most of it. Yet he was drawn to her, his thoughts dwelling on those dark brown eyes, sad smile and the thick dark hair that clung to her tear-drenched face. He couldn't get her out of his mind.

It was one of a number of uncertainties and perplexities that were plaguing his thoughts. Should he go home? How could he find Jesus? Where was Shifra? For the first time in his life his mind was a riot of conflicting emotions.

Chapter XXXIII

Shifra was growing weary. She had to remain vigilant at all times, worried that her employer, whom she'd robbed, would turn up at any moment and have her arrested, or worse. She'd rented another room, still in the lower city but further away from where she worked. She knew where all his main clients lived so was especially careful to avoid them. If she stayed away from his shop and clients, hopefully she would never see him again. The fear was always there though, lurking in the pit of her stomach.

The sensible thing of course would be to leave the city and go somewhere else. That way she would be sure to never see him again. There were two reasons why she stayed. Two men: Asher and Jesus.

She hadn't forgiven herself for not meeting Asher at the temple when she said she would. There were mitigating circumstances, of course, but she still should have been there. Sometimes the frustration and disappointment grew too much and she wanted to scream. She returned to the temple often, hoping to see him there. She scoured the crowds, walked past every inn and market stall in the hopes that she would find him. It had been weeks since that day at the temple and she had not seen him since. He had probably cursed her when she hadn't shown up, despising her in his heart for snubbing his warmth and kindness. If only he knew how sorry she was, if only she could speak to him again and explain how she had been tormented inside ever since.

And then there was Jesus. If she wasn't thinking about Asher she was thinking about him. Something had happened to her that day as she had stood in the crowd. She didn't understand how, but it was something to do with him. It had to be. Now she couldn't find him. Apparently, he didn't always appear publicly in the temple courts or in the synagogue. His life was in danger and so he often tried to keep a low profile. That wasn't easy when he commanded such a following. Everyone had heard of him and told of all sorts of crazy things he'd done. How much of it was true? Did he really heal people? Had he really confronted the religious leaders, challenged and condemned them? Was he a prophet?

She couldn't leave Jerusalem yet, no matter how dangerous it was for her. She longed to see Asher again and she was desperate to find Jesus. She would stay here as long as it took. Sooner or later something would happen that would change her fortunes. She'd had a setback, but still felt positive about the future. Something was happening, something good.

Chapter XXXIV

The autumnal heat wave was over and the temperatures in Jerusalem had plummeted. Indeed, it wouldn't be long before the winter months were upon them.

Asher was approaching the synagogue in the lower city. It was small and rundown, not much to look at and surrounded by the old and shabby lodging houses of Jerusalem's poor. In the city of the great temple, synagogues such as this were superfluous to many. Yet here it was the heart of this small neighbourhood, a place of prayer and study. The local community were devoted to it, as was evidenced by the number of wizened old men and women that could always be found therein.

Asher liked it. It was a refreshing change from the ostentation of the temple courts where piety and compassion were in short supply; usurped instead by the arrogance and greed of the elders and their fawning supplicants.

He heard the commotion before he saw it. Outside the synagogue a small crowd had gathered. At the centre were a few elderly gentlemen dressed in the distinctive robes of the Pharisees. They were clearly agitated; the small mob appeared to be exacerbating their frustrations.

Asher quickened his pace and pressed in among the crowd so he could see what was causing the disorderly spectacle.

It soon became clear that at the centre of the crowd, in front of the Pharisees was a small man dressed in rags. He was almost skeletal in appearance, filthy and unkempt. His hair was ragged, matted and reached almost to his shoulders. His beard was a mess, as though someone had cut chunks of it out with wild and careless abandon. Despite the hideous ensemble, the most noticeable feature was that mud appeared to have been smeared over his face. His wide eyes were peeking out from a well of dried and stained mud. It looked like it had been there for some time and he had made no effort to wipe it off. There was a wild, almost crazed expression on his face, but it was joyful. Despite the occasion and the aggressively charged atmosphere he found himself in, there was something jubilant about him. He didn't appear to be scared or in the least bit intimidated by the distinguished men that stood before him.

Asher had managed to push through most of the crowd and was now right in the thick of the action. He could see there was genuine anger in the faces of the Pharisees. 'Promise before God to tell the truth. We know that this man is a sinner,' one of them barked at him, sneering at him as though he was a piece of filth.

'I do not know whether he is a sinner. I do know one thing—that although I was blind, now I can see,' the man replied. There was a confidence in his voice, an assurance that shocked everyone. Not least the Pharisees who seemed unable to believe what was going on.

'What did he do to you? How did he cause you to see?"

He answered, 'I told you already and you didn't listen. Why do you want to hear it again?' the man was defiant and unafraid. If he had set out to deliberately antagonise them, he could scarcely have done a better job. 'You people don't want to become his disciples too, do you?'

A roar of laughter engulfed the crowd. The man's combative sarcasm had disarmed and enraged the learned men. Some in the crowd shook their heads in disapproval but most were laughing heartily, some even jeering the men they were supposed to respect. Loath to pass up an opportunity to poke fun at their superiors, it was clear by their facial expressions that this was a source of great enjoyment. Asher too couldn't help but smile at their discomfort. In his experience, men like this were odious and deserved to be taken down a peg or two.

His opinion of them was immediately vindicated when they began hurling abuse at the man. They called him a sinner and a wretch. One of them said he was no better than a worm and spat on the ground. 'You are his disciple! We are disciples of Moses!' one of them said, arrogance saturating every word. 'We know that God has spoken to Moses! We do not know where this man comes from!'

There was a murmur among the crowd. Some of them agreed with the teachers of the law but others were evidently more inclined to side with Jesus.

The man replied, 'This is a remarkable thing, that you don't know where he comes from, and yet he caused me to see! We know that God doesn't listen to sinners, but if anyone is devout and does his will, God listens to him.'

The men looked thunderstruck. They looked as though they couldn't comprehend where this man's arguments were coming from. Asher too, looked at the man in disbelief. Where had he found the confidence, the audacity to address these men in this way?

The Pharisees were dumbfounded and the crowd had fallen silent so the man continued.

'Never before has anyone heard of someone causing a man born blind to see. If this man were not from God, he could do nothing.'

The realisation of what the man was saying suddenly hit Asher like a runaway horse. The man had been born blind! And now he could see. Was this evidence of one of Jesus' miracles? He'd heard story after story of what Jesus had done but now he was face to face with someone who was claiming that Jesus had healed him. Not just any healing either, but he had been blind from birth! That was clearly why he had a wild, exuberant expression on his face.

The Pharisees were incredulous. It looked as though they might literally explode at any moment. 'You were born completely in sinfulness, and yet you presume to teach us?' one of them yelled in a shrill, uncontrolled voice.

With that, he nodded at those who were obviously his acolytes, standing nearby. At once they pushed through the crowd and manhandled the man out of the way. They grabbed him by each arm and marched him off. Some of the crowd cheered in delight that despite his ignominious departure, he had clearly bested his accusers. Others nodded in agreement, clearly approving of what their leaders had done.

Asher watched as the man was taken away, amazed at what he had just witnessed. He was getting closer. It felt somehow as if he was being drawn into something. This was more than another second-hand account. This time he had seen with his own eyes and heard with his ears someone who claimed to have been healed by Jesus himself. He turned away from the synagogue, his mind whirring with what might happen next.

Chapter XXXV

The Feast of Lights. It was winter and Jerusalem radiated with the light of a thousand torches. Myriad fires could be seen scattered across the countryside, throughout the Kidron Valley and all over the Mount of Olives.

It wasn't one of the main Jewish festivals for which all Jews everywhere were expected to make a pilgrimage to the Holy City. Yet it was popular nevertheless and the city swelled with the influx of Jews from across Judea, Idumea and beyond.

Nearly two hundred years ago Antiochus Epiphanes had invaded Jerusalem, slaughtering the people without mercy. In an act of deliberate provocation, he had erected a statute of Zeus in the temple and sacrificed a pig on the altar. He could scarcely have done more to profane the temple and humiliate the Jews. In response, Judas Maccabeus had encouraged the people to take arms. They did, and were able to drive out the defilers. The Festival of Lights was dedicated to the memory of that victory and the subsequent cleansing of the temple.

Varius had seen it all before. He was in Jerusalem having pestered his superiors for months to send him back. He had grown weary of the Galilee and the unceasing responsibility of guarding the imbecile, Antipas. The skirmish with the rebels that had led to the capture of their leader, Barabbas, still haunted his thoughts. It had been months ago and ever since, he and his men had exacted sweet revenge as the man lay rotting in one of their dungeons. Varius had visited him often to begin with, pummelling him for a few minutes at a time whenever he felt the need to let out his frustration or gain retribution for his fallen friends. Many of the other men did the same. They had to show some self-discipline and give him just enough time to recover before the next round of beatings. Otherwise he would have been beaten to a pulp long ago and that wouldn't have been a sufficient or prolonged enough punishment for scum like him.

When Varius had heard that Pilate was visiting Jerusalem for the Festival of Lights, he had ensured he was on the detail. The fact that Barabbas was being transported to the city too, made it even more important that he went. Now he was languishing in the cells of the Praetorium and no doubt his fate would soon be sealed. A criminal of his notoriety would soon find himself nailed to a cross. A punishment most suitable for the likes of him.

He had another reason for wanting to be in Jerusalem. As yet, the renegade preacher Jesus had still not been apprehended. That had been the whole point of the exercise which took him to Scythopolis and then to Mount Gilboa. The snivelling rat - the Rabbi - had assured him he was in the area but then Barabbas and his crew had turned up. Had he been in the area? Had he something to do with what happened? These men were all dangerous whether they were violent rebels like Barabbas or whether they hid their fanaticism behind a façade of love and peace.

The Rabbi must have returned to Jerusalem for he had heard nothing more from him. The stories of Jesus persisted though and so there was bound to still be an appetite for his apprehension. He was often in Jerusalem and its environs apparently. If Varius was to track him down, this city would be the best place from which to search.

His thoughts had become consumed with finding this man. In the beginning he had questioned why that was. Why had he been so willing to collude with the Rabbi? Why had the stories of this man bothered him so? Why was he willing to traipse across the countryside looking for him in order to arrest him? Was he obsessed?

Clearly he wasn't obsessed. But neither was he an idiot. He'd been in this country for years now and it was as though the people were under a spell. This blind devotion to their ancient religion was everywhere. It permeated every layer of society from the learned to the illiterate. It made some obscenely wealthy and powerful, and kept others in poverty. It was a scourge which the Romans had, for some reason, tolerated and so had the Greeks before them. Why? To keep the peace? To stave off rebellion? It didn't make any sense. Why weren't these people made to see that what they were believing, what they were building their lives around, was a sham? Why hadn't the Romans and the Greeks before them ground them into submission? If they insisted on placating some deity, what was wrong with the Roman gods? Would Augustus and Jupiter not suffice?

The more he ruminated upon it the angrier he became. Now there was a wandering preacher, a charlatan, who was playing upon the gullibility and ignorance of the people. He was the latest in a long list of would-be Messiahs and he had attracted quite a following. The people in this country needed to be saved from people like him.

He wasn't obsessed. It often seemed like he was the only one of sound mind in a country of senseless extremists.

Sometimes his thoughts didn't centre upon the religious curse the country was under. Sometimes he thought about the good times he'd spent over here. His time in Caesarea had been a high point before he had been exiled to the Galilee on account of Asher. His Jewish friend. Had he seen him that day in the shadow of the mountain? It was in the midst of the battle with the rebels. He had thought, for a brief moment he had seen his friend but then the madness of battle had consumed him and he had surged into the fray once more. It wasn't until hours later, on the march back to Tiberius that he had remembered. Had it been him? It would seem incredible if it had been. What would he have been doing there out in the wilderness. The thought had briefly assailed him that he had been in cahoots with the rebels. That was patently absurd and he had dismissed it immediately. He wasn't even sure if it had been him.

He had almost reached the Antonia Fortress in the north of the city. It was late and he'd been on patrol all day. Despite the number of people in Jerusalem, there had been little to concern him. Pilate hadn't moved from the Praetorium and there was a large enough Roman presence to ensure the crowds were behaving themselves. Most of that presence was concentrated in and around the temple courts. If there was to be any trouble it would no doubt begin there. He had not been tasked with patrolling the temple area. Instead he was given the considerably quieter - and therefore infinitely more boring - job of patrolling the northern part of the city, specifically around the Pool of Bethesda. There had been little to do other than break up a few fights. People tended to drink too much during these festivals. Ironic, given that they were meant to be the most pious times in the Jewish calendar.

He made it back without incident and, having handed in his weapons and armour, headed straight for the baths. Here he rested for several hours in a steaming hot bath, two Greek slaves attending to his every need.

In the bath beside him relaxed one of his colleagues. He couldn't remember the man's name. He didn't know many of the names of the people he was surrounded by and he had little inclination to learn them. 'Long day?'

Varius smiled and nodded. He had no desire to engage in conversation with anyone. If this fellow insisted on talking to him, he would have to cut his bath short and go and get something to eat.

'Where've you been?'

'Northern city. Pool of Bethesda mostly.' Varius kept his eyes closed and his answer short. The man would get the message.

'That's a good one. Nothing doing up there.'

Varius nodded.

'I've been at the temple all day.'

Varius said nothing.

'That Jesus showed up again.'

Varius sat bolt upright as if someone had thrown an eel into his bath and it had bitten him on the bottom. The man got a fright to see him react thus. 'Are you alright?'

'Yes I'm fine. What happened? What did he do?'

'Caused a ruckus, as usual.'

'You've seen him before?'

'I've seen him a few times. I've been in Jerusalem for years. My posting hasn't changed.'

Varius was intrigued. 'What does he look like?'

'Normal. He just looks the same as the rest of them. There's nothing special about him. Not to look at anyway.'

Varius was surprised by this information though he wasn't sure why. 'So what happened?'

'He was in the temple courts - Solomon's Colonnade, I believe they call it. A crowd gathered around him as they always do.'

'His devoted followers,' Varius sneered.

The man shook his head. 'Not all of them. Some of them hate his guts.'

'The leaders?'

'Oh, they really hate him! But there are plenty of ordinary folk who hate him as well.'

'I thought he had an admiring rabble that follows him everywhere he goes?'

'He does have that. He has disciples who are his closest followers and a larger group of admirers too. But not everyone loves him, is all I'm saying.'

'Go on.'

'I wasn't close enough to hear exactly what he was saying but he obviously said something to upset them. He usually does.'

'Why? What happened?'

'A lot of them started picking up stones to throw at him. It was the leaders first and then some of the others followed their example. Others in the crowd, those who supported Jesus started fighting with them. They were trying to stop them from stoning him.' He laughed at the memory of the encounter. Varius hung on his every word. 'We rushed over to make sure things didn't get out of hand but he managed to calm them all down.'

'What did he say?'

'I don't know, something about him and his father. I've heard him before and I honestly don't take much notice of what he says. The Jews are fanatical about their religion. I tend to ignore the details.'

'So then what happened?'

'Well, I think his disciples were getting nervous. They rushed him away. We stayed where we were and eventually the crowd dispersed. The leaders disappeared into the temple. They were irate. If I could give that man some advice I would tell him to watch his back. They're after him all right. It's only a matter of time before they get their hands on him.'

'Do you think he's dangerous?'

'Dangerous! What, him? He's not dangerous. He talks a load of gibberish if you ask me. Those who follow him around like little lost sheep will get bored soon enough. And like I said, the leaders he keeps antagonising will soon put an end to his antics.'

'What can they do?'

'I don't know. I'm sure they can devise something.'

'So you think we should just ignore him?'

'Why not? What business is it of ours?'

Varius was getting annoyed by the nonchalant attitude of his colleague. 'It's our business to keep the peace in this infernal country. If people like him go around riling everybody up eventually it will be us who has to deal with it.'

The man in the bath dismissed the notion with a casual wave of his hand. 'He's nothing to do with us.'

'Imbecile,' Varius muttered under his breath, rose from the bath and left.

The following day, despite his protestations, he was once more assigned the task of patrolling the northern city. He petitioned his superiors to be sent to the temple courts where he hoped he might catch a glimpse of Jesus. He was to be disappointed that day and for several days following. He cursed his bad luck. He was here in the city, so was Jesus and yet he hadn't managed to even get a glimpse of him, never mind actually formulate a plan to arrest him.

A few days later his heart sank and then emotions of anger and frustration came bubbling to the surface once more. He was walking near the Gihon Spring when he overheard a conversation about Jesus. An old raconteur of the marketplace had it on good authority that Jesus had left Jerusalem and was now on the other side of the Jordan. Varius cursed loudly and punched a bag of fruit in utter frustration, then marched away, his mood soured for the remainder of the day.

His fortunes would change one day. He had to be ready to seize the opportunity when it presented itself.

Chapter XXXVI

Asher followed the road east from Jerusalem. He had travelled it many times but not for years. It was comfortably familiar. He found that he could recognise trees and bushes by the roadside. There were small huts out on the distant hills that he knew and the smells lingering in the air all reminded him of one thing: home.

He'd finally decided to leave Jerusalem and head back home. He was utterly depressed and deflated at not being able to locate either Shifra or Jesus. He felt he'd come so close that day at the synagogue when the blind man had told everybody how he'd been healed. But ever since then he'd not seen anything. Someone did tell him that Jesus had returned and spoken to the man again, but that discouraged Asher even more. It seemed he was destined to miss out.

He'd grown weary looking for Shifra too. He was always on the lookout for her, and had offended many young women by staring at them for too long. Once he had gazed at someone for so long, he had almost shouted her name across a crowded street. He had realised just in time that it wasn't her and saved himself from abject humiliation.

He'd left early and was walking slowly along the road to Bethany. Most people on the road were heading in the opposite direction, going to sell their wares in the city. His eyes were fixed on the ground for most of the way, the rising sun commanding him to avert his gaze.

Soon his hometown came into sight and Asher stopped, a mixture of emotions swirling around within him. There was something so comforting in seeing the streets and houses he knew so well. He had been away for years but nothing had changed. It was exactly as he had left it. In some ways he felt as though he had been here only yesterday and all the adventures he'd been on had been a dream. Had he really lived in Jerusalem, the Galilee and Caesarea? Had he confronted a bear, befriended Romans and survived a storm? It all seemed unreal, and now he was walking down streets and passing houses he had passed a thousand times.

The closer he got to his parents' house the more people recognised him. One old lady, whose name he couldn't remember, stopped suddenly from the flour she was grinding and gasped in surprise. He hurried on as she clutched her chest with one hand and waved at him with the other.

He was suddenly filled with trepidation. How would they react when they saw him? What would he say to them? They were bound to ask him endless questions. What if they'd changed? What if everything had changed? He forced those thoughts out of his mind and buried the fear. He had to just get on with it. He should have come home a long time ago and he should at least have stayed in touch more.

Regardless of the terror that was trying to well up within him, he was looking forward to seeing his parents and Hannah too.

It wasn't long before he saw their house. He walked forward nervously and approached the front door. He had been trying to imagine how they would react and was determined to march straight in and get it over with. When he arrived there though, his strength left him and he paused on the threshold. After a few moments' hesitation, he took a deep breath, composed himself and thrust open the door.

It was still early and his parents were sitting having breakfast. They turned when the door flew open and he walked in. There was a prolonged silence during which everyone stared at each other. An olive which had been perched precariously on his mother's tongue, dropped to the floor and rolled away. His father froze.

A huge grin broke out across Asher's face when he saw his parents. 'I'm back!' he announced joyfully and spread out his arms.

By the time his mother reached him, her cheeks were already wet with tears. 'My son, my son!' she repeated between kisses, her strong hands clamped around his head. It was incessant and overwhelming. When he managed to break free from her vice like grip, she surged forth once more and wrapped her arms around him, burying her head in his chest, the muffled sound of, 'my son, my son' was all he could hear emanating from below.

He looked at his father who was standing awkwardly in the background. He had a huge smile on his face and Asher thought he could tell that his father too was crying. With some effort he managed to extricate himself from his mother's grasp and edged toward his father. They embraced finally and Asher felt the love he'd known all his life.

'It's good to be home.'

His mother's eyes grew narrow and before he had time to dodge, he felt the crashing blow of her hand on the side of his head. 'You are a naughty boy, Asher, a very naughty boy!'

'Ow!' he yelled. 'What was that for?'

'How long have you been away? Years!' She turned to her husband for confirmation. 'Has it not been years, Alon?'

His father shrugged nonchalantly.

'Bah!' she said, disgusted. 'What's the use of asking him anything?'

'You couldn't write? Communicate somehow?'

'I'm sorry, mother, you're right. I should have let you know where I was.'

'And what you were doing! Do you have any idea how many nights I have lain awake wondering where you were and what you were doing? Nothing! You could have been dead for years for all we knew! Isn't that right, Alon?'

Asher's father rolled his eyes which caused another flurry of abuse to flow from his wife's mouth. He couldn't help but smile. He loved to see the fire in his mother hadn't gone out and his father was as phlegmatic as ever. They were a great team and now that he was in their presence once more, he realised how much he'd missed them.

Her faux ire abated, she commanded her son to sit down and have some olives.

'Where's Hannah?' he asked.

'She is where she ought to be, son. With her husband!'

The words were delivered with so much force, Asher felt it in the pit of his stomach. 'She's married?'

'She has been married for more than two years now.'

'To whom?'

'Lahahana, son of Shealtiel.'

'Lahahana? My friend?'

'He's your brother-in-law now,' his father said dryly.

'She married Lahahana?' Asher was struggling to understand this unfathomable turn of events. His sister and one of his closest friends had got married.

'She's not just his wife,' his mother said with relish.

'What does that mean?' he replied, his voice laced with frustrated confusion.

'She's also the mother of his children.'

It was fortunate he was already seated. If he hadn't been, he would have fallen and hurt himself.

'She has children?'

'She has a son we call Azor and another child on the way.'

'You're an uncle,' his father added.

The joy at seeing his parents had been usurped by the utter devastation of this news regarding his sister. There were a mixture of emotions all battling for supremacy in his mind. Disappointment that everyone had gone on with their lives without him, bewilderment that his little sister was now a wife and mother and irritation that one of his best friends had married his sister. Most of all he felt guilty and ashamed. He was ashamed that he hadn't been there for his sister for one of life's most important moments. She would have been devastated that he wasn't there to share it with her and he would no doubt feel the full force of her anger when they met.

'I'm an uncle?' he finally said, struggling to control the swell of emotion.

'You have two nieces and a nephew so far with another on the way?'

'Two nieces?'

'Your brother Daan? He has two daughters. Twins. They are almost three years old.'

Suddenly Asher felt very small. What had he been doing these last few years? His brother and sister had been moving on with their lives, marrying and having children. What had he accomplished in comparison? Nothing! He'd been on a fool's errand, galivanting across the country from one useless encounter to the next. He felt foolish all of a sudden and embarrassed.

'I've missed so much,' he said solemnly.

His mother was about to embark on another ill-thought-out monologue when his father spotted the danger, 'Yael' he said quietly and nodded at their son.

Asher was crestfallen, the weight of the news he'd heard weighing heavily on his shoulders.

'We've missed you,' she said, gently resting a hand on one of his shoulders. 'What have you been doing all this time? Where have you been?'

Regaling his parents with the news of his travels was the last thing he wanted to do at that moment. 'I'll tell you all about it, I promise. First tell me more about the family. About Hannah and Daan. What have I missed?'

Yael took great delight in telling, in fantastic detail, all the news concerning the family. It took hours and stretched long into the afternoon. And the longer he sat there, in his old house, in the company of his parents, hearing all about his brother and sister, the warmer and more joyful he felt. The melancholy that had settled over him when he had first heard the news was gradually disappearing and he soon found himself wallowing in the joy of the good and special times that had befallen his family while he'd been away.

His mother and father hadn't changed a bit. She was as boisterous and fiery as ever; he was quiet and serene, just as he had always been. The love between them had always been obvious despite their differences, bringing joy to Asher's heart to behold it once more.

'Now, son,' his mother said after several hours, 'What about you? What have you been up to?'

Asher was finally ready to tell the story. It took hours, for his mother had a thousand questions to ask, queries to make and remonstrations to unleash. She reproached him more than once on his stupidity and carelessness. Why were you out there alone in the middle of bear territory? Who gets in a boat when they don't know what they're doing? Why on earth would you want to fraternise with Romans? The whole story would have taken an awful lot longer had he not decided to leave out many of the sordid details. He had no desire to tell his parents that he had fallen in love with the daughter of a Roman General, ended up in prison or wandered around the wilderness for a year with a religious madman. And the fact that he had very nearly been crucified? That would cause their hearts to stop. The consequences would be catastrophic if they ever found out about any of that. There were some things parents didn't need to know. There were some things parents had to be shielded from at all costs.

It was too cold to sleep on the roof in the winter so he slept on a makeshift pile of blankets downstairs in the main room. As he lay on his bed in the darkness, he felt a joy and a comfort he had not felt for a long time. It was the inner peace that comes from being home, being around family, being where one belongs.

Travelling from place to place and meeting all sorts of people had its allure but there was nothing so soothing to the soul as being back home again.

He woke early to the sound of his mother pottering about in the kitchen. She was already preparing breakfast, the smell of which enveloped Asher like a warm blanket. His father had already gone to Daan's to inform him of his brother's return. There would be a great feast in the evening involving all the family. Alon would get a choice lamb from the market and they would all celebrate the return of their oldest son.

After he had eaten, he walked across town. His mother had told him where to find his sister's house and he was still familiar with the old town. He had spent the best part of twenty years roaming these streets.

He saw her from a distance as he approached the house. He could see her on the roof of her small home weaving a fabric on a loom. It was a strange and disconcerting sight: his sister, the matriarch.

He stopped in the street outside her house and waited for her to look down at him. He was curious to see how she would react. Would she be pleased to see him or angry that he had been away for so long?

After a few minutes he got tired of waiting, 'What's happened?' he yelled. 'You get married and forget how to be hospitable? Ignore your own brother and leave him standing out in the street!'

At the sound of his voice she dropped what she was doing and gasped, her eyes wide with shock.

'Asher! You're home!' she replied and a huge grin spread across her face. She moved to rise from her chair but it was clearly an effort given the late stage of her pregnancy.

'Don't move, don't move, I'm coming up,' he shouted and then ran up the stairs. When he got there, he momentarily forgot her condition and pulled her up roughly from the chair and threw his arms around her. She

197

responded readily. When they let go, there were tears streaming down her cheeks.

'Are you alright? Are you hurt?'

'I'm pregnant,' she smiled. 'I cry several times a day.'

'Really? Why?'

'I don't know. Your body does strange things when you're pregnant. Yesterday I saw two children playing together in the street and ended up sobbing for hours.'

They laughed together for several moments and then sat down, gazing at each other fondly.

'I wasn't sure how you'd react when you saw me,' he said.

'Why?'

'I'm so sorry I missed your wedding and the birth of your son.'

'You have no reason to apologise. You were getting on with your life so I got on with mine.'

'I should've been here. I missed everything.'

'A lot has happened since you've been gone,' she conceded.

'Lahahana?'

'Are you mad?' she winced. 'He's always been worried how you'd respond when you returned.'

'It was a shock, I won't pretend otherwise. Is it right for you? Do you love him?'

'We do love each other, brother. You know our parents. They wouldn't have married me off to someone if they thought I would be unhappy.'

'I never knew you had feelings for him and he certainly never mentioned anything to me.'

'I never noticed him until you left. He would come over to the house sometimes to talk with father. I think he was probably just missing you. Gradually we began talking to each other so that finally it was obvious he was no longer coming over to see father.'

'Well I'm happy for you, little sister, though I shall have some words for Lahahana when I see him!'

'Don't make fun of him, Asher. He'll be a nervous wreck when he hears you're home.'

'And so he should be,' he smiled. 'I might be a few years too late but he shall have to have the big brother talk whether he wants it or not!'

'It's good to see you, brother. What have you been doing all this time? Where have you been?'

'In the north mainly. I spent some time in the Galilee and in Caesarea. Jerusalem too for a time.'

'Doing what?'

'Working. I ran a man's household in Chorazin, worked in an inn in Caesarea, an olive yard near Sepphoris. Met lots of people.'

'To what end?'

'To what end? What do you mean?'

'Did you find whatever it was you were looking for?'

'Why did you say that? What makes you think I was looking for something?'

Hannah rolled her eyes. 'I know you brother, remember? Nobody knows you better than me, not even mother and father.'

'I don't know what I've been doing all this time. Sometimes I wonder if there was any point in me leaving at all.'

'You must have had some wonderful adventures.'

'Maybe one or two,' he said coyly.

'You've had more than one or two. Interesting and funny things happen to you. They always have.'

The siblings spent the rest of the morning, lunch and into the early afternoon clawing back the lost time. This time Asher spared none of the details of his epic journey north. He could always confide in his sister and now, even though they had been apart for years, nothing had changed. He was able to divulge to her all the secrets he had kept hidden from his parents. He told her everything. She was delighted with the story of his dalliance with the beautiful

Diana and horrified that he had ended up in prison as a result.

He thought twice about telling her about the crucifixion. Perhaps that was too much. But then she noticed the scar on his wrist and he had no choice. The tears flowed again when he told her.

When he regaled her with the tale of how he had spent a year in the Judean wilderness with a small band of religious fanatics, she could scarcely keep the look of amused incredulity from her face. She was a captive audience and he delighted in reliving all the year's experiences for her.

Halfway through the afternoon, their father arrived. He found them laughing hysterically on the roof of the house, little Azor playing peacefully on the floor beside them.

'So, you have met your nephew then?' he panted, having climbed the steep stairs.

'Yes!' Asher responded with fake enthusiasm. He had barely paid any attention to the child, so pleased was he to be back conversing with his little sister.

'All the arrangements are made for tonight,' Alon went on.

'What's happening tonight?' Hannah asked.

'You are all coming over for a special meal to celebrate the return of our firstborn!'

'I have been to see Daan and got a perfect lamb from the market. Tonight we shall have a great feast.'

'That sounds wonderful, father!'

'You'll speak to Lahahana?'

'We shall come over as soon as he returns.'

'Good,' he turned to Asher. 'Come with me, son. You can help your mother and I prepare for this evening's celebrations.'

He hugged his sister once more and then left with his father. He was experiencing a thrill of emotion. Despite all he had seen and done over the last few years, it was the opportunity to spend time with his family that had elicited a real sense of excitement within him.

At numerous times throughout the evening he found himself looking around the room at his family. It felt so good to be with them again. They were a few years older now, of course, but it didn't seem that way. He watched his brother Daan playing with his daughters, and Hannah too looked a comfortable and happy mother. It was as it should be. They were contented and fulfilled.

He had enjoyed it too, seeing Lahahana for the first time. It was strange to begin with, and uncomfortable seeing him as his sister's husband. It had not been a pretence when he had warned him to treat her well, on the pain of angering her older brother. Lahahana assured him that his intentions were honourable and that he had a deep affection for Hannah whom he said he would die for. Asher believed him and as the conversation wore on he felt more at ease that one of his former best friends was now his brother in law.

Asher was the centre of attention. It was normally a situation he would abhor but in the presence of his family he was quite comfortable. He did most of the talking and was peppered all night with questions of his travels. He was happy to oblige, understanding that his failure to keep them adequately informed had meant they'd been starved of information about him. They knew nothing of the Galilee and were eager to hear of his time working for Gareb and Hiram but they were most interested to hear about Caesarea. The large Roman city on the coast seemed like a foreign world to them. Though they were familiar with Roman occupation, especially when they visited Jerusalem, Caesarea was an altogether different prospect. He told them of the grand buildings, the hippodrome, the theatre, the temples and the harbour. They were intrigued to hear it but none of them seemed desperate to visit.

He caught Hannah's eye once or twice and caught a curious expression on her face. He knew what it meant for they could read each other like a papyrus. She knew he was holding back, not telling them all he could. She had a smirk on her face, clearly delighted that she knew something they did not. She would never betray him, he trusted her implicitly.

The evening wore on, the wine continued to flow and the children slept. It was long into the night but there was a collective, unspoken urge to ensure the evening never ended.

Finally, when he felt as though he had said enough, he asked, 'So, enough about my adventures! What's been going on here since I've been away?'

'Here in Bethany?' Daan replied grinning, 'The centre of all that is licentious and wicked?'

'The epicentre of rebellion and revolt,' Lahahana smiled.

'Bethany! The heart of Judea and jewel in the crown of Rome's glorious empire!' Hannah announced grandly.

They all laughed at the irony. Nothing significant had ever happened in Bethany. It was a sleepy, backwater town in the shadow of the great Jerusalem.

'You may laugh,' Alon began, 'but what about all the shenanigans here a few weeks ago?'

'Oh yes!' Asher was intrigued. 'Something happened? Something to rock our quaint little town?'

There was a sudden change in the atmosphere that he felt immediately. He looked around the room at the others who were all exchanging furtive little glances. They had all gone quiet and none of them seemed willing to engage.

'What's this? Everyone has gone very coy all of a sudden. Now I am intrigued.'

A few agonising moments of silence passed before Hannah finally spoke. 'It was Lazarus.'

'Lazarus? What about him?'

'He died.'

Asher felt a pang of sadness. Lazarus, and his sisters, Mary and Martha, were well known and well liked in the town. He was a few years older than Asher so they had never been close friends, but in a town as small as Bethany, you were either friend or foe, with everyone.

'That is sad, what happened?'

'He's not dead anymore,' Hannah replied quickly in dry, matter-of-fact style.

Asher thought he'd misheard. 'Sorry?'

'He is no longer dead.'

'What is that supposed to mean?'

There was a collective silence that quickly began to irritate Asher. This, it seemed, was something nobody wanted to talk about. Eventually, Hannah continued.

'Have you heard of Jesus?'

When his sister mentioned that name Asher felt as though someone had punched him in the stomach with all their might. This man! He had been shocked into silence and so said nothing. Hannah continued.

'He is a friend of the family. He visits with them often, staying in their home. He is from the north, Nazareth I believe, and is some kind of preacher.'

'He is more than that,' Alon broke in. His face was solemn and his voice, grave. The atmosphere in the room had completely changed. There was a heaviness in the air, an intensity that was difficult to define. It wasn't unpleasant but it was almost palpable.

'Father was there,' Hannah said looking at him earnestly.

He responded to her unspoken plea to take up the story. 'He hadn't been sick for long. Whatever it was ravished his body quickly. Nobody knew what to do. The physicians were at a loss. Mary and Martha were inconsolable. When he died, all the usual proceedings were carried out to the letter. He was wrapped in burial cloths and placed in the tomb. He must have had many friends for the town was heaving with people who'd come from Jerusalem. I sympathised with the sisters for having to put up with so many.'

He stopped speaking, seemingly unwilling to carry on with the story. The family waited patiently for him to continue. Even Yael was unusually patient, understanding that the retelling of this story was not an easy task.

'He had been dead for a few days when Jesus showed up. I had seen him once or twice before, but he had always kept a very low profile. I paid no attention to him. This time when he came there was great tumult throughout the town. Perhaps people had an inclination that something was going to happen. I heard the noise from the street and went outside. He was walking purposefully, Mary and Martha by his side and a great mob of people all about. There were all kinds of people too. The young, the old, the sick and infirm, priests and Rabbis, they were all there. I went too.'

Asher was astonished that he was listening to his father tell such a story. He couldn't recall his father ever stringing this number of words together before, yet alone words of such magnitude.

'He walked straight to the tomb Lazarus had been laid in days before and commanded for the stone to be rolled away. I wasn't close enough to tell, but when they rolled the stone away, the people close to the front recoiled dramatically. The stench apparently was fierce.'

'Then what happened?' Asher was desperate to know more.

'He said, "Lazarus, come out!"'

'And then what?'

'He came out.'

A prolonged silence followed. Asher struggled in vain to understand his father's words. 'What do you mean he came out?'

'He walked out, covered in burial cloths.'

'You can't be serious.'

'I saw it with my own eyes, son.'

Asher studied his father carefully. He had never heard him speak of such things before and he wouldn't joke about something as serious as death. As he looked closer, he felt sure his father's eyes were filling with tears.

'You actually saw this happen?'

His father nodded.

'I don't believe it! Then what happened?'

'Chaos. The crowd erupted. His sisters rushed to him, tearing the cloths from his face. I shall never forget the look on his face. He looked shocked and calm at the same time. Bewildered but at peace. Some in the crowd immediately began proclaiming Jesus to be a prophet, some were even calling him the Messiah. Others were enraged. They could barely contain their anger. Many of them stormed off in the direction of Jerusalem. I assume to report what they had seen to the Sanhedrin. Jesus and the family went back to their home and I came back here. I heard that many went looking for him the next day but he had gone, stole away in the middle of the night.'

'How long ago did you say this happened?'

'A few weeks ago.'

'So you have had lots of time to think about it. What is your explanation?'

'I don't have one.'

'You can't explain what you saw?'

'I have explained it as best I can.'

'But father, what you are saying is incredible.'

'I know it is, son, and not a day has gone by when I haven't thought about what happened.'

'What do you say about him? Who is he?'

'I don't know.'

There was fear in his father's voice. Asher felt for him. Nobody else in the room had spoken. It was clear they were afraid too.

'Have you heard of him? This Jesus?' Lahahana finally asked.

'Have I heard of him?' Asher almost burst out laughing. Had a more ludicrous statement ever issued forth from the mouth of man?

'The whole country has heard of him! I would not be surprised if the whole world had too. He has had the Galilee in an uproar for years now. In Jerusalem, when people hear he is there the place gets turned upside down. And he has been here a number of times, you say?'

'Several.'

'He must do it quietly, come here when he wants to escape the crowds. Otherwise you would be in no doubt as to the man's reputation.'

'Who do you say he is?' Daan asked.

'I have no idea. I have looked for him many times but it seems I have just missed him time and again. Perhaps if I had never left home, I would have found him right here.' There was a note of frustration in his voice.

'What have you done since? Have you gone looking for him? Any of you?'

Everyone either shook their heads, stared at the floor or avoided eye-contact. There seemed to be a collective embarrassment that they had done nothing about this momentous turn of events.

'He's gone. Nobody knows where,' Daan finally said. 'Some say he spends a lot of time beyond the Jordan, others say he returns to Jerusalem quietly, while still more say that he has returned north.'

'So you have enquired?'

'I asked a few people.'

Asher was reeling. He had heard many stories of this strange man from Nazareth but nothing like this. He had raised someone from the dead! And right here in his hometown? Who is he and what was going on?

The festivities were over, an acceptance had settled over the whole group that the party had finished and it was time to return home.

When Asher retired to his bed he couldn't help but run his father's story over and over again in his head. When he finally drifted off to sleep it was Shifra of whom he thought. What would she make of this story? Would he ever get the chance to tell her?

Chapter XXXVII

The journey hadn't taken as long as she'd expected. She knew Bethany wasn't far away, but still she seemed to have travelled the road east from Jerusalem surprisingly quickly. She had chosen a time of day when there would be most people on the road. If experience had taught her anything, it was that young women were victims. They lived in a man's world and very often they had to succumb to their every whim - whether that be through marriage or far less honourable means.

It was early and the road was packed with people travelling to Jerusalem to tout their wares. There were few going in her direction and she warranted some suspicious looks from people. They were no doubt wondering what she was doing on the road by herself and why she was heading away from Jerusalem instead of toward it.

The last few weeks had been suffused with frustration. She had been on the lookout constantly for three men, none of which she'd seen. She was grateful she hadn't come across her former employer. She'd robbed him and ran away, but seeing as he'd beaten her she felt no remorse. It was the least he deserved after what she'd had to put up with for so long. She hadn't seen Asher either, which was a source of great disappointment. She had definitely felt something when talking to him in the temple courts, something she couldn't define but liked. She would never forgive herself for not meeting him as arranged. Despite her committed vigils throughout the city ever since, she had not laid eyes on him again. Most of all she was despondent at not having seen Jesus. He was the one she was most keen to see.

She'd heard plenty of stories now and heard many people talk about him, what he'd done and said. There were all sorts of tales about the miracles he'd performed. She especially liked it when someone told her of how he had challenged the religious leaders. They were always so arrogant and self-righteous, but apparently Jesus knew just how to handle them. She had been told how he had put them in their place, embarrassed them in front of the crowds. They hated him for it and were just looking for a way to stop him. She loved him for that alone. Anyone who had the courage to stand up to those hypocrites must be of trustworthy character.

Unfortunately, the more he challenged the religious leaders, the more irate they became. In response, Jesus wasn't going about as publicly as he was before. That was making it more difficult to track him down. She had felt sure she would be able to find him but he had proven frustratingly elusive. She had heard a story of him healing a man born blind. When she had gone in search of him she couldn't find the man. When she'd asked about him she had got conflicting stories so was at a loss to know where to go next.

The weeks had passed and frustration had been replaced by despondency, until yesterday, when she had heard from someone who claimed to have followed him everywhere, that he often visited friends in the nearby town of Bethany. It was not known for sure that he was there but she was assured he was no longer in Jerusalem. It was getting more and more dangerous for him there and so he was trying to be more secretive in his movements. She was encouraged to go to Bethany and ask for the home of Mary and Martha, two sisters who were known to be friends of his.

It hadn't taken much to convince her. She had left early the next day and now here she was, on the Jesus trail. When she shielded her eyes from the rising sun, she could make out the small town of Bethany in front of her. It looked like a very quiet, nondescript sort of place and she instantly understood why Jesus liked it. It was close enough to Jerusalem to be near all the action but far enough away to provide a haven from the crowds and from those who sought to hurt him.

She felt a nervous anticipation growing within her as she approached the town. What would she do if she found him? What would she say if she got to speak to him? She suddenly felt nervous and hesitated in going on. Yet something within her urged her forward. She longed to see this man again and was desperate to find out if what people said about him was really true.

She approached a marketplace where the stalls were already set up ready for the day's trade. Some of the traders yelled at her, beckoning her over to look at their fresh fruit or fine baskets. Others eyed her with suspicion or thinly disguised disdain. There were some towns that never welcomed strangers. Yet despite the odd truculent expression, most people seemed to be friendly and welcoming.

She decided not to ask any questions yet. The last thing she wanted to do was draw attention to herself. Inquiring after Jesus was bound to raise eyebrows. If he did come here to escape the crowds, they might be very protective of him. She would have to be very subtle in her pursuit. Watching and waiting was the best tactic to employ to begin with. Maybe she would see him without having to ask. That would be a stroke of fortune. She walked purposefully through the market not wanting to appear as if she had nowhere to go. Her eyes darted this way and that, examining every face and inspecting every small group of people. It didn't take long before she'd exhausted the search of the marketplace and soon found herself wandering down what appeared to be the backstreets of Bethany. Old women sat in the doorways of their homes weaving or sewing. Small children ran around in the street while their mothers caught up on the local gossip. I bet they could tell me what I need to know, Shifra thought. These young mothers probably know all there is to know of what goes on around here.

'Young lady, are you lost?'

She glanced around to see an old lady staring at her, a look of concern etched across her face.

'No, I'm not lost. I'm just having a walk, that's all.'

'Nonsense! You're lost. I know someone who's lost when I see one. Come here!'

There was a firmness in the old lady's voice but a kindness too. She could tell immediately that it was out of concern, not malice, that the old woman was beckoning her over.

'Come and have some bread and wine,' she said, 'and I shall see if I can help you find whoever it is you are looking for.'

Shifra smiled. It felt so good to be treated nicely. First Asher in the temple courts and now this old lady. To experience normal, cordial human interaction was something she'd become a stranger to. Now it was happening again and it felt good. She followed the old lady into the house, accepting that she was lost and didn't know where to go. It wouldn't do any harm to accept her hospitality. Who knows? Perhaps she would know where Jesus could be found.

The house was simple but Shifra could tell immediately that the old woman wasn't poor. The high quality furnishings and fabrics were the signs of a comfortable but not wealthy family. She sat down on a small wooden chair while the old lady disappeared into another room in the back. Suddenly she found herself sitting alone in a stranger's house. Without warning she could feel her old fears and anxieties beginning to surface once more. What was she doing here? Was she in danger? Where had the old woman gone? What was she doing? Was there anyone else in the house? How could she have been so stupid – walking into a stranger's house on her own?

'It's not much,' the old woman appeared from the back room carrying a small tray of bread and a flask of wine, 'but it's better than nothing and you look like you need something.'

Shifra sighed with relief and was suddenly conscious that her heart was racing. She had almost panicked and fled. Ridiculous paranoia. She was a modest, harmless old woman offering a simple and universal act of kindness. Shifra rebuked herself silently. Would she ever be completely free of those silent fears that lurked within her? They sought to master her, and once had. Not any more though, not any more.

The bread was warm and delicious. So preoccupied was she with finding Jesus that she hadn't eaten breakfast. In fact, she had missed many meals over the last few weeks but had barely noticed. Now she was eating though, she suddenly felt ravenous. When she glanced up she noticed the old woman looking at her with some surprise.

'You look like you haven't eaten in a week! Are you alright?'

Shifra had to swallow a mouthful of bread before she could reply. 'Yes thank you, I'm fine. I left early this morning and haven't had anything to eat.'

'Left where?'

'Jerusalem. I walked here this morning when the sun rose.'

'Ah. Do you have family here?'

'No, I'm looking for a friend of mine. I haven't seen her for a long time but I know she lives here in Bethany.'

'What is her name, perhaps I know her?'

Shifra put another large morsel of bread into her mouth to give her time to think. Should she just invent something?

'Mary,' she finally managed, while still chewing.

'Oh dear! You shall have to be more specific than that! There are many people of that name here.'

Shifra took a drink of the wine the old woman had kindly given her. When she glanced to the back of the room she suddenly saw the curtain move. There was someone there. Her eyes darted to the old woman. Was this a trap? Had she been lured here for some nefarious purpose? The old woman's countenance hadn't changed. If she had ensnared her here for some diabolical purpose, she was a master at hiding it.

She glanced toward the curtain once more. It hid the back of the house from visitors. There could be anyone back there, she thought and the fear began to kindle within her once more. Suddenly a shadow appeared behind the curtain. There was definitely someone there. She looked across to the front door. She would have to push past or leap over the old lady to get out. She could do that. The shadow behind the curtain grew larger. She readied herself to run. Her heart was racing and she could feel the bread in her hand disintegrating as she tensed up.

The man was getting closer. His large shadow behind the curtain was now huge. She edged toward the edge of her seat, ready to leap into action. She could see his fingers on the edge of the fabric. It was now or never. He ripped the curtain aside and she leaped to her feet, ready to barrel toward the door.

'Shifra!'

She stopped, dumbstruck, 'Asher!'

'You two know each other!'

'What are you doing here?' he had moved into the centre of the room and was standing right in front of her.

'I… I…' she searched for the words but they had deserted her.

'Were you looking for me? How did you find me?'

'No… I…'

'She's looking for a friend of hers, a female friend,' Yael interjected, placing enormous emphasis on the gender of her sought after companion.

'I can't believe you're here. I thought I would never see you again.'

'I... I...' she cursed herself silently for her inability to speak. What had happened to her? She must look like an imbecile. His mother must now be thinking she was a deranged lunatic.

'Why didn't you show up at the temple anyway, like we agreed? I waited for hours.'

'I'm sorry, I'm sorry,' the words finally burst forth like a torrent. 'It's a long story. I did come back eventually but you weren't there. I've felt so guilty ever since.'

An awkward silence ensued during which nobody knew what to say. Yael looked from one to the other, wondering what was going on and how this strange girl knew her son. Asher suddenly realised that his mother was looking at them with suspicion and decided further discussion had better take place elsewhere.

'Come to the roof and we can talk, mother probably has work to do. Don't you mother?'

A stern raise of the eyebrows told her son she didn't much appreciate being told she was unwanted but she acquiesced.

Asher led Shifra outside and to the roof.

'So what happened? Why didn't you come?'

'It was my master, my former master now, thankfully. When I returned to the shop I was really late. I had been at the temple for hours and was supposed to be collecting a payment for him. When I returned I made the mistake of telling him exactly where I'd been and what I'd been doing. At the mention of Jesus' name, he flew into a rage and started beating me.' She paused with a shudder, remembering the ferocity of the attack.

'He beat you?'

'Unconscious. By the time I came around I had a thumping headache and was aching all over. I don't think I was thinking straight because I only remembered I was supposed to meet you hours later.'

'I think that's understandable, given the circumstances.'

'I raced to the temple as soon as I remembered but it was too late.'

'I'm sorry. I should have stayed longer.'

'Don't be silly. It wasn't your fault. I felt so guilty afterward. You were so kind to me that day.'

She paused, looking at him with admiration. She couldn't help but smile. He was tall and handsome and he was kind. A man who was actually kind and not violent or aggressive.

Their eyes met and they connected for the briefest of moments. It was something she had never felt before and she could feel herself getting hot. She hoped she wasn't blushing but she almost certainly was. She looked away, hoping he hadn't noticed.

When he spoke, it was quiet and gentle. 'I returned to the spot many times, you know, hoping you would be there. I scoured that place for days on the off-chance that you would be there.'

She almost blurted out, 'me too!' but stopped herself. She had done the same thing! How come they had not seen each other again? All those days and weeks searching for each other in the same place and never setting eyes on each other. And then, as if by a miracle, she had ended up in his family home!

A few moments of silence followed. She contemplated what had happened and how wonderful it was that she was now sitting talking with him on his parents' roof. It made the previous weeks' longing all the more worth it for this moment.

'What about him?' he suddenly asked. 'Did you see him again?'

'Who?'

'Jesus of course!' he smiled, 'That's who we were looking for remember? Did you find him?'

She sighed with disappointment and shook her head. 'No. I haven't seen him again since that day. He has been in Jerusalem though. I can't understand how I could have missed him.'

'I know exactly what you mean. I have heard endless stories of him and rumours that he was here and there but never actually found him. I did find someone who claimed he had been healed by him.'

'Really!' Shifra longed to hear more stories. Anything she could hear about him would momentarily satisfy the longing she had, to know him more.

'He healed a blind man, or so the man claimed. I found him when he was being interrogated by the religious leaders. It was hilarious. He humiliated them.'

'Jesus?'

'No, the man born blind. They questioned him and challenged him, they tried to embarrass and belittle him but it made no difference.'

'I heard about that!' Shifra exclaimed excitedly. 'You were there?'

'Not for the miracle, only for the aftermath.'

'That's better than nothing. It's closer than I've come.'

'So you've had no joy either?'

'None whatsoever. Yesterday someone told me that he often came here, to Bethany, because he had friends here.'

'Mary and Martha?'

'You know them?'

'I've known them all my life.'

'Is it true? Do they know him?'

'Oh, they know him alright!'

'What does that mean?'

'A few weeks ago, my family told me a story about Mary, Martha and Jesus.'

'What happened?'

'Well it's mostly about their brother, Lazarus, whom I also know by the way.' He was enjoying being the font of all knowledge, Shifra could tell. He had a cute grin on his face as though he was desperate to impress her.

'So what happened?' She was eager to hear more.

Asher regaled her with the entire story, including as many of the small details as he could remember. She sat open mouthed, listening to the tale.

It was incredible! It was fantastic! It couldn't be true, could it?

When he'd finished, he sat back with a satisfied look on his face. He knew he had just told her the most wonderful story she had ever heard and he was glad he was the one who got to share it with her.

'So what do you think?' he asked.

'It's unbelievable! I don't know what to say! Do you believe it?'

'My father was there. He witnessed it with his own eyes. When you meet him you'll realise, he's not given to flights of fancy.'

'But raising the dead to life! It can't be!'

There was a few minute's silence. Shifra struggled to take in what she had heard and she could see Asher was deep in thought too. Was it possible? It seemed outlandish and ridiculous. Yet it didn't seem beyond the realms of possibility for this man. It wasn't that strange given what she'd heard about him so far. If he could heal a man born blind, why shouldn't he be able to bring back the dead? And something had definitely happened to her that day in the temple courts. But raising the dead to life! It wasn't possible. Was it?

'So what are we going to do?' she asked.

'What do you mean?'

'About Jesus! what are we going to do now?'

Asher shrugged his shoulders in a nonchalant fashion that surprised and disappointed her.

'Shouldn't we go and find him? That's what we said we were going to do in Jerusalem.'

Asher was nodding quietly. Shifra watched him curiously. She definitely expected more of an enthusiastic response. He seemed to be rather apathetic about her suggestion and that did surprise her.

At that moment his mother appeared carrying a tray laden with more food and wine. There was more bread, fruit, almonds and figs. She seemed like a feisty character but she obviously loved her son and doted on him. She was no doubt very proud of him. Now that he was back having been away for so long, she probably showered him with attention.

She kept a keen eye on him as he thanked his mother for the snacks and then began tearing off pieces of bread. She expected her to stay and join in their conversation, but to her relief she went back inside as swiftly as she had appeared.

'You like being back home?' she smiled.

'When you've been away for as long as I have, it is nice to return to some home comforts, I have to admit that.'

'You look like you've settled back in nicely. I bet it feels like you never left.'

'It does feel like that actually. Especially when I'm around my family. It's almost as if I was here only five minutes ago and never went anywhere. Apart from the fact my siblings are now married parents. I wasn't an uncle when I left!'

'So what's the plan now?'

'What do you mean?'

'Now that you're back, are you going to stay? Or are you going to leave again as you did before?'

'I don't know. Part of me wonders why I ever left at all. What did it accomplish?'

'Do you want to spend the rest of your life here, in this sleepy little town.'

He seemed almost offended. 'It might be small and sleepy but I've had some pretty wild times here you know! And there are some characters here, let me tell you'

'Like Lazarus?'

'Oh, I see what you did there. Nice way of getting the conversation back onto Jesus.'

'It seems like you're not interested in finding him anymore.'

'I never said that.'

'But it's what you're thinking. What about all the stories and near misses. What you just told me about Lazarus is incredible. You don't want to go after him? Find out the truth?'

He was quiet for a few moments before he began nodding his head lethargically. 'Maybe. You know why it's getting more and more difficult to track him down, don't you?' he finally asked.

'Why?'

'Because they think he's dangerous. He's upsetting more and more people - powerful people. My father said that some of the leaders who were there at Lazarus' tomb were leading members of the Sanhedrin. He's in danger and he knows it. That's why he is doing less and less out in the open. He's being more secretive so that they can't track him down. That's why we haven't found him. Perhaps he doesn't want to be found.'

'That's not true. What about that day at the temple? You could hardly get more public than that and there were hundreds there.'

'That was weeks ago. The longer it goes on, the more precarious his situation is. He needs to be careful that he doesn't annoy the wrong people.'

'I don't think he cares,' she said with exasperation, 'So why should we?'

'You don't care about the danger you might be in?'

'What danger would I be in?'

'If he's in danger then his followers are too.'

'I'm hardly one of his followers! I've only seen the man once.'

'But you're captivated by him. You long to see him again, don't you? You're desperate to find him.'

'I thought we both were.'

He didn't respond but stared into the cup of wine he was caressing with both hands.

'We don't know anything about him,' he finally said. 'He could be just another deluded fanatic.'

Shifra had now reached breaking point. She stood up, knocking a plate of almonds to the floor. Her disgust was evident.

'You're pathetic!' she spat. 'Well you can sit here, drinking your wine and enjoying your mother's hospitality but I've seen enough. I do want to find this man and discover what he's all about. Something happened to me that day in the temple courts and I want to find out what it was. He has the answers, I know it.'

She stared down at him, her contemptuous gaze willing him to retaliate. He said nothing but gazed up at her, still in shock at the passion with which she'd railed against him.

'You should never have come home,' she sighed, 'Your senses have become dulled and you're steeped in apathy. Well I'm not prepared to sit around eating and drinking while there might be someone out there who can offer some hope.'

She walked away leaving him wallowing in his own indifference.

As she walked away down the street and around the corner she felt tears welling up in her eyes. They were tears of disappointment, mourning for what could have been.

Chapter XXXVIII

The brothers in the Sanhedrin had discussed little else for months. This Jesus was dominating their deliberations, their discussions with the people and even their dreams. There seemed to be no respite from the man's pernicious influence. Eliashib had decided weeks ago that the man needed to be stopped by whatever means necessary. He knew there were some on the Sanhedrin who concurred but there were many who didn't: spineless cowards who just wanted to bury their heads in their scrolls and manuscripts and ignore what went on in the real world.

He had been given some encouragement some time ago when Caiaphas, the High Priest, had stood before them all and as good as said he believed Jesus should die. He had said it was better that one man dies for the people than the whole nation perishes. That had been following the debacle in Bethany. Lazarus!

Eliashib shuddered when he thought back to the episode which had happened several weeks ago now. The reports, when they came back, suggested that Jesus had raised this man back from the dead! Back from the dead! It was ridiculous and intolerable. Some of them had said they had witnessed it with their own eyes. He had been incredulous. It simply proved that the man was cleverer than they had hitherto given him credit for. He was now not just a charlatan but a sorcerer too! Who knew what kind of dangerous and nefarious arts he was dabbling in. Perhaps he was putting people under a spell and that was how he commanded such large followings.

The one positive to have come out of that sordid episode was the fact that more and more of the brothers were now coming around to the idea of a more radical solution. Unfortunately, it was becoming increasingly difficult to locate the fiend. He had met with Varius a number of times and tasked him with finding Jesus and hauling him before the Sanhedrin. He had agreed reluctantly but had consistently failed to apprehend him. While Eliashib suspected that Varius was earnest in his desire to see the man brought to justice, he was certain he wasn't wholly on board with the plan. Dragging Jesus before the Sanhedrin was probably not what the Roman wanted. He would probably prefer to be more clandestine, stealing him away secretly and locking him in a Roman dungeon where he could be left to rot.

That would not do for Eliashib or any of the others. If this was to be done, it had to be done properly. The man needed to be publicly accused and punished. Only then would the people see him for what he truly was.

Regardless of how it was to be done or who was going to do it, the task had seemed inordinately difficult of late. He had been appearing in public less and less often. Indeed, since the whole Lazarus fiasco, there had been precious few sightings of him, let alone miracles. Despite his public persona and the legions of followers he commanded, he seemed remarkably adept at hiding from the authorities.

More than once, Eliashib found himself cursing that day on the slopes of Mount Gilboa. He had been sure he and the soldiers Varius commanded were bearing down upon the wretch. Yet the brawl with the rebels that followed had ensured they had never known if Jesus had been in the vicinity at all.

Now he and others of like mind had to watch and wait for the next time he would show himself. Winter was in retreat, giving up on itself in the face of an emboldened spring sun. Soon it would be Pesach when huge swathes of people would descend on Jerusalem for the most important of the Jewish festivals. Surely he would not be able to resist returning to the temple for the most sacred of occasions. When he did, they would be waiting and there would be no more mistakes.

Chapter XXXIX

Varius had got what he had longed for: a permanent post in Jerusalem. Yet it had proven to be nothing but a prolonged period of frustration. His desire to hunt Jesus down had proven fruitless. He had been in Jerusalem alright, several times, but Varius always seemed to be in the wrong place at the wrong time. He had heard stories of his antics in the temple courts and here and there around Jerusalem but he had never actually caught sight of the man. It was spring now and sightings of him were getting more and more infrequent. Some said that he rarely visited Jerusalem anymore. So the man's not stupid, Varius thought. He knows his life's in danger here so he has decided to give the place a wide berth.

According to a number of people he had questioned, he was now spending more and more time elsewhere. Apparently he could often be found in Jericho and the land beyond the Jordan. That was too far for Varius to go, especially when he got little respite from soldiering duties. He had also heard that he was a frequent visitor to Ephraim, a small town north of Jerusalem or in Bethany a short journey to the east. He was loath to wander around those places looking for the scoundrel. It was beneath him. He had passed through Bethany before and had no desire to return.

Yet the longer it all dragged on, the angrier and more frustrated he became. It was eating him up inside. He had to get his hands on this fellow and see him punished for all the damage he was doing up and down the country.

He had even met with the Rabbi a number of times. He was more desperate than any he had met to track this Jesus down. It wasn't out of any desire for justice or compassion for his flock that drove him though. He was solely concerned with his own lot and how quickly he could ingratiate himself with his superiors. He was a slimy one that Rabbi, and Varius was becoming more repulsed by him every time they met. He had begged him to become more involved in tracking Jesus down, to the point where he had even offered to pay him to traipse around Jericho looking for him. The more encounters he had with the Rabbi, the more determined he was not to help him. He still wanted Jesus arrested, but not out of a desire to assist that twisted old goat.

Pesach was coming and Varius knew that was the most important of all the Jewish festivals. He had witnessed it before and expected hundreds of thousands of pilgrims to descend on the city. Surely Jesus would turn up then. Would he show himself in public? If he did, Varius had to be there.

Chapter XL

Shifra handed over the money and slumped down on the bed. She shuddered every time she thought back to that day when she had been beaten by her employer for having the temerity to tell him what Jesus had done in the temple courts. She was relieved she had taken his money though, for that had sustained her for weeks as she had travelled all over the region. She had plenty left too, so there was no danger of her having to grovel to some other angry ogre to provide her employment.

She stared at the bare wall in front of her. She was back in Jerusalem having failed to locate Jesus. Her room was basic, in the north of the city, hopefully a safe distance from her former master. The menial rent was fine with her; she didn't need anything lavish. As long as it was dry and mostly free of rats and insects, then it was good enough for her.

She sighed deeply and wondered what to do next. She had been fighting for weeks against the relentless melancholy that sought to overwhelm her. It seemed that whatever she tried, wherever she went, she ended up failing. She couldn't make anything work. It was as though she stumbled from one disappointment to the next and there was no respite. There seemed to be no light on the horizon, no comfort, no hope.

She had left the great city weeks ago and headed for Bethany where she hoped to find Jesus. She had found Asher instead. The instant euphoria and excitement she'd felt at finding herself in his family's house was quickly usurped by a bitter disappointment and eventual rage. She had rehearsed those moments over and over again in her head but just could not understand why he had behaved so. How could he have changed so much in those few short weeks? Was he really content just to stay at home and do nothing? Achieve nothing? It was if he was in some kind of stupor or sleep, like his soul was slumbering.

She had gone from there to the land east of the Jordan, venturing as far south as Machaerus, the great desert fortress of Herod Antipas. She had heard that another popular preacher by the name of John had been killed there a year before. Nobody had seen Jesus though. She had gone north to the other Bethany, the one in Peraea but had had no luck there either.

In desperation she had decided to stay in one place to see if he would pass through. She chose Jericho, hoping that the traders and merchants that passed through would have some news, maybe Jesus himself would turn up and perform a miracle or at least someone, somewhere would know where he was. For weeks she had stalked the marketplaces and busy street corners, hoping for some news. Day after day, week after week, she had been disappointed. She began to wonder if she had dreamt the whole thing. Did this person exist? Was she pursuing a phantom? How could it possibly be that she had not found the one whom she had so earnestly sought?

In exasperation she had left Jericho over a week ago and made her way to a small town north of Jerusalem called Ephraim. She had been told by a group of small children that he had friends there and often visited. When she arrived, she found the people very cagey and withdrawn. They did not like her and were minded not to answer any of her questions. Were they protecting him? Are the town in cahoots to ensure nobody finds out about their famous guest? Or are they just surly and irritable? Suspicious of outsiders and keen to keep at bay the outside world?

She had admitted failure there too and with a heavy heart had returned to Jerusalem. She had seen him there once, so who knows? Maybe he would return.

The inescapable feelings of sadness and frustration were lingering within her. She could feel them lurking there in the depths ready to master her if she'd let them. Yet it wasn't like it had been before. No matter how sad and frustrated she got, it wasn't like it was before that day. The utter dejection and hopelessness of those years were all-consuming. It was different now. She had something to live for, something to pursue, a path to follow.

Preparations were already underway for Pesach. Jerusalem would swell to five or six times its size when the pilgrims arrived. Roads had to be repaired and strengthened, bridges mended, buildings cleaned and maintained. Accommodation for those who could afford it was being renewed and land was being cleared for the thousands who would live in tents on the outskirts of the city. Merchants were stockpiling their wares, priests were practising their sermons and the attendants in the temple would be working night and day ensuring all was in order for the most important and prestigious of all the Jewish feasts.

Jesus would definitely be here for Pesach. Wouldn't he?

Chapter XLI

They had been in Jerusalem for a few days already. They seemed to have spent less time here of late but there was no question of them not being here for Pesach. Pilate had wanted to be here early to oversee the preparations. The city looked in turmoil but Sarah knew there was method to the madness. There were crowds on every street. Mobs of workers rushing from one task to the next. There were boys driving all kinds of animals to their destination, hoping to escape the ire of the city's public. Despite the chaos, Sarah knew that everything would be ready on time, it always was. The people of this city had been making these preparations since time immemorial. No matter how hectic it looked, she knew that everything would fall into place. It always did.

She had grown accustomed to the luxury of Caesarea. Even for the servants, life there was a cut above anywhere else, even Jerusalem. As most trusted servant to the most powerful woman in the country, Sarah got to benefit from some of the trappings of power.

She liked and admired Claudia. She was a gentle and thoughtful soul - in many ways the complete opposite of her powerful husband. Pontius Pilate, Prefect of Judea, could be an obnoxious and surly brute. Not to Claudia, however. He was usually the personification of chivalry and honour when it came to her. Sarah had heard him many times talking with his generals or servants. His true character shone through clearly then. He could be petty and vindictive when he wanted to be. A ruthless edge ran right through him, which some discovered too late.

Despite her comfortable surroundings in Caesarea, she did enjoy her sojourns back into the Holy City. She preferred not to stay for long. There were too many happy and painful memories. The two had seemed to collide and were now indistinguishable from each other. It had been over four years since Shifra had been taken from her, but she had never forgotten. She thought about her every day, still wondering if she was still alive somewhere. There were no tears anymore. They had dried up long ago. They were dull, emotionless musings now, fleeting thoughts that disappeared as quickly as they came. They never left her though. They were always there.

It was late in the afternoon and getting noticeably warmer. The winter months had been consigned to the past and spring was just starting to gain momentum. She missed the cool sea breeze that would blow through the palace at Caesarea and the glorious scent of the blue lupin and corn marigold.

Sarah rued the fact that when she did return to Jerusalem, it was usually at the time of the important festivals. There was something repugnant and a bit scary about Jerusalem at these times. Pesach was the worst of them all. More than once she got trapped in a street with an excitable mob. It was frankly terrifying, and she had no wish to venture out into Jerusalem more than was strictly necessary. She was content to stay within the confines of the Praetorium as much as possible.

At present she stood in the corner of a sheltered garden within the confines of Herod the Great's old palace. He really had done a stunning job creating these places. He may have been an odious tyrant, responsible for all manner of wicked atrocities, but none could argue with his architectural flare.

Her chores for the day were complete so she stood in the shade watching her mistress. Claudia had been unusually clingy of late. She had, over the years, become more and more dependent on Sarah and often treated her more like a trusted friend than a servant. She didn't have that kind of relationship with any of the other staff and that made Sarah feel important. Someone actually valued her.

There had been a subtle but definite shift in her mood over recent days. It was undefinable but obvious to Sarah, although probably to no one else. Especially not to the lummox that was her husband.

It had been a day before they'd set off for Jerusalem that she'd noticed a change in Claudia's mood. She had become more distant and melancholic and could often be found with a solemn, pensive look on her face.

She had that look now and Sarah was beginning to worry. There hadn't been any major conflict with Pilate, nothing out of the ordinary anyway. Perhaps it was coming back to Jerusalem that was gnawing at her. Pesach was a trial for everybody. Perhaps she shared Sarah's loathing of the whole maddening affair.

She decided to interfere. Walking gently but purposefully toward her mistress she casually looked around to ensure no one was in ear-shot.

'Are you alright, mistress? You don't look so well.'

Claudia smiled weakly. 'Is it that obvious?'

'You haven't been yourself since we left Caesarea. Is there something wrong?'

She nodded slowly. 'There is something wrong Sarah,' she said dreamily. 'But I'm not sure what it is.'

Not the response she was expecting, Sarah didn't know quite how to respond. 'Are you unwell? In pain?'

'No! No! Nothing like that! It's something deeper, something ethereal maybe.'

Sarah was bemused. 'I don't know what that means.'

Claudia was forcing her fingers into her temples. 'Neither do I, Sarah, that's the problem. Neither do I.' She looked up into the sky over Jerusalem and said, 'I wonder if it's something about this place.'

'Jerusalem?'

Claudia nodded.

'But we've been here many times before and it's never bothered you like this in the past.'

'Maybe this time it's different. It feels like there's something in the air. Can you sense it?'

'Sense what?'

She shook her head slowly and gritted her perfect white teeth. 'I don't know,' she said, exasperation saturating every word. 'There's something in the air. I can feel it.'

'Pesach's coming. The city's bursting at the seams. Maybe that's it.'

'No. That's not it. It's more than that. Something's coming. I don't know what it is but something's about to happen.'

She looked into Sarah's eyes, an expression of foreboding written all over her face. 'I'm frightened,' she said.

Chapter XLII

Shabbat. Varius wandered the streets of Jerusalem observing very little. The city was already bursting at the seams, despite the fact Pesach was several days away. No doubt in the next few days thousands more would arrive to fulfil their religious obligations. Not today though. It was always eerily quiet on Shabbat, when most people stayed indoors and did very little. The Jews were forbidden to work, of course, and most of them took it very seriously. That was why, despite the importance of the week and the impending Pesach festival, Jerusalem's streets were quiet.

He was not on duty today and rather than remain in the barracks, he decided to go for a walk. The temple was the last place he wanted to see so he headed for the west of the city. It was true, if there was any place he was likely to run into Jesus, it would be there, but he couldn't face it. Not today.

He trudged through the streets slowly, eyeing with suspicion those who were out and about. What was their excuse? Why weren't they tucked away behind closed doors like the rest of their people. There were the cripples and the beggars, of course, the idle and lame. They were ever-present and ubiquitous. He ignored their pleas for alms as he always did.

He passed through the narrow streets of small houses. They were crammed together, ramshackle in appearance, looking as though they could crumble at any moment. The

Praetorium towered above them and cast a sinister shadow over the west of the city. Sinister for the people that lived nearby, but glorious for the Romans that now occupied it. Pilate would be in there now, here in Jerusalem to oversee the festival. He did it out of pure necessity, Varius knew. At the first given opportunity he would return to Caesarea and leave the supervision of Jerusalem to others.

In the background he could see Golgotha: a loathsome place where the city's criminals were crucified. It neighboured a refuse sight where everything that was unwanted and rejected ended up. No doubt it was for that very reason that it was chosen as the sight of crucifixion. Perhaps the rebel Barabbas would end up there soon. He was languishing in a dungeon awaiting sentence. Varius would have liked nothing better than to see him finally sentenced and hanging from a cross.

The next few days would be busy. The thousands of Jews that were to descend on the place would need to be reminded who was in charge. Varius was quite prepared to be the one to do the reminding.

Chapter XLIII

The desert was a solitary place and Asher loved it. He always had. Since his youth he had on many occasions walked out into the desert alone. He loved standing on one of the clifftops looking out over the Great Salt Sea. On clear days he could see south to the fortress of Masada or even east to that of Machaerus. He sometimes came out here with his friends and frolicked in the pools and waterfalls that provided welcome relief from the harsh desert sun.

It was when he was alone out here that he felt truly content. Other than an occasional bird or brave ibex, he was undisturbed for hours, days even. He often imagined what it would have been like for King David to have hidden in these ravines and canyons. It was here that he had fled while escaping from Saul. Did he write any of the Psalms from these very caves and by the side of these palm-covered streams?

Over the years, it had been here that he had done his best thinking. When he had become a man and learned in the scriptures, he had sought refuge here to ponder the gravity of it all. Becoming a son of the commandment was a solemn commitment and not one to be taken lightly. He had also come here to escape the incessant nagging of his mother to choose a wife and the subtle but perseverant prods of his father to take on more responsibility in the family business. Nowadays his thoughts were consumed by two people: Shifra and Jesus.

The way Shifra had left aggravated him. He couldn't stop thinking about it. About her. She had been really angry, accusing him of being apathetic and indifferent. Was he?

She was so full of fire and energy. She was desperate to find Jesus and wouldn't stop. Had he ever been like that? He had wanted to find Jesus, see who he was and what he was up to, but she seemed to have an altogether different motivation. Why had he been looking for him anyway? And what was he going to do if he ever caught up with him?

The truth was he had really enjoyed being back at home and had loved being with his family again. Some of them had moved on with life, but they were still his family and he loved them. He was just beginning to settle down again, feel comfortable and content. Then she had turned up.

It had been weeks since he had seen her but she was still on a mission to find this man whom she believed had changed her somehow. He knew she would be amazed by the story of Lazarus and she was. She was like a coiled spring, eager to burst forth.

The story hadn't had the same effect on him. It was amazing and incredible to hear and the more he heard of Jesus the more astonishing it all seemed. But did he want to uproot again and go traipsing off around the country looking for him?

A sudden thud beside him covered him in water and caused him to reel in shock. He glanced over to see a large rock tumbling to a stop a few feet away. Instantly a roar of laughter erupted in the distance above his head and echoed through the small ravine in which he'd taken solace. Looking up toward the ridge, he immediately recognised the form of his friend Asa. The two of them, with Lahahana had come here many times.

'What are you doing?' Asher shouted, still reeling from the shock and clutching his chest.

Asa was creased over and unable to answer. His hilarity had intensified into silent laughter.

Asher took a deep breath, gathered his wits and reluctantly climbed back up to where his friend sat, exhausted at having laughed so hard.

'I'm glad to see you're enjoying yourself Asa.'

'Forgive me Asher. I couldn't resist.'

'You could have killed me. Had that rock been any closer you would have been scraping my brains from every nearby tree.'

'Come now Asher, you know I'm a crack shot. I could hit the nose of a jackal from a hundred paces.'

He simply shook his head. 'What do you want anyway?'

'I've been sent to fetch you. You're wanted back in town.'

'Why? What's happened?'

'Nothing's happened, don't worry. An old friend of yours wants to speak with you, that's all.'

'Shifra?' his heart leaped.

'No! Who's Shifra?'

A pang of disappointment struck him but he recovered. 'Who is it then?'

'Ezekiel.'

'Old Zeke!'

The mention of the old man's name brought a sudden elation followed quickly by overwhelming guilt.

'Zeke!' he said with a grimace. 'I've been back for weeks and I haven't been to see him. How is he?'

'What do you care?' Asa mocked with a look of complete solemnity.

'Come on Asa. Is he alright?'

'I don't really know to be honest. I don't know the man. He must have got word to your mother that he wanted to see you urgently. As soon as Shabbat was over, she sent me out here looking for you.'

Without further ado they began walking back to Bethany. The day had worn on and they had to shield their eyes from the sun and a harsh desert wind that was beginning to blow in from the west. On the outskirts of the town, they parted. Asa to his own wife and family, and Asher to a small house on the southern edge of the town.

Having knocked on the door, he waited, and eventually a small, rotund woman with narrow, shifty eyes appeared.

'Ah! So you finally decided to pay a visit, did you?'

'Hello Judith, is Zeke around?'

'You finally condescended to spending some time with a weak old man?'

'Is he alright?'

'You finally found time in your busy schedule to remember an old friend?'

'Are we going to do this all night?'

Judith, Zeke's daughter, was a feisty individual. She was fiercely protective of him and guarded him like a small child would a favourite toy.

'Don't take that tone with me, young man! If it was up to me you wouldn't get anywhere near him. Weeks you've been back now, weeks! And this is the first time you've been over, and why? Because my father sent for you, that's why!'

He had already been feeling guilty and didn't need it to be compounded by this woman. Now that he knew Zeke had sent for him, it was even worse. He decided to say nothing but wait for her to get it all off her ample chest. A few minutes later, having exhausted her speech, she stepped aside.

Zeke was looking a lot older and frailer than he had the last time they had spoken and Asher was surprised at his appearance. He was sitting up in bed, munching on some sweet chestnuts.

'Zeke my friend, how are you?'

'It's good to see you again Asher.'

'I am so sorry I haven't been over sooner. I feel terrible.'

'Don't be ridiculous! A young man like you has enough on his mind without having to worry about old men like me.'

'Still, I should have come over sooner. How are you?'

'I'm old. I don't get out much these days. My body aches and my muscles object at having to drag it around all the time. I'm not dying though! My mind still works.'

'I have no doubt.'

'I want you to tell me all about your travels, Asher. You have been away a long time and I can see in your eyes that much has befallen you.'

'It felt like I had been away for an eternity but then as soon as I got back here, it was as though I had never left.'

'Returning home is always like that. For better or worse.'

Asher proceeded to tell his old friend all that he'd been up to. For several hours they talked, disturbed only by the intrusion of Judith who insisted that her father ate and drank an appropriate amount. Zeke had many questions which Asher tried to answer as honestly as possible, without divulging some of the details which might have upset or offended the old man.

'He's been here, you know?' Zeke finally said after a few moments had lapsed.

'Jesus. The one you said you'd gone looking for.'

Asher nodded. 'I know. My father told me about what happened with Lazarus.'

'What do you think?'

'What do I think about Jesus? I don't know. Does anyone know?'

'Are you going to find out?' the old man asked gently.

Asher looked at his friend and smiled. He always knew which questions to ask. He always knew how to get to the heart of the matter.

'Your friend sounds like she's determined to find out.'

'Shifra?'

He nodded and appraised Asher some more. 'You're not keen?'

Asher sighed deeply, 'I don't know, Zeke. I don't know what I'm doing. In some ways I feel as though the last few years have been a total waste of time. I feel like I'm no further forward than when I left. And now that I'm back home I wonder whether I ever should have left in the first place.'

'We've had this conversation before.'

'I know we have, Zeke. Lots of times. The last time we had it I was yearning to get away from this place and you told me to go. You told me I would find what I was looking for.'

'And have you?'

'Have I found what I was looking for? I don't even know what that is! It's been over four years since I left and I'm no further forward.' The frustration in his voice was palpable.

'You're not the same person that left here four years ago. You found something.'

Asher looked bemused but had no words for the old man.

'You're frustrated and you've still got a multitude of questions. But they're not the same ones you had when you left.'

'Well you're going to have to help me out Zeke, because I don't know what's going on.'

'I think you did find something. Or you've almost found something, but it scares you. You haven't realised it's fear because we're good at denying what's going on inside. Deep down, deep, deep down in the core of your being, you're afraid.'

'What do you think I'm afraid of?' Asher had massive respect for the old man, but he wasn't convinced.

'The unknown, maybe. We're all afraid of the unknown,' Zeke let his words hang in the air for a few moments before continuing. 'That's why you're so happy to be home, in your father's house. You're safe there. You're comfortable. You're loved and cherished. Everything is certain, everything is as it always was. And it feels good. Yes, it feels so, so good.'

Asher dwelled on the old man's words. It was true, he did feel happy and comfortable at home. The place he couldn't wait to get away from a few years ago had become his sanctuary. And now, if he was honest with himself, he didn't want to leave.

'You're in danger.'

Zeke's sudden warning startled Asher and broke him out of his contemplation.

'I'm in danger! What do you mean?'

'It is said that comfort is the curse of old age, but it's not. Comfort is the curse of the dreamer, the adventurer, anyone who wants to break free from the mundane and pursue the extraordinary. You need to break free from it or it'll control you; it'll define you. Years from now you'll find yourself bogged down in such apathy and indifference that you'll never escape. Don't let fear control you, Asher, no matter how subtle it is. One day you'll regret it, but by then it'll be too late.'

There followed a prolonged silence during which Asher felt the force of the old man's words. They were frustrating and terrifying, but they were resonating with him as they always did. He'd always had the uncanny ability to penetrate to the heart of what Asher was going through. It often seemed like Zeke could see inside his head. Now was no different.

He felt like he couldn't take any more. He couldn't handle any more wise words just now. They were already weighing heavily upon him to the point of being burdensome.

'I think I should go now, Zeke. You've given me more than enough to think about for one night,' he said kindly, 'as usual.'

'Come and see me again in a few days. We should talk more, you and I. Especially if you're planning to stay here in Bethany a while longer.'

There was a mild rebuke in there somewhere, Asher understood. He smiled, nodded deferentially at his old friend and then left quietly so as not to raise Judith's ire.

It was late in the evening when he stepped out into the street. The air was cool and the moon was bright. He bristled in the cold and wrapped his cloak tighter around him as he made his way home.

It became apparent almost immediately that there were far more people about than there ought to be. Most people out at this time of night would invariably be Bethany's more disreputable citizens. Yet for a supposedly sleepy town, there appeared to be a remarkable amount of activity.

The further he walked the more he realised that there seemed to be a definite movement of people in one direction. He decided to see what was going on and so, as he had done before, he followed the throng. A few narrow streets, tight turns and jostling crowds later, he realised where they were headed. This was the neighbourhood in which Mary, Martha and Lazarus lived. Crowds of this magnitude, especially at night, could only mean one thing: Jesus was in town.

He turned another corner and had to halt abruptly for the number of people teeming in the streets made it impossible to venture further. He knew where Lazarus lived with his sisters and they were nowhere near. The whole town must have come out, regardless of the hour to see if they could get a glimpse of the travelling preacher. Perhaps news had spread to Jerusalem already. That would account for the large crowd.

There was a buzz in the air, a palpable sense of excitement that seemed to indwell the whole crowd. This must be what it's like wherever he goes. He wondered whether Shifra was there. She was determined to find him, so much so that they had parted acrimoniously because of it. Now, as he stood here in the crowd, knowing that Jesus was near, his mind was a quagmire of emotion. He had been amazed when his father had told him what had happened to Lazarus but then he hadn't really done anything about it. Shifra had rebuked him for it and while it wasn't a rebuke, Zeke was definitely questioning what he was doing with his life.

Not for the first time in recent weeks, his mind was a whir with frustration and confusion. What was he supposed to do?

He wrestled with the conflict within him, the different parts of his nature warring with each other. Fear won. He turned to walk away.

The crowd had grown in the short time he had been standing there. The layers of people behind him were already ten-thick but he had to get out. He pushed himself back through the crowd in the opposite direction, forcing his way past people who reacted angrily, pushing back and jeering at him as he barged his way through. That only served to sour his mood. By the time he had extricated himself from the morass, he just wanted to get home and put the last few hours behind him.

Chapter XLIV

Shifra had awoken early and, having dined on a meagre portion of sweet chestnuts, had spent the morning wandering in the northern part of the city. The temple dominated the scene and the Antonia Fortress in the foreground was a constant reminder of the iniquitous Roman presence. Yet despite the former, to which she was indifferent, and the latter which she considered an abomination, Shifra found this part of the city more peaceful than most - as peaceful as one could be at this time of year when Pesach was only five days away and the city was bursting at the seams.

She found herself, as she had on many occasions, sitting in the shade by the pools of Bethesda. They were large and deep, surrounded by colonnades and elegant porches. The sick and infirm were everywhere. They used to come here believing that an angel would visit and stir the waters. Whoever got into the water first would be healed. Jesus had visited some time ago and healed a lame man. She had been told that story a number of times. Perhaps it was why she, like many others, gravitated to the spot. She wondered how many of the cripples there now were waiting for an angel to stir the water or hoping that he would return. Whatever the reason, there were many of them there and she recognised the same faces every time she returned. She felt at home among the lowest of society: the weak, the despised, the rejected. She could identify with every one of them.

As she was talking to a blind man and his friend she began to hear a distant rumble. It was coming from outside of the city, beyond the eastern wall. She ignored it at first but it was growing louder. Others had heard it too and were whispering to one another. Some were trying to quieten people down in an effort to hear what was going on above the activity around the poolside.

In a few more moments it became apparent that the noise was a crowd and, by the sound they were making, a large one.

'It's a riot!' someone shouted. 'The people are in revolt! Down with the Romans!'

Those around him looked at him in disgust and told him to shut up. He'd awakened fear in some of them who quickly got to their feet and ran off.

The crowd as one were tuning in to determine the provenance of the noise. And the more Shifra listened, the more she was intrigued and excited about what she was hearing. It didn't sound like a riot and it didn't sound like an army. This was something altogether different. She continued to strain her ears to the sound. The noise she could hear was jubilant. It sounded like a celebration. Pesach was days away! What could people be celebrating with such wild abandon?

She had to go and find out. Leaving her friends to wonder on, she leaped to her feet and headed south through the city. Others were doing the same, drawn by the enticing sound of a carnival. There were people running in every direction but as she drew adjacent to the great Roman fortress she noticed a surge of people heading for the Sheep Gate. It was to the north of the temple complex and so-called because people would bring their sacrificial lambs through here on their way to the temple. In a few days' time this place would be a riot of pilgrims eager to fulfil their Pesach duties. She could scarcely imagine it being any crazier than it was at this very moment as people rushed to see what was going on.

The noise from beyond the city walls was growing by the second. Shifra felt herself being pushed along by the crowd. She could have gone in no other direction had she wanted to. This was exciting and adventurous. Something about this whole affair felt good. She was surrounded by men and women of all ages who were happy and excitable. She couldn't remember witnessing anything like it. The surge of positive emotion was incredible.

As she neared the Eastern Gate the crowd started to thicken and slow down. Above the heads, Shifra could see palm branches being waved in the air. What is going on? She was being squeezed, crushed by the force and volume of those around her. It reminded her of that day in the temple courts when she had first seen Jesus. She felt a jolt of anticipation. It couldn't be him, could it? He could gather a crowd, but nothing like this, surely?

A young woman stumbled into her, barged from behind by others more enthusiastic and boisterous. She didn't apologise but said, 'What is going on?' in an almost hysterical tone.

Shifra tried to explain she had no idea but before she could, another woman leaned across her and shouted, 'It's Jesus! People are saying it's him!'

'It can't be!' Shifra said. 'It feels like the whole city is here!'

She struggled to look around once more. There were thousands of people everywhere she looked. All kinds of people too. She could see the rank and file of Jerusalem as well as Roman soldiers, priests, Rabbis, the rich and the gentiles. It seemed like they were all here, converging on this one spot. And the noise was terrific. It was a beautiful, joyous noise. Above the crowd now, there was a myriad of palm branches, waving above the heads of the people.

Shifra was galvanised into action. She had to get closer. If it was him she needed to see him; she needed to get to the front of the crowd. She steeled herself to be aggressive and began to push herself forward. Most of those in the crowd were far bigger than she but she pushed on, squeezing through the crowd, ducking under people's arms and even crawling between their legs. Some tried to push back, actively stop her from moving forward but she pressed on. Some were getting angry with her, some resentful that she had the temerity to not accept her place in the crowd.

The roars of the throng grew louder as she approached the front. She was only a few people away from the origin of this seething mass of humanity. She could see through the gaps of arms and legs, the open road in front of her. It was covered in palm branches and cloaks.

'Hosanna!' people kept shouting. 'Hosanna!'

She surged forward even more and with every step, with every surge, with every aggressive fibre of her being, she could feel the old Shifra returning, the feisty, sassy one - the girl she'd been a few years ago before her whole world had crumbled away.

'Blessed is the King of Israel!' the man in front of her shouted.

She looked to the east and saw movement for the first time. She could see people walking toward her through the crowd. They were walking on either side of the road trying to push the crowd back, pleading with them and shouting at them. They looked shocked and terrified at what was happening.

There was mayhem and hysteria everywhere. She had experienced nothing like it. Then she saw him.

He was riding on a donkey, the men on either side of him trying desperately to stop the people grabbing and clawing at him. That day at the temple she had seen him only from a distance but now here he was. Right in front of her. She noticed little of his physical features but was immediately struck by the look in his eyes.

He was not sharing in the joy and excitement of the crowd. He was not laughing or smiling. If anything, he looked sad, lonely, as if what was going on around him was a curse rather than a blessing. And in his gaze, Shifra thought she could detect a paternal compassion, as though he knew these children didn't understand but was loath to blame them for it. And then, momentarily, his gaze shifted from faces in the crowd, to above it. The great temple loomed large over all of them, and for him she detected a foreboding. The look on his face was intense and determined; his mind was on the future.

In the solemnity of his gaze she saw majesty. There was power in those eyes. He was not a victim. He had not been taken by surprise or forced against his will. He was in control. And though the events that were transpiring all around him were wounding him, he was enduring it for their sake, not his.

He sat in dignified composure, a solitary, peaceful figure surrounded by a raucous, cacophonous rabble. The boisterous behaviour of the crowd seemed completely at odds with the character of the man, and somehow inappropriate. The shouts, the yells, the laughter - meant in approbation - were wounding him. She wanted to yell too. Though not at him, as they were doing. She wanted to yell at them. Tell them to stop, you're hurting him. He doesn't like it, he doesn't want it.

Then he looked at her.

It was fleeting and lasted a fraction of a second. But in that moment, when his eyes met hers, she felt as though his gaze had penetrated her very soul. In an instant she felt that same swell of emotion that she'd felt that day at the temple. Tears filled her eyes and she cried.

Jesus passed by on his way into Jerusalem and toward the temple. Once he and his companions had moved on, the crowd surged in behind them, propelling them along. Shifra had no desire to tarry in the crowd any longer and sought to move in the opposite direction. The whole scene had changed in the blink of an eye. She saw the look on his face, the obvious concern and compassion which he felt for them. In contrast, the roar of the crowd was ringing in her ears and it continued unabated. Cries of, 'Hosanna!' continued to be sung by the masses.

Now that she had seen him, she had no desire to celebrate. She had to fight against the crowd who were all moving in the opposite direction from her. She was barging into people, ducking and crawling, falling and fighting her way through this mass of people all desperate for a piece of this gentle man. Finally, she attained some respite and sank exhausted on the doorstep of a stranger's house. For the next few minutes the street got quieter and quieter until she was the only one left. Everyone else had followed the mob into the city. Gradually the grating noise of the clambering masses died down and she felt somewhat at peace.

It was then that her emotions took hold of her once more. There was no sobbing like there was last time. As she thought back to that moment when she saw him up close, when his piercing dark eyes had looked into her heart, she wept gently. Only this time her tears were for him. That sad, lonely, incredible man, fawned over by a rapacious rabble, unaware of how they were hurting him.

The encounter had left her drained. The noise had been carried away on the cool city air so that she could only imagine where they were now and what was happening. She hoped that it hadn't lasted much longer for everyone's sake. The Romans were sure to be very suspicious of such an episode and who knows how they would react if they felt threatened. Pilate was in town and, like all men of power, he was probably a proud and stubborn fool. How would he respond if he heard reports of the crowd hailing Jesus as king?

She decided to go home, rest and consider thoroughly what had just happened. She retraced her steps with a shudder, passing through the Sheep Gate and the shadow of the Antonia Fortress. The temple cast a long shadow behind her but she didn't want to think about what might be going on there now. Is that where Jesus had gone? What was he going to do once he got there? How would the Jewish leaders respond to all this?

No sooner had the thought crossed her mind than she had to jump out of the way as a group of men rushed toward her. It was immediately obvious that they were men of distinction. The ornate, flowing robes of the members of the Sanhedrin marked them out as powerful and privileged. Their acolytes scurried around them, before and aft, shoving people out of the way so their distinguished masters could advance unmolested.

No sooner had they passed than a jolt of recognition flashed through her mind. She knew one of them. Who was it? Then, like a sucker punch which left her feeling ill, the realisation dawned on her with nauseous clarity. Uncle Eliashib!

Chapter XLV

The atmosphere among the brothers was febrile.
'This whole sordid affair has gone far enough!'
'Were you there? Did you see it?'
'I was there. I saw the whole thing.'
'It was an outrage!'
'An abomination.'

The clamour to denounce the recent actions of the Nazarene had caused chaos to descend upon the Sanhedrin. Brothers who had witnessed his triumphal entry into Jerusalem had retreated to the Hall of Stones with alarming speed, desperate to express their indignation. There was panic and fury, disbelief and consternation. The brothers, scarcely able to contain themselves, shouted at and over one another in apoplectic ferocity. Those who hadn't been there sat in awe, as their compatriots seethed and frothed at the mouth, passionately denouncing the man who had just ridden into Jerusalem proclaiming himself to be king. Eliashib was among them.

He stood in a small cluster with some of the brothers he knew and some he didn't. Caiaphas wasn't there, neither was his father-in-law, Annas. The Sanhedrin looked to them for leadership and so, in their absence the brothers resembled a group of wild, petulant children, all competing for attention and desperate to make themselves heard. Gamaliel, an elder statesman of the Council tried in vain to bring some order to the proceedings but he was drowned out by the anxious cries of the brethren. The noise and bedlam of the occasion soon overwhelmed the participants and they descended into small groups to air their grievances. Such was the anger and anxiety on display, that nobody could command an audience of everyone present.

'I have been saying for months that something had to be done about this man, but who would listen? Nobody!' Eliashib screeched, looking around with an accusatory stare.

He found himself surrounded by brothers he didn't know. He would usually have been more guarded in what he thought, but the abhorrence of the occasion led him to forego any inhibitions.

'Were you there?' asked one.

'I saw the whole thing,' Eliashib said.

'Well tell us plainly what happened. Some of us weren't fortunate enough to witness it.'

'Fortunate!' he spat. 'There was nothing fortunate in being present for such a calamity. So gross a spectacle would have filled you with horror, made you sick to your stomach. It is a wonder the Almighty didn't strike down everyone present. Remember what happened to Uzziah the Hittite?'

'Get on with it, will you? Nobody wants to hear a sermon. Just tell us what happened!'

The insolence of the man annoyed Eliashib, but he pressed on. 'I was studying in the temple when I heard the noise of the crowd outside. The longer it went on the more unbearable it became so I went to see what had occurred. When I got outside it was plain that the commotion was coming from beyond the city wall so I moved out into the streets to get a closer look. At that moment I took my life into my hands for the mob were everywhere, all heading toward the Eastern Gate. At first I couldn't tell what was happening, but then people started shouting,' he paused and shook his head.

'What were they shouting?'

'They shouted "Hail to the King of Israel!"'

Some of the others gasped. 'They didn't!'

'They actually believe him to be the rightful King of Israel?'

'That's what they were shouting, all of them, as one voice, hailing this man, this preacher, this con-man from Galilee, to be a king.'

'And how did he respond?'

'He was riding on a donkey!'

The men drew back in horror as if suddenly hit by an unseen force.

'He was riding on a donkey? In fulfilment of Zechariah's prophecy?'

'No doubt he did it deliberately to portray himself as king. But it gets worse,' Eliashib cautioned.

'Worse?'

'The crowd were crying, 'Hosanna!''

'Hosanna? They don't claim him to be the Messiah?'

Eliashib nodded solemnly.

'This is unbelievable! How has it been allowed to get this far?'

The question stoked Eliashib's ire. 'It should never have been allowed to get this far and if people had listened to me, the man would be languishing in a prison cell somewhere.'

'If the man claims to be a king then he is guilty of sedition! Surely the Romans will have something to say about that! Pilate could have him executed!'

'Does Pilate care? The man has been roaming the country for years preaching to the crowds and pretending to heal the sick. The Romans have done nothing about it.'

'Pilate doesn't care. Jesus is nothing more than a minor irritant to him.'

'He'll be more than that now,' Eliashib said, 'After what happened today, he'll be forced to accept that this Jesus has become a serious problem. They can't let any man gather crowds like that especially when they're proclaiming him to be the King of Israel. What about Caesar?'

'The Emperor probably knows nothing of what goes on over here.'

'Well Pilate knows and he should care too. He should be standing up for his Emperor and doing something about this Jesus.'

'But what if he doesn't? He hasn't done anything so far. Are we just going to stand by and wonder if the Romans are going to act?'

'There's a worse prospect than Pilate doing nothing?'

'Which is?'

'He could blame us. Why have we not dealt with this criminal ourselves? Why have we let it get to the point where the man has become a hero to the people, commanding large crowds that parade through the city? Who knows what he might do in response. He could take away our temple!'

There was a collective gasp of horror.

'No!' Eliashib snapped. 'We can't just stand by and do nothing. There's been too much navel gazing already. We must stop wringing our hands and take action. Decisive action.'

'What do you propose, brother?'

He let a brief hush settle over their conversation. The dramatic effect secured, he said, 'He's guilty of blasphemy, the penalty of which is death.'

'Blasphemy!' one of them was shocked. 'Has he said anything to warrant such a charge?'

'The crowd were crying, 'Hosanna!' He's claiming to be the Messiah!'

'As abhorrent as that declaration is, I'm not sure it's enough to justify a charge of blasphemy.'

Eliashib was visibly frustrated. He had hoped and expected them to seize upon his plan with gusto.

'To be guilty of blasphemy he must lay claim to divinity. Has he? Has he claimed to be divine?'

'He has done so on a number of occasions. I have heard many of the brothers attest to that very thing.'

Eliashib was pleased, 'Then you see. The man is a blasphemer and deserving of death.'

'This is incredible! Who does this man think he is and on what authority does he act?'

'He's a madman, delusional and dangerous.'

'We have to convince Caiaphas to do something about it. He must be arrested and brought before the Sanhedrin. Let's see how he does under our questioning!'

'Where is Caiaphas anyway? He should be here by now. Surely he's heard what's happened.'

'Would he be able to hear anything from his ivory tower?' Eliashib sneered.

A sudden commotion from the other end of the hall caused them all to turn. Eliashib expected that Caiaphas had arrived with his entourage at last. But it wasn't him. It was a woman, a girl. She had run into the hall, closely followed by the temple attendants who were clutching and clawing at her but struggling to keep up. Her demeanour was of anger and determination. She had forced her way in here on purpose. Obviously with an axe to grind.

Eliashib, along with many others, shook their heads and clicked their tongues that anyone, let alone a woman, would have the nerve to burst into their meeting. She was obviously a lunatic. Mad as a basket of grasshoppers.

She moved around quickly, darting out of the way of those who tried in vain to accost her. She was shouting something, but he couldn't make out what it was. She was embarrassing herself, the poor wench. If she didn't bring herself under control she would face the lash. A good scourging was nothing less than people like her deserved.

Yet the more he looked at her the more he felt her face looked familiar. An awful feeling suddenly occurred to him. Was she one of the very few women who had managed to seduce him? Was she one of the wicked harlots who lurked in the shadows of this great city, tempting and coaxing men into sin?

'Eliashib!' she suddenly yelled.

Had he heard correctly? Had she just said his name? Time seemed to stand still. He looked in horror at the woman, his body froze and he could feel his face redden. Out of the corner of his eye he could see brothers looking at him quizzically. Maybe he had misheard. Maybe she had said something completely different.

'Eliashib!' she yelled again. 'Brother Eliashib from Joppa. I know you're in here.' She was pointing at the crowd of men, an accusatory glare etched on her face.

He didn't know what to do. He was so hot he felt as though he might burst into flame at any moment. He could feel the beads of sweat collecting on his brow. More people were staring at him now but there was a growing anger directed at her too.

'Who does this woman think she is?' someone shouted angrily.

'Get her out of here!'

'This is an outrage.'

'You have no right to be here!'

Eliashib didn't know what to do. Should he turn and run? He wanted to get as far away as possible but that would just focus the brothers' attention on him. Should he stand his ground and confront her? That could be humiliating. He didn't even know who she was!

He could feel himself starting to panic. The girl was causing a commotion and nobody in the hall seemed to be able to apprehend her. He began edging away, hoping to disappear into the crowd. It was impossible. He could feel people staring at him and he could tell they were moving out of his way making it impossible for him to hide.

Suddenly one of the brothers stepped forward and raised his voice above the clamour of the crowd. 'Silence everybody. Silence, please!' It was Gamaliel, one of the elders of the brethren. A hush gradually settled over the gathering. The girl too seemed to be calming down.

Eliashib didn't know what to do. He could feel his heart racing and he was breathing as though he was out of breath. The sweat was pouring down his back and his robes felt itchy and tight. The descending silence was terrifying.

'Young woman!' Gamaliel began in a stern voice, 'Your presence here today is most irregular! What do you have to say for yourself?'

The girl was visibly trying to calm herself down: forcing herself to control her emotions. She was surrounded now by members of the Sanhedrin and the guards whose job it was to maintain order - a job at which they had spectacularly failed. Some were muttering under their breaths and glowering at the girl.

For a few agonising moments Eliashib waited to see what she would say. Did she really know him? Was she really talking about him?

'I am truly sorry for the interruption, brothers,' she began, her voice quivering. 'It was never my intent to dishonour or show any disrespect to such an esteemed gathering of learned men.' She paused, gathering her thoughts. 'However, a few moments ago I saw someone enter this building, this very hall. Someone from my past who was the source of much pain to me and my family. I confess my emotions got the better of me and I forced my way in here to confront him.'

The hall listened in enraptured silence now. The girl was articulate and confident. She had mastered her emotions and was in full control. Eliashib listened with horror at what she was saying, desperately trying to figure out who she was.

'Who is it you are accusing,' Gamaliel asked, a gentler tone was now evident. 'Who is it you believe has wronged you?'

'It is my uncle,' the girl said.

In the fraction of a second before the girl announced his name to all and sundry, Eliashib had a revelation. A hideous, jarring flash of recognition as to who the girl was. He suddenly went cold, his memory reverting to the remembrance of his dead brother and his family.

'Eliashib from Joppa. He is my uncle and he is responsible for a grievous sin against me and my family.'

Chapter XLVI

Sarah hated coming into the city now. The festivals were the worst, for the streets and marketplaces were so crowded. If it had been up to her she would have stayed in the palace for the entire duration. She no longer had any desire to fulfil the requirements of Pesach. If God punished her then so be it. She would leave it to the others to offer their lambs in the temple. They could commemorate the great deliverance of the past. Apathy had become a way of life for her a long time ago.

Yet here she was, wandering the streets of Jerusalem during the greatest of all the Jewish festivals. She had been tasked with finding some specific herbs from the marketplace. One of Claudia's older servants was unwell and Sarah had reluctantly agreed to be the one to venture into the city to acquire what was needed for her care.

She had heard the commotion long before she had seen it. Yet despite what everyone else was doing, she had no desire to see what was going on. She hated the crowds and from what she could hear from beyond the temple area, this was a large and raucous one. There was something different about the noise they were making however. They didn't sound angry and aggressive as they usually did. If anything, they sounded joyful, triumphant even.

Whatever was causing the commotion, she had no desire to get involved. She had to go against the flow, forcing and pushing her way through the crowded streets. She made it to the chaotic marketplace and procured the herbs. Had she not been able to skilfully deflect the barrage of questions that came her way, she would never have made it out in one piece. Everyone wanted to know what was going on. The whole city seemed to be in an uproar and everyone apart from her was desperate to get involved.

She was forced to return by way of the temple where the crowds were even larger. The closer she got to that hallowed ground, the more of the great and the good she could see rushing about in abject panic.

There seemed to be more members of the Sanhedrin appearing by the minute. Their aged faces were twisted into expressions of fear and anger. Their old and feeble bodies moved at a speed they hadn't been accustomed to for many a year. Sarah couldn't help but smile at the preposterous spectacle of these old fools.

But then she saw him and her smile vanished. Eliashib was rushing in the same direction as all the others. He was younger and sprightlier than they were, but he still looked and moved like a bird of prey. His tall, skeletal frame, his small beady eyes and sunken cheeks and his spindly, claw-like fingers sent a shiver down her spine. Suddenly, it was no longer scorn and derision that dominated her thoughts but anger. Pure and unrestrained anger.

In that moment she was minded to march in there after him. She took off toward the Hall of Hewn Stones with scarcely a thought of what she would say or do when she got there. He represented the most painful time in her life. A time when she had lost her husband and her daughter. He had proven himself to be the epitome of indifference. When normal men would have shown compassion, he had proven heartless. When most would have shown mercy, he had been cruel.

Chaos reigned.

She could have walked straight into the headquarters of the Sanhedrin. People were rushing here, there and everywhere. Some were elated, others angry.

She stopped at the entrance to the Hall of Hewn Stones. What would she do if she went in there? What would she say? Then, her courage left her. Her anger dissipated and she stumbled to a low wall and sat down, exhausted.

That fight had been lost a long time ago. What could she do about it now? Yet she hadn't forgotten and she certainly hadn't forgiven. She could never do that.

She remained there for some time, thinking about what had happened to her these last few years. She had been so happy until Elishama had got sick, she had had everything. When he died it was as though she had suddenly become cursed. She had wondered whether his life had been blessed and she had lived under and benefited from it. Upon his death, she no longer had that protection and events had quickly spiralled out of control. The culmination of which had been the abduction and murder of her daughter.

She had found moments of happiness since. Life in the employ of Claudia had been more than she could ever have hoped for. Yet there was a terrific scar across her soul, one which was not as painful as it once was, but it was always there.

She was roused from the melancholy of her past by the tumult in the city. Wherever she looked people were rushing about in an excited state. The cause of the pandemonium must be great indeed.

There was a terrific noise coming from within the Hall of Hewn Stones. She could hear it from where she sat. Whatever was going on in there had just intensified, the noise level reaching fever pitch.

She looked toward the entrance and saw an old man stumbling out, angry agitation written all over his face. He saw her looking at him earnestly and crossed toward her, jabbing a furious finger in her direction.

'Who do you lot think you are?' he hissed, his eyes full of hate and his decrepit old finger thrusting inches from her face.

Sarah recoiled in disgust. 'What are you talking about?'

'How dare you barge in there and accuse one of the brethren! How dare you!'

'I haven't done anything of the kind!' she protestcd, standing now to her feet.

'Well one of you has! One of you women! And you're all the same! How dare you burst into that room, into the presence of such distinguished men and bring accusations against them. You deserve to be scourged! All of you!'

He muttered something incompressible and, having given Sarah one more hateful look, shuffled off down the stairs and disappeared into the crowd.

She was slightly shaken but that soon passed. What was going on in there? A woman was in there bringing accusations against a member of the Sanhedrin? Now this she had to see!

Chapter XLVII

Shifra was trying desperately to maintain her composure. She didn't know what had come over her but when she had seen her uncle, it was though she had been consumed with an unquenchable rage. Memories of her mother and father had come rushing back, and so too the callous behaviour of her uncle.

Now she stood in the Hall of Hewn Stones surrounded by the Sanhedrin, the most powerful and important council in the land. She had rushed into their midst without any thought for the consequences and now she had to try and justify her audacity. They had the power to punish her severely and probably would. There was no turning back now. Eliashib was in here and she had to make sure he answered for the way he had treated her family.

'What is this grievous sin you speak of?' Gamaliel asked.

'Why are you even questioning her, brother?' someone shouted. 'She has no right to be heard here!'

'Let her see how she likes the end of the whip!' yelled another. 'Then she might, in future, think ill of such an outrageous endeavour!'

'Brothers, please!' Gamaliel's voice was calm, almost soothing. Shifra warmed to him immediately. There was not the indignation in his voice that that there was in the others'. 'Please go on,' he said.

Shifra took a deep breath, tried to ignore the accusatory glares of those who surrounded her and composed herself.

'Several years ago my father died. His name was Elishama and he was an upright and good man, respected by all the people. He was not affluent but made a good living, supporting me and my mother admirably. Unfortunately, when I was fifteen, he became ill. We had to watch as the disease took hold. He wasted away before our eyes and eventually died. Apart from us, his only family was a brother by the name of Eliashib.' She could have sworn that at the mention of that name a subtle ripple of recognition fluttered through the assembled audience.

'That man, my uncle, is in this room. Correct me if I have erred brothers, my knowledge of the scriptures and of the great traditions of our people is pathetic in comparison with yours. But should this man not bear some responsibility for the welfare of his brother's wife and daughter?'

There was an outbreak of hushed tones and murmuring among the assembled brothers. She had their attention and those who were previously outraged at her presence were now willing to discuss the matter.

One of them stepped forward, a younger man. 'Why do you think your uncle should have been responsible for your welfare?'

Shifra felt nervous and alone but was relieved they were willing to engage with her. 'Because my mother and I were forced to live in penury, toiling in the fields to eke out a living.'

Another man stepped forward now of a much sterner disposition, 'If you squandered your inheritance then that is your fault and your fault alone! Do not lay the blame at your uncle's feet.'

'What inheritance?' Shifra snapped, almost laughing at the absurdity of the remark. 'We were given a pittance, to pay for rent. That scarcely lasted a few weeks. We lost our home, lost my father's business and were left with almost nothing. I can assure you brother there was no inheritance!'

'My girl,' her accuser continued patronisingly. 'The law is quite clear. When your father died, you as his only child, inherit everything. If your father was as successful as you claim then the inheritance should have been ample to provide for both you and your mother.'

Shifra was baffled. 'Then please explain to me brothers why it is that neither I nor my mother saw any of that inheritance.'

'None of it you say?'

'None of it.'

'Then what happened to it?'

A realisation was beginning to dawn on Shifra. The matter was worse than she had realised. 'My uncle claimed the inheritance,' she said.

A ripple of shock ran through the crowd. Some were gasping in horror, others were shaking their heads while some continued to eye her with suspicion.

'Your uncle claimed the inheritance, you say?' Gamaliel asked.

'Yes. He claimed the house and the business as well as all my father's possessions. My mother was given a paltry sum to help us rent suitable accommodation.'

'And your uncle is here?'

At this moment, a small man, also dressed in the distinguished robes of the Sanhedrin approached Gamaliel and began whispering in his ear. Shifra waited nervously. It felt like the proceeding was shifting in her favour but it was difficult to discern the feelings of the group.

'Brother Eliashib!' Gamaliel's voice boomed over the congregation. 'Are you present and what do you say to these very serious accusations?'

Movement in the crowd to Shifra's right caught her eye. Brothers were moving out of the way to leave one man standing alone. She could see immediately that it was him. He looked like an old vulture, isolated on a barren tree, eyeing his surroundings with fear and suspicion. The confidence had gone. He looked shaken and afraid. He stepped forward slowly, unwillingly. Those nearest to him backed away as if he were leprous. He moved grudgingly toward his accuser yet remained silent.

'Brother is this true?' Gamaliel asked, his tone gentle but firm.

Shifra looked at her uncle. He was only a few steps away from her now. He had not aged well in these last few years. His countenance was darkened, his ashen features more repulsive than she remembered. He still looked like a sly old bird. There was still nothing appealing in his aesthetic. The outward symptoms of a sin-sick soul.

He seemed unable to speak. He raised his eyes slowly from the floor and the look he gave startled her. Full of venom and hatred, his resentful eyes betrayed a heart that was blacker than night, consumed with bitterness.

'Brother Eliashib,' Gamaliel repeated, 'Is it true?'

'It is true!' the voice was loud and confident but it was not Eliashib's. It was female and familiar.

Shifra spun around and saw her standing at the entrance of the hall.

For a moment what she was seeing failed to register. She wondered what she was looking at. Was she seeing a ghost? It couldn't be her mother! After all this time, it wasn't possible!

The eyes of everyone present rested on the two women.

The two approached one another slowly, cautiously.

'It can't be,' Shifra muttered quietly. 'It can't be.'

The two now stood a short distance apart. A second later they fell into each other's arms. They held each other tightly, each refusing to let go.

'Mother!' was all she could think of to say. Her mind was an explosion of emotion. How could this be real? Was this really happening?

Yet it was happening and it was real. That familiar touch, that familiar smell. It was her mother. The sound of her voice, the feeling of being ensconced in her mother's arms. It was real. It was her.

'Women, please!' It was Gamaliel again. His voice was warm and compassionate. 'This is a precious moment. We can all see and we are not immune or unmoved by such a spectacle.'

Shifra broke from her mother's embrace reluctantly but held tightly to her hand.

'There is a lot more to this story, I think, but there is also a serious allegation that has been made.'

'Everything she said is true. I will vouch for that and swear to it if required,' her mother declared.

Shifra couldn't help but stare at her mother in wonder and disbelief.

She quickly gathered her wits and said, 'The abhorrent way in which he treated us is merely the beginning. I can give a full account of other moral failures.' She looked at her uncle defiantly but addressed the crowd, 'Moral failures which cast a dark shadow over him and your whole assembly.'

'Then the matter should be heard but I suggest now is not the time,' Gamaliel announced as if he were a judge presiding over a courtroom.

At that moment, the doorway of the hall was darkened. In walked a large entourage of finely dressed men. The two at the front were clearly the most distinguished of the group. They exuded authority. Shifra guessed it was Caiaphas the High Priest and his father in law, Annas. They were the ones who held all the authority in the Sanhedrin. The others would bow to their leadership.

Caiaphas strode into the centre of the room, eyeing the women with disdain. 'What is the meaning of this?'

He didn't wait for an answer but ordered Shifra and her mother to be escorted out. She was happy to leave, knowing that Eliashib's days were numbered and eager to talk at length with her mother.

Caiaphas was angry. As they exited the hall she could hear him bellow, 'This whole city is in an uproar. We need to act and we need to act now!'

The two women rushed outside, shaking with emotion. Her mother stopped suddenly, stood in front of her and grabbed her shoulders with both hands. 'Shifra is it really you?'

The tears started flowing now. 'It's me, mother. I can't believe it. I can't believe what's happening!'

Her mother pulled her in once more. For the next few moments they were locked in an embrace which all the legions of Rome could not have broken.

Eventually they let go and stared at one another earnestly. 'I thought I'd never see you again,' Shifra said weakly.

'My daughter, I've thought about you every day. I am so sorry about what happened. I am so sorry I couldn't protect you.' Her mother burst into tears, not from joy but out of pain and regret. The memories of that day came flooding back and the torment of not being able to help her daughter came to the fore once more.

'Don't torture yourself, mother. There was nothing you could have done.'

'I looked for you everywhere. I searched everywhere for you for weeks and weeks but everywhere I turned there was no trace of you to be found. Forgive me, Shifra. I failed you.'

'Nonsense! You're talking like a foolish woman, mother, and I know you better than that.'

'We have much to speak of and I don't want to let you out of my sight again. What is your situation?'

'I rent a room in the northern part of the city. It's rudimentary but it's all I need.'

'Come with me. I can offer you better accommodation than that.' Her mother began marching off down the street, dragging Shifra behind her.

'Where? Where are we going?'

'The Praetorium!'

Shifra thought she'd misheard. 'The Praetorium! Why would you want to go there?'

'I work there for the Mistress Claudia.'

'Pilate's wife?'

'I came to Jerusalem looking for you and ended up in her employ. Most of the time she's based in Caesarea with her husband but they always come here for the big festivals.'

'As does everyone else in the world!'

'You will be comfortable there and we will have time to talk,' she stopped and looked into her daughter's eyes. 'We have a lot of catching up to do Shifra and I want to know everything.'

Shifra winced inside. She didn't want to tell her mother everything. Yet maybe she should. She would have found the prospect nothing less than repugnant a few weeks ago but now, since that day at the temple, she found she could confront her past. It no longer had a hold on her. She'd been set free.

She looked at the back of her mother's head as she dragged her through the streets in the direction of the great Roman palace. Her mind was in a whirl. In one sense, it still didn't seem real. Yet in another part of her mind, memories from her childhood were coming rushing back. Times when she and her mother had rushed through these very streets or the ones in Joppa, hand in hand. Rushing to or from some festival or family gathering. Her father was there too, racing ahead, she and her mother always struggling to catch up.

What a day! First she had witnessed Jesus enter the city to rapturous applause; then she had seen her wicked uncle and confronted him before the Sanhedrin; then her long-lost mother, from nowhere, had burst back into her life! These were incredible times. Something within her told her it wasn't over yet. There was more to come.

Chapter XLVIII

Varius was on edge and so were many of his colleagues. There was something going on in Jerusalem and it was making them feel uncomfortable. The large Jewish festivals brought a plethora of problems. The size of the crowds was bad enough, you couldn't move in some parts of the city because of the seething masses everywhere you turned. Many of them were troublemakers too.

There were the zealots and fanatics who abhorred their Roman overlords. They were active all over the country, trying to incite the people to rise up against the Empire. It was an absurd and futile mission, of course, but they were unyielding in their ignorance. There were the priests and religious leaders who toadied up to authority when it suited them. They then did their best at whipping the people up into a frenzy when they were offended by something. The Pharisees, the Sadducees or the Essenes; they were all the same really: mindless religious idiots with a disturbing amount of power over the weak-willed.

Then there were the followers of the Nazarene. The city would be full of them now too. He and they appeared at all the major festivals and this Pesach was no different in that sense. What was different was what had been happening here the last two days. The place was in an uproar and the leaders, both Jewish and Roman were all wondering what was going on, what was going to happen next and what they were going to do about it.

He hadn't been there for the great one's arrival into the city, but he had heard all about it. Apparently the crowd had been hysterical, waving palm branches and proclaiming him to be the King of Israel. There had been some concern that the crowd might turn violent as they had many times before. Varius still remembered with relish the time he had confronted an angry crowd outside the Praetorium. There had been no violence this time though. The crowd had been jubilant not angry; instead of aggression there had been singing and dancing.

All the same, he knew there had been conversations among his commanders about what was going on. They were getting distinctly nervous about this Nazarene and what might happen if he ever managed to galvanise the crowds into military action. There was more and more talk of them doing something about it. Varius cursed his missed opportunities. He had been aware of this man for years but had never managed to apprehend him. Now his stock was rising and soon everyone would be after him.

He sat on his bed pondering the recent events. There was definitely something strange in the atmosphere, something he'd never felt before. You could almost feel it, touch it, smell it. It was indefinable, but it was there. It was something to do with the Nazarene, of that there was no doubt.

'He's at it again, your friend!' The man in the bed next to Varius was from the north of Italy, not far from where the Barbarians dwelt. He had a touch of the savage in him as a result. He collapsed down on his bed wrapped only in a towel, and with a mischievous grin on his face.

'My friend?'

'Your friend the Nazarene.'

'Oh, he's my friend now, is he?'

'You go on about him often enough!'

Varius rolled his eyes. That accusation had been levelled at him more than once. 'So he's been at it again, has he? What this time?'

'Went berserk in the temple,' his friend said with nonchalance while he scraped a pumice stone across his stubble.

Varius sat up, intrigued. 'What does that mean? Were you there?'

'I got there once all the fun was over. I saw the aftermath though. The market traders were flapping about in a rage, their produce and profits scattered all over the floor. There were animals running around screeching and snorting and so were the beggars,' he chuckled. 'Anyone with a keen eye on the main chance was in there, seeing how much they could get away with.'

'But what had happened? What had he done?'

'Apparently he said something about his father's house and then lost the plot. He was attacking people, tipping the tables over, shouting at the traders, whipping the animals. Basically, causing a fuss and drawing a whole lot of attention to himself.'

'Why though?' Varius asked earnestly. 'Why did he do it?'

'I don't know! He's a crackpot. The man's as crazy as they come. One minute he's riding into the city on a donkey of all things and the next he's trashing the temple.'

'He's trouble,' Varius said pensively. 'He's up to something.'

His friend shot him a look of derision. 'Rubbish! There are too many people giving this man way too much credit. Either he'll disappear as soon as he appeared or he'll get what's coming to him soon enough. I've seen a hundred like him.'

Varius was more intrigued than ever. First his grand entry into the city and now this. What was going to happen next?

Chapter XLIX

His new-found pariah status among the brethren galled him to the core. A leper could scarcely have been treated with more disdain. Most of them ignored him completely, some shied away, awkward and embarrassed, afraid that they too would get infected by association. Very few had the decency to speak to him. And how long would it last? It was intolerable.

The wretched encounter at the Hall of Hewn Stones had been two days ago. He nearly exploded with rage every time he thought back to that day. It started with the charlatan preacher riding into the city to great fanfare. It had ended with those wretched women humiliating him in front of his brothers.

The injustice of it all was infuriating. That they would have the audacity to accuse him of dishonesty and immorality beggared belief. He had always known there was something malevolent about the woman but it seemed the daughter was no better. They had obviously been conspiring all these years as to how they could persecute him. This pretence that they hadn't seen each other for years was clearly an act of subterfuge, designed to manipulate the Sanhedrin. It had worked. The brothers obviously believed that he was guilty or else they would not have despised him as an outcast.

He had to prove them wrong. He had to clear his name. He sat now on a stone bench, not far from where the nefarious encounter had taken place. It was dark as he sat in the shadows, brooding over and wallowing in the injustice of it all. He was hoping to accost some of the brothers and persuade them to join him. If he could get some of them alone, he might be able to encourage them to help.

Everything seemed to be dark of late. His thoughts, his mood and his future all seemed to be suffused with an iniquitous black presence. It dominated and controlled him, clouded his thinking, robbing him of all hope. It seemed fitting somehow that here he sat, lurking in obscurity. He and the shadows were one. He watched the brothers walking to and fro as he sat disconsolately, hidden in the darkness. He had given up approaching them. So many of them had spurned him to his face that he could no longer bear the shame and humiliation.

He knew the chances were infinitesimal, but he still clung to the vain hope that Caiaphas would walk by, perhaps even Annas. They were the most influential. If he could just get to speak to them and convince them that the women were lying, then maybe he could escape from this disaster yet. If only he could convince those who were held in great esteem, this sordid affair might not ruin him.

Their timing of course couldn't have been worse. They had conspired to make their accusations at a time when the whole of Jerusalem was in a frenzy not just because of the advent of Pesach but because of the furore Jesus was creating. The brothers of the Sanhedrin were becoming more and more concerned by the man. It was Jesus who would be consuming their time and thoughts, not him. This small matter of Eliashib's reputation and future was insignificant next to the terror Jesus was inflicting upon them.

It was like rubbing salt into an already nasty wound. Had they listened to him previously when he had warned them about the growing influence of the Nazarene, then much of the current calamity could have been averted.

He shook his head in silent frustration and was about to bow once more to a wave of melancholy when he looked up and recognised someone. He wasn't a member of the Sanhedrin but nor was he one of the rabble who had managed to sneak in. He dressed in such a manner as to indicate that he was well-off but not rich.

It was the way he moved that secured Eliashib's attention. He was walking slowly, in a furtive, stealthy manner as though he was at great pains not to be noticed. If he kept looking over his shoulder with the speed and frequency he had thus far, he would injure his neck. Eliashib was suspicious of him immediately. Who was he and what was he doing here? He was sure he had seen him before but couldn't place where.

He began moving into the further recesses of the complex. Eliashib decided to follow, though his heart was racing and a fear began to mature within him. Though he didn't dress like one, the man could be a thief or a murderer. Who knew what kind of devilish scheme he was involved in?

Eliashib had no desire to place himself in any danger. He simply wanted to know what the man was up to. Fortunately, it was dark and he was able to keep a safe distance, his black robes helping him blend into the ubiquitous shadows.

The man was creeping forward faster now and with purpose. He rounded a corner ahead and Eliashib lost sight of him. He quickened his pace and jogged forward. What was he doing? He must have taken leave of his senses! Yet he pressed on.

He rounded the corner just in time to see the man turn through an archway ahead. Eliashib knew that led into a small courtyard. He approached the archway cautiously and rounded the corner. He stopped suddenly, a bolt of terror coursing through his body. The man had stopped in the courtyard only a few feet away. Eliashib winced, ground his teeth and stepped back slowly, hoping desperately that the man hadn't heard him. What was to stop him turning around and planting a knife in his chest?

Trying to breathe quietly but fighting the clamour of his racing heart, he edged back around the corner and waited. Everything was quiet. The man hadn't moved. Eliashib breathed a quiet sigh of relief. He waited for several moments, cursing the cacophony of his own heart and willing himself to breathe more quietly. He was about to creep away when he heard voices. They were barely audible but he could hear them and they were coming from the courtyard. The man was talking to someone.

He risked a glance around the corner and saw there was now a small cluster of men in the courtyard.

The moon was bright and the starry host were providing ample illumination. They bathed the courtyard in a faintly blue lustre, enough to chase away the encroaching shadows.

The man he'd followed was at the centre of the group. There were four of them in total. Eliashib looked carefully to see if he recognised the others. It was Caiaphas! The High Priest! What was he doing here? He recognised the others too. They were his attendants, never far away from their illustrious master. This was suspicious. Why was arguably, the most important man in Jerusalem meeting this shady character late at night in a small out-of-the-way courtyard?

He strained his ears to hear what they were talking about but couldn't. They were speaking in hushed tones. The conspiratorial nature of this clandestine encounter only added to the suspicion.

There was a pause in the conversation. For several moments none of the men said anything. Eliashib held his breath. Then, almost imperceptibly, Caiaphas nodded to one of his proteges. He pulled from beneath his robes a small bag which Eliashib guessed was full of money. So Caiaphas was giving this man money! For what, he wondered.

The man holding the purse tipped the contents into one of his hands. The silver coins glistened in the moonlight.

Eliashib could see from where he stood that this transaction involved a lot of money. The man started counting out the coins and dropping them into the bag. Eliashib watched him carefully as he did so. He stopped at thirty, closed the bag and offered it to the man who took it from him carefully. Thirty pieces of silver. That was a large sum of money, four months wages for some.

What was Caiaphas up to? If he could find out, he might be able to use it as leverage. It was almost certainly something underhand, for why else would they be meeting in such secrecy? And if he could get the upper hand against the High Priest then he would almost certainly be able to make this ridiculous accusation go away.

The man turned to walk back from whence he'd come. Caiaphas and his attendants walked with him. They were moving toward Eliashib.

Panic seized him. He had nowhere to go. He couldn't make it to the next corner in time to get out of sight and he couldn't run anymore. He felt he was only moments away from a heart attack as it was. Running would only exacerbate the problem and hasten the end. He thought his heart would burst from his chest at any moment and he could feel the sweat collecting along his brow.

He stood still, pinned to the wall, eyes closed and teeth clenched. They were getting closer. He could hear them.

He risked a glance out of the corner of his eye, hoping that they would pass through the archway and move in the opposite direction up the corridor from where he stood. If they did, they might not see him. If they didn't, there was nowhere to hide.

The man he'd followed passed through the archway and turned away from Eliashib. The others followed, none of them glancing at the bulky shadow to their left. Eliashib held his breath for as long as he was able. They rounded another corner and disappeared. He almost collapsed to the floor in relief but managed to stagger around the corner and into the courtyard. The light of the waxing moon was most welcome and seemed to wash over Eliashib, calming his nerves and soothing his spirit. That had been too close. He was still shaking.

When they had crossed through the archway he had caught another glimpse of the man's face. It had been just enough to trigger his memory. He knew where he had seen him before. He had been with the Nazarene! Eliashib was sure the man was one of Jesus' followers. In fact, he was certain he was one of his closest followers, one of the disciples indeed. Now what purpose could the High Priest possibly have in conniving with him?

Chapter L

Sarah awoke suddenly. Someone was shaking her and whispering something in her ear. She was startled but gathered her wits quickly. It was Graciela and she was saying something about Claudia.

'What is it girl?' she asked, irritated and confused at having been pulled from the deepest and most wonderful portion of sleep.

'The master wants you."

'Pilate! Why?'

'It's the mistress, she's having trouble sleeping.'

Sarah sighed heavily and heaved herself out of bed. She shot a glance to her daughter who was still sleeping peacefully in the bed next to hers. She still couldn't believe it was her. But it was. She was actually there.

She draped herself hastily in her garments and rushed out of the room. Now that she was awake, the inept Graciela had returned to her room. She made her way through the servants' quarters and into the suite of rooms that housed the most powerful Roman in the country, and his wife Claudia.

She approached the bedroom cautiously and knocked. Claudia responded quickly, beckoning her to come in.

There was no sign of Pilate. 'Is the master here?' she asked.

'No,' Claudia answered, a faint notion of disgust evident in her tone. 'He has retreated to another bedroom. My restlessness is keeping him awake and he has no patience for it or me.'

'How about compassion?' Sarah asked boldly.

'He has never had any of that for anyone, least of all me.'

Claudia always looked beautiful. Now she sat near the window, the fading light of the moon casting her in a weak but solemn glow. A faint breeze swept through her hair and made her shiver. Her cheeks were wet with tears that glistened in the moonlight like diamonds upon the water.

'What is it mistress? What's wrong?'

'It's that man Jesus!' she snapped. 'I have dreamt about him again!'

'Again?'

'Yes. Again! It is the second night I have had the same dream. A reoccurring dream, Sarah! It must mean something.'

'We all have bad dreams sometimes, mistress. Nightmares are not uncommon. I will fetch you some strong wine and you shall soon be asleep.'

'No. I didn't say it was a bad dream or a nightmare. It wasn't terrible or frightening. Quite the opposite in fact, though it has troubled me greatly.'

'Well what was it?'

'It was him. You know the one. The Nazarene. The preacher who has been causing so much trouble.'

'Yes, I've heard of him. My daughter is quite taken with him.'

Claudia's eyes lit up. 'Is she? What has she said?'

'She told me about his entrance into Jerusalem the other day. The crowds were cheering for him, claiming him to be king, waving palm branches around and shouting, 'Hosanna!''

'Yes, I have heard all about it. It must have been quite a scene.'

'She also told me that yesterday she heard he created havoc in the temple, turning over tables, shouting at people and generally causing mayhem.'

'Yes, I had heard that too.

'He sounds like just another crazy fool to me, mistress.'

'Yet your daughter doesn't share your opinion?'

'No. She is much more sympathetic than I.'

'And why is that?'

'I believe she encountered him a few weeks ago when he was teaching in the temple. Something happened which had a profound effect on her.'

'What was it?'

'She said that a woman had been dragged before Jesus by some of the priests. She couldn't tell exactly what was going on but there was something in the way Jesus treated the woman. It affected her deeply.'

'I wonder what it was,' Claudia was pensive, gazing out of the window now, into the cool, dark night.

'She wasn't sure what it was but she did say that this Jesus seemed to treat this woman in a way no other man would.'

Claudia turned her head, her eyes wide with curiosity and a faint smile beginning to creep across her face. 'Don't tell me. He was kind to her?'

Sarah nodded slowly. 'Yes, I think so. Shifra said that he did seem to be treating her with kindness and compassion which was completely at odds with how everyone else was treating her.'

Claudia turned quickly to the window. From where Sarah stood, it looked as though she was struggling to hold back tears.

'Mistress what is it? Have I said something to upset you?'

Claudia shook her head but said nothing. She continued to gaze outside.

'Is it your dream? You haven't told me what happened.'

It was several moments before Claudia spoke, but when she did her voice was calm and composed. She was making every effort to repeat the contents of her dream with great accuracy.

'I am sitting in the middle of a beautiful garden but I am alone. I am very alone. There are stunning trees and flowers all around me. The scent of them is delicious and there is a lovely warm breeze blowing through the canopy, rustling the leaves and tickling the flowers. Amazing as the scene is, I cannot enjoy it. I am troubled. Deeply troubled. There are tears running down my face and I am sad. But I don't know why. The beauty of my surroundings is breath-taking but my melancholy, unconquerable. Then I see him. Jesus. He is walking toward me through the garden. It seems to take an eternity for him to reach me but eventually he does. He sits down next to me and smiles. He doesn't say a single word. He just smiles. It's not a shallow, fake smile. It's warm and loving. And the way he looks at me, I feel as though he knows me, and he cares. I feel as though he can see right through me, into the very centre of my heart, and he still cares, he still smiles.'

She paused. Sarah didn't know what to say but the longer the silence lingered, the more uncomfortable it became. 'Have you seen this man, mistress? Do you know it is him in your dream?'

'I haven't seen him, but I know that it is him,' she answered dreamily.

'But it sounds like a mostly pleasant dream. Not something which should distress you.'

'I know Sarah, but it does distress me. I wake up and I am troubled, agitated. I can't help thinking about it. I can't help thinking about him.'

Sarah was at a loss for what to say. She had never been one to take things like this too seriously and she certainly wasn't a counsellor. She did know Claudia very well and it was obvious she was greatly troubled.

'He is not a lunatic, Sarah. I may never have met the man but I know that much. I am inclined to side with your daughter,' she paused. 'And I am envious of her. Perhaps I could meet with her tomorrow?'

'Of course, mistress. I am sure she would be honoured and delighted to spend some time with you.'

'The dream, the dream!' she continued. 'I have had it twice now. Will he disturb my sleep again tomorrow? I fear this is not over yet.'

Chapter LI

Asher sat on a desolate hill on the outskirts of town. He had, for the last few hours, watched as the sun had made a graceful retreat through the western sky. It had disappeared from sight for a while, hidden behind the low-lying clouds that had blown in from the coast. When it re-emerged, it bathed the Holy City in a fiery red that was more terrifying than beautiful. Gradually the sun faded away and the city was bathed in darkness, a stark silhouette against the blackening sky.

There was something sombre about the whole scene. He had been sitting there for hours and couldn't shake the grave feeling he had. It was as though there was something in the air, a heaviness, something weighty and burdensome. There was a brooding, unsettled restlessness concentrated on Jerusalem. Yet he couldn't discern whether he was feeling something that was genuinely in the air, or whether it was a product of his own tormented soul. He had often come up here, gazed across the hills toward the great city, sometimes longing to be there, sometimes wallowing in his own existential crisis.

For the last four days he had been in turmoil. On the same evening, he had spoken to Zeke and then discovered that Jesus was in town. The old man had unfurled a load of cryptic comments and asked him questions that forced him to analyse himself. When he'd left, the streets were packed with people trying to see Jesus. Seemingly, he was at

Lazarus' house, but Asher had grown weary of the whole pursuit and had gone home disgruntled.

He had felt frustrated ever since. It was a relentless, incessant agitation that wouldn't go away. He felt as though some invisible monster was gnawing at him and wouldn't stop. And the more frustrated he got, the more irritable he became. He had snapped at both his parents and quarrelled with his sister.

He had come up here to get away from everyone. He had to think about what was going on and he couldn't do that surrounded by people who were constantly wittering on and irritating him.

Yet he couldn't escape it. His frustration was deep-rooted and couldn't be fought off. His conversations with Shifra and Zeke plagued him. He had lain awake at night rehearsing them in his head, wishing he had said this or done that. When he awoke in the morning, those same thoughts bombarded him once more. And there were the ones about Jesus too. They were the worst. He lurched from one frustrated memory to the next and there was no reprieve.

He suddenly recalled, all those years ago, standing on this very hill overlooking Jerusalem. Zeke was there that night too and he had told him to go in search of something. He had done it too. He had finally mustered the courage to leave home and head out into the unknown. Maybe he should do so again.

In a flash, he was inspired. He leapt to his feet, straightened out his robe and marched forward in the direction of Jerusalem. Darkness had fallen now and there was no clear trail. He stumbled a few times and nearly fell but he had decided to forge his own way through the hills and fields. He would stay off the road, make his own way.

He had no idea why. He didn't know where he was going or for what purpose. He would just head toward Jerusalem and see what happened.

He marched forward in determined fashion. There were small fires littered across the hillsides. The shepherds would be huddled around them telling each other stories, or the teenagers would be revelling in their rebellion. Some would be thieves and roustabouts. He would just have to hope he didn't fall upon any of them.

The longer he walked the more nervous he became. He could hear creatures scuttling about in the dirt nearby. His mind started playing tricks on him. He was convinced he could hear snakes slithering around him and the hiss of a cat nearly made him jump out of his skin. Yet he pressed on.

At the summit of each hill he was comforted to see the dimly lit silhouette of Jerusalem drawing closer. Yet at the bottom of each large hummock, the night seemed blacker than ever.

He walked on cautiously, his hands outstretched and his feet tentatively searching for hidden obstacles. He'd managed to avoid several errant trees but their nefarious branches had attacked his face.

Eventually he got close enough to hear the sounds of the city. He could just make out certain noises being carried effortlessly on the wind. Despite the hour, there was always someone around, something going on. Yet they were faint indeed, for before him was a large hill that was completely obscuring the city from his view. It was the Mount of Olives. Jerusalem was just on the other side but from where he stood, there was nothing but darkness.

The pale moon was concealed by a layer of dense cloud. There was nothing for it but to surge forward. Once he made it to the summit, Jerusalem would be laid out before him and the light of a thousand torches would beckon him forth.

Reaching the top was no easy feat. He found himself scrambling on hands and knees, surprised by how steep it was. He had no idea what time it was nor for how long he had been climbing. More than once, he felt something scurry across his hand or by his leg. He closed his eyes, gritted his teeth and climbed on.

After what seemed like an eternity, he reached the top. Pushing his way through a cluster of trees, he glimpsed the city, bathed in a warm, golden glow. That was his reward for the arduous journey across the hills from Bethany and up the dark side of the Mount of Olives.

He sat down, exhausted from the climb and in need of rest. Not only was it the middle of the night, but he had walked, climbed, tripped and stumbled his way to the summit. Now he relaxed and listened to the dulcet tones of the city. He realised for the first time there was a slight chill in the air. His exertions had made him immune but now that he had stopped, he could feel it on his skin and hear the rustling of the leaves in the surrounding trees.

Before long he could feel himself drifting off to sleep. His eyelids heavy, his body weary, he tilted his head back and closed his eyes. He was soothed by the swaying of the trees, the gentle movement of the wind and the ubiquitous sound of nocturnal life.

He awoke with a start after what seemed like only a few minutes. The air seemed colder and it felt like the wind was picking up. He was still on the summit of the Mount of Olives and more exposed to the elements. Deciding to walk down toward the Kidron Valley, he stood up gingerly and made his way down the hill. It was easier now that the light of the city could illuminate his path. The clouds were starting to thin a little and the moon could be seen trying to poke through. Without a grand plan, he pressed forward hoping to find more warmth in the valley below. There were many olive groves in this area which would provide ample shelter from the chill night air.

He pressed on. The cluster of trees were growing thicker now. He was having to duck and weave his way through them but thankfully he could see enough. He had a strange sensation that he recognised where he was. He knew there was an oil press nearby; the abundance of olive trees in the area confirmed his suspicion. The locals called it Gethsemane.

Tired from stooping down and weaving through the trees, he paused for a moment and leaned on a particularly old and gnarled olive tree.

There was little wind down here, a welcome escape from the harshness of the cool night air. It was quiet too. Eerily so. The animals and insects of the night must have vanished and there were no sounds coming from the city.

But he could hear something.

He concentrated his mind, trying to figure out what it was. Curious, he walked toward it, hoping it wasn't something dangerous. He crept silently forward, gently moving branches away from him. If it was somebody up to no good, he didn't want to disturb them. Having stealthily moved for about a minute or so, he stopped. There was an opening in the grove ahead and there was definitely something or someone there.

He crouched down to get a better look. There was someone there. He was curled up on his knees with his head in his hands and he was rocking slowly back and forth. Asher was behind him but could tell from his demeanour and the movement of his body that he was in distress. He spread his hands flat on the ground in front of him. He was saying something but Asher couldn't hear what it was. Is he mad? Is he dangerous? What is he doing out here in the middle of the night?

If he was a lunatic then Asher had to get away as quickly as possible. Who knows what he might be capable of? He might leap upon him in a second and slash his throat.

Yet there was something that told Asher he wasn't in danger. He didn't know who the man was. He didn't know what he was doing or why he was there. Yet he felt like he couldn't look away.

The man stood up and spread his arms out, palms upturned toward Heaven. The hood of his robe fell back to reveal dark hair. He was of average height, slight but muscular.

He'd raised his voice but Asher still couldn't make out what he was saying. He was almost certainly praying.

Then, in the next moment, he suddenly dropped his head and held it in his hands. His shoulders started convulsing, his whole body shaking. After a few moments, the torment became too much and he collapsed to the ground. With one hand he steadied himself and with the other he supported his head. His whole body shook violently.

Asher looked on helplessly. He felt as though he too might break down in tears. The man was obviously in agony, his heart breaking. A man of sorrows.

The thought briefly crossed his mind that he should help him, ask him how he could be of comfort. But he couldn't bring himself to do it. Whatever was going on with this man was deeply personal and Asher would almost certainly be more of a hindrance than a help.

Asher watched in anguish as the man continued to struggle. Finally, he seemed to be calming down. He altered his position so that he was now sitting cross legged, his arms wrapped around his body, his head bowed. He was holding on tightly as if he was in tremendous pain. Asher could make out part of the man's face now. If it hadn't been so dark, he might have been able to describe him.

Then suddenly the man relaxed. His shoulders dropped and his arms loosened. It appeared the torment was over.

A sound from a short distance away made Asher jump. There were noises emanating from beyond the grove. It sounded like there was a group of men nearby. Were they not alone? He was concentrating on the noise when he suddenly noticed the praying man walking forcefully away.

Asher didn't know what to do. Should he follow him? What was going on?

He paused for several minutes, wondering if there was danger lurking beyond the trees. The man had acted swiftly, confidently striding toward the disturbance. He didn't seem afraid.

Finally, Asher plucked up the courage, rose to his feet and made his way gingerly toward the ever-increasing noises he could hear nearby. There was some sort of fracas going on, of that there was no doubt. He could hear men shouting and arguing. Voices were raised in fear and anger. Asher could make out many lanterns and torches through the olive trees. Whoever it was, there were a lot of them.

He could feel the fear rising within him. That fear intensified a few moments later when he saw a retinue of Roman soldiers, swords drawn, surrounding a small band of men. The praying man was at the centre. He was being restrained by one soldier while the other bound him with a rope. The others nearby were protesting meekly, seemingly unsure of what to do. The Roman soldiers snarled in anger, eager to attack the frightened men.

The praying man was saying something. His demeanour was astonishing. He looked neither frightened nor confused. And although he was the one bound and held captive, it was he who Asher felt was really in control. It looked as though he was the one trying to bring some calm to the situation. It was he who was trying to appease the soldiers and speak comfort to his friends.

Then, the realisation hit Asher like a thunderbolt. It was Jesus. He was the man he'd watched praying. He was the tormented man, struggling and wrestling with some great burden. He was the one he'd heard so much about but had never seen. He was the one who had made such an impact on Shifra. He was the one whom so many were either in love with or terrified of.

They were arresting him! So they had finally tracked him down, in the middle of the night, on the outskirts of Jerusalem. The Jewish leaders and Romans would be delighted about that, but what would the people think?

They began to hustle him away. The Roman in charge barked some kind of order and his men drew their swords. Asher watched on sadly as Jesus was bundled off out of sight. Panic seemed to engulf his friends, who didn't know what to do. The soldiers began grabbing at them, swords drawn, only too willing to teach these troublemakers a lesson. One of them shouted something and they all began to flee. Asher lay still, cowering under a tree. He was close enough to see the fear in their eyes.

They were running in every direction, chased through the olive trees by soldiers, torches held high, and swords drawn. One of the young men was grappling furiously with one of the guards. He managed to tear himself away but left most of his clothes behind him in the process.

Asher was unable to move. Fear had overwhelmed him and he was terrified that if he moved, someone would see him and assume he was one of them. The men had fled, pursued through the olive groves by the relentless Roman soldiers. Some of them had flown by close to where he now sat.

He remained there for several minutes, too terrified to move. Eventually stillness descended once more. All he could hear was his beating heart. He judged the time was right to move away so he carefully got to his feet and began to move toward the city in the opposite direction to where they had taken Jesus. He carefully swept aside the branches of a small olive tree and found himself standing in a tiny clearing. The clouds had blown away, unleashing the moon to bathe the place where he stood in a pale, weak light.

'You! Stop!'

He froze. He couldn't see from where the command had come. In the next instant he heard the horrible, grating noise of a sword being drawn from its scabbard.

Chapter LII

'Don't move a muscle, you dog, or I'll run you through!' At last he had caught one of them. These mindless fools who followed the charlatan all over the country, hanging on his every word. The rest might have got away but he had this one. He could dispatch him right now and nobody would be any the wiser. One less deluded fanatic for the authorities to worry about.

'Turn around!' he barked.

The man did so, slowly and carefully. Varius edged closer, his sword drawn. He was tempted to stab him immediately, give him no chance to pull out a dagger. He was about to yell at him once more, tell him to get on his knees. But then he saw his face.

'Asher?'

Asher hadn't said anything but when he recognised Varius he was profoundly relieved.

'Asher, what are you doing here?' His words were laced with all sorts of emotion. Confusion yes, but anger too. He shook his head and dropped his sword. 'Don't tell me you're with Jesus! Don't tell me you're one of his followers too!'

Asher seemed to have gathered some composure. 'I'm not with him, Varius, but I was hiding among the trees. I saw the whole thing.'

'You're not with him!' Varius was incredulous. 'Then what are you doing out here in the middle of the night?'

Asher sighed. 'It's a long story. How are you?'

Varius was struggling to deal with this unexpected turn of events. He hadn't seen his friend for years but he'd longed to. The way he had left Caesarea had been a source of great regret. He had tried to help but was unsure if he'd succeeded. And now, all of a sudden, here was Asher, seemingly in the company of the rebel leader, Jesus.

'I'm on duty Asher. I came here with a number of my colleagues to arrest the insurrectionist.'

'Arrest him! Insurrectionist! What are you talking about Varius? This man is no threat to you!'

'So you are with him then?'

Now it was Asher's turn to look bemused. Varius could tell from his manner that he'd expected a warmer response from his old friend. He was too suspicious of Asher's motives and still grasping for comprehension, to comply.

'I'm not with him, Varius, but I've heard enough about him to know that he's no insurrectionist! He hasn't got a violent bone in his body from what I can see.'

Varius didn't know what to do and his words failed him. He could feel an anger bubbling away within him, but that it should be directed at an old friend of his was deeply troubling.

'He's a charlatan, Asher, a conman. He's followed around by a bunch of empty-headed dreamers who believe he's their Messiah.'

'You must have heard the stories. You must know the claims people make of this man. He heals the sick. He raises the dead.'

'He's a magician, Asher! A sorcerer! He has cast a spell on these people,' Varius couldn't help but raise his voice in anger. 'He has bewitched you!'

'But what harm has he done? Is he a threat to Rome?'

'He is a rebel and the leader of a rebellion! Did you not here about his procession into Jerusalem a few days ago? The crowd were proclaiming his kingship!'

'He offers them hope! He has the words of life. It is the religious leaders who should be concerned about him, not you. He exposes their corruption and moral bankruptcy.'

'You're a fool, Asher. I don't know what's happened to you these last few years but you appear to have taken leave of your senses.'

'On the contrary, my old friend. This night I feel as though I am seeing with more clarity than I ever have before.'

They stared at one another for several moments. As they did so an idea began to form in Varius' head. In his mind he was taken back to the slopes of Mount Gilboa and the failed attempt to apprehend Jesus in the Judean wilderness. He recalled that in the midst of the battle he had seen someone he recognised. It was only for a fraction of a second but it was the face of someone he knew.

'It was you,' he said quietly, the realisation dawning. 'It was you that day by Mount Gilboa.'

'What?'

'The day we were ambushed by a violent pack of animals, followers of Jesus, intent on destroying us and staging a rebellion. It was you. I saw you there.'

Varius watched as Asher's countenance changed. He was remembering the same event.

'Yes!' he said. 'I saw you there. I saw you fighting those men.'

'You were with them.'

Asher was shocked. 'No! I wasn't with them,' he realised the assumption Varius was making.

'You were there.'

'But I wasn't with them.'

'Then account for your presence.'

Asher muttered something.

'What?' Varius snapped.

'I was wandering around, that's all. I got lost.'

'Where were you going?'

'Nowhere.'

'What were you looking for?'

'Nothing.'

'You need to be honest with me Asher. I am becoming impatient.'

It was then that Varius realised that Asher had changed in the last few years, or he had or they both had. The warmth and affection he once felt for him had gone. He was now angered by the man he had once called a friend. His ignorance was astounding. How he could have been duped along with all the others was depressing and frustrating.

'Why were you there?' he repeated.

Asher sighed and shook his head. 'I was looking for Jesus,' he admitted.

Varius had to grit his teeth to control his mounting fury. 'Then you have been lying to me, old friend. You were part of that man's rebel pack that day and you were with him again tonight.'

Asher pleaded with him. 'Nothing of what you just said is true. I have never been part of any rebel group and I was certainly not involved with the men that attacked you that day by Mount Gilboa. Neither am I a follower of Jesus.'

'You're a liar.'

Asher shook his head in desperation. 'Why are you so angry? What has he done to elicit such rage within you?'

Varius said nothing but stared in fury at the man he no longer knew.

Asher was emboldened. 'I am not his follower. Not yet.'

Varius was becoming more agitated. He reached once more for his sword.

Asher saw the movement. The look on his face changed.

'I'm leaving now, Varius,' he said tentatively and turned to walk away in the direction of the city.

'You're not going anywhere,' Varius growled, his words laced with malice. 'Not until I say so.'

Asher kept walking. Varius lost control.

He raced at Asher and within a few seconds he was on top of him. He pushed him in the back with all his might.

Asher flew through the air and ended up sprawled in the dirt. He might be big and strong but he was not a soldier or a warrior. He was not a Roman.

Asher was on all fours struggling to get to his feet. Varius grabbed him by one shoulder and spun him around. Holding him by the corner of his robe he punched him in the middle of his face as hard as he could. Asher's nose exploded, blood splattering over both of them. Varius raised his fist to level at him again but Asher managed to pull away. He swung a foot in Varius' direction and connected with the side of his knee.

Varius howled in pain and staggered back. Seeing a possible advantage, Asher leaped to his feet but his assailant was covered in armour. He didn't know what to do. He looked around for something to hit him with or throw but saw nothing.

Varius recovered, annoyed that he had been hurt by someone from whom he was expecting no resistance. He untied his helmet and threw it to the ground, surging at Asher once more. They grappled with one another for several moments. He was a trained and experienced Roman soldier but Asher was tall and strong. Eventually they threw each other away, Asher gasping for air, Varius snarling like a rabid beast.

Varius rushed toward him once more, fists raised. He threw a punch at him but Asher dodged, he threw another and connected, this time with a glancing blow. Asher replied with a punch to Varius' side but his armour cushioned the blow. He winced in pain as Varius landed a punch on the side of his head. Then an uppercut to the jaw.

Asher reeled in agony, staggered backward and fell over. Varius pursued the advantage, stomping and kicking at his friend who was scurrying away backwards through the dirt. Blood was still streaming from his broken nose and his jaw was aching.

Varius suddenly cried out in pain. He hadn't noticed Asher get his hands on a large rock that was lying in the shadows. He swung it at his assailant, aiming for the same knee he had kicked moments before. The pain was terrific and coursed through him like a bolt of lightning. He roared in pain and fell to the ground.

Asher was struggling to his feet, driven to anger himself. He raced toward Varius and swung a fist at his now unprotected temple. Varius dropped to the floor, unable to protect his face and his knee.

'Please Varius!' he said. 'I have no quarrel with you. Let me go in peace.'

His platitudes stoked Varius' ire once more and he leaped painfully to his feet, unsheathing his sword as he did so. In one swift motion he swung his sword at Asher's head connecting with an enormous thud. Asher fell to the floor, unable to withstand such a blow.

Varius stood over, him blade inches from his friend's chest. 'Next time I shall use the blade of my sword and not the hilt.'

'Do you really want to kill me, Varius?' Asher winced. 'Is that really who you are?'

Varius looked down at his friend's terrified face. He could snuff out his life in an instant. He had done it to so many others and not lost a moment's sleep. This was different though. Despite his anger, deep down he didn't want to kill his old friend.

'How could you be so stupid?' he shouted, his sword still resting on Asher's chest. 'How could you let yourself be led astray by something so absurd?'

Asher said nothing. He looked scared and confused, tired and in pain. He didn't know what to say.

Finally, Varius stepped away, slid his sword back into its scabbard and picked up his helmet. He stopped for one brief moment to look back at Asher who was still lying in the dirt. 'Stupid fool', he thought before turning and walking away.

He would have to catch up with the others. They were taking Jesus to the High Priest. He didn't know what was going to happen next, but he knew the night was far from over. Whatever else was in store, it would help him forget about Asher. Just once more deluded imbecile in a country that was full of them.

Chapter LIII

Shifra awoke early and stared at the ceiling for some time. In her wildest dreams she never would have imagined that she would sleep inside the walls of the Praetorium, once one of Herod the Great's greatest palaces. Yet here she was and it was all on account of her mother. Her mother! They'd been reunited after all these years. It was incredible! Miraculous! She thought back to that meeting in the Hall of Hewn Stones where she'd confronted her uncle, Eliashib. She was anxious and afraid but the anger within her had driven her on to confront him. Then her mother had turned up.

They had spent the last few days catching up on all that had happened. Shifra told her everything. Even though she hadn't seen her for so long, she was still her mother and she found she could talk to her just as easily now as she could have done back then. It was traumatic and they both cried. Her mother was hysterical and inconsolable when Shifra told her what had happened to her at the hands of the bandits. She was consumed with guilt and no matter how much Shifra tried to absolve her of any blame, the torment weighed down upon her like the heaviest of burdens. She tried to tell her that in recent weeks she had found peace and that for the first time in years, she felt hope. It was difficult to get through to her mother though, so upset was she about what had happened to her daughter.

Their attempts to talk at length were constantly broken up by her mother's mistress. It appeared to Shifra that the Lady Claudia was greatly distressed about something but her mother wouldn't say what it was. She spent hours with her, even during the night. Shifra hadn't seen Claudia or Pilate and for that she was relieved. She assumed that any contact with the Roman elite was bound to be troublesome so she preferred to stay hidden in the servants' quarters.

The sun had risen and she could hear that some of the servants were already about their business. It was the Day of Preparation, during which the myriad Jews from across the city would be preparing for Pesach and the important meal they would eat together after sundown. Shifra wondered if the Romans did anything differently today or whether they were keen for the whole thing to pass over as quickly as possible.

Her mother wasn't there, probably attending to Claudia, so she crept from her room to the kitchen where she snatched a piece of bread and then quietly made her way along the subterranean corridors. It wasn't long before she'd negotiated her way out of the servants' quarters and out into the street.

She felt immediately that something was going on. The atmosphere in Jerusalem was always charged during Pesach but this was different. The street wasn't busy but there were more people on the move than there would normally be at this time of the morning. Was it just because of Pesach or was there something else afoot?

She decided to walk around and see if she had discerned correctly. Her gaze was drawn to two young women who seemed to be dashing about in a frenzy. She watched them for several minutes as they frantically knocked on one door and then rushed inside. They only stayed for a minute or two before exiting swiftly and heading to the next house where they repeated their actions.

She decided to intercept them.

Waiting patiently outside the house they had just entered, Shifra hoped they had something interesting to say. If she just positioned herself right here, then they would come out at any moment and she could question them.

Sure enough, in less than a minute, the two girls emerged. They were slightly older than her and were breathless with excitement.

Shifra stood in front of them, arms outstretched to prevent their advance. 'Something's going on; what is it?'

The girls looked at one another, their faces a picture of fear and exhilaration. 'It's Jesus!' one of them gasped. 'He was arrested during the night.'

'Arrested!' Shifra was horrified, 'What for?'

'We don't know,' the same girl replied. 'All we know is that during the night he was arrested and he has already gone before the High Priest and Herod Antipas. He has been returned to Pilate.'

'Pilate! But why? What's going to happen to him?'

'We're going there now to find out.'

'Going where?' Shifra was getting agitated. She didn't understand what was happening.

'To the Praetorium of course. That's where Pilate will put him on trial.'

'Put him on trial! But I still don't understand what he's done wrong.'

The girls lost patience with Shifra at that point and pushed past her. They made for another house where they burst in to deliver their news.

Shifra was left standing in the street. She felt as though she had been punched in the stomach. She didn't know what to think, say or do. After a few torturous minutes, she decided to go to the Praetorium too. She wouldn't go back from where she came from; she would head for the public courtyard and hopefully she could find out what was happening.

Surely it was a mistake. She knew the religious leaders were upset with Jesus and that his teaching made them uncomfortable, angry even, but to arrest him! Surely not. And what did it have to do with Pilate? The Roman Prefect wouldn't get involved, would he?

Chapter LIV

Eliashib had woken early and performed his morning ablutions, prayed and studied the scriptures. Dawn had broken a few hours ago. It was an important day, a holy and precious day. Other than Yom Kippur, there was nothing more important, no ritual more sacred to the Jewish people than their commemoration of Pesach, when God had delivered his people from the hand of the Egyptians. Today everyone would be making their preparations for the Seder, ensuring that they were fit in both body and mind to thank the Almighty Yahweh for his deliverance.

Nobody was more heartfelt in their preparations than him. He had studied the scriptures for decades and knew better than any other the meaning behind their rituals. He knew the scriptures better than anyone and so the whole festival had a greater resonance for him than for any other. He was certain that no one else, not even the brothers of the Sanhedrin would have been up as early as he was this morning. He was on his face in the early hours petitioning the Almighty while the others were still asleep in their beds.

As for Caiaphas! He was going to have a very uncomfortable conversation with Eliashib one of these days. Unfortunately, the demands of Pesach would mean that would have to wait a few days, but he would confront him eventually. When he did, he would find out what that clandestine meeting was all about and secure from the High Priest a promise of support. Then he would be able to return into the fold of the Sanhedrin from which he had been abhorrently ostracised.

He decided to seek out some of the brothers and petition them once more. He had to make some of them see sense and get them to support him. The diabolical accusations of those wretched women were threatening to ruin his future and destroy his career. He had to stop them somehow and the only way he could see to accomplish that, was to garner enough support from the brethren.

Ensuring he was suitably attired in the prestigious robes of his office, he sauntered out into the street; his haughty manner hiding the fact that he was currently a pariah, an outcast. Persona non grata.

He hadn't been walking for long when he noticed the people in the street eyeing him strangely. It wasn't usual for that to happen, given how important he was, but this time there seemed to be something different about their gaze. He continued to stride through the street confidently, head held high, his demeanour discouraging all but the most foolhardy from approaching him.

'You ought to be ashamed of yourself!' a woman suddenly spat, anger flashing in her eyes.

He suppressed a momentary feeling of panic. What was she talking about? Does she know? Had the accusations made against him been made public? Does the rabble know?

'Disgusting!' shouted an old man, leaning on a crutch.

'Disgraceful!' yelled a young woman, while her friends shook their heads in obvious contempt.

Eliashib fought the increasing urge to return home and bolt the door. It was intolerable to be treated in such a way. Who did these reprobates think they were taking to? How dare they address him in such a manner.

An old man sidled up alongside him and whispered, 'Well done sir, well done. You lot have done the right thing, no question. That man deserves everything that's coming to him.'

Eliashib was bemused. What did that mean? What was going on?

He quickened his pace, gazing at the faces as he passed. On closer scrutiny he realised there was a wide variety of emotions on display. Some were angry, some pleased, others were shaking their heads in disgust while others applauded. It was baffling and somewhat disconcerting.

He hadn't walked for long when he realised that there was a definite movement of people in the opposite direction from which he was heading. There were more people on the streets than usual for this time of the morning but they didn't seem to be going to the temple.

He stopped when curiosity got the better of him. Turning, he began to walk in the direction that others seemed to be travelling. It was very unlike him to do such a thing. He was used to being the leader not the follower, but nevertheless he was eager to see what was going on. Could whatever it was account for the strange way people were behaving?

He hadn't reached the Praetorium but he could already hear the roar of the crowd. There was definitely something going on there but he didn't know what it was.

When he arrived, he saw a mass of people spilling out into the streets around Pilate's residence. There was something going on in the courtyard. There was an unsettled atmosphere that scared him. The crowd were agitated about something, but they weren't of one accord. He could see a plethora of emotions on their faces and from one extreme to the other. He noticed some were laughing almost deliriously while he noticed one young man weeping into his hands. Most were jostling one another, standing on the tips of their toes, hoping for a better view.

Eventually, he spotted a brother on the edge of the crowd. He made his way over and questioned him sharply. 'What is going on here, brother?'

'You haven't heard?'

'Heard what? I am in the dark!'

'It's Jesus,' the man said with a grin. 'They arrested him last night.'

'Jesus! arrested!' Eliashib was shocked and elated.

'They've dragged him before Pilate.'

'Pilate! Shouldn't we question him first? It's our laws he's broken.'

The man shook his head in disdain. 'They've already accomplished all that. He's already been before Annas, Caiaphas, the Sanhedrin and Antipas. It's Pilate's turn now.'

Eliashib was angry and confused. 'How could he have gone before the Sanhedrin and why was I not informed?'

'It all happened in the dead of night,' he looked at Eliashib without compassion. 'While you were sound asleep.'

'But that's not lawful! He should have been questioned before the full Sanhedrin. Questioned properly and lawfully.'

'Caiaphas must want it done as quickly as possible. It's Pesach, you know!'

'I know it's Pesach!' Eliashib snapped back, thoroughly irritated with the man.

He decided to edge closer and see if he could gain entry to the courtyard where this man, this rebel, this fiend whom he'd been chasing for years was finally going to face justice. He got as close as he could but there were too many people in the way. Despite the early hour, the crowd was dense and the Roman presence, formidable. He managed to single out a soldier who he hoped would help him get into the courtyard.

'I'm sorry, Rabbi, it's just not possible. I'm here to keep your kind out, not let you in.'

Eliashib was irritated by the man's attitude. How dare he lump him in with the rest of the rabble. 'I should be in there, sir! I have been an integral part of this man's arrest!'

'You're not getting past me,' the man's stare was cool and defiant.

Eliashib noticed another brother standing beyond the Roman barrier, on the edge of the courtyard. If he could just join him, he could witness the proceedings. 'Please! One of my distinguished brethren is not far from us. He can attest as to how important it is I am allowed entry.'

'Look Rabbi, I don't care who you are or who your friend is, you're not getting past!'

At that moment the brother turned his head and looked directly at Eliashib. He gesticulated wildly and pleaded with his eyes for him to intervene but to no avail. The brother looked at him with thinly veiled disdain and averted his gaze.

Exasperated and annoyed, he gave up and accepted that he was not to be granted admittance to the trial. Suddenly a shout began to erupt from the people in the courtyard. It spread through the crowd like wildfire. It was one word.

Crucify.

Chapter LV

Varius felt nothing but contempt. He stood, high above the courtyard amidst the grand marble pillars of the Praetorium, looking down upon the crowd. A crowd baying for blood. They had been massing there from the early hours, eager to see what was going to happen to the man who, days before, had been hailed the King of the Jews. They were a mad bunch: some of them desperate to defend their hero, others frantic to secure his punishment. Varius despised them all. He had lived in this country long enough to know them. He had even learned their language. Familiarity had most certainly bred contempt and that was all he felt for them now as he gazed down upon the crowd.

It had been a long but exhilarating night. He had tried to put his altercation with Asher behind him, but in the quieter moments the memory returned to haunt him.

He had caught up with his colleagues as they dragged Jesus across the Kidron Valley and to the home of the High Priest. Once Annas had questioned him he was taken before the Sanhedrin - that obnoxious gaggle of amoral hypocrites. Varius had not been privy to the so-called trial but had been told by one of his colleagues that it had been a sham. What did he care? The man would be punished in the end somehow, justly or otherwise. Convinced of his guilt, he had been dragged before Pilate. Varius had been one of the many tasked with ensuring he arrived in one piece to each of his inquisitors. Pilate had sought to distance himself from the whole sordid affair and commanded Jesus appear before that oaf Antipas. Varius was loath to go anywhere near him again but orders were orders. Antipas could get no sense from the man so resorted to ritual humiliation instead, draping him in a purple robe and belittling him, much to the amusement of his fawning sycophants.

He'd then been returned to Pilate who was now going to have to decide what to do with the man. It was obvious from his demeanour that he didn't know what to do. The crowd were vociferous. Above all, he wanted to maintain the fragile peace that existed between the Romans and the Jewish hierarchy. Varius was keen to see what would happen next. What would Pilate decide?

He looked on in disgust as the crowd began to call for the scoundrel's execution. Not only execution, but the worst and most humiliating execution of them all - the one the Romans reserved for the most heinous of crimes, the most reprehensible of criminals. Crucifixion was the worst way to die. Pilate wouldn't sentence Jesus to that. It was inconceivable he would bow to the wishes of the crowd even if he did want to remain on good terms with their leaders.

He had already commanded that Jesus be flogged. That was where he was now. Some of his colleagues had taken Jesus into another, smaller courtyard, nearer the barracks, where he would be scourged. That was bound to appease Pilate, although perhaps not the crowd. Once the prisoner returned, Pilate would announce that he had received his punishment and the crowd would have to accept it.

For Varius, it was appropriate and proportionate. The man would be taken away by his followers to some remote part of the country where he would never be heard of again. It would send out a clear and unmistakeable message that would-be Messiahs were not welcome in Palestine.

There was some movement on the platform from which Pilate had addressed the crowd. A murmur of recognition rippled through them as they realised something was about to happen. Varius was eager to see too. Although supposed to be keeping a keen eye on the crowd, he couldn't avert his gaze from the platform.

From a hidden door at the rear, a number of soldiers appeared and took their positions facing the crowd. Slowly the prisoner emerged and, as one, the crowd fell silent.

He struggled to walk, shuffling forward painfully so that he was visible to everyone assembled. A unifying gasp of horror swept through everyone present, including the soldiers, including Varius. A robe had been thrown over his shoulders and tied shoddily. It was streaked with blood. His arms, legs and feet were all stained with blood too, the robe concealing the open wounds and gashes from which the blood flowed. Most horrific of all was the crown of thorns that had been forced upon his head. Varius knew immediately that his colleagues would have seen it as a hilarious joke - a crown for the King of the Jews.

He could hear some in the crowd begin to weep and others jeer. Once they had got over the shock, they reacted to this man in very different ways.

Varius was indifferent. He had seen much worse. Was it cruel? Possibly. Was it humiliating? Yes. The man had courted controversy for years and now he was receiving the reward of his labours.

Pilate appeared and sat on the Judge's seat. Varius was too far away to see the expression on his face but could tell from his body language that he was tormented. Perhaps he knew that the punishment he had already meted out was entirely appropriate yet the crowd and the religious leaders wanted more.

He held up a hand to silence the growing murmuring of the crowd. Upon their silence he announced, 'You have brought me this man as one who was inciting the people to rebellion. I have examined him in your presence and have found no basis for your charges against him. Neither has Herod, for he sent him back to us, as you can see. He has done nothing to deserve death. Therefore, I will punish him and then release him.'

Varius watched as the crowd roared their disapproval. The scourging wasn't enough. The humiliation wasn't enough. They would only be satisfied once they saw the man crucified. The dissenters in the crowd were gradually being silenced so that in the end only those calling for the man's execution could be heard.

'This man claims to be the Son of God and for that he must die!'

Varius was close to the man who shouted the accusation and suddenly realised why this Jesus had provoked such a reaction within them. For Varius he was a charlatan and a conman, a sorcerer even, but to those who were now calling for his execution, he was far more than that. By claiming to be divine, he had violated their religious sensibilities and offended them beyond all recourse. It was their stubborn adherence to their religious doctrines that caused them to be so incensed by this man. Were they not so blindly entrenched in their own inane beliefs, they might have been able to see that he was a nuisance, a troublemaker, nothing more.

Pilate looked irritated by the stubborn refusal of the crowd to abide by his decision. He raised his hand to speak once more. 'It is customary in such proceedings, that the Prefect release a prisoner sentenced to death,' the crowd fell quieter still. 'I propose to release this man to you for I find no charge against him that warrants a death sentence.'

Much to Pilate's irritation, the crowd erupted once more. They were clearly not impressed with Pilate's offer to release the prisoner. Varius could not help but shake his head in disgust at the bloodthirsty cravings of the people. He looked across at Pilate who had given an order to the soldiers around him. A few of them disappeared from the platform, returning a few moments later, dragging a prisoner with them. They positioned him at the front of the platform alongside Jesus, who was still fighting with all his might to stand up.

Varius had to stare in earnest at the man who had been brought out. It was none other than Barabbas, the man who had staged the attack on him and his men on the slopes of Mount Gilboa. The man was a rebel and a murderer, far more dangerous than Jesus and a far greater threat to Rome. Varius had apprehended him, imprisoned him and had him routinely flogged. He had been the one who had him transported to Jerusalem to face justice. Now what was Pilate doing? What role did Barabbas have to play in what was already a deranged and horrific spectacle?

Chapter LVI

Sarah looked on anxiously as Claudia wept. Jesus had been tormenting her for several nights. She had been unable to sleep, repeatedly seeing him in her dreams. She had warned anyone who would listen that something terrible was about to happen. Sarah had heard it a hundred times, causing her to lose patience with her mistress.

She'd even had the misfortune of being present when she harassed Pilate. She'd warned him over and over again to have nothing to do with him but he had never taken her seriously. Sarah could tell by the way he looked at her that he had little respect for what she thought. She implored him to listen to her, begged him to leave this man Jesus alone. Pilate laughed at her, dismissing her warnings as the fantastical claims of a deranged woman.

Then Jesus had been arrested and everything had become emphatically worse. Claudia had become hysterical when she heard that the man would stand trial before Pilate. Sarah had tried to calm her down but it was useless. It was as though something had taken control of her and she couldn't shake it lose. She was usually so calm and level-headed. This whole affair had turned nasty and Claudia looked as though she didn't know how to cope.

Pilate had lost all of the nonchalance he'd been exhibiting too. His carefree indifference had vanished. He now looked like a man with the weight of the world on his shoulders. He was irritated that the matter had been brought before him at all. He would have preferred it had Caiaphas and the other Jewish leaders just dealt with it themselves. His plot to send the man to Antipas had backfired too.

It was the vitriol of the Jewish leaders that was the problem. They were determined to secure the death penalty. Each time Pilate discussed it with them he became more and more exasperated. They were stubborn and completely unyielding in their desire to see the man executed. And because they couldn't do it lawfully themselves, they had forced the matter upon Pilate.

He was behaving like a wounded animal, angry and irascible. Sarah could see he was struggling with the options laid out before him. He didn't want to create more friction between himself and the Jewish elders but he also wanted to ensure he asserted Roman authority. He seemed to genuinely believe the man was innocent and was reticent to pronounce a death sentence.

Sarah didn't envy the decision he had to make. She could hear the roar of the crowd and it sounded as though it was becoming increasingly nasty. Pilate was under pressure to crucify the man.

Claudia had collapsed on one of the sofas and was weeping uncontrollably. Sarah had given up trying to comfort her. It was an impossible task. Pilate came in again, desperation evident on his face.

He looked at his wife, pleading with her for some support but recognising with despair that he would find none. Maybe he wasn't the iron-willed tyrant Sarah had taken him for. Maybe he did care what his wife thought after all.

Sarah watched him, a powerful, tortured soul, struggle with the power he'd been given. The power to set the man free, or crucify him.

Having paced around for several minutes, it finally looked as though he was reconciled to his fate. He sighed deeply, stood erect and fixed a look of determination on his face. In one powerful, sweeping motion, he marched out toward the waiting crowd.

Chapter LVII

Pilate stood alongside the prisoners, both of whom had already fallen victim to Roman justice.

'Who would you have me release?' Pilate bellowed, 'Jesus? or Barabbas?'

Varius couldn't believe what he was seeing. Many of his colleagues were looking at each other in dismay. Did Pilate really just offer to release Barabbas, a dangerous and notorious criminal? One who was responsible for the murder of Romans? Why would he offer the crowd such a choice? Why would he even contemplate releasing such a man? Perhaps he was confident that the crowd would never approve such an act and therefore Jesus would have to be released.

'Barabbas!' men in the crowd began yelling. 'Release Barabbas!'

Varius was astonished, and judging from Pilate's response so was he. It seemed the crowd were determined to see Jesus crucified.

Pilate appealed to them again and again but their response was the same. 'Crucify him!' they roared. 'Crucify him!'

Varius watched as the macabre spectacle unfolded, conflicting emotions competing for supremacy in his mind: anger that Pilate would contemplate releasing Barabbas, disgust at the crowd who were desperate for blood, and exasperation that one deluded fanatic could cause so much mayhem.

Pilate looked exasperated too. He had called for a soldier to step forth and stand alongside him. He held a bowl of water in his hands and had a towel draped over one arm. The crowd quietened as they wondered what he was doing.

He dipped his hands in the bowl of water and then ostentatiously held them aloft and said: 'I am innocent of this man's blood. It is your responsibility!'

The crowd reacted in anger, goading Pilate for his weakness and mocking him. 'His blood is on us and on our children' they yelled.

Varius was dumbstruck. In the next moment, though he couldn't hear what was said, Pilate must have given the order. Barabbas was unshackled and released to the crowd while Jesus was dragged from sight and marched into the bowels of the Praetorium.

Chapter LVIII

Asher didn't know what to do. He felt as though a thunderstorm of emotion was rumbling inside of him. The fight with Varius had shocked him and he was still shaken by the Roman's anger. He would never have conceived that their friendship would end in such a fashion. There had been something deeply troubling about his attitude: a restless violence that ran deeper than probably either of them knew.

Once he had calmed himself, he mustered the courage to follow the retinue of soldiers through the Kidron Valley. He kept a safe distance away lest someone, especially Varius, see him and once more accuse him of being a follower of Jesus. He discovered too late that they had taken their prisoner into the house of Caiaphas the High Priest. There were Roman soldiers and temple guards everywhere, there at the behest of the Jewish elders.

It became quickly apparent that he was not going to get in to see what was going on. The arrest had clearly been planned and carried out with the customary ruthless Roman efficiency. He assumed Jesus would be questioned, perhaps flogged then released.

He had stood outside the house of Caiaphas for several minutes wondering what to do. He suddenly became aware of the pain that was consuming his face. Others who were hanging around too started to glance at him suspiciously. He obviously looked like a shady character, his bruised and battered appearance suggesting he was a dangerous brigand or unpredictable drunk.

Nursing his broken nose, he'd walked into the city where he sought out an old acquaintance. Initially less than pleased to be woken in the middle of the night, he and his wife had welcomed him in when they saw the state of his face. It was swollen now and the bruising was starting to spread across his cheeks and around his eyes. Having done all they could, the couple retired to bed, finding some blankets for Asher to sleep on before they did so.

As he dozed off his thoughts drifted away from his mangled features and onto that scene in the garden before Varius had shown up. He had been transfixed on the man praying before he had known it was Jesus. Now that he knew, he desperately wanted to know more about him. He had so many close calls and near misses that he had given up hope of ever seeing him. Then, almost magically, he had stumbled across him all alone in the middle of the night. The more he thought about those precious minutes the more he wanted to know and understand what he was doing. This was no ordinary man, and the prayer he was engaged in was no ordinary prayer.

The more Asher thought about that scene in the garden the more he got the distinct impression that Jesus was involved in some terrific struggle. It was as though he had the weight of the world on his shoulders. What else could account for the distress he was clearly in? He had wept violently, seemed crushed one moment and then resolute at the end. He was fighting for something, maybe for someone.

He had awoken late that morning, the exertions of the previous night exhausting all his reserves of energy. The couple on whose hospitality he had thrown himself were gone and the house was empty. He helped himself to some bread and dried figs that had been left out for him and left to see what was going on in the city. What had happened to Jesus?

He now sat outside the city in a desolate spot. The arid country before him a reflection of the emptiness he felt within. The city was abuzz with what had happened during the night and throughout the morning. Asher had slept through it all.

He had found out by speaking to men on the street that Jesus had been taken before Pilate and accused of blasphemy. His sentence had been pronounced quickly and he had been taken to the place called Golgotha where he was crucified.

When Asher heard the news, he felt as though someone had stabbed him in the stomach. Crucified! How could this have happened? Could he really have offended the religious leaders so much that they sought the most cruel and horrific of Roman tortures?

Having heard so much about him and then seen him with his own eyes praying in the garden, it seemed insane that such a fate could befall him. The world had gone mad. The jealousy and paranoia of the religious leaders was unfathomable, the casual cruelty of the Romans, terrifying.

He decided to walk home. An all-consuming melancholy had enveloped him. It was heavy and depressing, weighing him down and conceiving a hopelessness within him that he'd never felt before. At times he felt as though he might burst into tears and that made him even more confused and distressed than he already was. Why was he feeling this way? He had not even known the man and only seen him once for a matter of moments. How had these events affected him so badly?

Struggling to understand his emotions, he walked on into Jerusalem. There was a strange mood in the city and it seemed to Asher there weren't as many people out on the streets as there should be at this time on Pesach. There were people running around frantically in their attempts to prepare the family meal before the sun went down.

He looked at people carefully as he walked, looking for signs on the faces of others that they were feeling as he was.

There were some who seemed unusually jovial, triumphant even, but there were others who seemed like a deep sorrow had settled upon them. He noticed tear-soaked cheeks on more than one person he passed. The death of this man had strangely affected the city. There was an unusual feeling in the air.

As he approached the temple area the crowds increased. It was a hive of activity, as it always was on this day. The smell of death hung in the air and made Asher feel nauseous. Morbid curiosity drove him into the courtyard of the temple where he could see the people offering their sacrificial lambs to the priests. They were performing the rituals, killing the animals and sprinkling the blood on the altar.

This ritual act was a serious business, undertaken by the Jews for generations. It had been decreed by the Almighty that this was the method by which they would receive divine favour. God's wrath would be averted; their sin would be atoned for.

Asher had been here many times before and watched as his father had presented the Paschal lamb. Yet for the first time he looked on in bewilderment. A growing unease was taking root in his heart. What was this really all about? Was the blood of lambs really expected to assuage man's guilt?

He looked on with a growing sense of despair. Suddenly a gust of wind swept around the courtyard taking everyone by surprise. People staggered to and fro, clutching onto their robes and holding onto others for support. In the next moment a shadow seemed to fall over the temple. Asher assumed the sun was retreating behind the clouds but the shadow deepened. Gasps and cries of panic filled the air as darkness fell. Asher looked to the heavens too late. The sun was gone. In a matter of seconds, a shroud of darkness had fallen over the city.

People were now shrieking in terror and running in every direction. Some could be heard shouting above the din, telling people to calm down; it was just an eclipse. Yet the longer it wore on the more mysterious and terrifying the darkness became. This was no eclipse. Asher managed to back himself onto an outer wall of the courtyard where he couldn't be pushed and shoved by those who'd succumbed to fear. The darkness remained, though by now people were lighting torches.

Asher could now see by the flickering lights that surrounded the courtyard. Most people had fled in horror. In their wake they had left their sacrificial lambs, abandoned them on the floor of the temple. Hundreds of dead and dying carcasses littered the courtyard, mutilated, despised and deserted.

The ground started to shake. Asher heard a low rumble emanating from deep within the earth. It was as though one of the forgotten beasts of old was awaking from its slumber.

As he stood in the darkness, fear gripping his heart, he couldn't escape the feeling that these strange events were directly linked to what was happening right now, on the other side of the city, at the site called Golgotha.

Chapter LIX

It was quieter now. Most people had gone home. The excitement was over, the deed was done. Very few now remained on this desolate site known as Golgotha. Most of the soldiers had gone. There was no need for a whole century of soldiers to guard three dying criminals, even if one of them was a celebrity. At least his family was there and some of his friends. The crowds had deserted him though. Perhaps he wasn't all they had hoped he'd be.

Since she'd discovered the outcome of the trial, Shifra had been walking around in a daze. She didn't know what to do or where to go and she felt as though she had no one with whom she could talk. The horror of finding out he'd been sentenced to death had seemed so surreal and confusing. No matter how she looked at it, she could not figure out what was going on.

She'd been sitting by the roadside crying in frustration and confusion when the roar of the crowd had signalled the next macabre turn of events. She hesitated to find out what the tumult was about but when she did she fled. It made her feel sick to her stomach that they would parade him through the streets. She could hear the raucous cacophony of the crowd, jeering and mocking him. They had apparently made him carry his own cross to the site of execution. In his already weakened state, he couldn't make it.

She had no desire to watch that or be part of such a sickening spectacle. What was wrong with these people?

Why would they revel in such cruelty and injustice? Why would they applaud and celebrate the demise of any man, let alone such a man as this? It would have been bad enough had he been guilty of something, but to treat an innocent man in this way was disgusting.

She had deliberately run in the opposite direction, running as fast as she could until she reached the other end of the city, until the abhorrent noise of the crowd could no longer be heard.

It was there in the courts of the temple that she had first encountered him. She had thought about that day many times since but she still didn't really understand what had happened. She knew her life had changed. Something had happened to her that she couldn't describe.

She didn't stay long in the courtyard of the temple. The relentless sacrificing of the lambs seemed repugnant and pointless.

She wandered aimlessly around the city for several hours. Nowhere to go, nothing to do.

Eventually she decided that as a result of what had happened on that day, she owed him something. She determined to go to the place of execution. Others may mock and ridicule, the crowd may jeer and celebrate, but she would go and pay her respects.

When she got to Golgotha he had already been hanging there for hours. The gruesome sight was difficult to take in yet she forced herself to look. They no longer looked like men: battered, bruised and bloodied beyond all recognition.

She had cried some more until there were no tears left. The sky turned black, she hardly noticed. The earth rumbled beneath her feet, she scarcely reacted. The wind was picking up and there was a storm brewing, yet she remained.

At last, she could take it no more. She took one more look at that broken man. As he hung on the cross dying, she knew that any hope she had was dying too.

Chapter LX

Try as she might, she couldn't shake that depressing feeling of melancholy settling over her once more. She had known it too long, was weighed down and burdened by it, utterly crushed and laid low. Now she could feel it returning like an old enemy, a previously vanquished foe, intent on ensnaring her again.

She thought she'd been set free but the last few weeks had been torturous. Ever since the crucifixion everything seemed hopeless. She found herself wandering around the streets of Jerusalem, day after day, not knowing where to go or what to do.

Her mother was no comfort. It was amazing and unbelievable to have her back in her life but she didn't understand. She kept telling her to forget all about this preacher and move on with her life. She should find a husband and start a family. In the end Jesus had turned out to be just like all the others, she said. Just another deluded troublemaker. It always ended the same way. But Shifra knew that wasn't true.

'I'm going to speak to Claudia on your behalf. I'm sure she'll find something for you.'

Shifra rolled her eyes. Her mother meant well, she knew, but she couldn't help getting irritated by her sometimes. That made her feel guilty. After all they'd gone through: years of separation and the horrors of that time. She should feel elated to be with her mother. Every moment should be precious. But it wasn't.

Sometimes she felt there was a great chasm between them. There was something that had never been there before but which separated them now. They had always been so similar, but now she felt an irrevocable change had taken place that would mean their relationship would never be the same.

They sat in the outer courtyard of the temple. Shifra loved it here; there seemed to be so many poignant memories for her. Her mother, not so much. She came because she wanted to be with her daughter. Shifra would far rather have been alone.

'You'd like her, I think,' her mother continued. 'She's fair and kind and doesn't make the demands on her staff as he does on his.'

'I don't know, mother. Working for Pilate after what he did! I'm not sure I could bear it.'

'You've got to let that go, Shifra. You've got to move on. And anyway, you wouldn't be working for him. You'd be working for her. There's a world of difference.'

'You can't spend the rest of your life thinking about that preacher. He's dead. He's gone. You've got to think about yourself and what you're going to do with your life. Do you plan on spending the rest of your life wandering around Jerusalem in a daze?'

'Maybe.'

'Well that's all you've been doing for the last few weeks.'

Shifra gazed around the courtyard at the people. Jerusalem had returned to normal since the tumultuous events of the trial and crucifixion. She felt that a sombre mood had settled over the city in the succeeding days but eventually it had dissipated. The festival was over and the world's pilgrims had returned home.

On a few occasions Shifra had wondered whether something was going on. She witnessed people in small groups huddled together whispering something excitedly.

They would often break up and rush in all directions as if they had some terrific news. It reminded her of what it used to be like when Jesus was in town. The excitement and tension he created made her hairs stand on end when she thought of it. Not any more though. All that was over.

'We'll be leaving for Caesarea any day now and I want you to come. There's nothing for you here.'

Her mother was like a dog with a bone.

'I don't know, mother,' Shifra sighed. 'I don't know what I'm going to do.'

'At least give it a chance. Give Claudia a chance. I'll speak to her today; I am sure she'll be receptive.'

Shifra had not the energy or will to fight. 'Do as you please,' she sighed.

Gazing out across the courtyard, someone caught her eye. It was a young man ascending the steps and about to pass into the courtyard. Shifra couldn't make out his face but he reminded her of Asher. Her thoughts immediately returned to that day in Bethany when they'd last spoken. She had been so upset by his attitude. He had been so listless, she couldn't understand it. Appalled and disappointed, she'd wandered off alone, any hopes of having a companion to join her in the search, swallowed up by his indifference.

She continued to stare at him. He was getting closer. It still looked like Asher.

It was Asher!

Something leapt for joy inside her. For a moment she enjoyed looking at him. He walked confidently, was tall and handsome. A fine figure of a man.

But then the disappointment crept in. She had been so crushed by their last encounter.

She found herself staring at him, not knowing if she wanted him to notice her and come over.

But then he did.

His face lit up when he saw her and he strolled over purposefully.

She got to her feet nervously, and her mother, not sure what was going on, joined her.

'Shifra!' he said, with an illuminating smile that seemed to create an aura around him. 'I have hoped for so long that we would meet again.'

There was something different about him. She said nothing but looked into his eyes in an attempt to discern the source of this new feeling she was getting.

An uncomfortable silence was developing, of which she was blissfully unaware.

'Aren't you going to introduce us?' he said finally, looking at her mother.

This broke Shifra from the semi-trance into which she'd fallen. 'Sorry, I'm sorry' she said, shaking herself out of the daze. 'This is my mother, Sarah.'

'I'm honoured to meet you Sarah. My name is Asher.'

'Hello Asher,' her mother replied, her eyes wide with delight and mischief.

'Shifra never mentioned she was acquainted with someone of your…' she looked him up and down quite blatantly, 'natural talents.'

Although embarrassed, Shifra could not help but smile for in that brief moment it reminded her of who her mother used to be. Feisty and cheeky, scared of nothing and intimidated by no one.

'Mother! Behave yourself.'

'Oh be quiet, Shifra! So how do you two know each other?' she addressed Asher.

'We've bumped into each other a few times,' he said guardedly. 'In this very courtyard as a matter of fact.'

'Oh? Go on,' her mother was intrigued.

'It was the day,' he paused as if struggling to utter the next word, 'Jesus caused a commotion in this very place. I found your daughter sitting not far from here,' he said, a seriousness entering his tone.

Shifra hoped he was tactful enough to stop there. He was.

'Jesus!' her mother said with obvious disdain. 'That's all she ever talks about. I hope you can talk some sense into her. You're not besotted with him too, are you?'

There was a long pause. Shifra, who had been staring at the floor, hoping these awkward moments would pass, looked up attentively. What would he say? The ensuing moments seemed to drag on for an eternity.

'You know I think I might be!'

'Oh for Heaven's sake! Not another one!'

Shifra felt overcome with joy. She fought in vain to prevent a smile spreading across her face but the explosion of joy within her had no other outlet.

Asher turned toward her, ignoring her mother. His face had taken on a look of abject solemnity, 'Shifra… about the last time we spoke, that night at home,' he paused, struggling to gain command of his thoughts and words, 'I am so sorry. You were right. I was an ass.'

Those words elicited within her an unbridled joy. 'What's happened?' was the only rejoinder she could manage.

'I saw him!' his words were laced with stifled enthusiasm. He looked like a small child struggling to contain his excitement.

'You and most of the city!' her mother's voice broke in, threatening to destroy the moment.

'No. I saw him before he was arrested, alone in the middle of the night, in an olive garden on the Mount of Olives.'

Shifra was transfixed. 'What was he doing?'

'He was praying. I didn't know it was him at first and he didn't know I was there. But the longer I watched him the more intrigued I became.'

'Why?'

'I've never seen anyone pray like that before. I couldn't even hear what he was saying but I could tell that he meant it. He was earnest and passionate. I had the overriding feeling that he was involved in some great conflict. He was fighting for something.'

Shifra was mesmerised. His words rekindled inside her the feelings she'd had when she saw him. The feelings that had been lost these last two weeks in the wake of the recent calamity.

'What were you doing on the Mount of Olives in the middle of the night?' her mother again. Her voice shattering the ambiance like a shrieking cat.

Asher was pensive. 'I don't know. I was restless that night. I was out walking, decided to head for Jerusalem when I stumbled across him praying in the garden.'

'So that's it!' Shifra declared.

Asher and her mother looked at her in befuddlement.

'That's what's different about you. You've been with him.'

They smiled knowingly, all except her mother who had quickly grown tired of these inane reminiscences. She had decided to help break them out of their delusions. 'What do you think of the rumours that have been going around the city? Do you believe them?'

Shifra was puzzled. 'What rumours?'

'The ones about the tomb and his body.'

'I don't know what you're talking about, mother.'

Asher looked nonplussed too.

'You must have heard the rumour that his disciples stole the body.'

'Stole the body! What are you taking about mother? You've never mentioned any of this before!'

'I didn't want to excite you. You spend too much time talking about this man as it is.'

'So who stole his body? And why?'

'I heard them talking about it in the palace. Pilate was told by his own soldiers that the fellow's disciples came in the night and carried off his body.'

'Ridiculous! For what purpose? Why would they do that?'

'Who knows? These people are all mad. And so are you!'

'So what happened to his body?' Asher asked.

Her mother shrugged her shoulders. 'I don't know, but something must have happened to it otherwise why would there be all these rumours?'

'And why would these soldiers make something like that up?' Asher said. 'They'll be executed if it's true. That's the Roman custom.'

'None of it makes sense,' Shifra said, shaking her head. 'They hounded him in life. You'd think now they'd have the decency to leave him alone.'

They had no more time to ponder these mysterious rumours because suddenly, out of nowhere, a big, booming voice pulverised the atmosphere.

'Asher!'

They all turned around to see a large bearded man of hefty proportions and affluent dress marching toward them like a herd of elephants.

Asher grinned and stepped toward him. The man wrapped his arms around him, lifting him into the air and laughing. He was shorter than Asher but twice as wide. His deep, throaty laugh was infectious. Shifra and her mother couldn't help but smile as this ecstatic bear of a man enveloped their friend.

'Asher, my old friend, how are you? It has been many, many years. It has been too long!'

Asher managed to drag himself loose of the man's affectionate embrace, and turning to the women said, 'This is my old boss from the Galilee, Gareb.'

The man looked crestfallen. 'Was that all I was to you, Asher? Your boss!'

'Well, I mean,' Asher struggled for the words, 'My friend… Gareb is a very good, old and dear friend of mine who also just happened to be my boss.'

Gareb roared with laughter and slapped Asher on the back so hard he almost fell over.

'We had some rollicking good times did we not, my boy?'

Asher smiled. 'We did Gareb, we really did.'

'Aren't you going to introduce me properly?'

'These are my friends, Shifra and Sarah.'

They nodded politely. Shifra was still somewhat overcome by the force of the man's personality. She could tell Asher was too. Her mother had no such qualms.

'So what brings you to Jerusalem?' she asked.

'Business,' he smiled. 'Always business.' Then, turning to Asher he said, 'Where have you been, boy? You haven't come to see me for many a year!'

'That is a very long story, Gareb. It would take me many hours to update you on all that has befallen me.'

Gareb's eyes widened. 'Now that does sound exciting. You shall come to my home tonight for dinner and tell me all about it,' he turned to Shifra and her mother, 'And you two shall come too. I insist.'

'Thank you for the offer, we should be delighted. Will you be able to get away, mother?'

'I shall have to ask the lady Claudia. It will depend on her current mood.'

Gareb was impressed. 'You work for the lady Claudia? In the palace with Judea's eminent Roman family?'

Her mother nodded.

'I did not know I was in the presence of such influence, such gravitas!' he said smiling.

'I think you have more gravitas than the whole Roman Army,' her mother said smiling.

Gareb roared with laughter once more and threw an arm around her. Shifra could not help but smile at her mother's discomfort.

'How long are you in Jerusalem for?' Asher asked.

'As long as possible,' Gareb sighed, 'I had to get out of the Galilee. The tiresome Jesus activity has started again. Rumours this time, endless rumours.'

Asher and Shifra's attention was grabbed instantly. 'Rumours! What rumours?'

'Rumours of his resurrection, would you believe?' he answered shaking his head. 'Just when we thought this whole thing had died down (pardon the expression) people start whispering that he's not dead!'

'Not dead!' Asher and Shifra said in perfect unison.

'There are stories circulating now that he's back in the Galilee, up to his old tricks.'

Shifra and Asher looked at one another; their smiles were ones of shock and delight, scarcely able to contain their elation.

Chapter LXI

Eliashib sat alone in his house, the darkness his only companion. He had locked himself away for most of the last week, unable to expose himself to the humiliation that would inevitably occur if he dared step outside. Ever since those wicked women had accused him in front of the brothers, he had been a pariah. The most loathsome leper could scarcely have been treated with more contempt. Yet here he was, despised and alone, rejected by the brothers on the back of spurious and unfounded allegations.

How could this have happened to him? He was one of Palestine's most eminent scholars, respected nationally for his wisdom and knowledge of the scriptures. How had it all come to this?

Brooding on the matter for several days convinced him it was the work of the Devil. Beelzebub, that ancient demon, had inhabited the women who used to be his kin for the sole purpose of destroying him. And try as he might, he could not find any route to vindication.

He had tried to approach Caiaphas and the leading brothers of the Sanhedrin but he was cast aside. He had even tried to see Annas but the fawning toads that surround him were bullish in their refusal.

They were all preoccupied with the rumours that Jesus' followers had stolen his body. Eliashib didn't know much for he was no longer privy to their private conversations. From what he could piece together, something had happened at the scoundrel's tomb. The soldiers charged with guarding his body had claimed it had been stolen in the middle of the night.

Now they were all up in arms. Pilate was desperate for the whole matter to disappear and the Jewish leaders were incensed that the man's crucifixion had not brought an end to the whole sordid tale. Eliashib could not help but enjoy seeing the anxiety on his former colleagues' faces. Had they let him, he would certainly have been able to help them. He would have known what to do about these maniacs who, even though their leader was dead, were still causing trouble. After all, if they'd listened to him years ago, this man could have been dealt with then, and none of this would ever have happened.

So consumed were they with the matter, that nobody had any time for him. He had been left to rot, ostracised and rejected.

He had been told that eventually he would be put on trial before the Sanhedrin and that he would have to respond to the accusations made about him. A decision would then be made as to whether he could continue to serve among them.

He was under no illusion. Given the way he had been treated over the last few weeks, he had reluctantly come to accept that his time on the Sanhedrin was over. The shameless hypocrites had made their minds up already. Whatever he said would be insufficient to redeem him in their eyes. They had decided to believe the lies of two fallen women and cast him on the rubbish dump.

He had thought about spending all his time in the temple. If he could petition the Almighty, he might be granted mercy and attain victory over his accusers. Was not Daniel of old, cast into the lions' den despite his innocence? God had rescued him.

The temple was in disarray too. It had been damaged in the earthquake, the veil of the temple, torn in two. Now the way to God was even more uncertain. Would God still hear his prayers and answer his petitions?

The answer was no. There was no one who could help him now.

As he sat in the darkness brooding over his future, he fought to stifle the fear and panic that threatened to overwhelm him.

His superb knowledge of the scriptures haunted him until he felt cursed that he knew so much. He couldn't shake from his mind the words of the prophet Isaiah:

> 'He was despised and rejected by men,
> a man of sorrows and acquainted with grief;
> and as one from whom men hide their faces
> he was despised, and we esteemed him not.'

He found he identified with the suffering servant. Could the events of the last few weeks have drawn a more fitting parallel?

Chapter LXII

With mounting anger and frustration, Varius listened to the reports that kept coming in about Jesus and his followers. There were whispers of a stolen body and the punishment that would be meted out if it were true. There were stifled rumours that his body had disappeared and nobody could account for it. The empty tomb was driving the authorities wild.

He'd seen with his own eyes Caiaphas and the other Jewish elders complaining to Pilate, remonstrating with him to do something about the ubiquitous rumours that the man wasn't dead.

He felt nothing but disgust for those who had got what they wanted: crucifixion for the troublemaker who had embarrassed them all. Now they were terrified that even after death the man would continue to haunt them.

If it was up to him, he would wipe them all out - destroy every trace of their toxic religion and force the people to accept it. They could worship the Roman gods if they were so desperate for the divine. Those that were unwilling to comply would experience the same fate as their defeated Messiah.

He stood now in the office of his superior: the Legate responsible for many of the soldiers in Judea and beyond. He had requested this meeting, hoping his petition would be warmly received.

'Yes, soldier!' he barked as he marched into the room, past Varius who was waiting patiently, and sat in a cushioned chair behind a large, empty desk.

'I have come to petition you, sir.'

'Want to go home, do you? Get back to your pretty girlfriend and start a nice little family?' he goaded, disdain and sarcasm saturating every word.

'No, sir. I want to be posted to the Galilee.'

'Why?' his superior asked, his face a contortion of puzzlement and disgust.

'I have been posted there before, sir. It is an area I am familiar with and have heard that Pilate is sending an extra contingent up there.'

'Oh you've heard, have you? What exactly have you heard?'

'I've heard the rumours, sir, that there's trouble brewing in the Galilee. The man we crucified a few weeks ago: his supporters are refusing to crawl quietly back under the rocks from whence they came.'

'So what's it to you? Why do you care?'

Varius paused and thought carefully. He didn't want to come across too irate. He was a professional soldier and had to appear as such.

'These people are a scourge, sir, a disease. I have come across them before and would like to play my part in ridding this country of their kind, once and for all.'

His superior seemed to be softening to Varius' plea. 'Well I don't disagree with that,' he said pensively. 'Where have you come across them before?'

'When I was posted in the Galilee, sir. The renegade had the whole place in turmoil. Thousands of them followed him wherever he went.'

'And at the time did you deem him to be dangerous?'

'At one time I led a small contingent of soldiers, south of the Galilee to the city of Scythopolis. We were in pursuit of this Jesus when we were ambushed by Mount Gilboa. Several of my men were killed.'

'Yes, I recall hearing about that,' the Legate said casually. 'And you think the men that attacked you were his followers?'

'I believe so, sir.'

Several moments of silence passed while the superior man seemed to be weighing up his subordinate's request.

'It's true,' he finally said. 'Pilate is sending more of us to the Galilee at the behest of the Sanhedrin, that bunch of Jewish snakes - a fool's errand if ever there was one. Do you know there are reported sightings of him? That's not a joke either. There are people up there who actually think they've seen him!'

'They're fanatics, sir, lunatics.'

'I was there, damn it!' he suddenly yelled and pounded the desk with his fist. 'I was there when they nailed him to the cross. I've seen a thousand men crucified and am yet to see one for whom it's not fatal. Surviving a crucifixion! What are we to expect next? Jupiter coming on the clouds to meet us? Neptune riding the waves of the Great Sea?' he paused. 'Some of them say he was divine, you know?'

'They're crazy, sir, and dangerous.'

'So you want to play your part in snuffing them out, do you?'

'Yes sir. I believe I would be an asset in the pursuit of these rebels.'

'And what will you do when you find them?'

'Sir?'

'His followers. What will you do to them once you've tracked them down?'

'They will experience the full force of Roman justice.'

'And if it were up to you?'

'Like I said, sir, they're a disease, a scourge on this country. I would propose complete liquidation.'

The Legate eyed him keenly. 'This is personal for you, isn't it?'

'No sir, it's not personal.'

'Yes it is,' he said smiling. 'This is personal. Why? What happened?'

Varius paused for a moment. He needed to control his thoughts. An image of Asher flashed through his mind. And then Safiya. No matter how hard he tried, he couldn't forget about her.

'Nothing happened, sir. It's not personal.'

'Very well then,' the Legate said curtly. 'You leave at dawn.'

Varius nodded, saluted and marched out of his superior's office. He felt emboldened, empowered, like he had been given permission to go forth and fulfil his destiny. The strongest sensation assailed him that the last few years had all been building up to this moment. This was why he was here. This was his mission. This was his purpose.

He would pursue these men to the ends of the earth. And when he found them, he would destroy them.

Chapter LXIII

For Asher, this view never got old. He had stood on this hilltop all his life. Here he was again, gazing across the hills toward Jerusalem. He had come here years ago before he had decided to leave home and embark on his great adventure. He had come here again only weeks ago when he had later witnessed Jesus praying in the garden – a night which had changed his life.

This time it felt different. He was no longer tormented by disillusionment and frustration. This time he knew what he had to do. The only question now was, did he have the courage to do it?

His heart had been bursting with enthusiasm for the last few days. His reconciliation with Shifra had been profoundly satisfying and a huge relief. The revelation of Gareb had been electrifying. It was crazy and unbelievable. Shifra's mother had said they were insane to even contemplate its veracity. That Jesus might still be alive! It was impossible! Ridiculous!

Yet Asher could not help but feel one of the most powerful of human emotions welling up within him: hope. He knew it was absurd, but he couldn't help but feel excited and terrified by it.

He knew Shifra felt the same. They had left each other in the courtyard that day with a promise to meet again at the exact time and place two days later. That hadn't worked out so well for them last time but Shifra assured him she wouldn't let him down again. They had agreed to consider what to do next. Should they respond to what Gareb had told them about the rumours circulating in the Galilee?

He was going to meet her tomorrow. He felt sure he knew how she would respond. There was a fire inside her he'd never known in anyone else and he couldn't stop thinking about her. When his mind wasn't on the rumours coming out of the Galilee, he was thinking about her.

'Here you are!' he spun around to see her walking up the hill to meet him. His heart skipped a beat.

'What are you doing here? I thought we were meeting tomorrow in the courtyard.'

'I couldn't wait,' she said breathlessly. 'I had to see you.'

There was a moment's silence during which they looked at one another tenderly.

It was growing dark, the sun beginning to cower from sight behind the great city. A warm breeze blew gently upon them, sweeping Shifra's hair across her face. The dying light of the sun bathed her in a gentle glow. She was beautiful.

'Have you decided what you're going to do?' she asked.

'Yes, I've decided,' he said. 'I don't feel like I really have a choice.'

'I feel the same. It's like there's something within me propelling me forward. I couldn't fight it if I wanted to. And I don't want to.'

'You're going to do it then? You're going north to the Galilee?'

Her smile was intoxicating. She looked radiant as she stood before him - full of enthusiasm, full of life.

'Something's going on; I can feel it. When I find out what it is, I'm going to become a part of it. I'm going to join them,' she paused. 'Are you coming with me?'

He smiled. It was as though everything was falling into place all at once. Everything he'd wanted for so many years. Everything he'd longed for and searched for. It was all happening, now.

He looked at her, a joyous look of expectation written across her face. He longed to tell her.

A jolt of fear rose up within him. He suppressed it and took hold of her hand. She was startled, began breathing deeply and looked intently into his eyes.

'I'm coming with you,' he said, 'and whatever happens from this moment on, we do it together.'

Lost for words and overcome with emotion, she simply nodded. In the fading light he thought he detected a tear running down her cheek.

They stood together, gazing across the hills toward Jerusalem. The fading light of the sun and the radiance of a thousand torches announcing a new chapter, a new age.

At last they had a hope and a future, a destiny they were sure would be wonderful.

ABOUT THE AUTHOR

Apart from stints abroad in Australia and Canada, Marcus has lived in the north east of England all his life. He studied History at university before completing a PGCE in secondary education. He has worked as a History teacher since 2005, writing in his spare time. He is married to Fiona and has three young children.

If you enjoyed reading *In the Fullness of Time,* please consider leaving a review:

- www.amazon.co.uk
- www.amazon.com
- www. goodreads.com

Find Marcus online:

- www.marcuscoles.com
- Twitter: https://twitter.com/mcolesauthor
- Facebook: https://www.facebook.com/marcus.coles/
- All Author: mcoles.allauthor.com

Printed in Great Britain
by Amazon